## KATLIN'S FURY

W HAT A FOOL she had been! Taken in by fancy words and a handsome face. Her mother instilled in her manners and grace and a love for books. Her father trained her to run a business. Neither taught her how to recognize a scoundrel.

A gust of wind rustled though the pine trees, a soft whisper, loud in the silence. The odor of pine wafted over her, the familiar odor suddenly strange.

"What can we do, Patches?" she asked the cat in her arms. "He has taken our money and our means of transportation." Tears of despair ran down her cheeks.

She stood lost in thought for several moments. Cold rage enveloped her and burned away the tears. "He's using my money to get himself to the gold fields." With sudden determination, she set her jaw. "Well, he won't get away with it. I'm going after him."

# KATLIN'S FURY

## by Jacquelyn Hanson

*To F-10 — Thanks for ... ... Love — Jacquelyn Hanson Oct 12, 2012*

# KATLIN'S FURY

by Jacquelyn Hanson

Glenhaven Press        Modesto — 1999

KATLIN'S FURY
by Jacquelyn Hanson

Published by:

GLENHAVEN PRESS
Suite 675 - 109
2401 E. Orangeburg Ave.
Modesto, CA 95355

First Printing — November, 1999

1    2    3    4    5

Publisher's Cataloging in Publication Data
Hanson, Jacquelyn,
Katlin's Fury

Bibliography: p.

1. A Historical Romance based on Bayard Taylor's El Dorado.
2. New Orleans—Plantation life. 3. California Gold Rush,
4. Steam ships—Journey across the Isthmus, Panama City—
Old San Francisco—Early Sacramento. 5. Romance, Adventure

Library of Congress Catalog Card Number:    99-97178
                    Paperback   ISBN    0-9637265-8-7

Typeset with PTI LaTeX
Font: ITC Souvenir Light
Cover Art by Studio II

## DEDICATION

This book is dedicated to the memory of Bayard Taylor, a poet and writer with a sensitivity I can only envy. His book, *El Dorado*, was the inspiration for *Katlin's Fury*.

"A lady from Maine, who made the journey alone, was obliged to ford a torrent of water above her waist . . . ."

El Dorado, by Bayard Taylor, 1850

# Chapter 1

**K**ATLIN FELT AGAIN for the bag of gold coins. "It has to be here, Patches," she gasped to the black and white cat lying on the bed. "It just *has* to be here."

The cat acknowledged her comment with a little "Meow", and cocked his head to one side as he watched her continue to search. Katlin's heart thumped wildly against her ribs as she yanked piece after piece of clothing out of the trunk, tossing each article away from her until nothing remained but bare wood. Finally, she could no longer deny it. The money was gone. Dizziness swept over her as she rose to her feet, fingertips pressed to her temples. For a moment, she feared she might faint.

Caleb had left several hours before, riding Sunny. Long enough she would never be able to catch him, even if he had not taken her horse. Gone with not only her horse, but with every penny they had received from the sale of the store and its adjoining cabin. In a sudden panic, she ran to her jewelry box and opened it.

The only item missing was her father's ring, gold with a black onyx stone, a large diamond nestled in the center. The onyx ring, a family heirloom, had belonged to Katlin's great-grandfather. With a sigh of relief, she saw her mother's jewelry had not been touched. Probably, Katlin thought with a touch of irony, because he thought they were all paste. He had no way of knowing Katlin's family had been wealthy in Scotland.

What a fool she had been! Taken in by fancy words and a handsome face. Her mother instilled in her manners and grace and a love for books. Her father had trained her to manage a business. Neither had taught her how to recognize a scoundrel.

She picked up Patches, who immediately started a loud purring at the attention. Carrying the cat cradled in her arms, she walked to the front porch. There she stood, stroking the contented Patches, and stared down the trail where she had watched Caleb and Sunny ride away. Two tears spilled from the blue eyes, over her eyelids, and creased a path down cheeks that retained their porcelain fairness in spite of the amount of time she spent out of doors.

As she stood there, Katlin went back over the events in her life that had led her to this backwater village on the coast of Maine. She grew up in New York City, where her father worked in Stewart's Department Store selling fine satins and laces to ladies. They had a nice home, not luxurious, but spacious, and two servants.

Katlin's mother and father had married in Scotland, where both sets of parents were landed gentry. They did not join the masses of immigrants seeking to escape the dreary poverty then rampant in rural Scotland. They came to America because Martha MacKenzie was consumptive, and they hoped moving to America would help her regain her health.

Her health did seem to improve for a while, but Katlin's birth, March 1, 1828, two years after their arrival, cost Martha any gains she had made. Katlin remembered the servants caring for her because her mother became short of breath if she so much as lifted the child in her arms.

But Katlin was Martha's sole purpose in life. Looking back, Katlin thought Martha MacKenzie's determination to see her daughter grow up kept her alive for many years.

She taught the child to read, and imbued in her a love of fine literature. She insisted Katlin speak properly, correcting any bad grammar habits the growing child picked up from the servants. From the age of ten, Katlin read to her mother daily. At Martha's insistence, she even attended Miss Wayne's Academy for Young Ladies to learn all the social graces required of young ladies in proper society.

"Right," Katlin said to Patches, as the cat licked the salty tears from her cheeks. "As if the social graces matter up here in this godforsaken part of the world." Patches meowed his acknowledgment.

The move to Maine, when Katlin was sixteen, was Andrew MacKenzie's last hope of saving his wife's life. He felt perhaps the sea air, away from the miasma of New York, would help Martha improve, so he purchased the small department store. They did make a good living, for the store served a large area, and people soon learned that not only did Mr. MacKenzie have good stock, he was honest and fair.

But although the store thrived, the MacKenzies did not. Within a year, Martha was dead, and Andrew himself showed signs of the disease. By the time he, also, fell victim to the consumption raging through his body, Katlin had been managing the store alone for nearly a year.

Thinking back, wondering how she could have been such a fool, she realized what had drawn Caleb Martin to her store. She remembered his fancy talk.

"Never seen eyes as blue as yours," he had said. "And your hair! It's the color of spun gold." Stroking her hair, he had gone on to say how much he admired the proper way she talked, her knowledge, her fine manners.

He seemed to sense her dissatisfaction, to realize she wanted more from life than a small town in Maine could offer. She thought of how his dark eyes lighted up when he talked of California, and how men were getting rich in gold, where the gold just lay around for easy picking.

"Sure would love to go there," he had often sighed. "But it costs money for passage, money which I ain't got."

He moved quickly at the interest that sprang into her eyes. Thinking back, she could not believe the speed with which it happened. After they had been courting for only a few weeks, he came running into the store to announce an itinerant preacher had arrived in town.

"He can marry us," he said, swooping her into his arms and kissing her soundly. "Then we can sell the store. That should give us enough money to get us both to California and the gold fields. There we can be really rich! I hear there's a fine new American city they're a-building on San Francisco Bay. Gonna be the New York of California."

She had tried to tell herself she did love him. Thinking back, she felt perhaps some of her misgivings were her instincts trying to warn her. She thought of the love her parents had shared and wondered if someday she would come to love Caleb as her mother had loved her father. Katlin laughed at the irony. She loved the idea of getting out of Maine. Caleb loved the idea of getting his hands on her money. A marriage made in Heaven.

The sale of the store to a young couple just down from Boston provided them with the money he sought. Once the bag of coins had been stowed in the trunk, she thought bitterly, only Katlin stood in his way. He had to get rid of her. "I was a gullible fool, Patches," she muttered, "believing everything he said. What easier way to be free of me than to just ride out of my life? If only he had not taken Sunny!"

She turned to the cat with a sigh. "Well, Patches, he has stolen our transportation and our means of livelihood. And the Rathburns will be moving here soon. We were supposed to be leaving in a week. We won't even have a place to live. What are we going to do?"

A sudden gust of wind rustled through the pine trees, surrounding the small cabin with a soft whispering, loud in the silence. The odor of pine wafted over her, the familiar odor suddenly strange.

"What can we do?" she asked the cat, tears running unheeded down her cheeks. "Return to Scotland? We do have kin there." She recalled her mother's description of the cold and damp in Scotland and rejected that option out of hand. "Go to Boston or New York and get a job as a clerk in some store?" She stood lost in thought for several moments, rubbing her cheek against the cat's soft fur, then a cold rage burned away the tears. "He's using my money to get himself to the gold fields. Well, he won't get away with it, Patches." She set her jaw. "I'm going after him."

Three days later, as she packed for her departure, lost in her thoughts, a loud pounding on her door yanked her from her reverie. Not a gentle tapping. A series of whacks that shook the door on its hinges. Startled, Katlin looked up from the dress she folded.

"Open up," a man's voice shouted from the other side. "Don't you try and hide, Caleb Parker, or whatever ye're a-callin' yerself now. Don't you think fer a minnit you c'n get away with pretendin' to marry my sister the way you done."

Katlin's heart thumped against her ribs. Caleb Parker? Had he even lied about his name? With a gasp, she yanked open the door and faced the irate man standing on the stoop.

"Don't you try a-hidin' him!" the man continued, shaking his fist, "Was you in cahoots with him to marry my sister and swindle her outta her money?"

"Your sister? Don't tell me he married your sister!" Stunned into silence, relief and fear mingled in Katlin's breast. The reality came over her in a rush. If she had not been truly married to Caleb, he had no legal claim to her money.

She could rightly accuse him of theft. Shame brought a flush to her cheeks. What would people say when they learned she had been living in sin all these weeks? Would they be understanding and realize her total innocence?

Right, she thought grimly. Go to Constable Mahoney. Tell him your story. He'll have it all over town by nightfall. If she didn't confess to the sham marriage, he would just inform her Caleb, as her lawful husband, had every right to use the money from the store to go to California. You've heard the old hens cackle. It's a good thing I'm leaving town, she thought. She returned her attention to the furious man in front of her.

"Yep, my sister. Widder lady, she were. Coddled her right nice, he did. Got her to marry him, sold her little farm, then loped off with the money. Even took the money her husband left her when he died." The man thrust his jaw forward. "Where you hidin' him?"

Katlin laughed, a humorless, clunky sound in her throat. "You missed him by three days."

Understanding swept across the man's features. "You, too?" He shook his head. "I s'pose you had some propitty."

She nodded. "The store my father left me when he died a year ago, and this small cabin. We sold them both to a young couple from Boston. We planned to use the money to go to the gold fields in California." She paused to run her fingers along the side of the small table that held the lamp. The wood felt foreign to her fingers. She took a deep breath. "Caleb took the money and rode off on my horse. Needed the horse to get a cart to carry our belongings, he said. I didn't realize at first that he had taken all the money we received from the sale of the property. When he had not returned after several hours, I became suspicious and discovered he had taken every cent. Including," she added bitterly, "my father's onyx ring that has been in the family for generations."

Katlin suddenly realized she had not invited the man in. "Forgive my manners. I was just so shocked at what you said. Please, come in. Sit down. Would you like a cup of tea?" She hurried to the stove and pulled the kettle forward over the heat. "I suspect he's in Boston by now, seeking passage on a ship to California." And he probably sold my beloved Sunny, she thought with a pang. I hope he sold her to someone who will be kind to her.

Sympathy filled the man's hazel eyes as he took the seat she offered. "Poor lass. You got family here?"

"No, I plan to return to New York. We came here for my mother's health, but she died anyway. So did my father. I stayed because I had a living in the store, but that's gone now. There is nothing to keep me here." Especially once the tongues started to wag, she thought.

The man sighed. "I hate to give up the chase, but I got me a wife and young-uns and a farm to see to. Gall's me to see him get away with such outright thievery." He yanked off his hat as though just remembering it. "Sorry ma'am." He turned the hat around and around in his hands, then blurted, " 'Specially after I found out that 'preacher' wan't no preacher, but his partner in his scheme."

"What?" Katlin whirled from the stove and stared at the man, her eyes wide with shock.

"Yep. They'd camp outside a town while Caleb looked around for a single gal with a little propitty. He'd woo her, and when she agreed to get hitched, the partner would come in disguised as a travelin' parson and marry 'em."

"The unmitigated scoundrel," she snapped, resolution filling her. She would avenge not only herself but this poor widow. "I am going after him. Give me the particulars and your direction. I will try to get your sister's portion back to her."

He looked doubtful. "I hear tell that's a hard journey.

Not one really suited fer a fine lady like you to make Miss
... Miss ...."

"Miss MacKenzie, since it seems I am no longer Mrs.
Caleb Martin or Parker or whatever his name really is." She
set a cup of steaming tea on the table in front of her guest
and held out her hand. "Put her there, Partner." They
solemnly shook hands and Katlin smiled grimly. "Yes, I
know it's a hard journey, but I will get there, never fear.
And I will find him. If he hasn't spent it all, I will get some
back. Now, enjoy your tea while I fix you a bite of supper."

"Thankee, Miss MacKenzie. That's right kind of you.
Sorry for poundin' so hard on your door."

"Please, think nothing of it. In your place, I would probably have shot out the lock." She laughed at the shocked
look on his face. "In the morning, you get on your way
back to care for your family. Leave Caleb to me."

# Chapter 2

A WEEK LATER, on the fifteenth of June, 1849, Katlin arrived in New York City after what seemed, to her, an endless stage ride. She climbed down stiffly, worn out by the long trip. She at first thought of trying for a ship out of Boston, which was much closer, but felt she could get better prices for her mother's jewelry in New York. Since the jewelry was her only asset, she knew she had to get as much for it as possible.

Urchins immediately surrounded her.

"Buy some oranges, ma'am, fresh off a ship from Brazil," cried one.

"Shine your boots," offered a second. "Only a dime."

"Carry your bags," said the third.

With a laugh, Katlin engaged the third ragged boy to help her with her bags and shooed off the rest. She motioned to a hack driver hovering nearby.

"Please," she said, "I wish to go to a small but proper boarding house. I'm sure you know of at least one."

"Lovejoy's Hotel's a nice place," he suggested. "Only fifty cents a night, meals pretty cheap, too. Or Gunter's. Costs a little less."

"Thank you for the advice," Katlin laughed, knowing only too well that hotels frequently paid cab drivers to direct travelers to their establishments, "but I really prefer a boarding house to a hotel."

"Yes, ma'am." He tipped his hat to her and, in short order, Katlin and her baggage were deposited in front of a small brownstone in an area of town she knew was a little rundown, but still considered respectable. She had to be very careful of her expenses. The couple that bought the MacKenzie store had taken pity on her and given her some more money, admitting Caleb had sold out for less than the property's value.

Since she would be in New York for such a short time, the brownstone would serve her purposes. There, for the sum of four dollars a week, she engaged a small room that included her morning and evening meals.

The following morning, she set out to accomplish the first step in her preparations, the sale of her mother's jewelry. It broke her heart to do so, but she could think of no other way. The small cache of coins Caleb had missed (had her instincts also warned her not to tell him about that?) and the extra money the Rathburns had given her would not last long. If she had to work and save money for her passage, Caleb would have too much of a head start. And too much chance to spend all of my money, she thought grimly.

Taking a hack to Broadway where all of the fine jewelry stores were located, she entered the first one she came to and took out the string of matched pearls that had been her grandmother's. Her heart quailed and tears filled her eyes. She could not part with that. She replaced the pearls in her reticule and took, instead, a heart shaped brooch with a ruby surrounded by diamonds.

Katlin steeled herself, marched firmly to the counter, and laid the ornament in front of the jeweler.

"Good morning." She smiled brightly to hide the ache in her heart. Visions of the brooch pinned on her mother's favorite blue silk dress loomed in her mind. She pushed them firmly aside. "How much will you give me for this piece?"

\* \* \*

That began one of the hardest mornings of her life. Six hours later she returned to her room, exhausted physically as well as mentally. By dint of much haggling, she had hopefully gotten enough to get her to Sacramento and last her until she could either find work or get her money back from Caleb. The pearls remained in her reticule, as did a pair of emerald earrings that had been her mother's especial favorites. Everything else was sold.

She counted the money when she returned to her rented room. It would cost three hundred dollars for a cabin on the steamer, but only one hundred fifty dollars if she went steerage. The thought of being crowded into the hold with dozens of other passengers, probably most of them men, made her shudder.

Suddenly, the room seemed stuffy. Katlin felt she had to get outside or she could not breathe. She sat on the stoop of the brownstone and watched the sun set behind the building across the street, wishing she had Patches to hold. The cat had always been such a comfort when she felt alone.

Patches is better off in Maine, she thought, two tears rolling down her cheeks. The store had been his home all of his life, and the Rathburns were willing to take care of him, since Patches had immediately demonstrated his skill as a mouser. Much as she missed him, she knew taking him with her would be impossible, remembering stories she had heard of how sailors considered cats on board a ship bad luck.

Silly superstition, she thought. Cats would be a real asset in keeping down the rats. But she did not want to take any chances. If a sailor found she had smuggled a cat aboard and threw him overboard, she would never have forgiven herself for exposing him to the danger.

"Child, ain't you gonna come in and eat your supper?" The landlady's voice behind her roused Katlin from her thoughts. "Land sakes, you're such a skinny little thing you'll blow right offen the ship first breeze as comes across the bow."

Katlin rose with a smile, remembering she had not eaten since breakfast. "You're right, of course, Mrs. Johnson. Give me five minutes to wash up and I'll be right in."

The next afternoon, when she returned again to the brownstone, she was three hundred dollars poorer, but in her hands she clutched papers guaranteeing her passage on the US Mail Steamship *Falcon*, scheduled to leave New York on June 28, 1849, bound for Chagres, with passage onward from Panama City to San Francisco.

# Chapter 3

ON THE APPOINTED date, Katlin joined the throngs at the pier. A jovial crowd of well-wishers mingled with the departing passengers. Songs and laughter rang out. All seemed to eagerly anticipate the adventure. Cries of "Come back rich," and "Bring me a nugget" rang out amid hugs and farewells.

Katlin stood a little apart from the revelers and wondered if any of them realized the enormity of the venture on which they so eagerly embarked. The *Falcon*, she discovered, was a wooden side-wheel steamer with one deck and three masts, with a rounded stern. She looked at it with a certain amount of apprehension. It looked sturdy, but . . . .

She shook her head to clear it. A porter approached and offered to take her bags. She followed him aboard. Captain Arnold, a kindly, cheerful man, greeted her warmly. "Welcome, welcome, Miss MacKenzie. Be you any relation to Andrew MacKenzie as worked at Stewart's?"

Katlin nodded. "My father."

"Fine man," he declared. "Met him once, I did, one time when the wife pulled me into Stewart's to pick out material for some new drapes. Wife tells me he passed on, he did. Real shame, young man as he were and all. Please accept my sympathy."

"Thank you," Katlin murmured.

The Captain immediately turned to the porter and said, "Remove Mr. Anderson's baggage from Number Seven and put him in Number Nine. Miss MacKenzie will have Number

Seven." He turned back to her with a warm smile. "More amid-ships. Gives a smoother ride. Bit crowded, we are, what with every fool and his brother dashing off to California with a notion he's going to return a rich man, but I'll make every effort to see you have a comfortable trip, I will."

"I appreciate your concern, Captain Arnold, but you must be busy. I'll take no more of your time." She offered him her hand, which he gallantly kissed, and turned to follow the porter to the tiny cabin.

By the time she had stowed her belongings, the steamer had left the dock, headed down the harbor towards the open sea. Katlin returned to the deck and stood by the rail, her hat tied firmly under her chin, and surveyed her fellow passengers. She saw only one other woman, a girl of about sixteen who clung to the arm of one of the older Spaniards, a man Katlin assumed was the girl's father.

Katlin smiled at her and the girl offered a shy smile in return, but her father scowled and pulled her away. He had apparently determined Katlin traveled alone, for, she thought with some amusement, that look is one of disapproval if I've ever seen one. She knew something of Spanish culture, and knew unmarried women were never allowed to travel alone. I'll have to tell her father I'm a widow, she thought. Then maybe he will let us try and visit. She grinned wryly. Maybe she should have studied Spanish instead of French.

The Spanish contingency, twelve of them, stayed apart from the others, quiet and sedate. The Germans, a jolly and boisterous group, cheered and laughed loudly at each others' sallies. She laughed softly as she picked our her fellow downeasters, as sharp-set a bunch as she had ever seen. A motley assortment of indeterminate origin made up the remainder.

All greeted her politely. Several of the younger men made moves to join her, but Katlin turned away, looking out over the harbor at the receding line of the city. Very aware of her vulnerability as a woman traveling alone, she had no desire to encourage any of these eager strangers in any amorous overtures.

Turning from the rail, Katlin returned to her cabin. Too excited at the prospect of her journey, she had eaten no breakfast, and wondered how soon dinner would be served.

Late that afternoon, the steamer began to pitch and roll. Katlin clung to a guard rail that lined the bulkhead of the cabin. The wind increased in strength, whipping her skirts about her. With a growing sense of unease, she watched the crests of the waves grow higher and higher, the wind driving white froth off the tops.

A seaman approached her. "Got to go to your cabin now, Miss," he said politely, taking a firm grip on her arm. "Blowin' up a storm, she is. Gonna take a sea over the bow anytime." He smiled, revealing several gaps in his yellow teeth. "Don't want ye ta get washed overboard, now, do we?"

"Most assuredly not," Katlin agreed, keeping a firm grip on the hand rail. She accompanied him through the door into the interior. As she stepped over the high sill, she now knew the answer to why the sills were so high. Of course, she thought. If a wave washes the deck, a high sill is vital to keep the water out of the interior.

By evening, Katlin used all of her strength to keep herself in her bunk. All thought of supper had long since left her mind. Every time she lifted her head from the pillow, a wave of nausea threatened to overcome her and make her lose the dinner she had eaten at midday.

Heavens, she thought. Am I going to feel like this for the whole trip? Will I have to spend the whole time lying on this bunk?

The following morning, Katlin blinked awake to sunshine streaming through the tiny porthole above her head. The ship still rolled, but not as badly as before. She raised her head with a tentative motion. When no wave of nausea followed the movement, she tried sitting up. To her relief, she actually felt quite well, and realized she was hungry.

With a sigh, she rose to her feet. "I believe, Katlin Mac-Kenzie," she said to the image in the little mirror, "that you may survive this trip after all."

The seas calmed. Two days later, Katlin stood by the rail, her shawl wrapped tightly around her, for in spite of the warmth of the sun, the wind carried a surprising chill that penetrated to her bones. She tied her hat securely under her chin. At dinner, Captain Arnold had told her they would shortly be rounding Cape Hatteras, and she wished to see the famed Cape of Storms. Secretly relieved they would be passing the notorious graveyard of ships in fair weather, she kept her eyes on the horizon.

A shout from one of the men drew her attention to barrels bobbing in the water.

"What is that?" she gasped to a nearby seaman, pointing to a large chunk of floating wood.

"Fragment of a bulwark, ma'am," he responded grimly. "Looks like a ship's foundered here, recent-like." He nodded sagely. "Most likely during that storm we weathered couple days back. Cap'n's changed course to swing by 'er, check for survivors."

"Oh, no," Katlin whispered, her eyes fixed on the flotsam, which now increased to include broken stanchions and a shattered spar as the ship headed closer to the wreckage.

"There, Miss," the seaman pointed. "There's what's left of her."

Appalled, Katlin could only stare at the hulk of what had

been a magnificent sailing ship. The mainmast had vanished, the foremast broken off at the yard. The bowsprit had snapped off and lay across her bow. Spars and rigging drifted on the surge, up and down, up and down, in an eerie dance of death and destruction.

"The people," she cried to the seaman beside her. "Where are the passengers, the crew?"

The seaman only shook his head.

Katlin, staring transfixed at the scene before her, could only think of the unfortunate souls who had been on board when the ship struck the reef. As the wreckage passed slowly by the stern, in her heart she heard the despairing cries, the frantic prayers, the desperate pleas for help. Tears filled her eyes and slid slowly down her cheeks.

As she stood there, Caleb crossed her mind. Could he have been on board this vessel, now a scattered wreckage before her? She almost laughed at the irony, then shook her head. He would surely have left before these poor unfortunates. But still, the justice of the thought had its appeal.

On July second, they remained hove to off of Charleston Harbor overnight to await the arrival of the mail boat. As Katlin watched the packet come out with its load of mail sacks and several sea-sick passengers, she asked the young seaman who stood beside her, "Why don't we just go into the harbor? Why do we wait out here?"

The young man grinned. "Costs money. South Carolina law says if the ship docks, all the colored members of the crew have to be bonded."

"That's ridiculous."

"That's the law," he said, shrugging his shoulders. "So we just wait out here. Plus it's safer. Treacherous channel for the larger ships."

Katlin nodded, her mind reverting to the wreck off Cape Hatteras. "If the captain feels it's safer, it's fine with me."

During the afternoon, Katlin stood by the rail watching the distant shore. The air, warm and humid, stroked her face. She kept her hat brim pulled forward to protect her skin from the fierce rays of the sun.

The young seaman who had spoken to her in the morning, a clean-cut young man scarcely more than a boy, seemed to feel responsible to be her guide. He came up beside her again and, with a gentle smile, politely touched the brim of his hat.

She pointed to the lighthouse barely visible through the misty showers that rimmed the shore, vaguely wondering why it could be so misty on shore and so clear out here on the water. "What is that?"

"That's Tybee Lighthouse, Miss, off of Savannah. Marks a point of land we have to be sure and go around."

She smiled at the young man, suddenly aware he was not like the others. "Pardon me, I don't mean to be inquisitive, but you . . . ." She hesitated and shook her head. "Excuse me. It's none of my affair."

He grinned affably. "I don't talk like a seaman, is what you're trying to say." The blue eyes twinkled. "You're right. I'm not a seaman by trade. I'm studying law, but my lungs turned weak."

Katlin looked more closely and recognized the glint of fever in his eyes, the slight flush to his cheeks, all too reminiscent of what she had seen in her parents. She felt a surge of pity sweep through her as she realized the boy was consumptive.

"My family felt a year or so at sea would be good for me," he continued. "Captain Arnold, now, he's a fine man. I'll stay with him another six months, then go back to Harvard."

Or go home to die, she thought, with a twinge of sadness. She smiled and offered her hand. "Katlin MacKenzie. Pleased to meet you."

"Henry Allen, Miss MacKenzie," he said, solemnly shaking the hand she extended. "The pleasure is mine." He pointed to the mass of clouds to the west, piled up along the shore. "Going to be a beautiful sunset. Enough lightning in those clouds to make a spectacular show."

In comfortable companionship, they watched the sun slowly sink between the layers of thunderclouds, reds and purples interspersed with ribbon-like streaks of jagged white light. The lightning darted around the horizon, making angular patterns against the ever blackening clouds.

When the last of the sun disappeared, Henry offered her his arm. "And now, Miss MacKenzie," he said with a smile, "the night air is bad for my lungs, and it's time for your supper."

She laughed and accepted his arm. She had been lonely, not wanting to encourage any unwanted relationships with the passengers. It was nice to have a friend.

Early the following morning, Katlin again stood at her favorite spot on the rail. Captain Arnold joined her as she stood watching the coast glide by.

"Why do we go so close to shore, Captain Arnold?" she asked when he greeted her. "Isn't there more danger of hitting shoals or reefs this near to land?"

"Because we travel inside the Gulf Stream," he explained. "Gulf Stream'll take us north at five, six knots. Use it to our advantage on the return trip, we do, but try to avoid it going south."

Katlin nodded. "That makes sense." She smiled. "Besides, that way we can see something besides water."

"Oh, yes, the coastline of Florida is quite beautiful." He pointed. "That there is the lighthouse of St. Augustine. First European settlement in the United States, it were. Founded by the Spaniards sometime in the 1500's." He waved his arm to encompass the whole scene. "Shoreline's low along here. Got some right pretty beaches. Weather gets warmer the farther south we go. Sun burns quicker, too, so keep your hat on."

"I will," she promised. "Tell me, Captain Arnold. Is the *Falcon* the largest of the mail steamers?"

"Oh, no, Miss. It's the smallest. Just under 900 tons, she is. The other two, the *Georgia* and the *Ohio*, will both be over a thousand tons." He grinned. "But the *Falcon* were ready first, so she pioneered the run to Chagres on December first of last year. The *Ohio* won't be ready until September, and probably be next January before the *Georgia* goes into service. So, right now, the *Falcon* is the only one the United States Mail Steamship Company's got running."

"Aren't there a lot of people going to the gold fields?"

"Yep, but most of 'em take sailing vessels as far as Chagres. Aspinwall's Pacific Mail's got three runnin' on the Panama to San Francisco run, the *Panama*, the *California*, and the *Oregon*. All three of 'em bigger than the *Falcon*." He touched his hat. "Now if you'll excuse me, Miss MacKenzie, duty calls."

Katlin stayed by the rail after Captain Arnold left her, watching the passing coastline. Beaches of white sand were bordered by thickets of live oak and trees she did not recognize. Henry came by and told her they were cypress and mangrove.

"The white sand is from the coral." He pointed out the banks of coral they skirted, the surge covering and uncovering some of the taller heads. "Helmsman has to look sharp around here this close to shore. Some of those coral heads can take the bottom out of a ship." He started to cough, and coughed for several moments. He wiped his mouth with a handkerchief, then whisked it out of sight, but not before Katlin caught sight of the twinge of pink.

"The mangroves," he continued, "when you get closer, you can see they grow right down into the water. Roots make big mats. Can trap a small boat." He grinned. "Got to get back to work or the first mate'll have my hide."

She laughed. "Go. Just one question. By the lagoons, I see little huts. Are those fishermen?"

"That's where the wreckers live."

"Wreckers?"

He grinned at the blank look on her face and explained. "Wreckers make their living by scavenging anything salvageable off of ships that get too close and break up on the coral, or in storms."

Katlin gasped. "They're vultures! Waiting for some poor souls to lose their ship."

He nodded. "But these are pretty harmless. Some parts of the world, wreckers draw ships onto reefs or shoals with false lights. These just salvage those as wreck themselves."

She laughed. "I suppose that does make them one step above the others, but somehow waiting for a ship to founder seems ghoulish to me."

"Give them some credit, Miss MacKenzie. They have saved some lives by being on the scene so quick."

Katlin shook her head. "I suppose you can say that gives them some redemption."

After Henry left her, Katlin watched the passing shoreline, taking especial interest in the trim, duck-like craft of the wreckers cruising up and down close to the shore. Flying fish skimmed the waters every few minutes, disturbed by the passing steamer. Katlin never tired of seeing the fascinating little creatures soar across the water.

Loud voices in German and Spanish yanked her attention from the scenery. As she listened to the angry voices, joined by shouts from other men, a shot rang out. Katlin stood stunned, paralyzed by fright, unable to move. In the sudden silence that followed the shot, a thin, wailing scream sent shivers down her spine.

# Chapter 4

KATLIN KNEW the scream came from the Spanish girl. What had happened? She hurried aft as fast as possible, in the direction of the continuing cry, weaving her way through the men who crowded toward the scene. She reached the stern to see one of the German passengers standing between two stalwart seamen who held his arms in a firm grip. All three stared at the deck.

The scream subsided to a thin wailing. The girl knelt by the body of her father, his head cradled in her arms. Blood streamed from a hole in his side.

Katlin hurried and knelt by the girl's side. She felt the man's chest. No heartbeat. No breathing. This wound had been instantly fatal, no question about it. Katlin shook her head. How could a man be so alive one moment and so dead the next? She found herself wondering what it was that made such a difference. Why did a sleeping man look asleep and a dead one so . . . so dead!

She shook her head and turned her attention to the girl.

"Come, child," she murmured, turning her away from the gruesome sight before her. "Come with me."

"No!" the girl cried. "*No esta muerte. No puede estar muerte!*"

Katlin held her closely. Such a shock, she thought, to see your father gunned down before your eyes. No wonder the poor little thing denied the man's death.

A portly gentleman pushed his way through the crowd. "I am a doctor," he said. "I will examine the unfortunate gentleman." He met Katlin's eyes. "Take the child away."

Katlin rose to her feet and persuaded the girl to stand with her. Tears flowed from the dark eyes as she sobbed against Katlin's shoulder. While they stood together, the German man spoke. "He haf knife. He say he kill me!"

Another passenger spoke up, nodding. "Fella's right. Seen the Spaniard pull his knife and wave it at 'im."

With a venomous glance at the killer, one of the dead man's traveling companions spoke, in reasonably good English, "Because he give the insult to Don Fernando's daughter. In my country, no gentleman allows such an insult to pass."

A stream of German burst from the prisoner. Another German, who spoke some English, explained. "Fritz, he only ask the girl if she care to stroll the deck with him. Polite, Fritz is always polite."

"But he do not ask the permission of Don Fernando to pay court to his daughter," the Spaniard stated haughtily, with the air of one explaining an obvious fact to a rather dense child. "That is an insult not only to Senorita Elena, but to Don Fernando's family as well. He cannot allow his daughter to be treated as a servant girl."

"Maybe," Katlin said, "you men should make more effort to learn about other people and other customs. Maybe then you wouldn't always be at each others' throats." She shook her head in disgust and led the trembling girl away, towards the bow where they could be alone.

There they stood for a long time, the girl's head cradled against Katlin's shoulder. The warm offshore breeze wafted across the ship, redolent with the odor of the rich vegetation lining the shore. Gradually the racking sobs subsided to a quiet weeping.

The next morning, they buried the unfortunate Don Fernando at sea, his body sewn inside a shroud of sail cloth and weighted with ballast so it would sink. Elena clung to Katlin during the brief ceremony and, with a long, wailing cry, stared at the body of her father as it slowly disappeared beneath the waves. After the services, the doctor gave Katlin a sleeping draught to give to the girl. Katlin persuaded her to swallow it, then tucked her into her bunk, promising to stay with her until she slept. She could not shake the feeling that Elena was more frightened than grief-stricken.

When the exhausted girl finally drifted into an uneasy, drug-induced sleep, Katlin sought the captain to determine which of the Spanish gentlemen planned to take over the care of the unfortunate child.

"Ah, Miss MacKenzie, I'm right glad you're with us this voyage," Captain Arnold greeted her warmly. "Please, sit down. Never had anything like this happen on my ship. Never. In a dilemma, I am. Several men clearly saw Don Fernando attack the unfortunate German gentleman with the knife." He held the long, thin-bladed knife up for Katlin's inspection. "A wicked weapon, no?"

She stared at the knife and shuddered.

"But," he continued, "if I let him go, several of the Spaniards swear they'll kill him. If this Spanish feller's friends harm Herr Friedenberger, *his* friends say *they'll* fight." He put his hands to his head in despair. "What can I do? Next landfall's Cuba. Can't leave the German gentlemen there. Won't tie up in New Orleans for at least three days after that." He raised his head and looked at Katlin, indecision written all over his face. "What can I do?" he repeated.

"Confine them all to their cabins or let them kill each other," Katlin responded bitterly. Men are so stupid, she thought with disgust. Always so ready to kill, and always so able to justify their killing. "I don't really care which. My concern is the girl. Have any of the other Spaniards said they are family?"

Captain Arnold shook his head. "Only traveling together to the gold fields, they are. The one feller who speaks English, he says they never met until they boarded their ship for New York. All of 'em are rushing to California to make their fortunes in gold. None wantin' to be saddled with the girl. Seems the child is barely fifteen. In fact, he tells me the rest of the bunch tried to dissuade Don Fernando from bringing her in the first place, but seems her mother had died and he couldn't bear leavin' her."

"Didn't he have a servant to care for her? I thought they were so particular about always having a woman to care for young girls."

"He brought her *dueña*, but the poor woman took the cholera in New York and died." He chuckled. "I don't think the others missed her much. Say all she did were weep and wail over leaving Catalonia. By halfway across they were all for sendin' her back or pitchin' her overboard."

"So now Elena's alone, a child who has been protected and cared for all of her life. No wonder she's so frightened."

"Can you take care of her, Miss MacKenzie, least 'til we reach New Orleans?"

"And then what? Dump the child alone in a foreign country, not knowing a word of English or French?"

The captain wiped the beads of perspiration off his brow with a soggy handkerchief. Katlin pitied him. A kindly, gentle man, the dilemma had clearly left him at a loss to know how to find his way out.

Watching him, Katlin made her decision. She knew none of the men, all besotted with their dreams of easy gold, would help Elena. "I will keep her with me," she said, to her own surprise, almost laughing out loud at the relief on the captain's face. "I don't know how I will be able to care for her, but I cannot allow her to be abandoned."

Katlin returned to her cabin. Elena still slept, long dark lashes brushing her cheeks. The dark hair spread out on the pillow, emphasizing the fairness of her clear skin. Katlin looked down on the sleeping face. Fifteen years old. So young! And what a beautiful child. The enormity of what she had committed herself to swept over her in a rush. What came over me? she thought. I don't even know how I am going to take care of myself, now I've taken on the responsibility for Elena.

She knew California had a large Spanish-speaking population. Maybe some California family would take her in. Maybe that would be the answer. She only knew she could not leave the poor innocent to fend for herself.

Katlin shrugged. "We'll make it, child," she said to the sleeping girl, smoothing the dark hair back from her face, astonished at the maternal feelings that swept over her. "We'll make it."

# Chapter 5

THE *FALCON* cleared the end of the last island of the Florida Keys during the night. When Katlin approached the bow on the morning of July 5, she found the ship headed southwest across the smooth blue water of the Gulf of Mexico.

Henry joined her. "Making nine knots," he grinned, "now that we've cleared the Keys, and are out of the Gulf Stream. Next port o' call is Havana Harbor on the island of Cuba."

The horizon formed a far distant smooth, unbroken line. As Katlin stood gazing at the scene, Elena joined her at the rail. To Katlin's relief, she learned Elena had studied English, and actually spoke fairly well.

Elena greeted Katlin with some hesitation, as though she feared Katlin would be offended at her next words. "My father," she finally said, "he say I not to speak with you when I want practice my English. He say you travel alone, you, you, how you say? You not a good woman. Not good for company for me." She gave Katlin a shy smile. "Father wrong. You very good woman."

Katlin returned Elena's smile. "Thank you," she said, smothering a laugh. For all this child knew of the world, Katlin could be a madam collecting innocents for her bordello. She doubted Elena even knew there were such places. *I hope she doesn't ask me why I'm going to California. I don't want to lie to her, but I'm sure she'd never understand if I told her the truth, that I'm chasing the rat who stole my inheritance.*

The Spaniards readily accepted Katlin in the role of *dueña* to Elena. The captain persuaded the unfortunate Herr Friedenberger to spend the rest of the voyage to New Orleans in his cabin. He and his party would disembark there and await the next boat.

Katlin and Elena stood by the rail, close to the bow, watching the water of the gulf glide by. The sun, a white hot ball hanging in the sky, burned fiercely down upon the water. Katlin had never known the sun to pound so heavily. She felt it burning her skin in spite of the parasol she held over their heads. Her eyes burned from the glare as the sun's rays reflected off the water.

Around noon, Henry approached with a broad smile. "Captain Arnold has invited you ladies to join him. He wants to show you something." Henry escorted them up the two steps into the wheel house where the captain awaited them.

"Good afternoon, ladies," he smiled. "I thought you might like to take a look at our destination through the ship's glass."

"Oh, *si, si!*" Elena eagerly accepted the small telescope and, squinting, held it to her eye. "A mountain! I see a mountain."

He smiled at her enthusiasm and handed the heavy tube to Katlin. Through it, she saw a peak rising from the water.

"They call that *Pan of Matanzas*, the highest peak on the island. It's an extinct volcano." He grinned. "At least, they say it's extinct."

"Why do they call it 'bread of massacre'?" Elena asked.

The captain laughed. "You will have to pose that question to your countrymen. I have no idea. As we get closer, you will see the Iron Mountains rising in the background."

By mid-afternoon, they skirted the coastline of Cuba. Katlin and Elena watched the shoreline pass, very similar to Florida, a long stretch of white beaches, coral reefs, and breakers. Orange trees surrounded the houses that dotted the valleys. Fields of growing sugar cane lined the slopes.

"Smell this air," Katlin exclaimed, inhaling deeply. "Have you ever smelled anything so intoxicating?"

Elena looked puzzled and Katlin laughed. "Don't mind me. Just enjoy the scenery."

At six that evening, with Henry as their self-appointed guide pointing out the landmarks, the steamer chugged past the Battlements of Moro, an immense fortress with the feathery heads of palm trees rising above cream-colored rocks. The Moro itself stood atop a round bluff of dark rock. As they glided into the harbor, Henry pointed out the city of Havana, a collection of terraced houses of light and brilliant colors and Spanish public buildings.

"See the cathedral? That's where the ashes of Christopher Columbus are supposed to be buried." He swept his arm in an arc to encompass the whole scene. "The harbor is completely land-locked, protected from the worst of storms. Guns on the Moro can easily keep out any enemy ships. And inside, the harbor is two miles wide."

Katlin looked at the green hills surrounding the city. "And those palaces dotting the countryside?"

Henry laughed. "That's where the nobility live. They own the sugar plantations we saw along the coast." He smiled at Elena. Katlin was amused by how smitten young Henry was by Elena's dark, fragile beauty. "Your countrymen live very well here," he told the girl.

"We can . . . how you say . . . go . . . to the land?"

Henry shook his head. "Not this trip. They're scared to death of cholera, and they've heard about the cholera in New York. They have a different notion of how it spreads. They say it's not the miasma, it's direct contact. They won't touch anyone. We have to anchor in the quarantine ground, by the hulk of that old frigate that's aground." He shook his head. "That's where they isolate all of the yellow fever victims until they either get well or die. They call yellow fever the 'black vomit'. Folks that get it often die in less than 24 hours."

"How dreadful!" Katlin exclaimed.

"I fear the cholera more," Elena said simply. "My *dueña* died of it in New York." The dark eyes filled with tears. "Is it not from the touch that it spread? Others on the ship coming to New York, they die too."

Henry drew her hand through his arm and patted it gently. "We'll let the doctors argue that one out. Come, they're dropping the anchor. Come and see what happens."

Katlin watched the health officer receive the mail and the ship's papers at the end of a long pole and dip it in a large wooden pail.

"What's in the bucket?" she asked Henry. "Water?"

"No, vinegar."

"Vinegar?"

"Yeah, they seem to think it does something to keep them from taking the cholera."

"Does it?" Katlin had never heard that before.

Henry grinned. "Well, they seem to think so. Guess it can't hurt to try."

Boats arrived with barrels of water and baskets of vegetables. Cuban soldiers in white uniforms watched with diligence to be sure no one made any physical contact. Even the half naked slaves who worked the pumps were careful to dip the rope ends and planks in the water before touching them.

Katlin watched the whole scene with fascination. Her eyes witnessed so many new events at once that her mind could not take them all in. She smiled. What an innocent she had been in her sheltered life!

After supper, Katlin and Elena stood on deck and watched the sun set beyond the mountains ringing the harbor. As the reds and golds faded to purple, they stood in companionable silence enjoying the cool evening breeze that wafted over their perspiring faces, bringing welcome relief from the heat of the day.

As the light faded, the stars winked on, a few bold ones first, then more and more until the blue vault was dotted with points of light.

"Look at the stars, Elena," Katlin murmured. She led the girl to the ship's starboard side, drawing her attention from the shrouded forms being lifted from the abandoned frigate and stacked into longboats. Yellow fever victims, Katlin knew, remembering Henry's comment. Black vomit. What a horrible way to die! She shivered in spite of the warmth of the evening air. A mosquito buzzed her ear and she batted it away.

Katlin found herself wondering how diseases like yellow fever and cholera spread. She had always been told it was from the miasma, or mephitic vapors. Cholera, in particular, did seem to spread rapidly in areas where the miasma was the worst.

She had no experience with yellow fever. Could the Spanish be right? Could cholera spread by touching? If so, then it seemed logical that the caretakers would always succumb to the disease. It had to be something else.

"Some day," she sighed to the uncomprehending Elena. "Some day we will know."

The church bells tolled, a mournful, dreary sound that carried out across the water. Katlin shuddered. The sad song drove away the pleasure she took in watching the stars and the lights of the city floating across the bay. She took Elena's arm. "Come, let's go into the cabin before these mosquitoes eat us alive."

# Chapter 6

THE RHYTHMIC THROBBING of the engine and the clanking of chain in the hawse-pipe as the sailors hoisted the anchor woke Katlin the next morning. She blinked and yawned. Shouts and singing between the *Falcon* and other anchored American ships had awakened her several times in the night so she still felt groggy. Better get dressed, she thought as she stretched her arms over her head and yawned again. Elena will be at my door in moments, ready for breakfast. She smiled. The child had bounced back from her tragedy with a resilience of youth that Katlin envied.

Of course, Katlin mused, Henry's devotion and constant attention probably had a lot to do with Elena's speedy recovery. Her heart ached to think that Henry's consumption could easily mean Elena would suffer another loss. She refused to dwell on it. After all, some people lived for years with pthisis. It was a strange disease. She remembered how her mother lingered with it for so long, yet it took her father so quickly. She shook her head and dismissed the dismal thoughts. Henry would return to New York with the ship and Elena would probably soon forget him. Instead, she found herself looking forward to visiting the fabled city of New Orleans.

They ate a hasty breakfast, then Katlin and Elena joined Henry at the rail to watch the beautiful blue water of the gulf glide by the hull. Whitecaps driven by a brisk northeasterly wind sparkled across the tops of the waves. As the sun rose higher in the soft azure sky, it drove the temperature up to nearly ninety degrees. The deliciously cool breeze kept them comfortable, although they carefully stayed under the shade of Katlin's parasol.

"You can tell we're getting close to land by looking at the water," Henry advised, pointing out the changes in color. As they watched, the deep blue shifted to a deep green, then to a muddy green. "A layer of fresh water covers the salt water for fifteen to twenty miles out past the mouth of the river. All the silt that's building the delta is carried miles out to sea before the river finally dumps the last of it."

"But I see no land," Elena protested.

"It's still too far away," Henry said. "We won't see land until tomorrow. There are no high mountains like on Cuba. The land is very flat. We'll see the light on South Pass off to starboard about dusk. That guides us into the correct arm of the river."

"You mean there is more than one?" Katlin had not thought of that.

"Oh, yes. The Mississippi is one huge delta. There are five navigable branches and countless smaller ones."

After the sun sank below the horizon in its usual blaze of glory, they retired to the saloon for the evening. There, Henry regaled Elena with stories of the river.

"They call it the Father of Waters," he declared. "It's filled by snows high in the Rocky Mountains, melted ice from the lakes of Minnesota, even runoff from a thousand miles of springs along the western slope of the Alleghenies. All drain into the Mississippi."

The next morning, Katlin stood by the rail, eager to get her first glimpse of the mighty Mississippi. She looked over the side at the current of brown soap suds. Elena joined her and looked with dismay at the water.

"It look like they wash the laundry in the water, yes?"

Katlin laughed. "Yes. So much for the Father of Waters."

Snow and ice and mountain springs indeed! "Henry has a vivid imagination. He forgot to mention all the mud. But it is a huge river. Must be a mile wide. And how they ever know where to navigate between all of these sand bars is beyond me."

They watched the shoreline slowly pass by. Willow and cypress trees lined the banks. Gray moss hung in long streams from the branches of the cypress trees, drifting down into the water.

Often a shout came from the lookout, "Floater comin' up to starboard!" At the warning cry, the ship changed course and sailors hurried to fend off the log with long poles.

Once Katlin saw an abandoned cabin, the thatch roof collapsed. She wondered what had become of the builder. Had he died of fever, or become disheartened with the struggle to keep back the river? She shook her head. No way she would ever know.

As they neared the city, fields of sugar cane and corn already in the ear ranged from the levees that protected the cropland from flooding back as far as she could see. Houses of planters, low and cool with long balconies, stood surrounded by orange and acacia trees and a tree covered with pink flowers.

"That's the crape myrtle, Miss MacKenzie," Henry advised her. "Real pretty tree. You'll see lots of 'em here in Louisiana."

"And those huts with no trees?"

"Those are the slave huts. All the planters have slaves."

She looked closer at the parallel rows of low tiny shacks. They must be unbelievably hot. Some of them had small gardens. One garden even blossomed with color from a small flower bed. "Why don't they have any trees?"

Henry shrugged. "Dunno. Guess they figger that since the slaves are all from Africa they're used to the heat."

The *Falcon* docked that evening in New Orleans, and Captain Arnold announced they would spend four days in port before departing for Chagres.

A storm of protest greeted his announcement.

"Never git to the gold iffen we don't hurry."

"Gold'll be all gone by the time you get us there."

"Your company, it say nothing of such delays. They assure us ..."

The captain held up his hand for silence. "Your ship leaves from Panama City on August first. Be there in plenty of time to make the connection, we will. Enjoy the city. Be your last chance at a civilized place for a long time."

Katlin smiled. "Since we are assured of making our connection in Panama, Captain Arnold, I, for one, will enjoy the interval. It's been a long time since we've been on land, and I am more than ready."

He returned her smile. "Good time to visit, it is. Cholera's gone, and 'tis not yet the season here for yellow fever. Come in two, three weeks, it will, but we'll be gone long before then."

"Good," Katlin muttered, thinking of the frigate in Havana harbor, the shrouded forms being lifted into the longboats, and the mournful tolling of the bells. She would never again think of bells as a joyous sound.

"And now," he tipped his cap, "if you will excuse me, Miss MacKenzie, got to see to the peaceful departure of our German friends. Don't quite trust these Spaniards not to try and even the score with Herr Freidenberger."

Katlin just shook her head. It crossed her mind that Caleb may have come through New Orleans. Would he have sold the ring here? Not likely. He would still have plenty of money, between what they received for the store and what he had swindled from the poor widow. All she knew was he had not booked passage on the *Falcon*, for she had asked in New York. He had probably taken one of the sailing vessels that left Boston every day.

The following morning, Henry hired a hack and took Elena and Katlin sightseeing. The American part, all hustle and bustle, resembled the business section of any city in the north. Disappointed, Katlin asked if any of the old city remained.

"Oh, yes," Henry assured her. "In the French Quarter, all of the homes of the French planters remain pretty much the same. They have been converted into small shops and cafes."

"Good. Let's go there."

On the *Place de Armes*, she saw workmen busy demolishing a large structure and asked what it had been.

"That's the Cathedral. They're tearing it down to build a prison."

"A prison! Isn't that a little sacrilegious?"

Henry grinned. "Guess not many Americans feel too sentimental about a Catholic cathedral, especially a French one. And they are preserving the front wall, with its venerable old tower."

"Good," Katlin commented. "I'm glad someone has some sense of history."

A rumble of thunder interrupted them.

"I believe, ladies, that we are about to have our daily downpour," Henry remarked. "Suppose we have a cup of coffee at one of the cafes while it passes. New Orleans is famous for its *cafe au lait*." He directed the driver, who urged the horse to a trot.

Within minutes, they could have traversed the streets by boat. Water poured from the skies in a veritable deluge. By the time they reached the small cafe, located in a magnificent old mansion on Royal Street, Henry had to carry them from the hack to the steps in water almost to his knees.

To Elena, it was all a lark. She opened her arms to the rain and laughed as it soaked her hair. "It is warm, the water. It is not cold!"

Katlin caught her humor and laughed as well. "I don't think the horse shares your feelings. Look at him." The horse stood patient and resigned, water dripping off his muzzle and his sagging ears. "Have you ever seen an animal look so positively dismal?"

All three, dripping wet, shook with laughter as they passed through the doorway into the dimly lighted room. While they waited for the sunshine to break through the clouds, they dined on small delicious cakes and drank thick coffee flavored with sweetened milk and served in small cups.

Before returning to the ship, Henry took them for a drive out Shell Road to the cemetery. There he pointed out the unique above-ground burial crypts.

"Why do they bury their dead above the ground?" Katlin asked.

"Because the ground has so much water in it the dead rise to the surface if they're buried."

"What?" Katlin gasped, her mouth dropping open in astonishment.

Elena shivered. "Do they ... how you say ... come to haunt?"

Henry laughed. "No, they just pop up out of the ground and wait to be buried again. The way it works, each family has one of these crypts. Need to bury the next family member, they just shove the bones from the first one to the back. Bones fall off the ledge into a collection container below, and there's room for the next one."

Katlin shook her head. "Never heard of such a thing." She noticed Elena glancing about her uneasily. "I think we'd best return to the ship."

* * *

The morning of the fourth day, as the time scheduled for departure approached, Katlin watched as about 150 additional passengers crowded on board. The captain, knowing the size of the anticipated crowd, had asked Katlin if Elena could move in with her, thus freeing a cabin. Katlin had complied and, watching the motley crew come aboard, was glad she had Elena close to her.

Henry pointed out the gaunt Mississippi, Arkansas, and Missouri squatters and ne'er-do-wells who again sought their fortune at another locale. "They'll fail wherever they go, Miss MacKenzie. It seems to be their lot. I suppose if they drank a little less whiskey, chewed a little less tobacco, and worked a little more regular, their lot might change, but I don't see that happening. Guess they figure this time, all they need to do is go to California and pick their fortune up off the ground."

"Do you really think it's like that in California? Is the gold that easy to find?"

"Depends on who you talk to, I guess. Have seen men with some fine sized nuggets come back. But I've seen a lot more eager searchers return empty handed."

"And the well dressed gentlemen? Seems to be a large number of them."

"Gamblers," Henry said. "An ominous number is how I'd put it." He grinned. "Gamblers follow the easy money. None of these fellers ever roughened their hands with honest work. Don't want anything to keep those sensitive fingers from finding the marks on the cards."

"Marks?" Katlin felt suddenly aware of her ignorance.

Henry laughed at her astonishment. "They all carry their own deck of cards. They put little nicks on the edge to tell them which card they have so they can draw the one they want."

"That must be hard to do, without someone noticing what they are up to."

"These men are real professionals. Most of them have worked the river boats for years. Believe me, they know how. I've watched and watched, trying to catch one, but they're too clever for me."

Katlin only shook her head. She wondered if any of these men, fresh from the soft, easy life of a river boat, had any idea of the enormity of the journey they had embarked upon.

She noticed some of the latest passengers were a variety unfamiliar to her. Lanky, loose-jointed men, with large hands and feet. Their clothing looked awkward on them, and she felt they would appear ungainly no matter what style of clothing they wore. What struck her the most was the expressions of melancholy on the long, sallow faces. Each bore a small arsenal, and scowled at the foreigners. Katlin fervently hoped they would not have another incident like the one that cost Elena's father his life.

As Katlin watched the embarking passengers, one stood out. Tall, clean-shaven, well-dressed, his neatly trimmed curly blond hair just touched his collar. As he glanced over the assembled passengers, his striking aquamarine eyes met Katlin's and her heart lurched.

# Chapter 7

"MASSA COLIN, Massa Colin! I'se so glad you're home." The grizzled negress stood twisting her hands around and around in her snowy white apron. "Miss Michelle, she's been askin' for you. Thinks it be her time."

The young man unfolded his long legs from the gig, stepped down, and removed his hat to fan his face. His high forehead glistened with perspiration in the muggy Louisiana heat.

"I came as fast as I could, Mama Carrie. Those Cajun shipping clerks just can't be hurried. And I know if I didn't watch them myself, half of our shipment would wind up on the wrong boat — or on someone else's account books!" He ran his fingers through his reddish blond hair and replaced the hat. Handing the reins to the boy who stood beside him, he followed Mama Carrie's wide body into the house and up the stairs to the bedroom where his wife lay, one hand on her swollen abdomen. Michelle's dark eyes sparkled in her small oval face.

"I'm feeling the first pains," she told Colin as he leaned down to kiss her. "Soon our son will be born! Mama Carrie has sent for the birthing woman."

He hugged her slight body close and kissed her again before releasing her. She always seemed so frail. A surge of fear swept through him. She was so little! Could she bear a child safely?

But she eagerly anticipated the birth, and chattered on. "The baby dropped this morning. Mama Carrie says that means the birth will come soon. I so feared you would not be back from New Orleans."

"I came as fast as I could. And," he teased, "how can you be so sure it's a son? Maybe I have a daughter, with sparkling black eyes like her mother."

"Because ... Oh!," she gasped, grasping her abdomen again, "Oh, there's another one! Will it be over soon, Mama Carrie?"

"Shoo, now, you relax. Susie be back with the birthin' woman any minnit now."

The entrance of the midwife ended the conversation. The woman immediately took charge, sending Susie to boil water and ordering Colin out of the room.

Michelle clung to him as he kissed her again. "Next time I see you, my darling, I'm going to introduce you to your son. You'll see!"

Colin turned at the door and blew her a kiss. I love you, he thought. You are my whole life. She waved cheerfully and Mama Carrie shut the door.

Time passed slowly. Colin tried to work on some of his accounts, but found he could not concentrate. Relax, he told himself, relax. Women have babies all the time. If only she wasn't so tiny!

Her dark, fragile beauty had attracted him to her at their first meeting, shortly after his arrival in New Orleans from New York. Her father, a French merchant, had invited Colin, as the newest landowner, to a small soiree. From the moment she placed her hand in his and he looked into those sparkling dark eyes, he knew she was the bride he wanted.

Colin smiled at the memory of their whirlwind courtship. Michelle's father had wanted them to wait for at least a year. She, in her usual direct way, announced she loved Colin and wanted no one else, so why wait?

"When the cholera comes through, or the yellow fever,

he could be gone — poof!" she said. "No, I take my happiness now, while it is here."

They had done well. His plantation grew until they had many acres of corn and cotton, and field slaves, even house slaves.

Owning slaves had bothered Colin, well aware of the mistreatment many of these people had suffered at the hands of unfeeling owners. He tried to avoid the more flagrant abuses. He bought whole families at auctions whenever possible, to keep them from being separated. He built them small cabins, even planting trees around the cabins for shade to provide some relief to the sticky heat. He noticed no other plantation did so, but he felt better for the action. He did not even own a whip, and forebade his overseer to use one.

Colin received all kinds of advice from his fellow planters on his lack of wisdom on how to handle slaves, but he had a loyal group. Any slave who got out of hand was told if he was not happy, Master MacDougal would be glad to sell him to one of the other planters. That threat kept them diligent.

Carrie and Susie and Mama Carrie's husband, Old Anthony, the house slaves, were loyal as family. Colin often thought of them as such.

As evening approached with still no word from Michelle's room, Colin stepped out to catch the evening breeze, wondering how much longer it could be. He watched the moon rise above the horizon, full and a brilliant orange. A harvest moon. He hoped it was a good omen. He lay down on the porch swing and watched the stars wink out as the moon rose, paling the stars into insignificance.

He woke at dawn with a start, cramped from sleeping in the short swing. Susie shook his arm, tears streaming down her face. "Massa Colin, Massa Colin, wake up!" She broke into sobs.

He jumped to his feet and grasped her arms. "What's

happened? Tell me!"

"The babe, the babe. It were too big." She gulped back her sobs and repeated. "Too big."

He did not wait to hear more. Releasing Susie's arms, he ran up the stairs, two at a time, and burst into the room. The midwife looked up. Mama Carrie sat in a nearby rocking chair weeping, wiping her eyes with her apron.

Colin approached the bed and took Michelle in his arms. Her eyes opened. "I did give you a son, my darling," she managed to gasp out, "but," the eyes held a glint of the old sparkle, "you ... will ... have to ... " Her head fell back and her eyes closed. He clasped her close and held her until the rasping breathing stopped.

His eyes met those of the midwife. "Babe too big," she said simply. "Tore her up inside. She too frail."

"And the boy?"

"Never breathed a gasp."

"I see." He thought of his happy world of yesterday. How could it be gone so fast? He saw the fear in the midwife's eyes.

"I done all I could, Massa Colin. I done all I know how to do."

"I know. I don't blame you. Just leave me alone with her for a while."

The two Negresses departed. Colin sat alone holding his wife's body, rocking her silently back and forth, his eyes dark with pain. His son. The son he had envisioned riding around the plantation at his side, learning to take his place. The son Michelle gave her life to give to him.

And Michelle! How could he go on without Michelle? She was his whole life. He had never thought any loss could be so hard to bear. He stopped rocking her body for a moment and looked down at the beloved face, so still and white. The realization of his loss hit him. He buried his face in her neck and burst into racking sobs.

He went through the next months in a haze of pain. His arms felt empty all the time. He spent hours beside the grave where Michelle and Colin MacDougal III lay together.

Everything reminded him of her. When the orange trees bloomed, he remembered how she loved the smell of orange blossoms, and the time she brought in an armload of the flowers and a bee in one stung her. Riding in the gig reminded him of how she would take off her hat and let her long dark hair blow in the wind, to the scandal of the neighbors. Whenever he lighted the lamp in the parlor, he thought of how she had begged him to buy it for her, even though he felt the large red roses on the shade made it look gaudy.

In 1848, rumors came of a gold strike in California. Is that the answer, he thought. Get away from here? I can't keep running. I left New York when my mother died. Shall I leave New Orleans to run away from death again?

In the spring of 1849, he made his decision. Gold seekers passed through on every steamer. He would sell everything and join them. If the rumors of so much gold turned out to be deceptive, he could buy land and farm in California. He would at least escape the memory of Michelle, and get away from everything that reminded him of her every day.

By July, all preparations were complete. He sold his land to a neighboring planter who was also willing to buy his slaves, one he felt would also treat them with kindness. Several wanted to try making it on their own. These Colin gave the papers they needed for passage to a free state, along with enough money to last them for a while, and wished them well. Susie's husband was among those men, so she went north also.

He bought a small house in New Orleans for Mama Carrie and Old Anthony so they could stay in the city they loved.

He arranged with the bank to pay them a stipend so they could be comfortable.

Mama Carrie wept with gratitude. "Oh, Massa Colin, you is so good."

Anthony just clutched the papers saying he was a free man, his eyes moist, unable to speak.

"It's the least I can do, Mama Carrie, after all of your years of faithful service. If you have any problems at all, you can reach me through the bank. A second copy of all of the papers is with Mr. Scofield."

And so, on July 12, 1849, Colin MacDougal II joined the small party of adventurers and gold seekers on board the US Mail Steamer *Falcon*, bound for Chagres.

# Chapter 8

ALL IN ALL, an additional 150 or so men joined the *Falcon* for her onward voyage to Chagres. The multitude crowded the deck, many having booked on as deck passengers.

Katlin queried Henry about the arrangements for the additional travelers the following morning, as the *Falcon* again reached the clear, blue waters of the Gulf.

"Cheaper," he grinned in response. "Company offers half-price passage to anyone willing to sleep on deck. Make a lot of money that way. Weather's always warm enough this far south."

"Half of them look like they're drunk most of the time," Katlin remarked, with a disgusted glance at several men dozing in the sun. "The only time they ever move is to go into the forecastle for more whisky."

"And they chew the tobacco *all* the time," Elena shuddered. "To watch them, it is enough to spoil the stomach, yes?"

"Yes," Katlin agreed. She looked towards the bow. There, hat in hand, the wind riffling the reddish blond hair that curled about his head, stood the gentleman she had watched board yesterday. He stood alone, aloof from the other passengers. With them, yet never one of them, she thought. He's so far superior in every way. She caught herself. Forget him. Nothing is going to detract you from your mission. With a smile, she turned to Henry.

"And how long until we reach Chagres?" she asked.

"Usually takes about seven days, barrin' anything happening."

"And what could happen?"

"Well," he drawled. "This is hurricane season. Captain Arnold keeps a close eye on the glass. Starts fallin' too low, he heads for a hurricane hole."

"And what on earth is that?"

"Protected harbor. Tuck in, anchor, tie everything as secure as possible, and ride it out."

Elena's eyes widened. "It is dangerous?"

"Can be." He shrugged his shoulders expressively. "But Captain Arnold knows what he's about." He tucked her hand through the crook of his arm, patted it gently and smiled. "Don't worry. I'll take good care of you."

Katlin noticed the look of adoration that sprang into Elena's eyes and suppressed a smile.

Although Katlin eyed the skyline every morning, expecting at any moment to see a heavy bank of menacing dark clouds bearing down upon them, seven days passed without incident. On their fourth night out of New Orleans, Henry pointed out the light at the end of the island of Cuba as they passed between Cuba and Yucatan. Running the gauntlet of coral reefs off the coast of Honduras kept Katlin gasping in awe at the skill of the pilot as he navigated his way among the coral heads, often not visible more than half the time. She breathed a sigh of relief when they entered the deep, dark blue waters of the fabled Caribbean Sea.

On the seventh day, Katlin and Elena braved the rain, pitching deck, and cold, raw wind, hoping to see their destination.

Elena shivered. "It is cold, like the New York, yes?"

Katlin laughed and pulled her shawl closer. "More like the coast of Maine," she said, feeling colder at the memory.

"I thought the tropics, they are warm, yes?"

Henry came up in time to hear her and grinned. "Wait until the cloud cover passes. Come inside. Dinner will be ready soon, and we won't see land until tomorrow."

"Thank you. Come, Elena." They struggled along the deck, with Henry's help, into the haven of the main saloon.

The morning of their eighth day after leaving New Orleans, a heavy rain cloud lifted and the headland of Porto Bello stood before them. Golden cliffs jutted from the wave of green vegetation that rolled down to the sea, where frothy breakers foamed against the rows of mangrove trees lining the shore. The mountains, the captain told her, were the Andes of Darien. They towered beyond the coast, rising higher and higher until the peaks disappeared in the rainy mists. Passing through a narrow channel between two magnificent bluffs, they entered the land-locked harbor.

"Chagres lies another eight miles west, but the mouth of the river is so narrow we'll be 'most atop it before we see it." Captain Arnold tipped his cap to them. "You ladies enjoy the scenery. I got to get ready for landin', I do."

Katlin and Elena stood watching the strange exotic landscape drift by when a castle on the bluff appeared out of the mist.

Elena seized Katlin's arm and pointed out the massive edifice. "Look, another Moro," she declared.

"That is the Castle of San Lorenzo. Magnificent in its day, though I fear it has fallen sadly into disrepair." As Katlin and Elena turned toward the speaker, he touched his hat politely. "Colin MacDougal at your service, ladies." He offered Katlin his hand and smiled, a smile Katlin felt all the way to her toes. She found herself getting lost in the depths of those magnificent eyes.

She pulled herself back with an effort and placed her hand in his. The touch of his hand, even through her glove, sent tingles up her arm. "Katlin MacKenzie," she managed to choke out.

"Ah, a fellow Scotsman. And this lovely miss?" He turned to Elena.

Elena dropped a quick curtsey. "Maria Elena Velasquez de Rodriquez, your servant, *Señor*." Her dark eyes sparkled.

Uh-oh, Katlin thought. She noticed my reaction to him. Now she's going to be playing match-maker. She felt they should get back to a safer subject.

"There is a history for San Lorenzo, I assume?" Katlin forced her voice to be matter-of-fact, although she could almost feel it cracking.

"Yes," he replied. "It is where over three hundred defenders were slain by the pirate Henry Morgan and his band of buccaneers back in 1671. They scaled the walls and leveled the castle. Only thirty-three survived the fight. Some jumped to their destruction from that precipice, preferring death at their own hand to captivity by Morgan." He pointed to the site. "Morgan has become somewhat of a hero in the legends and tales that have sprung up about him, but he was not a man to cross."

"*Que triste*," Elena murmured in sympathy, her eyes glued to the spot.

"Yes, then he crossed the Isthmus and destroyed the city the Spanish founded on the Pacific side in 1519. I understand we will have the opportunity to view the ruins after we arrive in Panama City." He tipped his hat again. "So pleased to have made your acquaintance at last, Miss MacKenzie, Senorita Velasquez." He departed, leaving Katlin and Elena to stare at the bluffs below the ruined castle.

Katlin closed her eyes. In her mind, she heard the cries of the doomed defenders as they made their last, desperate leap into the sea. The ring of steel, the shouts of the marauders, the roaring boom of the cannon, surrounded her for the moment.

She opened her eyes and shook her head. The rhythmic thud of the engine replaced the sound of the cannon and clash of steel. Instead of despairing cries, she heard only the sound of the water as the wheel rotated, pulling them along their way. She laughed at her fantasies.

Someday, Katlin MacKenzie, she told herself, your over-active imagination is going to be too much for you. She thought again of those aquamarine eyes. Colin MacDougal. He may claim to be a Scotsman, but with the red in his hair and the color of those eyes, there had to be an Irishman somewhere. She shrugged. It was none of her affair. She had no time for romance, even if he was interested in her. She had a job to do.

At half past four that afternoon, they dropped anchor off the mouth of the river, near a flat, marshy area. Katlin, with Elena clinging to her arm, watched as two stalwart sea-men rowed Captain Arnold and his clerk ashore in the ship's boat.

Katlin's heart quailed as she wondered what to do next. The men gathered their belongings, preparatory to disembarking. She knew they had to cross the Isthmus to the Pacific side. Their fellow passengers had loudly discussed the labors involved in securing canoes to take them to the head of the river.

As she pondered the problem, Henry came to her side.

"Miss MacKenzie," he began shyly, twisting his cap around and around in his hands, "I had a long talk with Captain Arnold. We've all heard that the climate in California is good for folks with pthisis. I've quit my job on the *Falcon* and will escort you and Miss Elena to California."

Relief washed over Katlin at his words, and Elena squealed with delight. Katlin smiled at Elena's reaction, which brought a light to Henry's eyes as well, and said, "Thank you, Henry. I was wondering how we would man-age, with all of these fellows scrambling for every available canoe . . . " her voice trailed off.

"Rainin' cats and dogs on the river now. Best to leave

the ship in the morning. No decent place to stay on shore anyway. Chagres is a miserable hole. Low, wet, and filthy, with dead dogs and pigs, and carrion of every description lying in the streets."

Katlin grimaced. "You're right. It doesn't sound like a place we'd want to stay. Are there no hotels?"

"One, on the south side, called the Irving House, costs twice as much as hotels in New York, and not much for service. Better to stay right here."

"I'm convinced," Katlin nodded. "I just hope we can get a canoe quickly enough in the morning to get out before nightfall."

The ship's boat returned the clerk to the ship alone. The men mobbed him the moment he stepped on deck. "Pacific Mail Steamer the *Panama* leaves Panama City August first," he reported. "Gives you fellers ten days to git there. Hadn't oughta take you more'n five or six. Make yer deals with the canoe men in the mornin'."

He pushed his way through the gathered assemblage and disappeared into the chart house.

The passengers grumbled and began the laborious process of again storing their belongings below decks. The tropical night descended with its usual startling suddenness. Brilliant flashes of lightning burst every few moments from a heavy dark cloud that lay over the sea. Each flash illuminated the dark walls of San Lorenzo, the palm trees along the shore, and the green rolling hills that surrounded the bay.

"It is dangerous, no?" Elena clung to Katlin in fright at the display of pyrotechnics.

"Can be, if it hits you. But I think this is far enough away we are in no danger," Katlin hastened to reassure the girl. I hope, she added in her mind.

The display faded, and rain drops pelted them, so they scurried below deck to the haven of their cabin. As they prepared for bed, Katlin looked around at the space that had been home for over a month. She wondered, where will we be sleeping tomorrow night?

Elena interrupted her thoughts. "You have the look of the worry. Do not. My Henry will take care of us."

Katlin laughed. She wished she could share Elena's faith in a consumptive boy who had never been past Chagres and whose illness could become incapacitating at any time. She did not share her concerns with Elena, saying only, "Of course. Let's get a good night's sleep. It may be our last chance for a long time."

But sleep eluded Katlin. She lay beside Elena for what seemed like hours, listening to the waves gently slapping the side of the hull and trying to ignore the snores from the other passengers. She knew the importance of getting a good night's rest before setting off on their trek across the Isthmus.

Finally she rose quietly and ascended to the deck. She stood by the rail, letting the cool evening breeze waft over her, bringing the fragrance of the lush vegetation that lined the shore, along with an occasional whiff of smoke from a native fire. The clouds had passed, and stars studded the soft velvet sky.

As she stood there, watching the moon gradually ascend to dominate over the stars, she wondered if continuing to follow Caleb was foolish. He would probably use up all of the money before she found him. If she could even find him. If only she had not taken on the responsibility to care for Elena! The child would be better off if Katlin returned to New York with her.

The memory of Caleb riding away on Sunny returned, and so did her resolution. He would probably continue to lie and cheat other women if no one stopped him. She set her jaw. I will stop him, she vowed. I will stop him.

"Good evening, Miss MacKenzie." Colin MacDougal's

voice at her elbow startled her. She could just make out his features in the dim light, but she would never mistake that voice, or his height, or the cut of his shoulders.

"Are you unable to sleep?" he continued. "I found the atmosphere below decks intolerably stuffy."

She turned to face him, moonlight bathing her face, and smiled. "No longer. I think I will now sleep quite well, thank you. See you in the morning." She briefly offered him her hand. "Good night."


Colin leaned against the rail and watched Katlin disappear down the companionway. She stirred his pulses as no woman but Michelle ever had. Could it be possible to ever fall in love like that a second time? Did he wish to expose himself to be hurt that deeply again?

He chuckled. Come to your senses, man, he said to himself. She's not interested in you. I wonder what possessed her to undertake a journey of this magnitude by herself. Foolhardy? No, she did not impress him as a foolish woman. There was an intensity about her, a sense of purpose.

# Chapter 9

THE SUN CLEARED the bluffs to the east before Katlin
and her fellow travelers and all of their belongings reached
the shore. As they rounded the high bluff of San Lorenzo,
the channel opened into a shallow inlet. The cane huts of
the town of Chagres stood on the low ground that circled
the bay, 70 to 80 huts built of bamboo poles stuck into the
ground and fastened with bark or cords. Palm leaves covered the conical roofs.

Many piles of luggage lined the shore beside the canoes
dragged up on the shoreline. Americans rushed about trying to hurry the boatmen, who calmly repaired the thatch
covering on the boats with split palm leaves.

Other canoes showed no signs of the boatmen, and the
passengers scurried about, loudly demanding to know the
location of the men they had hired and paid the previous
evening to guarantee a swift departure.

Katlin had roused Elena at dawn, saying, "Come. We
must be ready to leave. If the canoes are as hard to obtain
as they say, we'd better get started."

Elena's response was typical. "Without the breakfast,
no?"

"Without the breakfast, yes." She sent the girl to talk the
cook into giving her a biscuit to tuck into her reticule.

But as Katlin stood on the shore and shook her head at
the chaos, she wondered if it mattered. Maybe she should
have let Elena sleep longer and have breakfast. Henry, beside her, laughed. "These natives know two more steamers

are due in tomorrow. They also know Americans are always in a hurry. Down here, in this heat, no one hurries to do anything."

"I can believe that." Although just nine o'clock in the morning, the sun's rays already pounded down on her head.

Henry advised the girls to stay with the luggage. "I'll see about a canoe. They call 'em 'bungos' here. You watch no one gets into our stuff. These natives, they're gentle and kind, but have a philosophy that says if something isn't watched, it's fair game."

He strode off and Katlin sat down on one of the trunks to wait. She opened her parasol to deflect the most direct rays of the sun and watched the people lounging in the doorways of the surrounding huts. Men and women alike, each wearing a single cotton garment, leisurely smoked their cigars. Naked children with shaved heads and distended bellies tumbled and played in the sun.

"*Mira,*" Elena whispered to Katlin, her eyes wide. "The children, they wear nothing."

"In this heat, I suppose it makes perfect sense," Katlin replied with a laugh.

Elena looked doubtful, but made no further comment. They waited, perspiring profusely in the sticky heat. Katlin's clothing clung to her body, holding the heat. She was glad she dispensed with the stays and wore only her chemise and drawers under her dress. She had, with some difficulty, persuaded Elena to do the same.

Half an hour later, Henry returned with Colin MacDougal and a young native man he introduced as Felipe.

"Felipe will take the four of us to Gorgona, at the head of the Chagres River," he announced. "For fifteen dollars apiece, he will promise to make the trip in three days. He has another man who will help him."

He added with a grin, "Felipe also says Jorge is very helpful, but will relieve you of all concern for your belongings if he can, so watch your baggage."

Katlin shook her head. "And when are we leaving? Any chance to get some breakfast before we go?"

Colin MacDougal smiled at her. "No use to try the Crescent Hotel. I already did. Perhaps one of the natives will supply us."

"Go with Mr. MacDougal, Miss MacKenzie," Henry said. "Take Elena. I'll stay with the baggage."

Katlin did not express the doubt she felt about eating anything that came out of one of those huts. With a shrug, she said, "Whatever you say."

They strolled by the native huts until they found one where the woman standing beside the door agreed to feed them. There, seated on a chicken coop, they dined on some pieces of pork fat, fresh bread, and a delicious fruit with a thick green rind streaked with red that Katlin could not identify. Their hostess brought them fresh spring water to drink, served in a coconut shell.

The dogs and pigs watched from a respectful distance. Elena eyed them uneasily.

"They've probably been hit for getting too close and have learned to stay away," Katlin reassured Elena with a chuckle.

Exhilaration swept through her as she wiped the fruit juice from her fingers. What an adventure this was turning out to be! Her misgivings left her. Could one reason be the presence of Colin MacDougal? He had an air of competence about him that she felt reassuring. Although, she thought with a grimace, he has no obligation to you, Katlin MacKenzie. He's probably as anxious to reach the gold fields as the rest of them.

As they ate, a man strode up and greeted them cordially.

"Howdy, folks. Any more of thet grub around?"

"Of course, please join us." Colin rose to give the man his space on the hen coop. "Are you going to California also?"

"Jest got back. Spent two months in the diggin's." He patted the money bag around his waist. "Got me $2200 in gold dust. Me an' the missus, we're gonna open a little store, and this'll git us goin'. And feast yer eyes on this!" He reached into his shirt and pulled out a dingy, ragged handkerchief. Triumphantly, he unwrapped a huge nugget of gold.

"Weighs four ounces," he bragged. "They's more like it, jest layin' around for the pickin'. I'd'a stayed longer, got more, but I wanted to git back to the missus 'n' the young-uns. She'll be a-worryin', she will."

Katlin shook her head. She began to understand the urge these men felt to get to their destination. She had seen that same look of obsession in Caleb's eyes. At that moment she almost felt some sympathy for him. It passed quickly. *He could have taken me with him. And that certainly did not excuse his cheating that poor widow. No, Caleb was a rat, undeserving of compassion.*

Other travelers passed by and heard the man's boast. It seemed to drive them into a more frantic frenzy to get started, and they rushed to prod their boatmen. One man emerged from a hut dragging a native on each side of him and marched to the canoe. Another waved his pistol about and made threats, which frightened Elena and annoyed Katlin. The natives totally ignored the blusterers.

"No use rushing 'em," Henry laughed. "They'll go when they're ready." He explained. "They've seen men make threats before. They know if the man shoots the boatman, he won't ever get there, so such actions only make Americans look foolish."

Katlin only shook her head.

By eleven o'clock, their belongings were stored in the broad, sturdy craft hollowed out of a single log, about twenty-five feet long and three feet wide. The boatmen rigged the thatch cover to protect their passengers from the fierce rays of the sun. With Henry's aid, Katlin and Elena boarded and settled onto the slab of wood that served as the seat. Katlin shifted on the hard wood and grimaced. It was going to be a long three days. The thatch did not cover the whole canoe, so Katlin raised her parasol.

"Go now for food, return quick," Felipe said. He and Jorge departed.

They waited, broiling in the blazing sun. Several men mentioned a fear of yellow fever. Memories of the victims of that dreaded disease suffering in isolation on the ship in Havana Harbor popped unbidden into Katlin's mind. The Black Vomit. A disease that, like cholera, could kill in 24 hours. She shivered as she remembered the moans of the dying, the still forms transported to shore after dark, the mournful sound of the bells . . . .

Stop it, she ordered herself, swatting at a persistent mosquito and wiping her forehead with her already sodden handkerchief. Don't bring on the fever by fretting about it.

Boys came by selling fruit and biscuits. Elena announced she was still hungry.

"You're always hungry," Katlin laughed. She dug some coins out of her reticule. "Have a biscuit. I'll have some more of that delicious unknown fruit we had for breakfast."

"Mango," the boy informed her solemnly, accepting the coins and giving her two of the green-red fruits.

"Mango," she repeated. "Thank you. I'll remember that." The boys departed and she borrowed Henry's knife and began to peel.

About noon, as Katlin wiped the last of the juice from the mango off of her fingers, Felipe and Jorge returned with a bag of rice, another of dried pork, and an armload of sugar cane.

"Go now," Felipe announced cheerfully. "Ten miles to Gatun. Be at Gatun before rains come. Spend night there, under roof."

"Guess that beats spending the night on the river in the rain," Henry commented philosophically. "The *Panama* won't leave until August first, so we got no need to hurry. Relax and enjoy the trip, ladies. It's thirty-nine and a half miles to Gorgona, another four and a half to Cruces." He patted Elena's hand, then turned away coughing.

When the paroxysm finally stopped, Katlin noticed he tried to give Elena a reassuring smile, but his efforts did not remove the worried look from her eyes.

California climate may be good for pthisis sufferers, Katlin thought, but if he doesn't live to get there, it won't help him much. With a sigh, she thought of how long Martha MacKenzie had lingered, yet how quickly her father had died.

She refused to worry about it. She positioned her valise so she could lean against it and lay back under the thatch canopy to watch the scenery and listen to Jorge sing, decidedly off key, but with great enthusiasm.

The moment they left the bay and headed up the Chagres River, Katlin felt she had stepped into another world. Nothing she had ever read or heard prepared her for the sheer mass of living greenery that surrounded her in this land of eternal summer. No trace of soil could be seen. Blossoms of white, yellow, and scarlet intermingled with the lush mass of leaves. Boughs of trees reached across from the banks, with streams of vines trailing into the clear, fresh water of the swiftly moving river. Butterflies and birds with brilliant plumes flitted in and out of the foliage.

Each turn of the river brought new delights. She thought, with a twinge of pity, of people who lived their whole lives in places like New York or Boston, never seeing such beauty as stood before her now.

\* \* \*

By late afternoon, just as the clouds massed on the horizon and a few stray drops of rain began to pelt them, Felipe and Jorge beached the canoe and pulled it up on the bank. As Colin and Henry assisted Katlin and Elena to alight, Jorge returned and spoke to Felipe in rapid Spanish.

Elena translated to Katlin. "He say he have the space for the night in a hut. We go quickly now, before the rain."

"Gladly." Several more large raindrops splattered on Katlin's parasol.

Elena looked puzzled. "He also say we sleep in the," she paused, "the hammock? What is that?"

"You'll find out," said Henry with a grin. "Come on. The rain will be here for real any second now."

Felipe escorted the party to a hut, really just one large room, where all of the living took place. Katlin looked about, but could see no signs of privacy anywhere. She wasn't about to say anything about their private needs to any of the men, so she had Elena ask the small native woman who stood by the cooking fire. With a soft laugh, the woman led them to a small bamboo enclosure with walls of palm thatch. Inside, Katlin saw only a patch of sand, but signs showed it had been used before.

"This only for *mujeres*," Elena informed her. "The men, they go into the jungle."

"Well, that's a relief," Katlin replied, appalled at first, then her sense of humor rose and the whole scene struck her as funny. She remembered the long, tedious days she had spent at Miss Wayne's Academy learning to be a proper lady. If only Miss Adams could see her now! She started to laugh, and Elena joined her.

They returned to the hut to find a partition of sorts across one corner of the room. Henry busily strung two hammocks between the poles that supported the roof. Her haversack and Elena's stood against the wall. He looked up from his work and grinned.

"Mr. MacDougal, he can be persuasive. He insisted you two ladies have some privacy."

"Thank you," Katlin said. "And thank Mr. MacDougal for us." She stretched her arms over her head and arched her back. "I'm stiff from sitting in that boat all afternoon." The sound of drums reached her ears. "Why do we hear drums?" she asked, startled as she remembered stories of drums being beaten before natives attacked.

"It's Sunday night. Big fandango. Two boys're pounding some wooden drums to get all the folks together. Everybody's gettin' decked out in all their finery."

"Can we go?" Katlin's curiosity, always easily aroused, surfaced at once.

"Best get some rest. Felipe says we head out at midnight to get up the river."

After a supper of pork and coffee and more of the fruit the boys had told her was called a mango, she sat cross-legged on the thatched floor and tried to write in her diary by the light of one miserable tallow candle stuck in a bottle. She had barely begun to write her perceptions of the scenery when she found her paper covered with fleas.

Between the flickering feeble light and the onslaught of the fleas, she decided to postpone her diary annotations and get some sleep. She managed to get Elena settled in the hammock, but not until their efforts reduced them both to fits of giggles.

"Try to get in more slowly," Katlin managed to gasp, controlling her laughter with difficulty. "You overbalance the wretched contraption when you try and jump on it." Elena kept turning the hammock over, landing on the floor. When Katlin began to despair of ever getting the girl settled, and was about to call for Henry to help them, Elena finally managed to get herself secured into the bamboo leaf cocoon.

Katlin learned some things about hammocks from Elena's

efforts, and managed to get herself into her own, secure for the few hours until midnight. Neither bothered to undress.

Sleep eluded her. Frequent quarrels among the natives gathered around the table drinking aquardiente kept awakening her. If the loud voices quieted for a while, one of the dogs would pass under her hammock, using it as a scratching post to rub off the fleas. The fleas, as Henry had warned her, were very acrobatic, and soon she felt them biting with regularity.

"Dog," she muttered sleepily, "go rub your fleas on someone else." That dog would oblige and amble off, only to be replaced by one of his companions.

At midnight, Henry roused them. They managed to extricate themselves from their hammocks without falling and silently made their way back to the boat. It took them until two in the morning to get the crew together and head out once more onto the river.

Felipe joined them with a third hand he engaged for another eight dollars. "Needs an extra hand. River's high, current's swift from all the rain," Henry explained. "He says the Chagres can rise up to forty feet in a single storm."

"Forty feet! That's incredible," Katlin gasped.

"Yep. They get up to 130 inches of rain a year on this side. Get it all between May and November."

At dawn, they reached a cluster of huts Felipe called Dos Hermanos. There they passed two canoes filled with fellow passengers from the *Falcon*. A stream of rapid fire Spanish passed back and forth between the boatmen.

Elena translated. "He say men crazy, not want to stop. Point pistol at boat man." She giggled. "Go all night, men very tired, go slow. Felipe say better rest, go faster. He tell other man we smarter passengers, listen Felipe."

Katlin only shook her head at the folly of those who felt such a need for haste they would risk their lives and the lives of their boatmen. "The *Panama* won't leave until August first anyway. What's the hurry?" she asked Henry.

"Other ships come by. Guess they figger if they get there a day or two earlier, they can get on a ship ahead of us." He shook his head. "Crazy, they are. Like to kill themselves pushing so hard."

The afternoon clouds started to gather. "Stop Palo Matida for rain, one hour, maybe two, then rain go," Felipe announced. He beached the canoe as a cold wind swept across them and the sky darkened. Scrambling for cover, they barely reached the hut before torrents of rain broke over them. Jagged streaks of lighting darted from the clouds to the ground, each followed by a crash of thunder that shook the very ground beneath their feet.

Katlin and Elena huddled together under a poncho of India rubber to keep out the cold air that blew in one side of the hut and out the other. "I think we're getting half of that 130 inches right now," Katlin muttered.

After an hour, the rain eased to a light drizzle, and the boatmen urged them back into the boats.

"In the rain?" Katlin asked when Colin offered his hand to help her rise. She tried to ignore the spark that shot up her arm at his touch.

"They say we must make Peña Blanca before dark, to spend the night there."

Katlin sighed, and they were soon under way again. She and Elena, cold and sodden, huddled under the India rubber poncho. Jorge sang with his usual gusto, following each song with another swallow from the brandy bottle.

"He's going to be too drunk to paddle if he keeps that up," Katlin commented to Henry.

Henry twisted his mouth into a wry grin. "It's the custom. Travelers keep the boatman supplied with brandy, he sings and drinks it. Can't break tradition, you know."

Katlin laughed, finding herself amused by the whole scene. Here she sat, huddled under a poncho in pouring rain, being propelled up a strange river in a tropical paradise by a boatman who not only serenaded her, but was about to get drunk and pass out.

She suddenly thought of Caleb and wondered, how far ahead of me are you?

# Chapter 10

THEY REACHED Peña Blanca and secured space for the night. Elena and Katlin shared the loft of the spacious hut, grateful to be assured of privacy and to be away from the dogs. The thatch above them crawled with vermin. A large rat scampered out of sight through a hole in the corner. Cockroaches as large as Katlin's thumb scurried away from the light of the tallow candle Katlin carried.

Elena emitted a little squeak of distaste at the sight.

"Go to sleep," Katlin ordered. "At least they don't bite." She thought of centipedes and venomous snakes with horror and wondered if any of them would put in an appearance. Her imagination pictured them crawling along the thatch and dropping down on her. She doused the light from the feeble candle and pulled the thin blanket over her head. In spite of her worries, fatigue overwhelmed her and she immediately fell into a deep and dreamless sleep.

It seemed to Katlin she had barely closed her eyes when she felt someone shaking her arm. She opened her eyes and made out Henry's face in the dim pre-dawn light.

"Come on," he urged. "Wake up. Felipe wants to start at sunrise. Says he hopes to make Gorgona tonight and the river's running high with all the rain."

Katlin sat up, relieved to find no snakes or centipedes had joined her during the night. "We'll be right there." Inwardly, she thought, I've slept in the same dress for two nights in a row, will probably sleep in it again tonight, and would give anything to soak in a nice tub of hot water.

When they reached the bank, the men hurried them aboard. Katlin gasped at the swiftly moving water.

"Can they pole against that?" Katlin asked, appalled as she watched leaves and small branches whirl by in the rapid current. "Won't we wind up back in Chagres?"

"That's why we hired the third man, to help pole. As the river rises and narrows, the current is swifter. 'Specially with all the rain the last couple days." Henry smiled at Elena as he patted her hand. "Don't worry. We'll take good care of you."

The men made good their boast, and managed to make fairly rapid progress up the river in spite of the current. Just as Katlin began to relax and enjoy herself again, a violent blow knocked her from her seat into the bottom of the boat. Elena landed on top of her.

"*Que pasa? Que pasa?*" Elena cried out in fright. The boat remained stopped while the current flowed around them. Henry and Colin hastened to help Elena and Katlin regain their seats.

"And what was that?" Katlin asked, surveying her muddied gloves and skirt with dismay.

"Hit a sunken log," Colin explained. "Happens all the time in the Louisiana bayous. Logs soak up enough water to sink just out of sight, but snag on the bottom. If the water's shallow, the log is high enough to catch the boat." He dipped his large handkerchief into the water and scrubbed the mud from the bilge off of Katlin's gloves. Their eyes met. The surge of emotion that swept over Katlin dismayed her. She pulled her hands free.

"Thank you," she murmured, turning away from those hypnotic aquamarine eyes. "Can the boatmen get us free? We're not going to capsize, are we?" Fright swept through her at the thought of being thrown into that turbulent stream.

The terrified Elena clung to Henry, her eyes wide.

Felipe hastened to assure them all would be well, that this sort of thing happened often, but they struggled for over an hour with no success, rocking the boat until Elena cried out in fright and grabbed Katlin's arm.

"*Vamos a morir*," she gasped. "*Vamos a morir*."

Finally, Felipe took a rope between his teeth, jumped into the water, and swam to shore. He fastened the line to a tree, and, with all five men pulling, they managed to yank the canoe free. It rocked as it came loose and almost knocked Elena and Katlin into the bilge again, but Katlin had braced herself and managed to keep them in place.

Felipe swam back to the boat and clambered over the side, grinning broadly. He took up his paddle again and cried out in triumph, "*Ahora, vamos!*"

With a sigh, Katlin settled back to watch the scenery again. A small monkey scolded them and scurried higher in the branches as they floated beneath his tree. They passed ranches where the jungle had been cleared and planted to corn, plantains, and rice. The ranches had names, according to Felipe, who pointed them out as they cruised past: Agua Salud, Varro Colorado, and Palanquilla.

Early in the afternoon, shortly after Palanquilla passed to the stern, the sky darkened and a storm swept down upon them. To Katlin, the rain came with a roar not unlike the sound of an approaching train.

With a shout at his crew, Felipe poled the boat towards the shore and found them a refuge of sorts under a broad sycamore tree. There Katlin and Elena huddled under the invaluable India rubber poncho and listened to the pounding rain.

And you thought you had seen rain in Maine, Katlin thought. It's like someone tipped over the whole cloud and poured all the rain out at once. She felt moisture leaking around gaps in the poncho as the thatch cover on the boat reached its saturation point and could hold no more. The tree above the boat filled its leaves with water, then dumped the contents, and straightened to fill again.

She and Elena lifted their heads together. Their eyes met. Katlin looked at Elena's sodden hair, with the rain streaming down her face, and thought she, too, must look half drowned. Jorge continued to sing and sip on the brandy bottle. The humor of the whole scene finally got to Katlin and she started to laugh.

When the storm passed over them, on down the river, they continued their journey. The banks grew steeper as the river narrowed. In late afternoon, Felipe pulled up to a small dock and announced they had reached the hacienda of San Pablo.

"*Casa de* Padre Dutaris, the *curé*. We spend night here. Still four hours, Gorgona, too far, too swift. Gorgona *mañana*."

"You mean we can spend the night in a real house?" Katlin marveled at her good fortune, thinking she would be able to at least change her chemise and drawers. She and Elena eagerly followed Felipe up the path, across an open, rolling savanna.

Gigantic palm trees towered above them, and huge acacias dotted the plains. Fat cattle and sleek horses grazed on the open grassland. From the top of the rise, a magnificent view of the river opened before them. As the sun beat down upon the hills, steam rose to make the cattle seem to float upon a cloud.

Elena chattered beside her. "Felipe, he say *curé* good friend. Wife of *curé*, she feed us good. The padre, he cheated by many Americans, so only feed those Felipe say *son bueños caballeros*." She waved her hand in the direction of the herd of livestock. "Also say padre rich man, have, how you say, *un mil ganados y caballos*."

The padre's son, a bright, intelligent lad of about twelve with sparkling black eyes and velvety brown skin, greeted them. Playing host in his father's absence, he invited them into the house where his mother stood by the cooking fire. Wonderful aromas arose from the pots on the hearth, and Katlin's stomach jumped in anticipation.

They dined on chicken, eggs, rice boiled in coconut milk, chocolate, and baked plantain, all of which tasted as delicious as it smelled. After supper, while Henry and Elena went for a stroll, Katlin sat on her hammock to write in her diary, pleased to find no fleas hopping on the page. The boy sat beside her and watched her write, then wrote his name for her next to what she had written.

"You're a charming young man," she told the boy, closing the book. "And you write very well. I'll treasure your memento. Now, as much as I enjoy your company, I am worn out and would like to go to sleep."

Henry returned with Elena and Katlin looked up.

"You weren't gone very long," she observed.

"The mosquitoes!" Elena exclaimed. "They eat me." She displayed a number of welts on her face and hands.

Henry chuckled. "They come up out of the fields in swarms as soon as the sun starts to set. Get in your hammocks and get under the netting. See you at four o'clock. Felipe wants to be underway at five."

"Five! Why so early? I thought we were only a few hours from Gorgona."

"We are, but we want to get there as soon as we can. The rest of the passengers from the *Falcon* will be taking all the mules and horses. Need them to get across and down to the city on the other side. If the river is high enough, we may go on to Cruces. Only eighteen miles from Cruces to Panama. Twenty miles from Gorgona." He grinned. "Sleep well."

They were under way by five o'clock the next morning as planned. Colin watched Katlin as she and Elena appeared.

"You look in good spirits for so early in the morning," he said, noticing her improved mood. He swept off his hat to her. "You are looking lovely this morning, Miss MacKenzie."

"Thank you," she replied. "They tell me a good night's sleep is good for the complexion."

"And a rosy complexion it is, with all of this sun. You and I have the same problem. We never tan, we only burn." Not like my Michelle, he suddenly thought, as memories of her golden skin tanned from the sun rushed unbidden to his mind. A wave of grief swept over him.

"Excuse me, Miss MacKenzie." He turned on his heel and strode away.

Katlin frowned at his retreating back. And what was that all about? She did not know whether to be intrigued or annoyed. She shrugged. Whatever bothered him was his problem, not hers. He was right, though. She did feel much better this morning.

A bath and a change of undergarments had done wonders for her morale. It made her even more anxious to get started. She had to get to California and find Caleb.

"Come on," she urged Elena. "They are waiting for us."

Halfway to Gorgona, they rounded the foot of a prominent mountain with a single palm rearing majestically from its peak.

"Mount Carabali," Colin announced, waving towards the mound. "If we wanted to stop and climb to the base of that palm tree, we could see both the Atlantic and Pacific oceans. We follow the same route Balboa took when he crossed in 1513 to discover the Pacific Ocean."

"Really?" Katlin stared. "How do you know?"

He laughed. "The padre's son told me. He's a clever lad."

"Does that mean we are almost to the top? Look how

hard the men have to pole!"

Felipe had collapsed, exhausted, but Jorge, his nearly naked body bathed in sweat, poled with such vigor that the boat shot ahead. The third man, his chest gleaming like polished bronze, tried to keep up. Katlin noted, with some amusement, that she heard no more singing. All of Jorge's energy went into poling the boat.

Shortly after eight o'clock, Gorgona hove into view on the south bank of the river. As he secured the boat, Felipe announced he wished to return to Chagres from Gorgona.

"We aren't going to Cruces?" Katlin asked. "The river certainly is high enough."

"*Cruces, mucha colera,*" Jorge muttered. "*Muy malo, mucho peligroso.*"

"If we can get horses or mules from here, we may be able to avoid Cruces," Colin said. "I had heard they have cholera there."

"We brought it with us from New York," Katlin muttered. "I'll bet the Spaniards are right. If it's the miasma, like the American doctors say, why does it follow us?"

Elena's eyes grew wide. "I fear the *colera*. My *dueña*, she die in New York from the *colera*."

"We can avoid Cruces," Colin said, "but the cholera's in Panama City as well. They say it's already killed a quarter of the native population."

"I'm surprised they let Americans come through, bringing disease like we do," Katlin observed. "Why don't they keep us out?"

"Bad for business," Colin chuckled. "The foreigners spend a lot of money on the crossing and while they're waiting for passage in Panama City. At Chagres, one of the returning miners told me there's a North American named Miller that lives here and owns a store. My informant said Miller will know the condition of the trail to Panama City. I'll go talk to him. Wait here for me." Colin strode off.

Henry, Elena, and Katlin waited with Felipe in the shade of a broad acacia tree. The sun grew hotter as it rose higher in the glaring, pale blue sky. Katlin fanned herself with the palm frond fan the boatman had provided. She looked with envy at the scant clothing worn by the natives. If we could shed half of these clothes, she thought, the heat would not be nearly so unbearable.

Colin returned in about ten minutes. "Mr. Miller says the road is open," he reported. "Several of the *Falcon's* passengers have already left, some on horses, others on foot, as horses and mules seem to be scarce."

"Maybe we need to go on to Cruces in the boat?" Henry asked. "We can't expect the ladies to walk."

Felipe, reiterating his fear of the cholera in Cruces, motioned for them to follow him to an adjoining hut. There the owner greeted them as he lazily swung back and forth in his hammock, not bothering to rise.

Katlin chuckled to herself. She noticed the natives stirred themselves as little as possible. Of course, in this heat, she could understand. She wiped her forehead with an already soggy handkerchief and fanned her overheated face.

"*Para amigos de Felipe,*" he intoned, "*tengo seis caballos.* Four to ride, ten dollar each. Two for baggage, six dollar."

"Done," Colin grinned. He shook hands with the venerable and dignified native and the deal was struck.

They paid off the boatmen to allow their return to Chagres, and gave each the dollar tip promised to them for making the trip in three days, although they had not quite made it in that length of time.

"I guess three days and a third qualifies," Katlin laughed. "We don't want them to think *all* Americans are out to cheat them."

"Yes," Colin agreed. "Better to part friends. He did get us an excellent meal at the padre's house. And horses and a guide for the rest of the trip."

Henry nodded. "Even though his reason for getting the horses was so he didn't have to go to Cruces and face the cholera. He didn't do it as a favor for us."

During the afternoon, a number of other canoes arrived. Katlin thanked heaven they had arrived early enough to get reasonably good lodging before the rest of the crowd showed up.

As it grew dark, the drums announcing a fandango began. Clouds of mosquitoes rose up about them in large numbers. Fires were built so the smoke drove away the worst of the annoying insects.

Colin strode up with Mr. Miller from the store. "We are invited to join the aristocracy at the alcalde's house for the celebration. Everyone else will be farther down the hill."

"What are we celebrating?" Katlin asked.

"Who knows? They just have a fandango whenever they feel like it."

In response to the alcalde's invitation, Katlin and Elena joined a group of ladies dressed in pink and white, who wore flowers in their hair. Katlin felt like a ragamuffin among them, but Elena, chattering happily in Spanish with the alcalde's daughters, was having a wonderful time. Violins and guitars struck up a lively tune, and Elena joined the dancers with enthusiasm.

Katlin watched the dancing for a while, then walked away to take a stroll in the moonlight. She thought this would be a nice chance to be alone, to think and enjoy the beauty of the tropical evening. The soft velvety air stroked her skin.

As Katlin strolled down the hill towards the river, she passed the second party of dancers, a much more raucous crowd than the alcalde's friends. She did not notice one of the revelers move away from the group to follow her. Lost in thought, she did not even hear him as he approached on silent feet to where she stood leaning against one of the palm trees.

"Lookin' fer company, little lady?"

One hand gripped her arm, the other closed around her mouth.

# Chapter 11

COLIN HAD WATCHED Katlin walk away from the dancing. He also noticed that, as she passed the group down the hill, one of the drunken revelers separated himself from his fellows and followed her. Colin wondered briefly if she had an assignation with the man, then dismissed that idea as highly unlikely.

"I'll bet he's up to no good," Colin muttered. He turned to Henry, who stood engrossed in watching Elena twirl and gyrate to the music, and repeated the comment loud enough for the boy to hear over the din of the revelers.

Henry's eyes followed Colin's as Katlin disappeared behind a tree, the man trailing twenty paces behind her. He nodded. "You're probably right."

"I believe I'll follow along, just in case. If she called for help, no one would ever hear her over all this racket."

"Be careful," Henry admonished. "Some of those backwoods yokels carry enough guns to equip a small attack force."

"If his intentions are amorous, I doubt he's armed. I'd better hurry, though, before they are both out of sight." He grinned. "Won't be any help to her if I get myself lost in the jungle." Colin strode off in the Katlin's direction.

Katlin felt the arm tighten around her, pinning her arms to her side as she kicked and struggled. She tried to bite the hand that covered her mouth, but the vise-like grip held her too tightly. Anger swept through her. How dare he grab her and try to force his attentions upon her in this outrageous way? The smell of whisky from the man's breath almost overwhelmed her. Drunk. So drunk she knew instinctively trying to reason with him would be a waste of time.

He lifted her from her feet, but she continued to kick, still more angry than frightened. Judging from the curses, some of her kicks were having an effect. But she knew, with an agonizing prescience, that his superior strength would soon overpower her. She caught a glimpse of his face in the moonlight and recognized him as a fellow passenger from the *Falcon*, one of the group that had boarded in New Orleans. One, she thought with disgust, of those who spent most of the trip to Chagres drinking or passed out on the deck.

But what could he hope to gain? If he forced his attentions on her, she could surely expose him. He had nowhere to hide.

Or did he mean to kill her? Suddenly, fear swept over her, replacing her feelings of anger. A body hidden in that jungle might never be found. The others would assume she had wandered off, gotten lost, and died. She had to free herself.

Fright gave her strength and she struggled harder. The hand covering her mouth slid up to obstruct her nose as well, and she found herself struggling for breath.

My God, she thought, frantic as she felt her lungs burn, he's going to suffocate me. Giddiness threatened to overcome her. I can't faint. I just can't! Colin, help me!

Even as the words came into her mind, she heard Colin's voice. For a moment, she thought she imagined it, but then she heard him say, "Let her go, you crazy, drunken fool. What can you be thinking?"

"Mind yer own bizness," her assailant snarled back. "This here's between me and the little lady." The grip on Katlin's face tightened and her eyes bulged.

Colin seized the arm that held Katlin's mouth and yanked the hand from her face. Katlin gasped for air, gulping large breaths into her oxygen-starved lungs.

"Git!" Katlin's assailant yelled at Colin. "She ain't no lady, or she'd not be a-travelin' 'th'out no man."

Colin reacted by slamming his fist into the man's face. As her attacker fell back, he released Katlin, who tumbled to the grass, her legs refusing to hold her. Colin knelt beside her to help her rise.

"Are you injured, Miss MacKenzie?" he asked, his voice filled with concern.

The moon shining behind him kept his face in a shadow, so she felt, rather than saw, the intensity of his gaze.

"No, no," she gasped. "I just have to . . . get my breath back." Over Colin's shoulder, she saw her assailant rise to his feet, and caught a gleam of moonlight on metal.

"Colin," she gasped, horror sweeping through her at the thought of Colin's danger. "He has a knife!"

Colin whirled to face the threat, but a loud explosion sounded, sending the sleeping birds screaming from the trees above them. The upraised knife fell as their attacker slowly crumpled to the ground.

Henry stood in the moonlight, the pistol still smoking in his hand.

"Really, Colin," he said. "I told you if you're going to save a lady, you should carry your gun."

Katlin started to laugh, almost hysterically. "I think perhaps the lady should have better sense than to take a midnight stroll alone." She bent over her attacker. "Is he dead?"

"I hope not," Henry said, dropping to his knees beside the prone body. "I've never killed a man. Just wanted to stop him. Figgered he had to 'a been drunk."

A number of people arrived, attracted by the sound of the shot. One carried a lantern. Colin knelt beside Henry. "Don't see any blood under him. Oh. Here." He rolled the man over onto his back and pointed to a crease along his skull. "You just grazed his head and knocked him out. He should recover shortly." The man's rapidly swelling right eye showed where Colin's punch had landed.

Henry grinned. "He'll have a headache to remember us by when he does. And he won't be able to tell if it's from the bullet, the sock in the eye, or the whiskey."

One of the man's traveling companions spoke. "I'll tend 'im. Dang fool. I tol' him not to mess with no high steppin' filly like Miss MacKenzie. Lady like her ain't fer the likes o' him."

Katlin laughed softly. Her knees still shook. She clung to Colin's arm as she rose, fearful she might not be able to stand unaided. Taking a deep breath, she thanked Colin and Henry for coming so promptly to her aid. "I must remember I am not in a small town in Maine any more." Her legs steadied and she released her grip on Colin's arm. "And now, I believe I've had enough excitement for one evening. Elena will be growing concerned, and it's time I retired. I suspect we will have a much harder day tomorrow."

Colin and Henry accompanied Katlin back to the hut where they had obtained lodging. No one spoke. Katlin's mind whirled. The man's words haunted her. Had he thought, because she traveled alone, that she was a loose woman? Did the others think that? Most important, what did Colin think?

When Colin bade her good night, he seemed to read her mind, for he gently kissed her hand and murmured. "Ignore the drunken fool's words." He smiled. "You are every inch a lady, and Henry and I will challenge anyone who says otherwise."

Her eyes filled with tears and her throat tightened. "Thank you," she whispered.

He squeezed her hands and smiled again. "See you in the morning."

Colin retired to his hammock, his mind in a turmoil, filled with admiration for Katlin's reaction to the attack. No screaming, no fainting, no spate of tears. No cry for vengeance, no demand the man's life be forfeit. She even showed concern for her attacker, understanding the whiskey had led to his uncouth behavior.

Yes, he thought, as he drifted off to sleep. Every inch a lady.

# Chapter 12

WHEN KATLIN ROSE the next morning, she felt battered and sore. Her muscles ached from the previous night's struggle. She lifted her left sleeve and surveyed the bruises on her arm with dismay.

Elena stared at the purple and green marks with horror. "He is monster! I wish my Henry kill him. He deserve to die."

Katlin shrugged. "He was drunk, Elena. Sometimes men do strange things when they're drunk." She laughed, a short, humorless bark. "I'm just glad Henry and Mr. Mac-Dougal followed me. It could have been a lot worse."

Elena shuddered.

"Forget it," Katlin advised. "We have more important things to worry about. We have to get to Panama City before the steamer departs for San Francisco."

"Good morning, ladies." Henry's voice reached them from the other side of the bamboo screen that partitioned off their sleeping section. "I've got your pantaloons for you."

Startled, Katlin darted around the screen and stared at the two pair of white duck trousers Henry carried over his arm.

"Sorry," he said, blushing as he held them out. "Don't usually take much interest in women's apparel, but the alcalde's wife, she tells me since you have to ride astride you'll need these. She gave 'em to me."

Elena looked puzzled while she figured out what he meant, then blushed as furiously as Henry.

Katlin grinned. She had surreptitiously worn pantaloons under her skirt before, when she and Sunny had wanted to go for a real ride. Memories of rides with Sunny washed over her, and tears filled her eyes as she thought of the horse she had loved so dearly. The horse Caleb stole from her. Rage burned away the tears. If riding astride was required, she would ride astride.

"Thank you, Henry," she said, taking the garments. "We will join you shortly."

It took some effort for Katlin to persuade Elena to don the masculine garb.

"My father," the girl demurred, "he say the lady do not, do not, how you say, ride the horse like the man."

"Your father, if he were here, would be telling you that sometimes a lady does what a lady has to do. There is no other way for us to get from here to the Pacific. Besides," she added, fluffing Elena's skirt about her over the offending garment, "no one can see what you are wearing underneath."

Katlin quickly donned her own pair of the baggy trousers, arranged her skirt, and gathered their belongings. "We do have to hurry. Henry and the guide will be ready to load the pack horses. They won't want us to keep them waiting."

The alcalde's wife and daughters came out to see them off. The horses, sturdy little mustangs, stood waiting patiently. Colin laughed when he saw them.

"I can almost step over them," he declared. "Look!" He swung himself into the saddle. His stirrups almost touched the ground.

"Relax," Katlin laughed. "It's only twenty miles."

Colin grunted. "It's going to be a *long* twenty miles."

"Short legs climb better," Henry advised. "Everyone uses these horses. Besides, if the horse slips, you don't fall as far."

"That's a comfort," Katlin observed dryly. "Do they fall

often?"

"Oh, yes," Henry said. "I've talked with fellows as have come back. The ground around here is mostly a kind of clay that gets slippery when it's wet. Makes the trail real slick, so, even as sure-footed as they are, the horses slip all the time, especially in the rainy season. Which it is now."

"So I've noticed." Katlin took a deep breath and grimaced.

The alcalde rattled off a long sentence in Spanish. Elena translated.

"He say, he send two servants to take pack horse. Not to worry about baggage. Will be deliver to *Hotel Americano muy rapido.*"

Katlin sighed. "I guess we'll just have to trust him. It'll be easier than having to lead them ourselves."

Their guide disappeared into the jungle. Henry followed. Katlin spurred her horse, and Elena hurried behind her. Colin brought up the rear.

Katlin ducked behind her mustang's head to evade the worst of the branches that slapped at her face. "Keep your head down," she called back to Elena behind her. "These branches can knock you off your horse."

The trail, bad enough when they started, grew deeper and darker the farther they went into the woods. The path narrowed until it finally became little more than a gully filled with mud that reached almost to the bellies of their horses.

Elena and Katlin both pulled their feet up to keep them out of the muddy water. The horse swayed and bobbed, making Katlin thankful she rode astride. She could not imagine keeping her seat riding side-saddle.

Katlin gasped as Henry's horse half slid down the steep side of the hill. Hers, without hesitation, followed. She heard Elena's little scream of fright behind her. The horse straightened at the bottom, then climbed the opposite side like a cat.

As Katlin watched, Henry's horse stepped in a hole and mud spurted up to cover him. Her horse followed, and a cascade of muddy water sprayed her as well. She looked down at her mud-covered skirt and shook her head in dismay. The native that led them wore only a pair of short pants. Now she knew why.

Their guide continued with seeming unconcern about the ruggedness of the terrain, climbing up one side of each hill, sliding down the other, then struggling up toward the crest of the next hill. Katlin thought the top of each crest would bring them in sight of Panama, but instead only gave her a view of the next one. The trail seemed to climb forever. All the twists and turns and ups and downs had confused Katlin's sense of distance.

Muddy water sprayed up over her at each step of her horse. Finally, in exasperation, Katlin snapped at Henry, "Can't this wretched creature step anywhere else except in the same hole as his predecessor?"

Henry laughed. "They're trained to follow. And that's what they do."

Katlin sighed. Since she had no choice but to endure the continual splattering, she concentrated on her surroundings. The mountain range they passed was broken and irregular. The trail passed over the lower ridges and projecting spurs, circumventing the main chain. A dense forest covered as far as she could see. Above her head, a roof of transparent green provided some protection from the fierce rays of the relentless sun. Chattering monkeys and screaming parrots filled the trees with a cacophony of sound.

The trail broke out of the jungle at one spot to follow the edge of a deep ravine. Bald vultures watched silently from the tops of trees. Katlin looked over the side down into the gully and saw the bodies of several mules. She shuddered, knowing the vultures waited for their cavalcade to pass before swooping down to devour the bodies. If one of us fell into that gully, there would be no way out, even in the unlikely event one were to survive the fall. The vultures would eat us, too.

Stop it, she ordered herself. No point in being morbid. These ponies act like they've been over this trail many times. I'm sure they're not about to fall into the ravine. She reminded herself again that mustangs were famous for their sure-footedness, and tried to take comfort from the thought.

The road leveled and passed a small ranch, but they did not stop, nor did anyone approach them.

After the ranch disappeared from view behind the maze of vegetation, their guide cried "*Alto!*" and pulled his horse to the side of the trail. Katlin and her companions did the same, and watched as a long train of luggage passed by, packed on the backs of horses and bulls. Katlin tried to see if her baggage and Elena's rode on one of the horses, but did not recognize anything.

"I guess," Katlin sighed to Elena, "we will just have to hope our belongings are on the next train." They watched the stream of animals, tied head to tail, file by in an eerie silence broken only by the shuffling of dozens of hooves.

At the next ranch they passed, one of their fellow passengers from the *Falcon* sat under a tree beside another, who moaned on the ground.

Colin hailed him. "What ails your companion?"

"Cholery," the man whispered hoarsely, his eyes wide with fright. "This here's my brother Will, an' he's a-dyin' o' cholery. Took it yestiddy, kept goin' as long as he could. Cain't ride no further."

Colin hesitated, but the man waved him away. "Nuthin' you kin do. Keep away so's you don't take it yerselves."

"Good luck to you, then. Hope to see you in Panama."

The man, his face bleak, made no reply, and Katlin's party rode on.

After they passed beyond the sight and hearing of the two men, Colin said, "I think the other fellow's going to die of fright, whether he takes the cholera or not"

"At least he's staying with his brother," Katlin observed. "Most of these men are so intent on reaching the gold fields that nothing else seems to matter to them."

They rode on in silence for the next hour. The vision of the dying man haunted Katlin. What a horrible disease! She remembered just two days before watching the young man talking and laughing with his brother. He had been alive, vibrant, eagerly looking forward to becoming a rich man in the gold fields. Now he lay at death's door, far from home, with only his brother as his companion. She shuddered. The horror of being left here buried in this foreign land would not leave her.

Engrossed in her thoughts, Katlin did not realize Henry and the guide had stopped until she felt her pony halt his forward momentum. She looked up and saw another passenger she recognized from the *Falcon* seated on the ground beside his horse, his head in his hands.

Henry dismounted and the man looked up. His cadaverous face bore the same look of bleak despair Katlin had seen on the last cholera victim they had passed. We need not have worried about avoiding the cholera in Cruces, she thought. We are bringing it with us.

Colin dismounted and approached the man. "Where are your companions?"

The man lifted his head. "Was a-travelin' wi' Will an' Abe Martin, 'til Will took the cholery too bad ta ride. Abe stayed with 'im."

Colin nodded. "Yes. We passed them."

"The rest ..." the man grabbed his abdomen and groaned. When the spasm passed, he whispered. "The rest ... went on. I tried ta keep up." He retched and spat greenish fluid on the ground beside him, then wiped his face with a grimy handkerchief. "'til the pain got so bad I couldn't ride. Had ta rest a spell."

"You had best return to Gorgona," Colin advised

"No!" the man gasped. "Got to go on. Got to get to Panama to ketch the steamer."

"But, my good man, you're too sick to ride," Henry cried. "You can't cross these mountains if you can't even stay seated on a horse!"

"Help me. Please help me. I kin make it iffen we go slow."

Henry and Colin exchanged glances. Their guide motioned for the party to hurry. Katlin heard a familiar rumble as black clouds gathered over their heads. It would rain soon.

"We can't just leave him here," Katlin cried, appalled at the thought.

"You're right. We can't." With a sigh, Colin nodded to Henry. Together, they helped the man back onto his horse. The guide returned, urging them forward with a rapid string of Spanish.

Elena's eyes grew wide. "He say, he say, more rain come, river go very high, very fast. Have to cross river."

Henry turned to Colin. "He's right."

"But I thought we left the river, at Gorgona," Katlin protested.

"We did leave the Chagres. But we have to cross the Rio Grande. It comes down from the mountains on the west side of the Continental Divide."

Colin nodded. "Yes, and feeds into the Pacific, and so we have to cross it." He shook his head. "No matter how deep it gets. There's no other way if we're going to catch the steamer for San Francisco."

Large drops of rain pelted down. Katlin and Elena enveloped themselves in their India rubber ponchos. With a roar, the deluge swept down upon them. They plodded forward, Henry and Colin taking turns holding their new charge on his horse.

The third time he fell off, Colin tied him on. Darkness fell before they reached a weathered hut where they could shelter for the night. The guide built a small fire and boiled leaves from a nearby plant. He refused to go near the sick man, instead handing the cup to Elena.

"He say the tea good for the *colera*," she explained, holding out the cup.

"Let's see if we can rouse him enough to take it," Katlin took the offered cup and shook her head as she looked down upon the miserable specimen of humanity huddled on the ground before her. Nausea almost overwhelmed her as the smell that suffused from the man's stained clothing filled the hut.

"Do not touch!" Elena cried. "You will die also."

"I have to try, Elena. If it can help him, we have to try."

But her efforts were in vain. The man had sunk so low into his stupor she could not get him to swallow. His arms and legs were rigid, as though the disease held him in spasms. She managed to get some of the herbal tea into his mouth, but it only dribbled out the sides and down into his beard.

Finally, she felt Colin's hand on her arm.

"Come," he said gently. "You've done all you can."

Her hands shook as she put down the cup and stood up. Colin folded his arms around her to comfort her, and put his cheek against her hair. "You are very brave, but you've done all you can," he repeated. "We have to leave it in God's hands now. Your hammock is ready."

In a trance, stricken by her inability to help the man, she allowed him to lead her away, certain she would never sleep. But she did not realize the depth of her exhaustion. She lay down fully clothed in the hammock and did not waken until she felt Elena's hand on her arm.

Katlin's eyes flew open as she realized daylight had returned and she had slept all night. "The man?" she asked.

Elena shrugged expressively. "He still breathes. We must leave him. The guide, he say the Rio Grande rising."

Katlin rolled out of the hammock. "We can't just leave him to die alone, Elena. No one should ever have to die alone."

Colin knelt by the man's side, his hand on the sick man's chest. Katlin could barely discern any movement from his shallow breathing. "The heartbeat is rapid," Colin said softly, "and very faint. See how blue his face is? That's the last stage of cholera. I fear the end is near." He smiled ruefully. "So, we have a dilemma, don't we?"

"We can't leave him," Katlin said firmly. "If the rest of you want to go on, I will stay."

"And who will guide you to Panama?"

"There'll be other parties coming through. I can follow one of them."

Elena put her valise on the dirt floor, sat down upon it, and announced, "I stay with Miss MacKenzie."

Colin's eyes met Henry's and the boy nodded.

"Have it your way, Miss MacKenzie," Henry sighed. "I'll get a grave dug while we're waiting, so's we can get goin' again as soon as . . . as soon as we can."

It took nearly an hour before the breathing stopped. Katlin sat beside the moribund young man with the same helpless feeling that had paralyzed her as she watched her father die. Some day, she cried mutely, her cry no less intense for its silence, some day we will have ways to prevent these senseless deaths. Someday we will stop diseases like cholera and yellow fever and consumption.

Katlin, feeling very inadequate to the task, recited the Lord's Prayer over the grave site during the brief ceremony. The guide stood back from the group, his battered hat in his hand, and crossed himself several times. Colin and Henry quickly replaced the dirt and tamped it down.

"We don't even know his name," Katlin said sadly. "We should have asked him for his name, or if he had kin while we had a chance. Surely his belongings will be waiting for him in Panama."

"We'll ask for any who traveled with the Martin brothers," Colin said gently, turning her from the grave. "Some of them may know who he was so we can notify his kin. Now, we really do have to get going."

Two hours later they reached the Rio Grande, after climbing down a series of clefts and gullies which seemed impassable to Katlin. She marveled again at the sure-footed little ponies. Once Henry's pony lost his footing and slid to the bottom. Henry only shook his head and remounted. They drew rein beside a stream of milky blue water which rolled and tumbled on its way to the Pacific Ocean.

Katlin gasped at the roiling water. "Shouldn't we wait for it to go down a little?"

"Guide, he say it only get worse," Elena said. "Say go now or go back to Gorgona."

Katlin shook her head. "I don't want to ride across. I'd feel safer on foot if I had something to hold."

"We'll run a line from one side to the other," Henry said. "Have the guide lead the horses over. You can walk over holding on to the line. Here." He handed Colin one end of the coil of rope. "Tie it to a tree. If I go down, pull me out."

He plunged into the river. Elena gasped when his horse lost its footing, but quickly regained it. As Henry's mount scrambled out on the opposite bank, the guide plunged in, leading the rest of the horses.

When their escort reached the safety of the other side, Henry secured the rope to another tree and called back. "It's not deep, just swift. Cross upstream of the line, Miss MacKenzie. The bottom seems even. No holes along the line. Just whatever happens, don't let go of the rope!"

"Stay with Elena," Katlin ordered Colin. "Hold on to her." With a long, shuddering stare, Katlin gritted her teeth, took a firm grip on the slippery line with both hands, and stepped into the raging water. The force of the current tugging at her skirts almost swept her away, but she braced herself and slowly moved forward, a step at a time, careful to place each foot solidly in front of her before moving the second.

In the middle, the water reached her waist, and the current tore at her. She stood still for a moment to catch her breath and be sure of her footing.

"You're doing fine, Miss MacKenzie," Henry called to her in encouragement. "You're over half way across."

"Thank you," Katlin replied grimly, and began to inch forward again. The continued pull on her skirts threatened to sweep her off her feet, and she wished she had discarded them and crossed in the pantaloons. As the depth lessened, she sighed with relief to realize it would get no deeper. Hand over hand, she crept along the rope.

"I've made it," she shouted in triumph to Henry when she knew she had succeeded.

With a grin, Henry waded out to help her clamber up onto the bank.

She collapsed onto the soft grass. "That wasn't so bad," she gasped to Henry. "Just have to empty the water out of my boots. Thank goodness the water isn't cold."

Katlin called encouragement to Elena as the girl took her first tentative steps into the water. "Just don't let go of the rope! Mr. MacDougal is right behind you."

Colin held Elena's arm as she started across, and he followed. With his other hand, he steadied the rope. As she inched forward, the ferocious torrent swept her off her feet.

Katlin screamed as Elena's head disappeared under the raging water.

# *Chapter 13*

KATLIN JUMPED to her feet and stood frozen with horror as she watched the milky blue water tug at Elena, threatening to pull the handful of gray material from Colin's desperate grip. The girl's long, black hair swirled about in the foamy eddy the current created around her.

Colin clung to the line with one arm. With the other, he clutched Elena.

"Henry!" he shouted. "Help me! I can't pull her back, the current's too strong."

Henry plunged back into the water, and reached them before Katlin could move. She arrived at the edge of the river in time to see Henry yank Elena's head out of the water. Elena coughed and choked, and wrapped both arms around the boy's neck, almost pulling him off balance.

As Katlin watched the two men battle against the current, she realized they would not be able to pull Elena back without help. The undertow had those wretched long skirts in its grip. Katlin looked again at the swirling water, then back at the struggling men. The guide stood holding the horses. He obviously had no intention of helping the trio struggling in the water. Katlin made her decision. Remembering her own difficulty with her skirts on the crossing, she peeled her dress off over her head. In chemise and pantaloons, she worked her way down the line until she reached the men straining with their burden.

Seizing Elena's arm, Katlin pulled it back over the rope, helping the groping fingers get a grip.

"Hold on to the rope, not Henry," she ordered over the

roar of the rushing water. "Move one hand forward at a time. We'll tow you." Elena still floated, her skirts held by the current. Inch by inch, the four of them struggled to shore and collapsed on the bank.

As Katlin, with a grimace, pulled her soggy dress back over her head, a spasm of coughing seized Henry. He coughed and struggled for breath until Katlin and Elena both forgot their own narrow escape in their concern for him.

Katlin had a few horehound cough lozenges in her saddle pack. She recalled they had brought some relief to her father whenever he was in the grip of a coughing spell. When the paroxysm finally released Henry for a moment, she offered them to him, trying to ignore the bright red blood that stained the handkerchief.

If Henry collapses, Katlin thought, suddenly frightened at the knowledge that he easily could, we'll never be able to get him to Panama. And we certainly can't leave him.

And if he dies? Katlin refused to accept that alternative. She had grown very fond of the boy in their short acquaintance.

Colin came over and knelt beside Henry as well. "Better? I'm afraid we have put you through a little too much exertion on this trip. We really have to move on. Will you be able to travel?"

Henry grimaced and took a deep breath. "I'll make it, Mr. MacDougal. Just . . . let me . . . catch my breath."

Elena continued to cradle Henry, stroking his forehead and telling him over and over again, mostly in Spanish, how wonderful and brave he had been. "*Mi corazon, tu tienes mucho valor,*" she murmured over and over. Henry understood very little of what she said, but he lay quietly accepting her ministrations with a contented smile. Katlin chuckled at the scene and rose to her feet. Colin did likewise. As he did so, Katlin noticed he cradled his left arm. Her eyes widened and she gasped, "Are you injured?"

"I think I dislocated my shoulder when I stopped Señorita Elena's rapid trip down the river. Also, I must say you were quite heroic, dashing to our aid the way you did. Not many ladies would have taken the risk, I fear. And few would have had the presence of mind to remove their long skirts before entering the water."

Katlin chuckled grimly. "As I told Elena earlier, sometimes a lady does what a lady has to do. I'd have had an easier crossing myself if I had removed them earlier. If we'd had Elena take her skirts off before crossing, she probably would not have fallen. Let me check your shoulder."

He grimaced in pain as she gently removed the sopping wet jacket and shirt, her heart racing at the sight of the strong muscles that rippled across his back and chest. She assumed her most professional air to cover her reaction. Probing the shoulder, she was pleased to feel no evidence of dislocation.

With a sigh of relief, Katlin told Colin, "It's only a bad sprain. Rest should take care of it. Let me bind it for you."

Colin grinned. "That's good. It sure felt like it came right out of the socket. I lost all strength in the arm. I couldn't pull her back, I could only hold her."

"You saved her life. She'd have washed down the river if you hadn't held her. The guide would have been no help, and Henry and I could never have gotten to her in time. Those wretched skirts would have dragged her under."

Katlin took a large scarf out of her saddle pack and managed to bind his arm next to his body. Replacing the shirt, she tied it around his waist to secure the scarf bandage and tried to get her breathing back under control. "That should hold you. Try not to use the arm for a while. It should be better by tomorrow."

He rose and pulled her to her feet with his good hand. Their eyes met.

"And are you also a doctor, Miss MacKenzie of the many talents?"

She twisted her mouth into a wry grin. "When you live in a small town in Maine, you learn to be many things. I'm also very good with a pistol, and I can load a rifle as fast as any man." She smiled and laughed grimly. "I can chop wood, kill a chicken, make soap, and perform many other unladylike skills. My mother always had servants to do all of those common chores. She would roll over in her grave were she to learn all of the things I have been forced to do for myself."

Colin returned her smile. "I think, Miss MacKenzie, that, whatever is driving you to California, you will do very well there. From what I hear, the country was made for ladies like you."

As she pondered his unusual statement, wondering how he knew she had a mission in California, the sky blackened, and a clap of thunder heralded the arrival of the regular afternoon rainstorm. As Colin and Katlin stood together, the sky opened and the deluge descended.

Katlin sighed, then her sense of humor rose to her defense and she laughed. "Shall we bother with our ponchos? We surely can't get any wetter!"

"You're right. And I do believe our companions are ready to depart."

Katlin mounted her pony, who stood in patient resignation with the rain dripping off his muzzle, occasionally shaking his head and showering her with muddy rain water. She jiggled the reins and took her place behind Henry and Elena, both showing the remarkable resilience of youth after their recent fright. Katlin's mind whirled as their entourage plodded along in the rain. Had Colin guessed how strongly she had reacted to him? She certainly didn't need any romantic entanglements until after she located Caleb.

And then what? Her mind still could not play out the events beyond locating him. Go to the law? From what she had heard, there wasn't much law in California. Confront him with her gun? Then what? Could she actually shoot him? She'd never killed anyone, or even thought of it.

He did take Sunny, though. Memories of Sunny swept over her, memories of the many hours she had shared with her beloved horse riding through the forests of Maine, the scent of pine trees wafting over her on the cool breeze.

Thoughts of Sunny searching her waistband for the lump of sugar she always carried brought tears to her eyes. She remembered what a comfort the horse, who always seemed to understand Katlin's feelings, had been when her father died.

If that monster did anything to hurt Sunny .... She shook her head and forced her thoughts from Caleb.

Concentrate on getting to California, she ordered herself. We have to go through Panama City, where a quarter of the population has already died of cholera. Then we face a sea voyage of several weeks with a boy seriously ill with consumption. A child of fifteen is looking to me for support, and I still have no idea how I am going to make a living in that wild country.

And then, she told herself grimly, you will have to find Caleb in a vast wilderness overrun by thousands of gold seekers.

She returned her attention to the path before her. One step at a time.


Colin watched Katlin take her place in line as though nothing had happened. He wished he knew what drove her. She was not ready to confide in anyone, let alone him. But she stirred his pulses as no one but Michelle ever had.

Michelle. He had never in the two years since her death gone so long without her image in his mind. Could her memory be fading? Or were a pair of magnificent blue eyes beginning to replace her? Nonsense. He shook himself and pulled his hat down further to keep the rain out of his eyes.

Urging his pony forward, he hurried to overtake his companions.

As he rode, the tingles inspired by the touch of her fingers on his bare skin as she examined and dressed his shoulder raced through his body again And he could not resist the feeling that, as they stood together, he'd only to lean forward a few inches to claim those damnably kissable lips as his.

He laughed at himself. Come to your senses, Colin Mac-Dougal. The lass has no interest in you at all. He returned his attention to the path before him.

As the sun faded, they reached a straight stretch of road with some evidence of paving. The vegetation cleared and he could see the guide at the head of the line, Katlin riding behind him, followed by Elena, then Henry. He hoped that meant they were close to the city. His eyes went back to Katlin. She rode proud and straight. Yes, Colin thought again, whatever she may say, however she may feel about herself, she is every inch a lady.

# Chapter 14

$A$T NOON of the next day, they crested yet another rise, and the familiar aroma of salt air wafted over Katlin.

"We must be close," she remarked to Elena. "If we can smell the ocean, we have to be almost there."

"I hope so." Elena wiped her muddy face with a sodden handkerchief. "I am so tired of the camping. A hotel will be nice, no?"

"No, I mean, yes," Henry grinned. "And you can tell we're getting close. Look at our guide." Katlin's and Elena's eyes followed the sweep of Henry's arm. Their guide had dismounted. He vigorously scrubbed his feet in a mud hole, replaced the filthy short trousers with a clean pair of white duck pantaloons he produced from his saddle pack, and donned a shirt. After cleaning himself, he proceeded to wipe the worst of the mud off of his horse before remounting.

Katlin laughed. "I guess he wants to impress the ladies in Panama. He will certainly look good compared to us. You can tell he's been over this trail many times."

When Katlin surveyed the muddy mass her clothes had become, she wished she had been able to do the same. She hoped they would reach the hotel soon, sighing with pleasure at the thought of getting into a tub and washing off the mud and grime of the previous five days. Of course, the only clothes in her possession were the ones she wore. They had placed all of their faith in the *alcalde* of Gorgona. He had assured them the native to whom they entrusted their luggage would ship it as promised.

Katlin twisted her mouth into a wry grin.  For all they knew, the enterprising native had a little *bodega* in partnership with the *alcalde* where they sold goods entrusted to them by naive Americans.  She shrugged her shoulders in resignation.  No point in worrying about it.  She carried her money, the pearl necklace, and the emerald earrings in a pouch she kept pinned inside her chemise.  If the rest disappeared, so be it.  They were a part of the life she had left behind her anyway.

Shortly afterwards, huts appeared on the side of the road, the same small, one-room shanties of cane they had seen in Chagres, more evidence their party approached the city at last.  Soon they traveled among stone houses and massive ruins of buildings overgrown with vegetation.

"There must have been a magnificent city here at one time," Katlin exclaimed to Colin, who rode beside her.

"Pedrarias the Cruel founded the first city in 1519, on a shallow bay about five miles from the present one."

"Why did they call him that?" Katlin asked.  "Or maybe I don't want to know."

Colin laughed.  "Because he set out to exterminate the Indians.  All of them.  He even executed Balboa.  Accused him of treason."

Katlin shuddered and exclaimed, "What a horrible man he must have been!"

"Spanish history in the Americas is full of such stories," Colin continued.  "If we have time, I'd like to visit the ruins of the old city.  They say it is quite impressive.  When Morgan sacked the place in 1671, he took out 150 mule-loads of loot.  It was the major trade route for the gold from the Incas, silver from Bolivia, and pearls from the Pacific.  Of course, the Spaniards had stolen it all in the first place, so I suppose one could see some justice in it."

"Why did they move the city? Why not just rebuild it where it was?"

"They moved it five miles to its present location because it's a much better anchorage. In 1821, as Spain lost her dominance in the New World, New Granada took over, and Panama became a state of New Granada. It remained a little backwater village until the Americans discovered they could cut months off of their journey by cutting across the Isthmus."

"And also avoid Cape Horn," Katlin said. "I've heard some stories of the Cape. Enough to convince me I never want to experience it."

Colin chuckled. "Agreed. The passage from New York to New Orleans cured me of ocean travel. The Gulf and the Caribbean can be bad enough, but at least there's no snow and ice."

"And yet you are going on to San Francisco?"

With a wry grin, he conceded he was. "But they assure me there will be no snow or ice. And they call the ocean the Pacific because it is supposed to be much more benign than the Atlantic."

Katlin nodded. "Yes. But an ocean is an ocean. I'll bet a storm on the Pacific isn't any better than a storm on the Atlantic."

Colin threw back his head and gave a hearty laugh. "Then, Miss MacKenzie, I will depend upon your medical skills to get me through safely to San Francisco."

She joined in his laughter for a moment, then her smile faded. "It may take our combined skills to get Henry through. My parents both died of consumption. I know how bad a disease it is, and how quickly it can kill."

Colin glanced ahead where Henry and Elena rode side by side, Elena chattering away, mostly in Spanish. Henry just looked upon her adoringly while she talked.

"Perhaps," Colin said gently, "love will help him survive."

"I've heard that. I've never seen any man love a woman more than my father loved my mother, and she lived with the disease for twenty years before it killed her. My father, after my mother died, lived less than a year." She sighed. "Almost as if he felt he had no further reason to live."

A rider from another party hailed them. "You folks *Falcon* passengers?"

"Yes, we are," Colin responded.

"Thought so. Recognized the ladies. You have a pretty good trip up the Chagres?"

Katlin laughed softly as Colin replied, "Relatively uneventful. And you?"

The man shrugged. "So-so. Couple o' men took the cholery in Cruces. Had to leave 'em there."

"We heard they had cholera there," Colin nodded, "so we got our horses at Gorgona in hopes of avoiding it. Did meet a couple of fellows with the cholera. You know a Will or Abe Martin? Their party went on without them."

"Nah, never heard the name. They's lots o' folks ahead, though. Mebbe one o' them'll know 'em."

"Thank you." Colin touched the brim of his hat in farewell. "Good journey to you."

The man rode away. Colin's eyes met Katlin's and he shrugged. "I never said it would be easy."

She smiled. "I know. Thank you for trying."

They rode on in silence between the rows of ruined buildings until they drew rein in front of the *Hotel Americano*.

Clouds gathered for the afternoon rainstorm as they dismounted. Katlin glanced at the blackening horizon and drew a deep breath. "Thank Heavens we can spend today's rainstorm under a *real* roof!"

Colin laughed. "They say it only rains half as much on this side."

"That's a relief, I suppose. Half as long or half as much water? Does it rain here all the time?"

"The dry season is from November to April. They don't get a drop then."

Katlin twisted her mouth into a wry grin. "If I ever return to this benighted country, remind me to come in the dry season."

He grinned. "I will. Now, I suggest we have an early supper and retire for the night so the maids can wash our clothing. Hopefully, our baggage will be here by tomorrow, but we have no way of knowing for sure."

"If it comes at all."

"Such a lack of faith in the good *alcalde* does not become you, Miss MacKenzie," he said with a chuckle that told Katlin he had thought of the possibility of the little *bodega* also. "I hope you had nothing of value in your baggage."

"Absolutely nothing except a few changes of clothing."

"Very wise. Since there seems to be no porter, Henry and I will carry your haversacks to the room." He pulled his watch from its fob and consulted the time. "I'm happy to report my watch survived its soaking in the river. Wash off the worst of the mud and join us for supper in, say, half an hour?"

Katlin nodded and took Elena's arm. "Half an hour."

The roar of rain on the roof drowned her reply.


The next morning, the maid knocked on their door and presented them with their clothing. A reasonable attempt had been made to remove the mud stains, and the dresses, while indifferently ironed, were at least clean.

A good night's sleep, in spite of a lumpy bed and not very clean sheets, did wonders for Katlin's morale. As she and Elena joined Henry and Colin for breakfast, Katlin felt energized, rejuvenated, and ready to face whatever the day would bring.

"And a bright good morning to you, ladies," Colin smiled in greeting as he and Henry rose when Katlin and Elena joined them. "You're both looking lovely this morning."

"Thank you," Katlin laughed. "Nothing like a bath, a night's sleep in a real bed, and some clean clothes to renew one's spirits. I never want to see another hammock. Oh, my!" She looked with dismay at the plate piled with eggs, rice, plantains, and a huge slab of bread the waiter placed in front of her. "Surely he doesn't expect me to eat all of that!"

"Eat up, Miss MacKenzie," Henry advised. "From what I hear, you won't get this much grub once we get aboard that steamer."

"Which is due in today," Colin added. "So, if you ladies would like to tour the city, we had better do it this morning."

Elena's eyes sparkled. "Oh, yes, I want to see, yes."

Katlin smiled at Elena's enthusiasm, then sobered. She met Colin's eyes. "We have to try and learn the identity of the unfortunate man we buried. Will we have time to do both?"

He smiled. "I made some inquiries this morning before you ladies joined us. It seems the gentleman's name was James McFee, an Irishman from New York." He drew a paper from his pocket. "His companions are going to send his belongings back to his widow, so I gave them the personal effects from his haversack." He handed Katlin the paper. "This is the direction of the poor lady. I thought you might like to write to her."

Katlin's eyes filled with tears as she stared at the name written on the paper. "Yes, of course. She must be told we did not allow him to die alone. I'll also tell her we gave him a Christian burial. It may give her some comfort, poor woman."

"Several other passengers from the *Falcon* are also at death's door with the cholera. I, for one, will be glad to be quit of this place as soon as possible." He shook his head. "At least they don't have yellow fever. I asked about and no one has ever heard of a case."

, Katlin sighed. "I'll bet, with all the folks coming through from New Orleans, that they get it soon."

"We'll hope not," Colin replied. "I lost several friends to it in New Orleans."

"I wish you had told me I didn't have to worry about yellow fever while I was sitting in that bungo in Chagres fretting about it."

Colin laughed. "You didn't ask. If you want to worry about taking something, worry about the ague. I understand it's quite prevalent here."

"Thank you," Katlin grimaced. "I'll remember that. If we're going to see the city, let's go."

As they left the dining room, a baggage train from Gorgona arrived. To Katlin's relief, she recognized their belongings.

"So the *alcalde* came through after all," Colin said.

"Did we ever doubt him?" Katlin replied.

"I admit the thought crossed my mind," Colin confessed.

"Mine, too," Katlin laughed. "So stow our baggage and let's go see the city!"

As Katlin, with Colin, Henry, and Elena, stepped onto the porch to begin their tour, a loud commotion attracted their attention. They watched as a horse drew a crude cart creaking and clattering down the street in front of them, a crowd of people laughing and following.

"Why all the excitement over a cart?" Katlin asked.

A red-headed young man stood beside her. He smiled and tipped his hat. "First cart ever built in Panama, Miss,", he explained. "Yankee mechanic as built it was headed for the gold fields. Ran out of money to get the rest of the way, so he set himself up in business here building carts."

Katlin turned to Colin. "I assume from that remark there are no buggies to rent. If we want to tour the city, we do it on foot or on horseback."

Colin nodded. "That's what it looks like. I prefer a horse, myself, for five miles to the old city sounds like a long walk to me."

The young man tipped his hat again. "Tom Beale at your service, ma'am. I'd be happy to guide your party on a short tour. I'm trying to get a ticket on a steamer north myself, but I've been here a month already. Plenty of time to see everything worth seeing, believe me." He grinned, and two dimples appeared on his freckled cheeks. "Nothing else to do, so I decided to find out as much as I could about the place, so's I could tell folks. Makes it more interesting, seeing the city, if you know the history and what's going on in the politics and such."

"Oh, yes!" Katlin's eyes sparkled. "I'm so glad we met you, Mr. Beale." She glanced at Colin, surprised to find him scowling. The frown disappeared as soon as she looked at him. She shrugged. Maybe it had been her imagination. Surely he was as interested in the history of the city as she.

"Why have you been here for so long?" Henry asked as they mounted their horses and prepared to begin their tour. "I'd'a thought you'd be halfway to San Francisco by now."

"Luggage didn't get across in time for me to catch the *Oregon* when she came through. Been trying to get on another one ever since. I'm not the only one. There's about seven hundred waitin' here for passage. Since about three hundred of us don't have tickets, they're gonna hold a drawing this afternoon for the fifty-two seats left aboard the *Panama*. I'm hopin' to get on her."

"What will you do if you don't?" Henry asked.

"Probably take a sailing ship, or wait two more weeks for a shot at a space on the *California*. A lot have taken sailing ships, even though it's about a seventy day voyage from here. At least a man can get passage. I hear some fellers have sold their ticket on the steamer for six hundred dollars, then taken a sailing vessel."

"Six hundred dollars! Why, that's double the price I paid," Katlin exclaimed.

"Not as bad now as a few months ago. Then as many as three thousand was tryin' to get to San Francisco." He chuckled. "Several small companies bought some native bungos and started north in them, thinking to paddle all the way. Most of 'em came back after about forty days, since they'd only got as far as the Island of Quibo, over in the Gulf. That's about two hundred miles."

"Hadn't they even looked at a map?" Katlin said, appalled at such innocent stupidity. "They could have died of hunger or thirst. Good heavens, they even could have drowned! What if the canoe capsized?"

"I suspect something like that happened to some of 'em, for not all as left made it back. No one seems to know what became of 'em. They could have gone ashore, I suppose, and made their way north overland. But that's a long trip across some pretty hostile terrain, from what I hear."

"If that is the case, we wish you luck in the drawing this afternoon, Mr. Beale," Colin said, "but if you seriously wish to give us a tour, please lead the way!"

Their new friend took them first to the cathedral, the most impressive sight in town, in his opinion.

"Built in 1688," he said in hushed tones as they entered. The coolness of the interior washed across Katlin's overheated face. Mr. Beale snatched off his hat as though just remembering it. "See the altar? All gold. It's from the original Jesuit church in the old city, the one Morgan sacked."

"And Morgan missed a solid gold altar?" Katlin exclaimed. "I find that hard to believe. Are you sure your informants weren't telling you a tall tale?"

Tom Beale met her eyes and smiled. "The priests covered the altar with white-wash so Morgan couldn't tell it was made of gold."

"How clever!"

"Wasn't it? Sit a minute and watch the services. They're right interesting."

As they watched, woman after woman walked reverently forward to the altar to light a candle, then step back, cross herself, and kneel for a moment.

"They're praying for the souls of relatives who have died from the cholera," Tom Beale whispered to Katlin. "They've been holding special masses like this all month, since the cholera has taken so many."

Tears sprang to Katlin's eyes as she thought of young James McFee, and Will Martin. Maybe she should ask one of the ladies to light a candle for them. She hesitated, not knowing the custom.

As she watched, four of the cruder element among the *Falcon's* passengers strode in, talking loudly. They did not remove their hats, in spite of Mr. Beale's admonitions. Instead, as Katlin watched in horror, they strode to the altar. One of them lighted his cigar on one of the votive candles. His companions laughed crudely as he puffed out several clouds of smoke.

Katlin, embarrassed at the uncouth behavior of her fellow Americans, wanted to put out the cigar on the man's forehead. Her thought must have shown in her face, for Mr. Beale murmured, "Let's get out of here."

"Yes, but please apologize to the priest for their boorish behavior. I certainly hope they don't think all Americans are such louts."

"I'm sure they have seen all kinds."

Beale offered her his hand to guide her down the several steps leading from the church back into the heat and, Katlin sensed, released it with some reluctance. Amusement at his reaction drove away some of the indignation she felt at the scene she had just witnessed.

She smiled faintly. I should have worn a wedding band and told everyone I travel to California to join my husband. She glanced at Colin, trying to read his mind. Would she have wanted Colin to think her married also? Quiet, she told her inner self. He's not interested in you. He's just being a gentleman.

As they returned to the street, Elena wrinkled her nose. "Why does the street smell so bad?"

"Yes," Katlin agreed. "The whole city smells like a privy."

"It is a privy, Miss MacKenzie," Mr. Beale laughed. "Watch out when you walk under any of these overhead balconies. The good ladies of the city and their maids just dump the chamber-pots out into the street."

Katlin found herself watching the balconies as they rode through the city. To her disappointment, half of the faces she saw were American. Signs on most of the shops were in English. She heard a native boy whistling 'Yankee Doodle' on the street, and a young senorita sat in the doorway playing a Negro spiritual on her guitar, singing the English words with a marked accent.

When they reached the remains of the old city, the air cleared and the miasma of the populated areas dissipated. Katlin took a deep breath as she stood by the ruins of the Jesuit Church of San Felipe and looked to the southeast, to the lofty mountains of the South American continent. To the northwest rose the North American continent. The panorama thrilled her. Rows and rows of pelicans swooped across the broad waters of the gulf, the white sand beaches sweeping in an arc that seemed a hundred miles long.

"We're standing in the middle of the world," she exclaimed. "This little strip of land connects North and South America. And it's all that separates the two largest oceans in the world." She thought that over, remembering how narrow that strip of land really was. She turned to Mr. Beale. "Why on earth hasn't someone built a canal across?"

"That idea's been bandied about for over twenty years, Miss MacKenzie," their young guide answered, his hazel eyes meeting hers. "More seriously since the canoe and mule line was established by the Royal Mail Steam Packet Company in 1846. But with the amount of rain that comes in the rainy season, building it could be a real challenge." He shook his head. "Plus the natives resist work in any form. Labor would have to be brought in from the States. And between the cholera and the ague, just keepin' 'em alive will be problem enough."

"Still," Colin added, rubbing his chin pensively, "With all of the traffic crossing to get to California, construction engineers are surely looking at it more seriously. The United States signed a treaty with the Republic of New Granada in December of '46. In it, the United States Government guaranteed the neutrality of the Isthmus. That sounds to me like they've got something in mind."

"They have, but to bring crews in, they run the risk of 'em using the job as a means of getting halfway to the gold fields for free."

"Good point," Henry laughed. "Get themselves this far for nothing, then catch the next steamer north."

"Besides," young Beale continued, "It's an engineering nightmare, because you have a twelve foot average tide on this side, compared with one foot on the other. They'll have to build a series of locks. A major undertaking, it is, but, mark my words, there'll be one across here some day. Until then, though, they are planning to built a rail line across. One of Mr. Aspinwall's associates, man name o' Stephens brought an engineer last year to survey for the best spot. They found a pass only three hundred feet above sea level, so they decided to go ahead with it.

"Now, of course, they have to do all the politicking.

They're trying to get funding from the Congress. They also have to get a contract with New Granada." He chuckled. "I suspect they'll be easier to deal with than Congress. Not many of those Eastern folks as cares much what goes on in California."

"I hope they hurry. A railroad would make that trip across a lot easier," Colin said, scowling as he watched Mr. Beale take Katlin's hand and tuck it in the crook of his elbow.

"You be careful, Miss MacKenzie," the young man said solicitously, "and watch your step. There are stones underneath these weeds, and the footing is precarious. Wouldn't want you to fall, now would we?"

"Certainly not," Katlin agreed, accepting the offer of assistance.

Much to Katlin's surprise, Colin interceded, removing her hand from Mr. Beale's arm and tucking it though his own. "We'd best return," he said. "With all the competition for the seats on that steamer, we don't want to get left behind."

Colin's possessiveness surprised Katlin. Was he jealous of Mr. Beale's attention? Did all of his assistance mean more than just a gentlemanly concern for her welfare? Nonsense. She dismissed the thought. He just wants to be sure we don't miss the steamer so we have to spend another month waiting for the next one.

"So soon?" Elena pouted as Henry helped her remount her horse. "But we have seen so little!"

"I'll make it up to you when we reach San Francisco," Henry promised. "Colin is right. We want to be there when that steamer gets here. Sure don't want the agent re-selling your tickets. And it's a good thing Captain Arnold gave me that letter to give the captain of the *Panama*. Otherwise I'd a' never gotten on myself. As it was, one of the clerks wanted to make me pay, but the other one said they'd better do what Captain Arnold said."

When they reached the *Hotel Americano*, Colin watched Tom Beale cling to Katlin's hand a little longer than Colin felt necessary. When he heard Katlin wish the young man good luck in the drawing for tickets, the wave of emotion that washed over Colin startled him. He wanted to wipe the smile off of the other man's face. He fortunately caught himself before he acted on his impulse.

He remembered his reaction on several occasions when he found her laughing with the young man during their morning's excursion. He could not understand his feelings. You've no claim to her, Colin MacDougal, he told himself. Be reasonable. She is an attractive woman, but remember, you swore you would never fall in love again.

Then why did he react so strongly to a possible rival? He caught Katlin's eyes upon him and, embarrassed to think she might sense his reaction, he shook away his thoughts and forced himself to say brightly, "Yes, Mr. Beale, we hope you will be able to join us on the journey north. Thank you for your time. We've enjoyed the tour. Too bad it could not have been longer."

As he and Tom Beale shook hands, Colin could taste the acidity of his own smile.

# Chapter 15

"**A**RE YOU PACKED?" Colin asked Katlin as soon as Mr. Beale departed. "We have no time to waste." Native porters crowded around them and offered to carry their bags. "The *Panama* is already taking on her passengers. We had best get aboard as soon as possible, to be sure we don't lose our seats."

"But we already have our tickets," Katlin protested.

"If these clerks can get six hundred dollars for a ticket, I would not be surprised if they re-sell ours unless we are there to prevent it."

Katlin laughed. "I see your point. Very well. Send the porter up in, say, half an hour. We'll be ready."

One hour later, Katlin, Elena, Henry, and Colin, with all of their baggage, stood on the shore and looked across the bay at the steamer riding at anchor about a mile and a half away. Knee-high breakers rolled ashore in a regular rhythm. Katlin watched the native boatmen slide their bungos through the line of foamy water. She could not keep a touch of fear from creeping into her breast. She watched the activities for a while, admiring the skill of the boatmen, reassured to note they did never seemed to upset the canoes.

Elena stared at the mass of native craft plying the distance between the shore and their destination and asked, "Why they leave the ship so far away?"

"Can't come any closer," Henry said. "Too shallow. Tide goes down twelve, fourteen feet. She'd be high and dry."

"Matter of fact," Colin chuckled, "they tell me that's how they make repairs. Bring the ship in, let the tide go out, do the work. Incoming tide re-floats her. Only place on the whole Pacific coast with that extreme a range."

The fierce sun pounded down upon them. Katlin opened her parasol for some relief from the relentless rays, almost wishing it would rain. At least the cloud cover would cool her down a little. She looked around, but did not see Tom Beale anywhere in the crowd. His thatch of red hair would make him easy to spot.

With a smile, Katlin noticed Colin glancing casually around as well. Did he, too, check to see if Mr. Beale had joined the crowd waiting to board the *Panama*? She recalled his reactions from the previous day. She shook her head. Granted, Colin MacDougal was an attractive man, but she refused to admit, even to herself, that she could be falling in love with him. Perhaps some day, after she settled with Caleb . . . .

"Ready, Miss MacKenzie?"

Colin's voice penetrated her reverie and she started. "Oh, yes, of course." It took her a moment to bring herself back to the realities. She looked with some dismay at the men wading through the surf to get to the canoes, wishing she still wore the pantaloons she used on the trip from Gorgona. "How do we get there? Do we have to wade?"

"Carry the *señoritas? Un medio, Senor.*" A muscular young native boy appeared beside her. His dark, sweaty skin glistened, reflecting the sunlight.

Colin grinned. "There's your answer." He dug some coins from his pocket and presented them to the young man, whose teeth gleamed white in his dark face as he tucked the coins out of sight. Elena squealed as he scooped her into his arms and quickly deposited her in the canoe. Katlin found herself following Elena moments later.

As the oarsmen rowed them swiftly across the calm, azure

waters to the anchored vessel, Katlin, crowded between Elena and the gunwale, trailed her fingers in the surprisingly warm water. She looked over the side and saw ripples of white sand on the bottom, with an occasional shell or tiny crab. At one point, the canoe disturbed a school of tiny black and white fish. Flocks of pelicans skimmed over the water, flying with a smooth precision that fascinated Katlin.

"Look at this," she exclaimed to Elena, waving her arm to include the long sweep of the bay.

Elena, clinging to Henry's arm as the canoe swayed from one side to the other with the motion of the oarsmen, sat and stared at the back of Colin's jacket. At Katlin's words, she looked up and out across the bay. "It is pretty, no?"

"Pretty! This has to be the most beautiful spot in the world."

"Smell the fresh air, Miss MacKenzie," Henry said. "We're away from the miasma of the city, and none too soon. Half dozen or more of the *Falcon* passengers didn't make the steamer 'cause they're a-bed with the cholera. I, for one, am real glad to be away."

Katlin shook her head. So death and desolation could follow even to as lovely a place as this.


They crossed the mile and a half to the steamer in a remarkably short span of time, and climbed the ladder to the already overcrowded main deck. The *Panama*, also a wooden side-wheeler, boasted two decks and three masts.

"This ship seems much larger than the *Falcon*," Katlin observed.

"She's 200 feet long, 33 feet wide at the beam, and over a thousand tons," Henry said.

"Why the masts, if the boat is propelled by steam?" Katlin asked.

Henry grinned. "In case something happens to the engine, or they run out of coal. Can happen. Matter of fact, the *Panama* left New York on December first of last year. En route to the Pacific, she broke a cylinder. Sailed back into New York Harbor on Christmas Day. Didn't make it to San Francisco until June of this year. This is only her third or fourth run."

"Well," Katlin remarked dryly, "I hope all of her cylinders hold together until we get to San Francisco."

Henry laughed. "We'll keep our fingers crossed. Now, let's get you ladies to your cabin and get your gear stowed before someone finds your cabin unoccupied and decides to use it. I suspect many of the passengers will be sleeping in hammocks strung all over the boat. I don't see how they can have cabins for all the folks that've bought tickets."

"Good idea." Katlin, Elena at her heels, followed Henry to the second deck and located their small cabin. It held two berths, one atop the other, a toilet stand with a small mirror, and a wash bowl with a water bottle and glasses. A damask curtain covered the berths, and bright red carpet decorated the floor.

"Oh, it is nice, no?" Elena bounced up and down on the lower bunk berth in her exuberance.

"Thank you, Henry. Yes," Katlin said to the excited Elena, "we should be quite comfortable here."

"Mr. MacDougal has a cabin just like this 'un on the main deck. He says I can use the top bunk so's I don't have to travel in steerage." He grinned. "If you've ever seen steerage, you'd understand."

Katlin laughed. "I've heard enough. I've no need to experience it myself. That's why I decided to spend the additional money to get a cabin."


The following morning Elena and Katlin joined Henry and Colin on deck to watch the last of the passengers arrive.

"Good morning, Miss MacKenzie, Senorita Velasquez," Colin greeted them. "You ladies look lovely this morning. I trust you slept well."

Katlin laughed. "As well as can be expected, I suppose," she replied. "How soon will we be departing?"

"The seamen tell me as soon as the last canoe-load of mail gets on board, and that, I suspect, is it right there." He pointed to a native bungo heavily laden with canvas sacks, low in the water from the weight, and listing to one side, where water occasionally lapped over the gunwale and up onto the cargo. "I'm sure it never occurred to them to use two boats rather than risk losing the mail overboard by putting it all in one."

"Probably not," Katlin agreed. She took Colin's arm and pulled him farther aft, away from Elena and Henry. She lowered her voice, although amid all of the din she need not have bothered, and asked, "How is Henry this morning? He looks pale. Did he sleep well?"

Colin grimaced. "Coughed a lot. And I think he's feverish. You think it's the consumption?"

"I suspect so. He's been pushing himself pretty hard the past week."

"Well, we'll just have to persuade him to spend the trip lying on deck in the sunshine. I hear that helps dry out the lungs."

Katlin sighed. "That's probably all we can do. I hope it's enough."

Ten minutes after the mailbags were transferred from the canoe to the steamer, the blast of the parting gun echoed across the bay. Before the echoes died away, the swish of the paddles heralded their departure, and the boat headed for Taboga.

"Taboga?" Katlin asked when told of their destination. "Where's Taboga?"

"In the bay, about an hour's run from here."

"And why do we stop there?"

"To take on water. Seems there's a spring of real good water in a ravine behind the village. All vessels as stop in Panama take on water at Taboga. Easier, too. It's a volcanic island, comes straight up from the ocean. It's also a coaling station. Coalers drop off loads at points along the route." He grinned. "I've heard of boats running out of coal and burning the furniture. Wind along the west coast is not very good for sailing. Taboga's got a deep, secure roadstead just a stone's throw from the beach, as opposed to a mile and a half like at the city."

As they approached Taboga, the beauty of the island amazed Katlin. The summit rose a thousand feet above the water, and banana, coconut, tamarind, and orange trees grew in unbroken terraces of luxurious vegetation all the way down to the beach.

A steamer lay on its side on the beach. Elena grasped Henry's arm and gasped, "Oh, look," she cried, "look! It is crashed, the boat, yes?"

Henry started to laugh. "It's not wrecked, Elena. Remember what we told you about the tides? Looks like she sustained some damage to her keel and is being repaired. Incoming tide'll float her off. You'll see."

Elena looked unconvinced.

"They use the tides as a ready made dry-dock," Henry explained. "I suspect some day, someone'll take a notion to build a couple of walls and a gate. That's all they'd need. That'd give 'em a longer time to make repairs. Way it is, they have to get the work done before the tide changes."

Katlin looked closely at Henry as he tried to convince Elena the boat really was undamaged. The flush of fever on his cheeks told her that, no matter how hard he tried to convince Elena otherwise, he had not recovered from the exertion of the trip across the Isthmus. He looked like he had lost weight as well. If they did not take good care of him, he could become seriously ill. She knew he did not want to show any sign of weakness in front of Elena, but somehow, they had to convince him to rest.

"Henry," she asked. "Did your doctor give you any medicine to take along when you joined the *Falcon*?"

"No," Henry grinned. "Says none of the medicines do any good, and some, like calomel, only make me worse. He's a firm follower of Samuel Thomson, my doc is. Says the best thing for consumption is rest, fresh air, and plenty of good food."

"With as many people as are on this boat, we're going to have to do some maneuvering to get you the food," Colin laughed. "I've already heard some of the passengers grumbling about the shortage of grub."

Katlin shrugged. "We'll have to try. But at least you can get plenty of the first two. The deck has all the fresh air you can breathe, and you don't have to work. You're a passenger now, remember?"

Henry laughed, the action bringing on another coughing spell. When he caught his breath, he smiled into the anxious eyes upon him. "I'll try," he agreed. "You don't have to hog-tie me."

Elena looked puzzled. "What does it mean, the hog-tie?"

Colin smiled and slapped Henry on the back. "It means he's going to be a good boy and let you and Miss MacKenzie wait on him. Right, Henry?"

The boy grinned. "Your wish, Miss MacKenzie, is my command."

The blast of the departure gun drowned her reply.


Colin made a thorough check of their fellow passengers. Many of the Spaniards who had accompanied Elena on the *Falcon* had successfully crossed the Isthmus and survived the cholera. He did not care for the looks of some of the rougher element. They could spell trouble. He knew relations with the Mexican government were not the best, with their defeat in the Mexican War still so recent, and he just knew these men would not be very diplomatic, recalling the boorish behavior of the four men at the Church of San Felipe. Too bad the captain could not find some pretense to keep them on board whenever the ship docked.

But he did not find Mr. Beale anywhere in the crowd of passengers. Apparently his attempt to obtain passage had not succeeded. He looked over at Katlin, who stood at the rail with Elena and Henry, her face flushed from the heat, the parasol providing a small amount of shade. Why am I so glad Mr. Beale did not join us? he thought. What is the matter with me? But he could not deny, even to himself, that the attraction he felt for Katlin was strong.

He shrugged. Probably best if he just kept an eye on her in case she needed help. She could certainly use a friend, going off to that wild country by herself with just the boy and the girl. Perhaps in time, his feelings would sort themselves out.

His decision made, he joined her at the rail. "I fear Mr. Beale failed to obtain passage, Miss MacKenzie." He watched closely for her reaction to this item of news.

Katlin shrugged. "Too bad. Poor man. Guess he's still stuck in Panama." She laughed merrily. "Maybe he can set himself up in business as a guide!"

She didn't care that Beale had been left in Panama. Colin met her eyes and smiled. She returned his smile and happiness rushed over him in a wave.

# *Chapter 16*

ALTHOUGH TWO FRENCHMEN had brought their wives, Katlin discovered she was the only American woman on board the *Panama*. Four women out of 250 passengers, Katlin mused. I'm glad I have Elena.

The bell for breakfast clanged at 9:00 AM the next morning. Katlin and Elena arrived to find every seat filled and the men gobbling every morsel of food in sight. A chicken the waiter placed on the table disappeared from the platter as though by magic, to reappear in sections on several plates.

As Katlin stood watching with disgust, Elena wide-eyed beside her, Colin appeared behind them. "Disgraceful," he muttered. He smiled at Elena. "Don't worry. They'll have a second seating as soon as these pigs are finished. Wait here." He scouted around the cabin and returned.

"There is a protected spot behind the mizzenmast that is semi-private with seats for only eight. I will fetch the two French gentlemen and their wives. The eight of us will preserve that section for ourselves so you ladies will not have to be exposed to the riff-raff."

"Thank you." Their eyes met and Katlin smiled at Colin with relief. She had not thought about what traveling alone might mean, and welcomed his assistance. She noted the absence of the fourth member of their party and asked, repressing her fears, "How is Henry this morning?"

Colin's brow wrinkled with concern. "He had a restless night so I left him sleeping. He had barely stopped coughing and gotten to sleep when some fellow's hammock line broke." He grinned. "If the thump hadn't wakened him, the yelp that followed would have."

Katlin laughed. "Only one thump? I heard at least three. Thank goodness Elena and I have a cabin. I had enough experience with hammocks in Panama to last me a lifetime. Thank you for taking Henry into your cabin. I'm sure he'll rest much better, and I'm glad you let him sleep. He certainly needs it." She glanced about at their fellow diners. "Do fetch the Frenchmen. Some of these men show signs of finishing." She shook her head. "At least, I assume they've finished. They've eaten everything but the plates."

"That's because they paid so much for their passage they feel they have to eat as much as possible to get their money's worth."

"I suppose that's why there was no coffee."

"Yes. They all think they have to drink at least three cups. Let me fetch our companions." Colin, fluent in French from his years in New Orleans, returned in moments. "They were standing just outside the door. The ladies had looked in and refused to join that mob. I've assured them we will have a secluded spot. Come on."

Katlin put her hand on the bulkhead for support as she crossed the rocking floor. Colin put a hand on her elbow to steady her.

A gentleman rose as she approached. "Finished, ma'am," he said politely "Please, sit down." The other men in the section Colin had chosen aft of the mizzenmast looked up and nodded as they noticed Katlin and her companions. One by one, they also rose, as though the presence of the ladies forced them to recall their manners.

"Thank you." Katlin accepted the proffered seat, and her companions followed.

Colin spoke in French to the two couples, then turned to Katlin. "Save places for me and Henry. I'll see if he's awake. If he's still asleep, I'll just take something back to him."

"Heavens, yes," Katlin agreed. "He needs all the rest he can get."

Colin returned before the waiters brought the trays of food for breakfast, Henry in tow. To Katlin's relief, the boy did look better, and he insisted he felt quite well. Elena fussed over him, and, when the food arrived, piled his plate high with beefsteak, biscuits, and sweet potatoes.

"Eat," she insisted. "The food, like the sleep, will help you be well again." She smiled at him, adoration shining in her eyes.

From across the table, Katlin watched the two young lovers. How tragic, she thought, that the consumption had the boy in its cruel grip. Poor Henry. Poor Elena. She sighed.

Colin, beside her, followed her glance and nodded. "We can only take care of him and pray," he murmured into her ear, so Henry could not hear the comment.


That afternoon, Katlin and Elena stood at the rail and watched the island of Quibo pass by the starboard side. High mountains disappeared into the clouds in the distance. They had made Henry a comfortable bed on deck out of a pile of blankets. Katlin raised her parasol against the relentless rays of the sun, which glared white-hot in the pale blue tropical sky. She appreciated the slight breeze raised by the passage of the ship. Not a single white-cap broke the mirror finish of the water. Long, gentle swells followed one after the other towards the horizon as far as her eyes could see.

"Heavens," she panted to Elena. "I used to think it would be nice to live in the tropics, but I've changed my mind. This heat drains every bit of energy out of me."

"It is hot, no?" Elena agreed.

"It is hot, yes," Katlin affirmed. "It must be ninety degrees, and it doesn't cool off that much at night, either."

"It will get cooler when we get farther north," Colin said as he joined them. He glanced at the sleeping boy. "And the heat will help dry Henry's lungs." He leaned on the rail and gazed out across the scenery. "Enjoy the land and calm seas while we have them. I hear we soon cross the Gulf of Tehuantepec, and will be out of sight of land for several days. According to the seaman I spoke with this morning, if the wind comes up, it can get pretty rough."

Katlin remembered when the *Falcon* had cleared New York Harbor and the waves began breaking over the bow. She did not look forward to a repeat of the feeling she had experienced while she clung to her bunk on that first and seemingly endless night.

"Will I be glad to get to Sacramento," she said with a rueful laugh. "I'm never setting foot on another boat."

Colin chuckled. "Be glad you're on a steamer and not a sailing vessel. I hear they can take up to ninety days from Panama. They have to sail way west to pick up the trade winds, then come back. And they sometimes get becalmed and make no more than two or three knots for several days."

Katlin closed her eyes and shuddered.

"Dinner will be at four o'clock," Colin said with a grin. "Seems we get fed only twice a day. I'll enlist the aid of the two French gentlemen and secure our spot behind the mizzenmast again. Please excuse me, ladies." He touched his hat to them and departed.

Elena pulled two bananas and a biscuit from her reticule. "Henry, he need to eat more than two times the day. When he awakes, I feed him." She joined Henry where he lay and sat beside him.

Katlin sighed. She might as well return to her stuffy cabin and finish the book she borrowed from one of her fellow travelers. If the boat started rocking, she would have no chance to read.

Two days later, they had lost sight of land, but fortunately the sea remained calm. Katlin watched the sun sink into the Pacific Ocean and wished she was a poet so she could adequately describe the beauty of such a sunset. Never in Katlin's life had she seen such a riot of color. As the sun settled into the water, it appeared to flatten, and the sky around it burst with a multitude of shades, from amber to rose, then red to violet, flashing flaming pyramids of light through the folds of clouds.

She watched as the sun vanished and the violet darkened to a deep purple. The evening star rose and shone brightly, to be joined, wink by wink, by more stars until thousands studded the night sky. The temperature, though still high, was tempered by an evening breeze and blessed relief from the blazing sun.

Katlin stood alone for a long time, enjoying the relative coolness of the evening, wondering what the next few days would bring. Colin's aquamarine eyes kept intruding on her mind. So many things threatened to make her care for him more she would allow herself. His concern for Henry, his gentle manners, his readiness to come to her aid when the man followed her in Panama . . . .

She forced the vision away and returned to her cabin to get some sleep. She fervently hoped that perhaps tonight, all of the hammock ropes would remain intact.

Colin, unknown to Katlin, had spent the time standing a little apart from her, watching in case one of the rougher element chose to annoy her. When none did, his eyes followed her trim figure as she returned to her cabin. Again he experienced the mixture of feelings. She was not like Michelle at all. Her pride, her determination, even the way she carried herself were so different. He shook his head. He could not explain, even to himself, why he felt so driven to protect her.

The wind rose. At first, it came as a welcome relief to the heat of the day, but when the ship's motion began to increase, he felt a twinge of alarm. Would this be one of the dreaded "Tehuantepeckers" the crew talked about? Where the north wind blew down across the Gulf of Mexico and crossed the isthmus from Coatzacoalcos to Salina Cruz, gathering strength as it crossed again over water?

"Come right down offen the land," the seaman had said. "Us bein' so far off o' shore gives 'er plenty o' fetch to build some big seas." Colin twisted his mouth into a wry grin as he recalled the sailor adding cheerfully, "Come down on ye with a roar like a freight train, it do. Kin upend a flat-bottom scow like this-un in a flash."

The ship rose and crossed a giant swell. Colin felt a sinking sensation in the pit of his stomach as the ship sank into the trough on the other side. He tried to dismiss the old seaman's scorn for the side-wheeler as the prejudice of sailors, steeped as they were in the tradition of sailing ships, against all steamers.

The ship crossed another giant swell. Colin again felt the sinking sensation, and caught his breath. Was the *Panama* seaworthy enough to weather some heavy seas?

# Chapter 17

KATLIN HAD JUST dropped off to sleep when she felt the ship rise and drop into the trough. She listened. The wind whistled through the rigging, audible over the thud, thud, thud of the engine and the swishing of the paddle-wheel as the steamer drove its way through the pitching waves.

A frightened cry from Elena brought her fully awake. "The storm!" the girl gasped. "The storm. The wind! We will die, no?"

"No, we're not going to die," Katlin assured the girl. At least, not right away, she thought, setting her jaw, determined to show no fear. "Be careful. If the boat starts pitching, you can get hurt." Or worse, she thought, you will get seasick. Katlin worried more about seasickness than sinking.

"Elena, Elena, are you all right?" Henry's voice reached them through the door. "Open up!"

Katlin struggled across the pitching deck to the door and opened it. Henry stood there, Colin behind him. Katlin felt a momentary embarrassment at being seen in her night shift, but quickly dismissed it. If Colin and Henry were here, they must be concerned for the safety of the ship.

"We are in no immediate danger," Colin reassured them, "but we should be prepared for any exigency. Get dressed in the pantaloons you wore across the Isthmus. If we have to swim for it, you can't do it in those long skirts. Join us in the saloon on the main deck when you are dressed."

The door closed, and Katlin hurried to follow his advice,

prodding the stunned Elena to do the same. "Come on, " she urged, digging their pantaloons out of her trunk. "Good thing we brought them along." Elena had been in favor of discarding the despised garments as soon as they reached Panama City.

Katlin took the precaution of securing her mother's emerald earrings, her grandmother's pearls, and all of her cash in the small sack she had used crossing the Isthmus. She tied the string securely around her neck, tucked the bag down inside her shirtwaist and stuffed the tails of the shirt inside the pantaloons.

"Move," she ordered, when Elena stood gaping at her. "Henry and Colin will be back to see what's taking us so long."

While Elena struggled into the ungainly trousers, Katlin ripped a seam down the side of a skirt so she could wrap it around her to cover the pantaloons, but in such a way that it could be easily removed should the need arise. With some difficulty, she persuaded Elena to do the same.

"Come on, we can sew the seam up again when we are out of danger. You don't want to be tangled up in your skirt if we have to swim. Remember your experience with those wretched skirts in Panama?"

When they finished dressing, they joined Henry and Colin in the saloon.

"We have changed course and are heading directly into the wind and the waves, towards the shore," Colin said as Katlin and Elena entered, carefully clinging to the bulkhead in the pitching ship.

"Why are we doing that?" Katlin queried.

"The crewman I spoke with assured me the closer we get to shore, the calmer the seas will become." Colin grinned. "He also said wise sailors follow the shoreline to avoid the heavy seas that can come with these winds."

"Then why are we out so far?"

"They tell me the owners of the steamers order the captain to cut across the bay, because it can save up to two days of travel time."

"They risk our lives and their ship to save two days?"

"So it would seem," Colin nodded. "In their favor, it must be said that these winds are not that common this time of year. In the winter season, they are more cautious."

Katlin grimaced. "That's a comfort, I suppose." She clung to her chair as the ship rose and dove into an oncoming wave and stopped for a moment, with a shudder. The steady thud of the engine reassured her as the ship climbed to the crest of the next wave.

The two French couples joined them. One of the ladies wept, the other had her jaw set in determination. Katlin met her eyes and the woman smiled.

"*C'est fou, ne c'est pas?*"

Katlin laughed. "Yes," she agreed. "It is crazy."

Colin turned to Katlin in surprise. "I didn't know you spoke French."

"Please," she smiled. "Give me some credit. My mother considered anyone who could not speak at least a minimum of French to be appallingly ignorant. I wish, for Elena's sake, she had felt as strongly about Spanish."

The crash of the next wave sent one of the oil lanterns smashing to the deck. Elena screamed as the fire, carried on the burning oil, raced across the slanting floorboards to the curtains covering the portholes. In seconds, flames climbed the bulkhead. Katlin heard the paint crackle as it blistered in the heat. Smoke began to fill the room. Fear swept over Katlin as she realized the danger they faced. Stories of the horror of a fire at sea rose unbidden in her mind.

Several men stripped off their coats and beat at the flames. Henry started to join them, but Colin pulled him back.

"Get the ladies out, Henry." When Henry hesitated, Colin gave him a shove. "Go!"

Katlin regained the use of her paralyzed limbs, and hustled Elena toward the doorway. Henry joined them and they burst into the welcome fresh air. A wave washed over the deck and nearly swept Elena away. Henry and Katlin clung to the rail with one hand, Elena with the other, and managed to get her back on her feet.

"Let's go aft," Katlin shouted to Henry. "We'll have some protection from the waves there. I sure don't want to go below decks until I know they have that fire out."

"The fire, the fire," Elena wept. "The ship, it will burn, and we will all drown, *verdad?*"

Katlin and Henry ignored her, and continued to work their way aft. Once they reached the stern, they found a protected spot in the lee of the elevated cabin next to the water barrels. As they huddled together, a fit of coughing seized Henry. Katlin held her breath, waiting for the gush of blood that had preceded her father's death. When it did not come, and Henry finally collapsed into Elena's arms, Katlin sighed with relief. Another reprieve, she thought. But for how long?

Katlin lost all sense of time as they cowered in their nook. The ship rose and fell with regularity. Each time it rose, Katlin held her breath, praying the ship would crest the wave and not overturn. The steady chug of the engine reassured her. Each time the ship sank into the trough on the other side, she released her breath with a long, tremulous sigh. Several times she drifted into a hazy sleep, only to be awakened by the next pitch of the ship. Stiff with fatigue and cramped from crouching in the small space, she tried to stretch her legs. Would the night never end? Several times she nearly decided to work her way back to see if the fire had been snuffed, but each time, another pitch of the deck made her decide to stay put. She took comfort in the fact that the area surrounding them remained free of flames.

As the first pink haze of dawn broke through the clouds lining the coast to the east, Colin rejoined them. His soot begrimed face told Katlin the fight against the fire had not been an easy one.

"Fire out?" Henry opened one eye.

"Yes, a couple of hours ago, but some of us stayed to keep an eye on it. It flared up several times, and we wanted to be there, just in case it decided to flare up again." Colin ran a weary hand through his blond hair and rubbed his smoke-reddened eyes. "We are close enough to land that you can see the coastline from the bow, and the seas are lessening, so we should be out of danger. If you ladies would like to return to your cabin, perhaps you can get a little rest."

Katlin accepted his hand and, with his help, struggled stiffly to her feet.

"That sounds like a good idea to me," she said with a prodigious yawn. "Come on, Elena." She and Henry lifted the half asleep Elena upright and, between them, got her into bed. Katlin tucked the girl in and, with a grateful sigh, sank into her own bunk. She slept almost the moment her head touched the pillow.

Katlin awoke the next morning to calm seas with not a breath of air. After breakfast, not wishing to spend one unnecessary moment in the stifling heat of the cabin, she took up her post on the rail. To protect herself against the fierce rays of the sun, she raised her parasol and fanned her face, already overheated in the heat and humidity.

Elena joined her. "The wind, it is gone, no?"

Katlin laughed. "Yes, and I have to admit I miss it already."

Colin strode up, took off his hat, and wiped his forehead. "I used to think New Orleans got hot. Now it seems a heavenly cool spot compared to this."

"Yep," Henry, who trailed behind Colin, added. "I always told my folks I had the tropics in my veins. Every time snow blew, I'd tell 'em I planned to move south to some tropical paradise as soon as I finished school. I've changed my mind. I'm ready to have a little snow blown in my face."

Hammering reached their ears. Colin cocked his head and listened. "Sounds like repairs to the main saloon are being made as we speak."

"Was there much damage?" Katlin asked.

"Mostly superficial," Colin said. "Couldn't get it to stay out because the pitch in the wood kept re-igniting. We finally pulled the wood from the bulkheads and threw it overboard."

Katlin patted his arm in sympathy. "You poor dear, you worked all night. No wonder you look so tired." Their eyes met, and Katlin felt herself being drawn into those magnificent aquamarine eyes. She shook herself to clear her head and removed her hand from his arm.

He returned her smile. "I'll take a nap this afternoon. We have about a week of weather and travel just about like this before we reach Acapulco. I'll have plenty of time to catch up on my rest."

Katlin turned to Henry, to get her jumbled thoughts off of her reaction to Colin. "And you, too, Henry. Get lots of rest. You had a bad spell last night." She did not mention the terror that had raced through her as she waited to see blood gushing from his mouth at any moment during those terrible hours while they huddled together between the water barrels.

"Yes, Boss," Henry grinned. "Between you making me rest all the time and Elena shoving food into me, I should be in the bloom of health by the time we reach San Francisco."

They heard shouts from the deck forward. Katlin turned to Colin. "What's going on?" she asked.

"Some of the blacklegs that came aboard the *Falcon* in

New Orleans are starting up a little game of *monte* on the deck astern. Unfortunately for the rest of us, they were lucky in the draw for seats, while honest folk, like our friend Mr. Beale, got left behind."

Katlin did not miss the glance he gave her when he mentioned Tom Beale. She laughed under her breath. I didn't mistake it, she thought. He *was* jealous of Mr. Beale's attention to her when they were in Panama. The tingle of pleasure that stirred her pulses dismayed her. Remember, she told herself firmly, no entanglements until you have settled with Caleb.

Colin continued. "Several of them were notorious for cheating in New Orleans. One reason they left. When their sort gets too well known, they have to look for newer pastures." He shook his head. "And there are always fools who think they can get the best of them."

Henry grinned. "The padre did, in Panama. They set up shop there and the good father won their five hundred dollar stake the first night. Must have had divine help. Anyways, they're going to have to build up their capital again."

"Which means they'll be a little careless," Colin growled. "Good. The sooner someone gets their number here on board, the better."

Katlin laughed. "Do you think gamblers ever learn? Why, I remember . . . ."

She stopped as a shot rang out. The sound reverberated across the water.

# Chapter 18

ELENA SCREAMED. Katlin's mind flew to the scene on the *Falcon* and the fight that took the life of Elena's father. She could tell from the look on Elena's face that she, also, remembered that terrible scene.

Colin and Henry hurried aft, in the direction of the still echoing gunshot, Elena and Katlin at their heels. They arrived on the scene moments after the captain. As the crush of men parted for him, Katlin caught a glimpse of one of the monte dealers sprawled out on the deck.

"Get a doc!" one of the men shouted. "We got a doc on board?"

Katlin spoke up when only silence greeted the call. "I have some medical knowledge. I will be happy to tend the man." A path opened for her. Colin followed. Henry stayed behind with the weeping Elena.

The man lay in a heap on his left side. Katlin rolled him onto his back. His right arm fell loosely to the deck. The limpness of his body told her the man had probably been dead when he landed. Blood oozed from a small hole in the center of his chest and from his mouth.

"He's been shot in the lungs," Katlin murmured to Colin. "His lungs are filling with blood. You know as well as I that there's nothing we can do to save him."

"Yes, I know." Colin grimaced.

"He's not breathing," she added. "He was probably dead before he fell."

The captain stood over her and watched as she felt for a heartbeat, but found none. She met the captain's eyes and shook her head.

"And now will someone tell me what happened?" The captain's stern voice rang out as he surveyed the silent men surrounding him. A stunned young man stood staring in horror at the still body on the deck. "I only wanted him to give me back my money. He took all the money I had, then I caught him cheatin.'" He babbled with fright. "I thought he was reachin' for a gun and . . . and . . . my gun just went off." His knees buckled and he sank to the deck. "I never meant to kill him, honest."

"Deliberate murder, it were." One of the other blacklegs spoke up. "Dan never carried no gun. Peaceful man, he were. I say string the blackguard up."

Murmurs of assent ran through the crowd. Katlin turned frightened eyes to Colin. "Surely they won't hang the poor young man. I'm sure this scoundrel was cheating him."

"Up to the captain," Colin said. "He'll check with witnesses, see if anyone saw the man reach for a gun."

"And if no one did?"

"Then they will probably hang him."

"No! Look, he didn't mean to kill him. Besides, the man was a crook. He cheated!"

"Cheating at cards is not a hanging crime. Murder is."

Katlin looked more closely at the dead man and recognized him as the one who had irreverently lighted his cigar on the votive candle at the cathedral in Panama. She felt again the surge of outrage that had washed over her as she witnessed the insult, feeling the pain of the devout Catholics who had watched in horror.

Somehow, it seemed to Katlin, the man had gotten his just reward. What a shame if the poor young man who was the instrument for that justice were hanged.

With a flash of insight, Katlin recalled how the man's arm had fallen when she turned him from his side. Following her impulse, she probed the man's shirt front. She felt a bulge and smiled at Colin. "Care to see what I just found?"

"What have you found, Miss?" the captain demanded.

For answer, she pulled out a small derringer that had lain hidden in the dead man's shirt. She held it up for the captain's inspection.

The captain grunted and turned to the blackleg who had insisted the young man be hung for murder. "So much for your friend's innocence," he growled. "He was reaching for his gun just like this feller claims." He scowled. "We'll put a stop to this once and for all. First man I see playing any games of chance gets clapped in irons until we get to San Francisco. Not gonna be any more of this on my ship. Do I make myself clear?"

He spoke to the seaman standing next to him. "Get some help and toss that carrion overboard. I want him off my ship. And get that deck swabbed down good."

He turned on his heel and strode away. Katlin looked at Colin in horror.

"Just toss him overboard?" she gasped. "No ceremony? Not even wrapping him for burial?"

"Come." Colin led her away. "You're not in a small town in Maine any more."

She shuddered and tried to close her ears to the splash as the man's body hit the water.


A week later, they entered Acapulco harbor at midnight. By the moonlight, Katlin could see the ring of mountains that surrounded the basin on which the city was built. Lights glittered along the shore.

Colin pointed out the white walls of the fort on a rocky point to the north of the harbor. "Look. The moon is so bright you can see the trees lining the Alameda."

As they watched, the ship's tender set out for shore, but returned almost immediately. Katlin heard shouts of "*fuero! fuero!*"

With a little gasp, she seized Colin's arm. "What are they saying?"

"Get out, if I translate correctly." He pulled her closer to him as the sound of a cannon shot echoed across the water.

"Why are they firing at us?" Katlin cried in fright. She clung tighter to Colin's arm.

"They're not. That's a warning shot. It didn't come anywhere near us."

"I suppose that's a comfort. What on earth is going on?"

"Here comes a seaman from the tender. Maybe he can tell us." Colin put a hand on the man's arm. "What's happened?"

The man shook his head. "Line o' soldiers on the beach with rifles. Said they'd fire on us of we came any closer." He grinned. "I make it a personal rule never to argue with a man's got a rifle pointed at me, so we turned around and come back. Seems they've heard the cholery is in Panama, and won't allow no one to go ashore. Fact is, they want us to pull back outside the harbor. Won't even let us stay this close."

Katlin remembered the young man they buried coming across the Isthmus with a shudder. "I can understand their fears," she murmured, "but weren't we to get fresh provisions here?"

"Guess we'll have to get 'em at San Blas, Miss," the seaman responded politely. "That's our next port 'o call, about three days from here."

"And if they have heard the same rumors at San Blas?"

The seaman shrugged and turned away.

Colin answered for him. "Then we will be on short rations until we reach Cabo San Lucas."

Katlin shook her head, thinking of the fights that could break out if they ran short of water. She saw Colin watching her and smiled. "You're right. I'm not in a small town in Maine anymore."

\* \* \*

When she rose the next morning, they had covered forty of the miles to San Blas, and followed the coastline. Majestic mountains rose in the distance. While not exactly cool, the temperature was a least a little lower. After breakfast, Katlin stood at the rail, welcoming the breeze, and thinking this coastline had to be the most beautiful in the world.

Two days after the incident with the gamblers, Katlin noticed a high peak rising above the surrounding mountains. When the captain paused briefly to wish her a good morning, she pointed it out to him.

"That there's the Colima Volcano, Miss Mackenzie. It's near Lake Chapala, in the Province of Jalisco. Stands 16,000 feet high, it do."

"It's very impressive," Katlin observed.

"Part of the mountain chain that starts in Canada, goes through the States where we call 'em the Rockies, then right down into South America. Where you crossed the Isthmus, that's the lowest they get in the whole range." The captain went on his way. Katlin continued to gaze at the distant volcano. What an education this trip was giving her!

The following morning, Thursday, August 13, their third day out of Acapulco, Colin pointed out the Islands of Las Tres Marias on the port side.

"We're approaching the roadstead of San Blas," he added.

"Is it a large town?" Katlin asked.

Colin grinned. "About the same size as Chagres, from what I hear. Not exactly a metropolis. Look, you can see it coming up now. We have to anchor about a mile off."

"Again?" Katlin sighed. "I would dearly love to stop someplace where we can tie up to a pier and not have to go ashore in those wretched canoes." The engines slowed. Katlin heard the clank of the anchor chain and shouts from the crew. Already an assortment of native boats approached.

An officious man in one of the larger vessels announced he was the *alcalde.*

"*Bienvenidos, bienvenidos,* welcome. *Hay muchos provisiones.* You need the fruit? The beef? The *agua,* of course." One of the larger launches carried two steers, evidently for sale. The little man chattered on in his mix of English and Spanish for a few more minutes, then departed.

Katlin turned to Colin. "Did I hear the word 'quarantine' anywhere in that conversation?"

"Not once," he grinned. "Must be bad for business. Care to take an excursion ashore?"

Henry and Elena strolled up arm in arm in time to hear the question.

"Oh, *si, si,*" Elena jumped up and down like a little girl and clapped her hands in delight. "We can walk up to the fort, yes?" She pointed to the Presidio about a mile beyond the town, standing atop a high, rocky bluff. "I have never been to a real fort."

"I understand it's been abandoned for some time," Colin nodded, "so I suppose no one would object to our visiting the area," Colin nodded. "It will cost us three *reales* apiece for a ride to shore, but I guess it's worth it."

The route of the *cayucas* took them through a line of breakers. Katlin held her breath in apprehension as the rows of white water appeared before them, but the boatmen seemed to take it in stride. In a few moments, she felt the keel of the *cayuca* scrape the shoreline and found herself deposited on the shore in ankle deep sand. Mustangs, mules, and donkeys covered the beach, interspersed with natives selling everything from strings of bananas and plantains to earthen jugs filled with cool water.

As they strolled among the huts of the little village, more natives sold limes and oranges, or tortillas and fried pork.

Colin enlisted the services of a native boy to guide them

up to the Presidio and they started off. The trail led them through a swampy jungle to the foot of the cliff.

"Oh, my," Katlin gasped as she stared at the trail. "It goes straight up!"

"If you ladies think it will be too difficult," Colin offered, "we can go back."

Katlin feared the trek would exhaust Henry, but she did not want to embarrass him by saying so. Fortunately, Elena made the decision.

"You go," she said to Katlin and Colin. "I wait here. My Henry, he stay with me."

Colin grinned down at Katlin. "Still game?"

Katlin saw he waited for her to back down, so she set her jaw and said, "Lead the way."

The barefooted boy started up the hill at a brisk pace. Katlin, determined to keep up, took a deep breath and followed.

Up they scrambled, through banana trees and thickets, over loose stones, and around boulders until at last they stood at the pinnacle.

Katlin took off her hat, shook her hair loose, and let the breeze blow across her overheated face.

"It's so gloriously cool up here," she cried. "And we can see forever!" The *Panama*, riding at anchor, appeared the size of a toy boat in the distance. Rows of trees outlined the river as her eyes traced it back to the mountains which rose until they disappeared in the clouds.

The dark blue of the deep ocean changed gradually to an emerald green as it approached the shoreline. White lines of breakers added to the beauty of the scene.

Colin joined her as she stood admiring the view before her. "Don't want to break the spell," he said with a smile, "but if you want to see the rest, we'd better begin. I think we have time for a stroll around what's left of the town." He offered her his arm and they entered the deserted courtyard.

The walls had broken down, and vines had grown over the gates and stone pillars.

The plaza opened out onto another, this one covered with tall weeds. Pigs rooted and grunted among the foliage. They looked so feral that Katlin clung a little tighter to Colin's arm, but the pigs ignored them.

"Look," Katlin murmured. "The church is going to ruin as well. What a shame! Those bells don't look like they've been rung for years."

"I understand Commander DuPont spiked the guns during the Mexican War, but the garrison had been abandoned even before that."

A slender young woman approached carrying a jug of water on one hip and some bananas balanced on her head. She smiled shyly as she offered her wares.

"I guess a few of the houses must still be occupied," Katlin observed. "But we are the only ones from the *Panama* to come up here. She must not get much business."

Colin laughed. "I'm sure someone from the family goes down the hill when the boats come in. Here, have a banana." He handed the woman two *reales* and took a deep drink from the *olla*. "Delicious. After that moldy, musty water we get from those scuttlebutts on the ship, it tastes wonderful."

Katlin finished her banana and took a long drink of the cool water as well. She sighed with pleasure. "I wish we could take some with us."

"We'll buy a jug in town to take aboard. I don't want to carry anything extra down that steep trail." Colin handed back the jug and thanked the woman, who curtsied and walked away. "Now, unless you want the *Panama* to leave us here, we'd better get started on our way back."

Katlin nodded. "You're right. This is a lovely spot, but I don't think I'd care to spend a month here. And Elena will be fretting." On an impulse, Katlin offered Colin her hand.

"But thank you for bringing me."

He smiled into her eyes and gently kissed the hand he held. "The pleasure was all mine, Miss MacKenzie."

Katlin's heart leaped into her throat and her heart pounded so loudly she feared he would hear it as the touch of his lips sent tingles up her arm, even through the glove. She took a deep breath to get her emotions back under control. No romance, she told herself firmly. That's what got you into trouble in the first place, when you let a pair of striking eyes sway your judgment.

As his eyes held hers, she realized how much she wanted to kiss those smiling lips and pulled her hand away.

"You're right. We really do have to get back." She turned and started down the well-worn path.


They found the trail back, downhill all the way, much easier than the climb up. Elena and Henry jumped apart when Katlin came into view, guilt written plainly on their faces.

Katlin smothered a smile. So Elena had sent her off with Colin to get some time alone with Henry. She sighed. Guess I don't make a very good *dueña*, she thought. Isn't the *dueña* supposed to make sure the girl is never alone with a man? Katlin shook her head. If Henry is dying of consumption, let them have a little pleasure. Ignoring the high color on Elena's cheeks, she smiled and said, "You missed a lovely view, but now we must hurry back or we'll miss the boat."

At that moment, as if for emphasis, the steamer's gun sounded the signal to return.

When they reached the beach, everyone else had already re-boarded. Only one *cayuca* remained on the beach, a hollowed out log about ten feet long. It rolled over the swells in a frightening manner.

"Lie flat," Colin ordered. "Keep the weight low in the boat."

Elena gasped and clung to Henry. Katlin crouched as close to the bottom of the boat as possible, her knees in the muddy water of the bilge. No one dared move a hand or foot for fear of upsetting the delicate balance that kept the clumsy craft upright.

When they reached the steamer and pulled up to the gangplank, the seaman receiving them berated Colin.

"Are ye daft, Mon, riskin' the young ladies in such a craft?"

Colin handed Katlin up the steps. Their eyes met and both laughed. Katlin, surprised to find she had found the adventure exhilarating, came to Colin's defense.

"I think, young man, that it was I who put Mr. MacDougal at risk."

# Chapter 19

KATLIN REACHED the deck the following day just as the sun broke through the morning mist rising from the distant mountains. She watched with interest as they approached the settlement of Mazatlán. After breakfast, she took Elena for their morning stroll, wending their way, with some difficulty, through the crowds of men lining the rails.

"*Mira, mira,*" Elena pointed towards the horizon. "Another ship!"

The plume of smoke grew steadily larger until they could see another steamship. Henry joined them and identified the approaching vessel as the *California*, sister ship of the *Panama*.

"She's on her way down from San Francisco. She'll anchor here in Mazatlán. Should pass by close enough for us to get some news."

Shouts soon began between the two ships.

"Still gonna be any gold left, time we git there?"

"You fellers hain't taken all the gold, hev ye?"

"True what they say, gold jest layin' around waitin' to be picked up?"

Katlin listened to the questions and laughed. "Seems all they want to know about is the gold. San Francisco could have burned to the ground, for all they care."

Henry grinned as the reassurances that the supply of gold remained plentiful flew back across the expanse of water separating the two ships. "That's what they came for, Miss MacKenzie, and that's all they're interested in." He tucked Elena's hand through his arm. "Come to the starboard rail.

They tell me Mazatlán is one of the prettiest parts of the whole trip.

The three of them joined Colin on the starboard side to see mountains that went straight down into the sea, split into chains of islands separated by narrow channels. Crags scarred the sides of the mountains, precipices of dark, red rock. Relentless ocean waves had carved deep caverns into the base of these mountains, each surge of the pounding surf digging deeper, each wave exploding in a burst of foam and spray as it dashed against the rock. The water struck with such force it often swept many feet up the face of the cliff.

Impressed by the force of the waves, Katlin could only marvel, "If a ship got too close, she'd be smashed to pieces!"

Colin nodded. "Happens. I hear a sailing vessel foundered here not two months ago. Wind drops suddenly, surge catches the ship, and puts her on the rocks before the crew can do anything to prevent it. Could happen to a steamer as well, should she lose her engine."

"Seen it, once," Henry added. "Sailing vessel almost went on the rocks off Cuba in heavy seas. Put out the long boats and had everyone rowing as most they could. Two more ships sent long boats to help, or they'd a' foundered for sure."

Katlin laughed. "Well, I certainly hope our engine is functioning properly."


"California!" The cry woke Katlin the following morning at sunrise. She sat up in her bunk and looked out to see only open ocean.

Elena jumped from her bunk and looked also. "Where, where?" she cried.

Katlin laughed and rose. "Get dressed. It will be off the starboard side. We can't see it from here."

They joined the throngs on deck. Everyone tried to catch a glimpse of the fabled land of gold.

"Oh, I cannot see!" Elena cried, jumping up and down, trying to peer over the crowds of backs in front of her.

"Let the little lady through," a stentorian voice roared out. "Let her see the Peninsula of California." As though by magic, a path opened in front of them and they reached the rail at the starboard bow.

Katlin scanned the sterile brown coastline through a glass offered to her by one of her fellow passengers.

"Why," she gasped, "it's bare rock! Nothing but a few cactus plants and some scrubby brush. Nothing like the mainland farther south. How can anyone possibly live there?"

"Valley of San Jose coming up real quick, Miss," the man offered. "Small river waters it, it do, and the town is nearby. River keeps the whole valley green. Could be a paradise, if someone with a little Yankee enterprise were to move in here."

"San Jose del Cabo," Katlin mused. "Wasn't a small body of American troops under siege here during the war with Mexico?"

"Yep. Lieutenant Haywood's bunch. They held out, though. Lucky for them the war ended so quick."

Katlin stared at the barren, yellow crags that glittered in the morning sun, and the line of shattered peaks that glowed violet in the distance. She shuddered at the thought of being blocked from escape by the sea, with the only way out across those desolate wastelands.

She shook her head to clear it of her dismal thoughts and said, "Come on, Elena. Let's go get some breakfast while there is still some left."

That evening, they passed the Cape, a granite bluff broken into three distinct pyramids of glistening white rock.

The ocean had carved caverns and arches, some as high as twenty feet. Some of the natural bridges arced so high that Katlin caught glimpses of the ocean beyond.

On the twelfth of August, they passed the island of Santa Margarita. Colin and Henry joined Katlin and Elena at the rail.

"Gotta watch real close in these parts," Henry laughed when Elena asked him why they moved so slowly. "Captain's being real careful. Says the charts are way off. They don't show any shoals at all, but the *Panama* found one and ran aground on her way down. Had to lay to all night. In the morning, they found they'd been going straight for the headland. If she hadn't snagged on the shoal, she'd have gone a-ground."

"Then I'm glad we are passing by here in the daylight," Katlin sighed. "This looks like a very desolate spot to be stranded."

Henry nodded. "They tell me a few months back a whaling ship got caught in the current and was lost. Her crew managed to get ashore, but they had to walk for days across a barren desert with no water and no trees. Like to never made it to the Valley of San Jose."

"I hope we don't try to emulate their example," Katlin remarked dryly.

Colin chuckled softly beside her. "I trust the Captain will make sure we don't."


Two days later, on August 14th, they crossed an invisible line in the water. They left the tropics, and the tropical heat, behind them, and picked up the northwesterly trades. The temperature dropped twenty degrees and more passengers chose to remain in their staterooms or in the saloon. Elena found the cool wind unpleasant and elected to stay indoors. Henry stayed with her.

To Katlin, the change in temperature was invigorating. The following morning, dressed warmly against the chill wind, she strolled the deck alone after breakfast. Most of her fellow passengers looked forward to the end of the journey. She overheard them talking eagerly about their anxiety to get to 'the diggin's'. She stopped by the rail and stared at the coastline gradually passing by, mile after mile of dismal, brown, barren hills.

A school of dolphins appeared and dove gracefully in and out of the bow wave. She watched them, smiling at their antics, until they seemed to tire of the game and headed out to sea, plunging and swooping with one occasionally making a high leap into the air before landing back in the water with a splash.

Intent on watching the dolphins, Katlin did not realize Colin had joined her until her spoke.

"Magnificent creatures, aren't they?" he said.

"Oh, yes." She turned to him, her eyes glowing. "They're wonderful! I'd never spent much time on the water before. I never realized it held so much life. When we rounded the Cape, I saw some wide, flat fish one of the crew told me they call devil-fish. I swear, they could do three loops through the air in one jump."

"Those were manta rays," he grinned. "Some species get up to twenty feet across, but only the smaller ones can perform those amazing acrobatic stunts."

"Fascinating. Yesterday I watched a turtle swim by that had to have been eight feet long. And in the afternoon, I saw a whale broach. He was far away, but he must have been huge. It saddens me to think of killing such magnificent creatures."

Colin nodded. "Need corset stays for the ladies, ambergris for perfume, and oil for the lamps. Someday, when we find ways to manufacture such items, maybe we won't need to kill the whales."

"I hope it comes soon," she said fervently. "I saw one of the whalers come into Penobscot Harbor once when I lived in Maine. It sickened me."

They stood in silence for a while, watching the pelicans glide in perfect formation over the water, then Colin spoke again.

"We are nearing the end of our journey, Miss MacKenzie. We will be in San Diego in another two days. Have you given any thought to what you are going to do next? Do you plan to stay in San Francisco when we arrive?"

"No," she replied. "I'm going on to Sacramento."

"And from there?" His aquamarine eyes met her blue ones.

Katlin hesitated. His eyes held her, and she felt he looked into her soul. Could he see what she planned? Of course not, she told herself. Don't be silly. How could anyone know? She'd never told anyone.

He took her hands while she remained mesmerized by his eyes. "I don't want to intrude on your private affairs," he said gently, "but I'd like to be your friend. Let's keep in touch."

Emotion swept over Katlin. She realized in a rush how lonely and vulnerable she really was, of how she had depended upon him during the trip across the Isthmus. Could their friendship ever develop into more?

No! She rejected the thought, remembering how smoothly Caleb had won her trust. Somehow, she would make her own way, depending on no one. Her father had taught her a great deal about merchandising. She would open a small general store in Sacramento, just like in Maine.

She pulled her hands from Colin's grasp and smiled. "Thank you, Mr. MacDougal. We must arrange to write. Now, I must join Elena." She walked away, leaving him staring after her.

Colin stood with his back against the rail and watched her departure. The wind riffled his sandy blond hair and blew a tuft of it across his forehead. He reached up to smooth it back into place, and rubbed his chin, deep in thought.

Whatever has happened in her life, she's not going to let it out, he decided. Had she lost someone, as he had lost Michelle?

No, it goes deeper than that, he thought. Someone has hurt her. Someone has given her a deep distrust of men. She's open with Henry, because she considers him a boy, but she pulls back from me.

And do I want more from her? He tried to straighten out his own feelings. Was he ready for another commitment? Could he banish the ghost of Michelle enough to be fair to another woman? To not constantly compare her to his first love? Could he ever love another woman with the same depth he had loved Michelle?

He shivered in spite of his warm coat. He would just have to be sure she didn't disappear into that mob in Sacramento. Somehow, he could not accept the idea of her walking out of his life forever.

With a sigh, he turned from the rail and followed her path through the companionway.

# Chapter 20

KATLIN ROSE EARLY on the morning they reached San Diego, and stood alone at the rail watching the sun rise behind the mountains to the east. Less than an hour later, the *Panama* rode her anchor line, rocking gently back and forth in the low swells in the protected harbor.

"What are those sheds for?" Katlin asked the seaman who strode by her.

"Hide-houses, Miss MacKenzie," the young man replied politely.

"Hide-houses? Oh, yes, like in *Two Years Before the Mast.*" The memory of reading Dana's book flashed into Katlin's mind and she recalled his description of loading the bundles of hides.

"Yes'm. Fer years, the big rancheros have raised cattle for their hides. Ships pick 'em up here and take 'em back to the States."

Katlin wrinkled her nose. "Something smells dead."

The sailor grinned. "Used to be worse. Injuns scrape the hides, but they never do a good job. Leave on a lot of meat and it rots. You c'n smell San Diego for miles out to sea, if the wind be from off the land."

"We don't have to bring any on board this vessel, do we?"

"Nope. Too bulky. Don't pay to haul freight on steamers. Sailing vessels do the haulin'. Not many folks know it, but most of the shoes they wear come from hides hauled in from California by sailin' ships." He pointed. "That there road, now, it's a real fine 'un. Follows the shore right to the town. San Diego's about three miles away. You look close, you can jest barely see it from here."

Katlin noticed several tents close to the hide-houses. Evidently not everyone had a permanent home. She also saw several recent graves and asked her companion about them.

"Oh, them's from some of the folks been tryin' to git to the gold fields by crossin' the desert." He grinned. "Most of 'em didn't have no notion what they was gettin' into. You'll hear a lot about *that* trip, I'm sure." He pointed to the shore. "See all those fellers hangin' around the beach? An' all those boats loaded and ready to go? Most of 'em come across and are gonna take passage on the *Panama* to get to San Francisco."

"More people? This boat's already got too many people!"

The seaman shrugged expressively. "More folks get packed in on each trip, the more money Mr. Aspinwall makes for his company."

The ship's gun sounded and the first boat left the shore, headed for the *Panama*.

"That first boat, now," her informant continued, "she'll be a-carryin' the Boundary Commissioner and prob'ly a couple o' army fellers. The next boat's got some of our new passengers."

Katlin paid no attention to the officials, but looked with great interest at her fellow travelers. Lank, brown, and weather-beaten, they bore long hair and beards. She noticed one Negro among their number, and found herself wondering how he came to be in their party. The faces of all of them showed signs of extreme suffering. Their clothes hung in tatters and they carried only small packages rolled in deerskin, along with the ubiquitous rifle.

"Didn't they bring more supplies than what they can carry in those little bundles?"

"Had to leave most of it along the way."

Katlin only shook her head.

Half an hour and fifty passengers later, the *Panama* again weighed anchor. By mid-morning, she had rounded Point Loma on her way north to San Francisco. As they cleared the rocks, Katlin turned to Henry, who stood beside her tossing scraps of bread to the seagulls, who screeched and fought over the tidbits.

"Why is there no light on the bluff?" she asked. "What happens if the ship has to pass here in the night, or in fog?"

"I hear an American just bought the whole area. My bet is he's planning to be ready when the United States Government decides they need one here, now that California belongs to us. Actually, not too much danger here. Whole area is pretty well charted."

Katlin snuggled deeper into her coat and shivered. "I can't understand why it is so cold. I thought this was August."

Henry laughed. "The seamen say the weather changes just past the Cape, and it gets colder the farther north we go. Even when the sun is warm, the wind is cold."

"And how are you feeling?" Katlin eyed him carefully, relieved to see no sign of fever on his face. "I haven't heard you coughing lately."

He grinned, a little sheepishly. "Actually, I feel much better. The cough hasn't been near as bad, and the fever doesn't seem to come up as much in the afternoon like it used to." He stared out across the water for several moments, then turned back to her.

"Do you suppose I could really get well?" he asked. "Does the climate out here cure consumption like some folks say?" He cast her an anxious glance. "I've, well, er, uh, Elena and I . . . ." He blushed.

Katlin laughed. "I've noticed." She sobered. "And you're concerned about becoming a burden to her."

"And about dyin'," he blurted. "I know what consumption can do. I've watched friends die with it. Never gave it too much thought before, but now . . . " His voice trailed off.

"Now you have a special reason to live."

He nodded. "I feel so much better after these past weeks of just layin' around, eating and sleeping. Do you suppose if I tried to work I'd get sick again?" He sighed heavily, a sigh that stabbed straight into Katlin's heart. "I can't take care of Elena if I can't work."

Katlin had been thinking long and hard about how she could make a living for herself and Elena in Sacramento. She smiled into Henry's earnest blue eyes and made her decision. "How would you like to go into business with me? That way we can be sure you get enough rest and don't get ill again."

Gratitude jumped into the boy's face. "Would you? Could you? Oh, Miss MacKenzie, you're so good!"

She laughed at his enthusiasm. "Well, we're not successful yet, but I did manage my father's general store in Maine. I plan to try my hand in Sacramento. There has to be an easier way to get gold than to dig for it. And Elena and I will need help."

Henry stuck out his hand. "Put her there, Partner. You've just hired yourself an assistant. I don't know much about runnin' a store, but I'm ready to learn. Just tell me what to do."

As they solemnly shook hands, sealing their agreement, Colin strode up with Elena. He smiled at Katlin. "Are we interrupting something?"

"Not at all." Katlin tossed a merry glance at Elena. "Elena and I have just hired Henry to help us in our store."

"We have a store, Miss MacKenzie?" Elena's eyes sparkled. "You never tell me."

"Of course we have a store," Katlin smiled. "All we need is a building and some merchandise to sell."

"That's all?" Colin laughed. "Seems to me that's the bulk of it."

"Oh, no," Katlin disagreed. "The bulk of it is here." She tapped her forehead. "Buildings and merchandise are easy to get. What's hard is knowing what to do with them once you have them."

The clang of the dinner bell interrupted the conversation. Colin offered Katlin his arm.

"Please," he said with a smile, "allow me to escort the mainstay of the new partnership in to dine."

In the afternoon they passed between the mainland and a beautiful island which rose from the sea, steep bluffs on all sides except for a natural harbor with white sand beaches protected on three sides. Through the glass, Katlin saw herds of goats covering the hillsides.

"That's Santa Catalina Island, Miss MacKenzie," Colin responded to her question. "The goats, they tell me, were placed on the island by the Spanish seamen so they could replenish their stores of fresh meat when they cruised up and down the coast. And, goats being goats, their numbers have increased."

"Look how they've stripped the hills of vegetation. It's a wonder they have anything left to eat at all. Is there a source of fresh water on the island?"

Colin shrugged. "My informant didn't say. There must be, or the goats wouldn't have thrived like they have. I understand there are four more islands we will pass during the night, just off of Santa Barbara. Then we get to round the Cape Horn of California."

"What?"

He grinned. "That's what they call it. The real name is Point Conception, but I hear it's windy and cold, with rough seas, and usually shrouded in fog."

Katlin shivered. "Sounds like a charming place. Where

do we stop next?"

"Monterey. Supposed to be a beautiful spot, if a little chilly. I suppose, compared to Maine, it's not so bad, but I find after living in New Orleans for five years, my blood has grown a little thin."

Katlin woke the next morning to pitching and rolling that reminded her of the day she left New York Harbor.

Cape Horn of California, she thought. Just great. I wonder how long this is going to last? Any thought of breakfast left her mind. She looked out of the porthole at the gray mist that met slate-gray water tipped with frequent white-caps and pulled the blanket over her head. Experience had taught her that lying flat helped. Maybe she could just sleep until they reached San Francisco.

Untouched by the motion, Elena giggled when the ship rolled her from side to side of the little cabin as she attempted to dress.

"Miss MacKenzie! Did you not hear the bell? Come, we will be late for the breakfast. My Henry and Mr. MacDougal will be waiting for us." Katlin groaned and took a deep breath. Maybe if she got out into the fresh air ... And she thought she had her sea legs! She dressed as quickly as possible in the pitching cabin and they emerged into the cold, damp air.

"Go in to breakfast," she told Elena. "I'll be fine right here." Katlin clung to the rail with both hands. "Just bring me a biscuit when you've finished."

After Elena, accompanied by Colin and Henry, left her to enter the dining saloon, Katlin noticed the Negro who had joined them in San Diego standing alone, a little ways down the rail from her. On an impulse, she joined him.

"Good morning," she smiled.

"Good morning, Miss," he returned politely, then grinned at her, revealing a row of white, even teeth. "You don't feel like breakfast either?"

Katlin laughed and held out her hand. "Katlin MacKenzie," she said, "and glad to meet a fellow non-sailor."

He returned her smile and accepted the gloved hand she offered. "Malcolm, Miss MacKenzie. Never had no other name, but now that I'm gonna be a free man, I reckon I've got to git me one."

"Not for my benefit, Malcolm, but you're right. You will do better if you can get a last name. I hear many freed slaves take the name of their former masters."

"Could do that, I suppose. He be a good man, he be. Offered to give me my freedom iffen I kin send him a thousand dollars worth of gold."

"California will probably be admitted to the Union as a free state, so I assume you are already a free man."

"Bargain's a bargain, Miss MacKenzie. I give him my word to send the thousand in gold and he's promised to send me papers sayin' I be a free man." A sudden swell lifted the ship and they both clung to the rail for a moment until the deck stabilized beneath their feet.

Malcolm added, "But if I'd 'a-known what a Hell I'd go through a-crossin' that desert, I'd 'a got me enough passage money to come from New Orleans on the steamer, the way you come."

"I've heard some reports of the hardships of the desert coming across. You were very brave to try it."

"Dumb's a better word, Miss MacKenzie. If I'd a' had any notion what I was gettin' into, I'd a' found some other way."

"Was it as bad as they say?"

Malcolm shook his head slowly from side to side. "Too bad fer words. After I crossed the Colorado River, it become a scorched landscape. Nothin' but burnin' salt plains and shiftin' hills of sand." He stared out across the water as though seeing it again. "No water, nothin' fer the animals to eat. Bones of mules and men scattered all along the sides of the trail. Corpses dug up by the wind blowin' the sand away. And the smell from all the dead mules!" He shook his head. "Wonder is we all never died from the miasma. Any man faltered, he'd be a goner. Anyone who stopped to help him took the chance of sharin' his fate."

Katlin did not move or speak, not wishing to break the spell. The suffering he had seen and endured washed over her with his words. She looked at the lines on his face, the pain in his eyes, and knew they would remain a part of him forever.

"I come across a man who'd fallen behind his party. He was lyin' on the sand and couldn't get up. I gave him some of my water and a few bites of biscuit. His mule had died of hunger, still tied to a clump of cactus. He begged me to find his party and send someone back to git 'im. I was afoot. No way I could'a carried him, so I went on. Caught up with his bunch the following night. They said he'd always come into camp a few hours after ev'ryone else, so when he hadn't showed up, they'd not give it much thought. Next mornin', some Mexicans come in and said the man were a-dyin'."

Malcolm set his jaw. "The leader of his party decided to go on, not to go back, because, as he said, if the man's dyin', ain't no point in riskin' other lives."

"I suppose he was probably right." Katlin thought of poor James McFee, whose companions left him alone to die of cholera. And of the Spaniards who were so willing to hand Elena over to a total stranger. "But I've noticed these men in the grip of gold fever. They can only think of one thing."

"I went back, Miss MacKenzie. Man oughten not to die alone. Forty miles on foot across that hellish desert. I got back in time to be with him when he died." The man's eyes filled with tears, and Katlin felt her own eyes sting. "I lifted his head and he tried to speak, then jist collapsed."

He stopped. Katlin put her hand on his arm in sympathy.

He took out his handkerchief and wiped his eyes. "I took his personal papers and what little money he had and buried him as best I could. Figgered I'd get someone to send the money and papers back to his family, if they's a direction." He smiled at Katlin, a little abashed. "Never did learn to read, o' course. It's agin the law in Mississippi to teach slaves to read. Maybe you could take care of it, Miss MacKenzie?"

"I'll be happy to, just as soon as we reach San Francisco. We can send it back on the return trip of the *Panama*. It's very thoughtful of you . . . ."

"Hey, you, what in 'ell you think yer a-doin?" The harsh words cut into Katlin's sentence. Astonished, she looked to see one of the ne-er-do-wells who had joined them in New Orleans.

"Nigras don't talk to white women back in Mississippi, where I come from!" The man grabbed Malcolm's shirt front and pulled him from Katlin's side. With his right hand, he swung and struck Malcolm's jaw.

Katlin screamed in horror as the hapless Negro fell to the deck, blood running from a cut on his lip. She rushed to his side and knelt, lifting his head and stanching the blood with her handkerchief. Rage surged through her. After all that Malcolm had done for that poor man in the desert, this was his reward? Her eyes like glints of blue steel, her voice frigid, she hissed from between clenched teeth, "I don't care where you came from, or what rock you crawled out from under. You're not fit to touch this man's boots. Don't you ever interfere with me again."

"Yeah?" he sneered. "I figgered you fer a lady, but reckon ye're jest a slut. Nigger lover. One o' them Faneuil Hall bunch. You been readin' the trash that Stowe woman writ, I'll bet. I'll teach this uppity nigger . . . ."

He stopped when he found himself staring into the barrel of Katlin's Colt.

# *Chapter 21*

"**W**HAT'S GOING ON HERE?" Colin's voice penetrated Katlin's consciousness, but she did not take her eyes off Malcolm's assailant. The barrel of the gun did not waver.

Colin seized the man's arm, threw him against the rail, and grabbed him by the collar of his shirt, lifting him slightly off his feet. "Are you annoying Miss MacKenzie?" When the man did not reply, he shook him. "Answer me!"

His hapless victim gasped. "Ye're a-chokin' me, man."

Colin's only answer was to tighten his grip. Katlin kept her pistol trained on Malcolm's attacker. Her peripheral vision noted that a crowd had gathered, attracted by the excitement, but no one made a move to interfere.

Malcolm sat up and shook his head. "Don't want to cause no trouble for you, Miss MacKenzie."

Katlin smiled grimly. "You're not causing trouble, Malcolm. The gentleman from Mississippi just has to learn that he's in California now." She rose to her feet, clinging to the rail for support, and tucked the revolver back into her reticule. With the incident behind her, her heart raced and her hands, so steady while she held the gun on their attacker, trembled.

Colin released his hold. As the lanky Mississippian scurried away, Colin turned to Katlin.

"Thank you." She gave him a shaky smile, trying to maintain an outward calm she was far from feeling. "Your timing could not have been better."

He swept off his hat and bowed to her. "Well, Miss Mac-Kenzie, I must say you never cease to surprise me."

"I told you. I am capable of many things proper society considers unladylike."

He laughed. "I now believe you."

Malcolm rose to his feet and Katlin introduced him to Colin.

"Sorry for the trouble, Mr. MacDougal," Malcolm said. "Plumb forgot about how Mississippi men feel about folks like me talkin' to their women."

"I'm not one of their women." Katlin clenched her jaw. "I'm from Maine, and I judge a man by his actions. You have proven yourself an honorable person, worthy to take your place among free men. I'll bet no one would ever see him risking his life to try and save a total stranger like you did."

"Thank you, Miss MacKenzie. Now, iffen you'll excuse me, I better git a cold poultice on this face o' mine. I can feel it a-swellin' already."

"Of course. I'm so glad we met. Bring me the personal effects of the gentleman you tried to save in the desert. I'll be happy to take care of them for you." She offered him her hand and he gallantly bowed over it before departing.

Colin stood beside Katlin and watched him leave. "Miss MacKenzie, I admire your courage, but you will have to be a little cautious in defying convention."

She laughed. "My father frequently said the same thing, usually when he caught me riding astride." On my beloved Sunny, she thought with a pang. Rage at Caleb for taking the horse from her exploded through her again. She took a deep breath and looked up to see Colin watching her face. She shook her head to clear it and smiled brightly at him. "And when did you say we would reach Monterey?"

The sea calmed into long, low swells, the fog lifted, and Katlin's spirits rose along with it. The *Panama* followed the coastline all day, and Katlin stood at the rail and watched as the low brown hills passed slowly by the starboard side. When the sun broke through the fog, brilliant sunshine sparkled like diamonds on the water. The hills glowed golden in the sun, and white surf crashed against the bluffs. They passed a huge offshore rock that protected a secluded bay.

The riot of color in sunset over the ocean never ceased to fascinate Katlin. As the sun settled in the west, the ship rounded Point Piños and entered the harbor of Monterey. A picturesque fort on the north side returned the salute of the *Panama's* gun. A fair-sized community of charming homes nestled among the pine trees lining the harbor.

Watching from the rail, Katlin exclaimed to Elena, "What a beautiful spot!"

"But it is cold, yes?"

Katlin laughed. "Yes. And I understand San Francisco will be even colder. We'll be traveling on to Sacramento. They say it's much warmer there." As the anchor chain rattled in the hawse-pipe, she noticed four weather-beaten sailing vessels standing at anchor close to shore. They had fallen into disrepair, and bore the desolate look of abandoned ships. "I wonder why those ships were just left to fall apart?"

"Probably the crews deserted for the gold fields." Colin joined them in time to hear Katlin's comment. "I hear there are many such vessels in San Francisco Bay. And that captains often keep their crews on board at gun point."

Katlin shook her head and shivered. "Of all things. Come on, Elena, let's move into the saloon. I'm freezing out here."

\* \* \*

On August 18, they at last reached San Francisco.

"Fifty-one days from New York to San Francisco," Colin reported. "Compare that to six or seven months rounding Cape Horn in a sailing vessel. We should anchor by this afternoon. If the fog lifts enough so we can see it, I understand the Golden Gate is quite spectacular. All of the rivers from the whole Sacramento and San Joaquin valleys drain into the ocean through this passage. When the tide is going out, ships have a real struggle. Often have as much as a five or six knot current to battle."

Katlin fell silent as the ship approached the fabled entrance. The fog fell away, and mountains up to 3000 feet high rose on the north side of the entrance. The bluffs on both sides glowed golden in the morning sun. She could understand why sailors had named it the Golden Gate. The island rock of Alcatraz, white with thousands of seagulls, appeared in the distance.

She knew she would soon reach the end of her voyage. The next step would be the trip up the river to Sacramento City. Then what? As the water fell away behind the *Panama*, bringing her ever closer to their destination, she tried to sort out her feelings.

She should just devote her energies to getting her store started. After all, both Elena and Henry counted on her for their support, especially if Henry was to continue to regain his health. But she also had to find Caleb, if for no other reason than to keep him from cheating other women as he had her and that poor widow back in Maine.

But how? There were no laws to help her, no government, not even a satisfactory mail service. An advertisement? Right, she grimaced, as though he would come forward willingly. And she had no way of knowing what name he used here. Surely he had changed it again.

And Colin MacDougal? Try as she might to push them away, those aquamarine eyes kept intruding on her thoughts.

Did she want to take the chance of trusting another man? True, he had seemed to prove himself honorable, but she felt his reserve. He did appear to take an interest in her, but somehow, she sensed he did not feel ready to make a commitment either.

She sighed. As she pondered her options, the *Panama* rounded the curving shore of the bay. Three hills rose to the west, forming an amphitheater on which the city grew, a montage of tents, plank huts, and adobe houses. Activity swarmed over the two piers that jutted out into the bay. Dozens of ships lined the beach that fronted the city. The ship's gun sounded to announce their arrival.

Whether you are ready or not, Katlin MacKenzie, she told herself, your voyage is over. The easy part of your trip is behind you. You can no longer postpone decisions. Do you really think you are up to the challenge of what lies ahead?

Colin stood a little apart from her. A number of other passengers crowded the rail between them, but from where he stood, he could see her face. He saw the conflict raging within her. He thought of the scene when he found her crouched over the fallen Malcolm, her gun ready to defend him, her eyes like blue ice.

She's a complicated lady, he thought. In some ways, her defiance of convention reminded him of Michelle. In other ways, she seemed so different, in a way that oddly disturbed him. As he watched, the wind blew her bonnet back on her head, allowing some of the golden curls to escape.

He shook his head. You're not ready to accept her as she is, Colin MacDougal, he told himself. Face it. Let her go. She has plans that do not include you. But somehow, as he stood staring, transfixed, the thought of a future without her seemed empty, without meaning.

She untied the bonnet and shook her hair loose to blow

in the wind. Colin's heart raced. He remembered how close he had come to kissing her when she dressed his shoulder on the banks of the Rio Grande as they crossed the Isthmus. He closed his eyes and again saw the vision of her with her chemise and pantaloons clinging to her slender body as they rescued Elena from the raging water.

Desire for her swept over him. He felt an impulse to push his way through the crowd and take her in his arms. Sweat broke out all over his body in spite of the coolness of the wind that swept across the rail.

Henry's voice at his elbow startled him and jerked him back to reality. He took a deep breath. And back to common sense, he thought with some amusement. Remember the Colt she carries in her reticule.

Henry continued to speak, unaware of the conflict raging within Colin. "Well, Mr. MacDougal, looks like we're about to arrive. Ready to go get yourself some gold?"

# Chapter 22

"**W**HERE WILL WE DOCK?" Katlin asked Colin who, with Elena and Henry, had reached her side. "Those piers already have more ships than they can accommodate."

"We anchor out," Colin replied as the chain rattled in the hawse-pipe. His calm demeanor hid the turmoil that still churned within him. With a splash, the anchor hit the water. "Ships that tie to the pier risk losing their crews. Remember the abandoned vessels we saw in Monterey? We'll go ashore by long boat."

Henry pointed to the rotting hulks lining the bay. "See there, Miss MacKenzie? Those are ships that . . . ."

He broke off as angry shouting reached them across the still waters of the bay. Pistol shots rang out, echoing past the startled passengers of the *Panama*.

Elena gave a scream of fright. Henry pulled her against the bulkhead to shield her. Colin seized Katlin in his arms and pulled her below the level of the rail.

"*Que pasa? Que pasa?*" Elena's cries continued. When the shooting stopped, Colin rose and assisted Katlin to her feet.

"Well," she gasped, a little out of breath at the suddenness with which Colin had thrown her to the deck. "What was that all about?"

Colin pointed to a long boat with fourteen or fifteen men skimming across the bay, headed for the opposite shore. Angry shouts from the nearby ship continued, and Katlin looked to see an officer waving his pistol in the air and shouting curses that came very clearly across the expanse of water.

Colin chuckled softly. "Looks like that ship just lost part of her crew. Fools. They're so crazed with gold fever they're willing to risk getting shot."

Katlin remembered the four ships in Monterey Harbor, and looked again at the line of wreckage along the waterfront. She shook her head and turned to Elena, who still whimpered in fear.

"Calm down," she told the girl sharply. "Take a deep breath. I can't take you with me into a lawless town like Sacramento City if you get hysterical at the sound of a few gunshots. They weren't shooting at us."

Elena's eyes widened at Katlin's tone, then she nodded. "You are right, as always, Miss MacKenzie. I was acting the foolish girl." She drew herself up to her full height. "I am Maria Elena Velasquez de Rodriguez, daughter of Don Jose Fernando Velasquez de Martinez. I will show no fear."

Colin, Henry, and Katlin burst into laughter. Henry grinned and patted Elena's hand.

"That's my girl," he said. "Bring on the world. We're ready."


Katlin fastened the last pin into her hair, tucked her hairbrush into her haversack along with her etui and a warm scarf, and snapped the lock on her trunk. As she did so, a loud knocking announced the arrival of the steward.

"Bags ready, young misses?" he called through the closed door. "Got to git 'em on the long boat so's ye kin go ashore."

Katlin opened the door and indicated the two small trunks. "This is all. We will carry our haversacks."

"As you wish, mum." The obliging steward hoisted their baggage onto his cart and moved to the next cabin.

Colin and Henry appeared and offered to help them with their haversacks.

"Long boat from the *Ohio* brought a lieutenant across," Colin announced. "He says he will give us a lift to the pier so we don't have to load you ladies in with the rest of the passengers. Are you ready?"

Katlin looked around the cabin one last time, picked up a tortoise shell comb Elena had dropped, and tucked it in her reticule. "Ready," she said.

As they crossed the deck to disembark, Malcolm approached her cautiously, a deerskin packet in his hand.

Katlin smiled. "Oh, yes, Malcolm. The property of the unfortunate gentleman you tried to help. Thank you. If there's any direction in here at all, I will see the man's family receives this."

"Thank you, Miss MacKenzie. You relieve my mind considerable. Wouldn't want no one to think I stole money from a dyin' man."

She offered him her gloved hand and he bowed over it gallantly. "Thank you, Malcolm. I plan to open a store in Sacramento City. It will be called *MacKenzie's Mercantile*." She smiled at him as he raised his eyes. "If you find digging for gold palls, look me up. I'm sure I'll have a place for someone of such proven honesty and loyalty."

He grinned, beautiful white teeth showing in his dark face. "I'll remember that, Miss MacKenzie. When I be a free man." He tipped his hat and walked away.

Katlin watched him descend the gangplank and take a seat amongst the steerage passengers and piles of baggage. The boat shoved off, so heavily laden the water reached almost to the gunwales.

Malcolm looked back as the boat headed for shore. She waved. He saw her, and returned her wave. She wished him well, and hoped she would see him again.

Colin took her arm. "The long boat from the *Ohio* is waiting. If you and Elena don't want to go ashore in an overloaded scow like that one, we'd better hurry."

Katlin and Elena followed the two men and were assisted into the long boat by a young lieutenant. The crewmen rowed them swiftly across the smooth water of the bay. The hull of the boat scraped to a halt on the sands of the beach beside the heavily laden pier, where a large vessel discharged her cargo. Two seamen jumped over the side and dragged the boat up onto the shore and began unloading baggage. The lieutenant helped Katlin and Elena to disembark with such care they did not even get their feet wet.

"Thank you," Katlin smiled to the young man.

"My pleasure, Miss. Don't get many lovely young American ladies in this godforsaken part of the world."

Katlin noticed several men buried in sand up to their chins. It seemed a strange sight, so she turned to their escort. "Lieutenant, why are those men lying in the sand like that?"

The young man shook his head. "Passengers off the *Brooklyn*, Miss. She got in a couple of days ago. All these men were suffering from scurvy. In fact, two of the passengers had died."

"Of scurvy? I thought proper food prevented that. And why bury yourself in the sand? What possible benefit can that have?"

The lieutenant shrugged his shoulders. "Not all captains feel obligated to see their passengers have proper food. And the sailors swear by the sand treatment. Claim it cures scurvy." He saluted as the seamen pushed the boat back into the water and scrambled aboard for their return to the *Ohio*.

As Henry gathered their belongings into a pile, among the many similar stacks of baggage lining the beach, Katlin stared at the men lying under the sand. She shook her head at such foolishness. Then again, what did she know? Maybe it did help. She turned her mind from them.

"Stay with the ladies, Henry," Colin ordered, paying no

attention to the hapless scurvy victims. "I'll see about some porters."

Katlin sat on her trunk and watched the activity around her while they waited. She wrinkled her nose. "What is that awful odor? Smells like a garbage dump."

Henry laughed. "It is a garbage dump. Smells worse now, with the tide out. When the tide comes back in, it covers up the worst of it. Everyone from the town and from the ships dumps their trash into the bay."

Katlin only shook her head. Tents and canvas houses were strewn helter-skelter over the barren brown hills before her. A ramshackle two story building boasted the claim of Fremont Family Hotel. Some hotel, she thought. I certainly hope we can find some better quarters than that. Then she chuckled, remembering the thatch huts crossing the Isthmus. Even the Fremont Family Hotel should be an improvement.

Something had bitten her on the ankle, and the spot itched ferociously. She wished she could lift her skirt and scratch. She surreptitiously rubbed the spot with her right shoe.

Elena shrieked and jumped up from her seat on her trunk. "A creature, it bite me," she cried, rubbing her leg furiously through her skirt. "What it is?"

"Probably sand fleas," Henry laughed. "Couple of the seamen warned me. Said San Francisco is famous for her sand fleas, built on dunes like she is." He grinned in sympathy. "Should be better when we get to a hotel and get away from the beach. At least, we will hope so."

Katlin sighed, remembering the clear, fresh air of the Maine coast, the quiet solitude, the scent of pine trees, the beauty of the surrounding countryside as she and Sunny rode through the forest. For a moment, looking across the littered beach, the pressing crowds of men, the cluttered beginnings of the town, smelling the garbage rotting on the beach, she wished she had never left.

Then she recalled the excitement of seeing so many new things, the thrill of new adventures beckoning, and that she neared Caleb's destination. Her doubts vanished. And Colin MacDougal. If she had not come, she would never have met Colin. Try as she might, those striking aquamarine eyes never left her for long.

Be still, she ordered the tiny imp in her mind. He's not interested in you. He's only being a gentleman. She blushed as she remembered his eyes on her when she had pulled off her dress to help rescue Elena from the river. She took a deep breath as she recalled the shock that ran up her arm as she probed the bare skin of his injured shoulder. Forget it, she told herself. He's a gentleman. If he learns why you are really here, and what happened with Caleb, he'll disappear from your life in an instant.

Deep in thought, she did not realize Colin had returned until Elena touched her shoulder. Startled, she looked up to see two swarthy boys in their early teens begin hoisting their belongings.

"No one wants to work as a porter, so I agreed to pay these boys two dollars apiece to help us."

"Two dollars!" Katlin gasped, thinking of the boy she had paid a dime to help her with her luggage in New York. "That's over a day's wages for a man back East. Isn't that a lot of money just to carry a couple of trunks?"

Colin twisted his mouth into a wry grin. "Welcome to San Francisco. Prices on everything are outrageous. But we do have a ways to go. Once we get to the crest of that hill," he waved his arm in a southwesterly direction, "there are hundreds of tents and houses."

"That's good," Katlin sighed with relief. "I began to fear we would have to find space in the Fremont Family Hotel." And put up with the sand fleas, she added in her mind.

Colin picked up his bag and small trunk. The boys followed with the girls' trunks. Katlin carried her haversack. Elena trailed behind, with Henry carrying her haversack for her. They trudged along single file, plodding though the thick sand, and paused for breath at the crest of the hill.

Katlin closed her eyes as a blast of sand from the furious wind that raced though the gaps in the hills covered them with a cloud of dust. When the gust passed, she saw hundreds of tents and houses scattered all over the hillside, with little or no pattern, strewn about like grains of salt, allowed to fall where they might.

Buildings of every shape and description, many barely begun, some only canvas sheds open to the front, stood all around them. Signs in a number of languages Katlin did not recognize adorned the fronts of these makeshift buildings. Piles of goods of all sorts stood in the open air, apparently for lack of a place to store them.

Colin pointed out the variety of people in addition to Yankees of every possible sort, from bearded miners in dusty trousers and flannel shirts to clean-shaven bankers in broadcloth suits. Native Californians wore brightly colored serapes and large sombreros, as did the Chileans from South America and the Sonorans from Northern Mexico.

"The Kanakas are a Polynesian people," Colin continued. "They come from the Sandwich Islands. The Chinese are the ones who wear their hair in a long braid called a queue down their backs. Has something to do with their dignity. Seems the highest insult is to cut off a man's queue. He can't show his face in public again until it grows back out."

"How odd," Katlin exclaimed. "And that ferocious-looking man with the huge knife?"

Colin laughed. "He's a Malay, from the South Pacific. That's a creese, and they all carry them everywhere they go. It's more important to their dignity than shoes."

"I can see I have a lot to learn." Katlin could only marvel at the variety of life in front of her. You wanted to get out of that small town in Maine, she thought. Well, you're out now.

"Why is it so cold?" Elena asked. "I thought this was the summer."

Henry patted her hand. "It'll be warmer, once we get up the river to Sacramento."

Katlin looked to the west and saw a huge fog bank creeping over the hill. "I suspect it's going to be even colder soon. We'd better find a place to stay."

They had reached the plaza, called by the impressive name of Portsmouth Square. On the uphill side, an American flag waved and snapped in the brisk wind from a pole in front of a long, single story adobe building. A large sign proclaimed this the Custom House.

On the downhill side stood the Parker House, a sturdy looking one story frame building at least sixty feet long. Colin headed for this establishment, and the boys deposited their luggage on the portico, received their two dollars apiece, and disappeared into the crowd.

Katlin sat down on her trunk and dropped her haversack beside her. Rubbing her aching arms, she looked around at the vast numbers of men crowded about.

"Can we get rooms here?" she asked Colin. "It looks like half of the *Panama's* passengers are trying to do the same thing."

"Stay here with Henry. I'll ask." Colin put his baggage beside hers. Elena and Henry also sat down on the trunks.

Katlin looked anxiously at Henry. He had not had a bad coughing spell recently, but two bright spots of fever glowed in his cheeks. He may be better, she thought, but he's far from well. We have to get him away from this damp climate. Maybe the heat in Sacramento will help dry his lungs.

The fog moved closer. The cold white disk of the sun

shone through, with wisps of fog moving across it. She shivered, pulled her shawl out of her haversack, and wrapped it around her.

Colin returned, accompanied by the proprietor.

"Not a room to be had in this establishment," Colin reported. "Not even floor space to unroll our blankets. But when I told this gentleman we had two ladies in our party, he offered to assist us in obtaining lodging across the plaza at the City Hotel. It's not as nice as here, but they should have a room for you ladies."

Katlin looked at the trunks. "Who will carry these?"

"They'll be fine here, Miss," the proprietor assured her, "until we get you settled."

An hour later, and twenty dollars poorer, Katlin had a room for herself and Elena in the garret of the City Hotel. The room was barely big enough for the two crude cots, which were covered with blankets, but no sheets. Two chairs, a rough table, and a small looking glass completed the appointments.

Katlin could stand up straight only in the center of the room, and there was barely enough space between the rafters and the bed for a person to crawl. She looked about the room and laughed.

"Be careful, Elena. Don't sit up in a hurry or you'll bump your head on the rafters." Katlin looked up at the roof and noticed gaps between the rough boards. Some effort had been made to patch the cracks with tar, but open spaces remained. She shook her head. "They say it never rains in California between May and November. I certainly hope they're right."

Henry appeared at the door with the baggage. "Gonna store our stuff in here with you. Colin 'n' me are bunking on cots on the big main room downstairs. He's bringing the rest. There are no porters. We asked the landlord and he said here every man is his own porter." He shivered and pulled a coat out of his trunk. As he shrugged into it, he said, "If that wind gets any stronger, it's gonna pick up the building, I swear."

Colin arrived, chuckling. "There's a newspaper merchant outside on the corner peddling copies of New York papers at a dollar apiece, so I dug out some papers I had used in packing my valise. Sold them to him for ten dollars!" He stored his trunk under Katlin's cot. "Now, if you ladies are ready for supper, they tell me the gong will sound in a few moments. We would like to get you seated before the crowds converge."

# *Chapter 23*

As THE SUN slid behind the horizon, the wind died.
The bank of fog which had hovered on the crest of the hill
all afternoon moved down, surrounding them with a soft
mist that muffled the sounds of the evening's activities with
an eerie silence.

Colin led Katlin to the table in the dining room. As she sat
down, a gong rang out and men streamed in, rapidly filling
all of the available seats. After the room reached its capacity,
men continued to enter, looking about with disappointment
as they realized no unoccupied chairs remained.

Katlin smiled at Colin "I'm so glad you thought to bring
us down a few minutes ahead of everyone else. Otherwise,
we could have wound up standing to eat like those gentlemen." She motioned to a disgruntled group gathered on
one side of the room.

Colin's eyes caressed her for a moment and he laughed.
"I can't take all the credit. The proprietor suggested it. I
think you will find this a real treat after the skimpy fare and
sea rations on the *Panama*."

Elena's eyes widened at the sight of the pitcher of milk
the waiter set before her. "Fresh milk! And *butter*, too!"

Katlin laughed at the girl's obvious delight. "Enjoy it.
We may not have such luxuries when we get to Sacramento
City."

They made full use of the sumptuous meal of hearty
California beef, rich biscuits with honey, delicious cheese,

and fresh vegetables. When she could eat no more, Katlin pushed back her plate and sighed with pleasure. "I can't eat another bite!"

A gentleman seated across from her smiled and said. "Save room for the pie, Miss. Cook here makes a real fine apple pie."

Katlin rolled her eyes skyward and sighed. "I'll try." She fell silent and listened, with some dismay at the numbers she heard, to the three men across the table discussing the outrageous prices charged for rents.

"Why," the pudgy gentleman in the middle said, "I have to pay $40,000 a year to rent my store, and it's only got twenty feet of street front to it, and just one story. Got half the goods from my last shipment stored outside. No room for 'em inside. Sure hope folks're right when they say it don't rain here 'til October, November."

"You think that's bad?" the man on his right declared. "I'm a lawyer. Wanted a place to hang my shingle. All I could find was a cellar about twelve feet square and six feet deep. Charging me $250.00 a month, if you can believe it. Out and out thievery."

"I have to pay my man-servant $200.00 a month in wages," interjected the third. "Have you ever heard of any-one paying that much? Says if he don't get it, he'll go try his hand in the gold fields. Blackmail. But I don't want to lose him, so I pay." He shook his head. "At least common labor has fallen to a more reasonable sum. All these disappointed gold seekers coming back are swelling the local labor force."

"Need 'em all," declared the merchant. "Building up to thirty houses a day, they are. Maybe we get enough built, rents will come down a bit."

The lawyer laughed. "Don't count on it real soon."

"Got to. I can't afford to rent any more space, and I got all that merchandise settin' outside. Starts to rain, it'll be ruined, especially the cloth and laces."

"Laces? Where you gonna sell laces, man? You see any of these miners buying lace?" He glanced at Katlin and Elena. "Excuse me, ladies."

Katlin had listened to the conversation with interest. "Excuse *me*," she said to the merchant. "I plan to open a dry goods store in Sacramento City. Would you consider advancing me some of your extra merchandise on consignment?" She smiled. "It would be better than letting the rain destroy it."

The man looked at her with interest. "You could be right. You got any merchandisin' experience?"

"Yes. My father and I owned a small general store in Maine. I managed it alone for a year after his death."

The man looked at her shrewdly, his eyes narrowing. "And why'd you leave it? Seems unlikely for a young lady like you to get gold fever."

Katlin knew this question would come, and had rehearsed the answer in her mind. She felt Colin's eyes on her as she replied calmly, "My father's death left me alone. I sold the store and returned to New York where I had relatives." Forgive me my little white lie, Colin, she begged in her mind. She braced herself for the next question, sure he would want to know why she had come to California, but the expected query did not come. Instead, a pudgy hand with a large gold ring on the pinky finger reached across the table.

"Phineas Walker, Miss. Pleased to make your acquaintance."

"Katlin MacKenzie." She offered her hand.

"Irish?" He frowned. His hand, reaching to meet hers, paused in mid-air. She shook her head and laughed, fully aware of the opinion many held of the Irish.

"No, not Irish. Scottish."

"Very well, Miss MacKenzie," Mr. Walker nodded, grasping her hand in a firm grip. "I am engaged for the evening with my two companions here, but perhaps we could get together tomorrow, say, ten o'clock? Here in the hotel? In the lobby?"

"Ten o'clock in the lobby," she nodded in agreement. "I'll be there."

"Now," he said, his eyes gleaming as he watched the waiter place a large wedge of golden apple pie in front of him, "that is enough business for the day. Let us enjoy our dessert."

After supper, Katlin and Elena dug their warm coats out of their trunks and strolled with Colin and Henry for a look at San Francisco at night. Katlin snuggled into the collar of her coat and wrapped her muffler around her neck and the lower part of her face.

"Who would ever dream it could be so cold in August?" she gasped to Colin as the cold mist swept over her. "We won't get lost in the fog, will we? I haven't seen fog this thick since I left the coast of Maine."

Colin pulled her gloved hand through his arm. For a moment, she leaned against him, then caught herself and pulled back. "It's all right," he said in a soothing voice. "We won't stay out long. We don't want you ladies to take a chill." He lowered his voice so only Katlin heard him and added, "And this cold, damp night air has to be bad for Henry's lungs."

Every building they passed had been turned into a gambling palace. Crowds of miners waving bags of gold dust pushed and shoved their way in to gamble the results of their efforts at games of monte and faro. Katlin and her party stood briefly at the doorway to the El Dorado and looked in. Katlin recognized, through the haze of tobacco smoke, two of the gamblers that had come with them on the *Panama*, two of the four who had been so disrespectful at the church in Panama City.

The miners in their flannel shirts, baggy trousers, and dusty boots contrasted sharply with the dandified suits of the professional gamblers. She saw no guns in evidence, but knew most of the men carried one, tucked into their waistband, or in a boot. With a shudder, she realized how easily any one of them could start shooting.

As they watched, one miner piled a large stack of one-ounce bags of gold dust on the table and lost the whole lot on one throw of the dice. He let out a wild yell and raced for the door. Colin pulled Katlin aside, out of his path, as his boots thundered across the wooden porch.

Katlin could only shake her head at such foolishness. She turned to Colin. "Let's go back to the hotel. It's been a long day, and I think I've seen enough."

He nodded. "Probably wise. I can't help but think this crowd will get rougher as the evening progresses."

The next morning, after a huge breakfast of eggs, biscuits, and beefsteak, Colin went to check on transportation to Sacramento City. Katlin and Elena, with Henry trailing along behind them, took the packet of belongings Malcolm had entrusted to her and started towards the Post Office. Mr. Moore, the new Postmaster, had arrived on the *Panama* with them, and invited them to come up and see his new station.

Strolling in front of the United States Hotel, another unprepossessing building similar to their own, they came upon a boy of about eight or nine digging in the dirt. Katlin stopped and watched with fascination as the child picked out fine grains of gold with the head of a pin that he moistened in his mouth.

"Can you really find very much gold like that" she asked, as he persisted in his task.

"Oh, yes'm, Miss. Miners drop some all the time. Found fourteen dollars worth yestiddy. 'Course, that were a good day. Helps Ma an' me, it do. She gits a dollar a shirt doin' washin', but it's real hard work, and lotsa men send their shirts over to the Sandwich Islands fer washin'. Don't wanna pay a dollar."

Katlin could understand not wanting to pay that much. It seemed a lot of money just to have a shirt laundered. "And is your father in the gold fields?" she asked.

"Oh, no. Pa died in '48. He wuz with the New York Volunteers. Come out durin' the war with Mexico. Liked Californy, he said, and decided to stay, he did. He sent for me an' Ma to join 'im. When we got here, they told us he had died. Inflammation of the lungs, y'know," he nodded sagely. "Was hard goin' for me an' Ma fer a spell, then all the miners started comin'."

The boy rambled on. "Some o' these miners, now, they don't wash the shirts. Jest wear one until it falls apart, then throw it away an' buy a new one."

Katlin smothered a smile at this ingenuous observation. "Can you imagine," she said to Elena as they strolled on, leaving the boy diligently pursuing his task, "what they must smell like by the time they decide it's time to buy a new shirt?"

Elena wrinkled her nose in distaste.

They neared the Post Office, another ramshackle building that looked like it had been constructed in haste. At least it boasted a shingle roof instead of the canvas so many used, or the flat boards with gaps like at the hotel. Crowds of men surrounded the edifice. Some shouted angry epithets, others pounded on the door and the barred windows. They could barely catch a glimpse of the building through the mass of humanity.

"I see why Mr. Moore said he would not allow anyone inside until they had sorted the mail," Katlin laughed to Elena. "He said the *Panama* carried over 25,000 pieces on just this last trip, so it's going to take him a while to get through all of that. He only has one helper. I don't think we're going to get any closer. Let's go back and see if Mr. MacDougal has returned with news of our departure arrangements. And I must keep my ten o'clock appointment with Mr. Walker. I can give Mr. Moore the packet this evening at supper and ask him to mail it for me."

On their way back, they passed a tiny studio, a six foot square frame tent. The sign read 'Osgood's Fine Paintings'. They stopped to watch him work. The young artist was putting the finishing touches on the portrait of a middle-aged gentleman that stood on an easel in front of the miniature atelier.

They admired the portrait. "Who is it?" Katlin asked the painter.

"That's Cap'n Sutter, Miss, Cap'n John Sutter. Asked me to do his portrait, he did. He's the gentleman as owns most of the land around and to the north and east of Sacramento City. Got a big Mexican land grant, he did, from Guvner Micheltorena. Back in '44 or '45, I believe."

"Oh, yes, the man whose worker found the first gold. I guess it's made him rich. No wonder he decided to have his portrait done."

Mr. Osgood shook his head. "I think it was a bad thing for him. He's got all those folks swarmin' over his land, buildin' cabins and stakin' claims and stealin' his cattle. Wouldn't surprise me if it bankrupts him."

"Oh, I hope not. That would be a shame. Did you go to the gold fields?"

"Yep, for about three months. Did pretty well, but it's hard work. Painter, I am. Easier ways to get gold than diggin' for it."

Katlin laughed. "I believe those were my exact words. I'm going to open a dry goods store in Sacramento. As these men settle down, they'll be bringing their wives, and the ladies will want calico and laces and table linens."

"You're probably right. I hear Sacramento is growing almost as fast as San Francisco."

They bid the young man farewell and returned to their hotel. Mr. Walker hefted his bulk out of his chair with some effort, and greeted her cheerfully. "And a good morning to you, ladies. You are both looking lovely this fine day. Come, join me. Care for a drop of refreshment before we begin?"

Katlin seated herself on the rickety bench opposite him and declined with thanks.

"Then let's get down to business," he beamed at her. "I'm not as foolish as my two companions last night implied. I do have some cases of linens and laces, true, but most of what I have is blankets, shovels, axes, and the like. Also several cases of those fine new revolving pistols of Mr. Colt's. Figger they're gonna get right popular. And a good selection of the new India rubber ponchos which, if it ever does rain in this accursed country, should be much in demand by the miners."

He chuckled and added, "Got some fine china, as well. From what I hear, lotsa the folks comin' over by wagon had to dump a lot of their stuff to get over the mountains. Figger the ladies will be ready for a few of the finer things."

By the time the gong resounded the call for the noon meal, he and Katlin had come to an agreement. He would give her two weeks to find an establishment, then ship her such cases of merchandise as he felt he could spare. She would send him the money when the material sold. They shook hands to seal their arrangement.

Katlin marveled at the trust among these men. In a country with no law, no lawyers to speak of, and no banks, people had to rely on that trust.

Colin arrived as Mr. Walker departed for the dining room. "Good news," he reported. "The schooner *James L Day* departs from Clark's Point tomorrow morning as soon as the fog lifts enough to give her visibility. Fare's only fourteen dollars for each of us, and that includes the boat ride out to the ship." He laughed. "No small matter, since I understand these scoundrels charge up to five dollars a person to row you out."

Katlin and Elena retired early. Katlin, exhausted from all the activity of the past two days, fell asleep immediately, but woke in the middle of the night. A bright moon shining through the tiny window cut a bayonet of light across her bed. Efforts to ignore it and return to sleep proved futile. She lay on her back with the light bathing her face, wondering what the morrow would bring.

She thought of her dwindling supply of money. The stories of the high prices charged for renting buildings here in San Francisco frightened her. She had not dreamed store space could ever cost so much. Would she be able to carry out her commitment to Mr. Walker? The responsibility for Elena and Henry also weighed heavily upon her, and she felt a moment of panic. What if she failed? What if Henry's illness worsened? Would Colin help her?

Colin's aquamarine eyes and gentle smile forced their way into her mind. She recalled her feelings as they walked about the town, her arm through his, sensing his nearness, his warmth, ever conscious of his strength, of his faint, masculine odor. She blushed as she relived the electricity that shot through her as her breast brushed against his arm, even through her heavy coat. Her breaths came faster and she felt her heart race.

She shook her head at her foolishness. Forget it, she thought. Face the facts. He's a gentleman, and no gentleman will marry you after what happened with Caleb. Taking a deep breath, she whispered to herself to be calm.

She sighed, a sigh that threatened to break down the wall

she had built around her heart. The moon moved beyond the window, leaving her in darkness once more, and she slept at last.

# Chapter 24

KATLIN WASHED QUICKLY in the icy water from the pitcher on the small table, and found herself trying to remember what it felt like to have a real bath, soaking in hot, sudsy water. Shivering in the cold, she peered through the tiny window, seeing nothing but gray mist. No hurry to get to the *James L Day*. It would be at least mid-morning before the fog lifted enough for their departure. Elena still slept, the blanket pulled up over her head.

Katlin finished dressing, and reached over, gently shaking the girl's shoulder. "Come on, we have to get down to breakfast, or there won't be any left."

Elena sat up quickly, forgetting the low ceiling, and exclaimed as she bumped her head on the rafters. With a rueful expression on her face, she rubbed the spot and said, "Today we go to the Sacramento City, yes? And it will be warm, yes?"

Katlin laughed at Elena's enthusiasm. "Warmer, yes, eventually, today, probably not. But we should be there by tomorrow for sure. Mr. MacDougal says we take the schooner part of the way, as far as Benicia, wherever that is, then transfer to a small steamer for the rest of the trip." She folded her night shift as she spoke, and tucked it into her trunk. "I guess the schooner draws too much water for the river, and the water in the bay can get too rough for the little steamer. Come on," she urged, as Elena dawdled in her dressing. "Get your things together or the boat will leave us here."

They took full advantage of the hearty breakfast the waiters again placed before them, and by nine o'clock, Katlin
and her three companions stood by the small landing at
Clark's Point. At the Point, the sun made some inroads
into the fog as the mist gradually lifted from the bay. Katlin
walked away from the others, toward the shoreline, and
could just make out the outline of the schooner, slowly
emerging from the mist like a ghost ship. Boats manned by
husky seamen busily ferried passengers out to the waiting
vessel.

Katlin stood on the shore and looked out at the trim lines
of the beautiful craft that lay at anchor, barely moving in the
calm waters of the protected bay. Colin approached silently
and stood beside her. As always, she was instantly aware of
his proximity.

He followed her gaze. "She is a lovely ship, isn't she?
Sturdy, too. Had to be, to weather the gales coming around
the Horn." He smiled, looking almost lovingly at the slender,
graceful lines of the vessel. "Steamships may be faster and
more practical, but they will never match a sailing ship for
beauty."

A sudden gust of wind lifted the last of the fog that
shrouded the ship, and she stood out in all of her majesty.
Colin is right, Katlin thought. She certainly never felt that
surge of admiration for the lines of the *Falcon* or the *Panama*.
She nodded. "Then I'm sure she can easily handle the
weather in the bay."

A fellow passenger spoke up. "Get some heavy winds
through here sometimes. Clear Alzatraz and the wind that
comes in through the Gate can lay a sailing vessel on her
side if the crew ain't on top of 'er." He shook his head.
"Worst danger, though, goin' up that river, ain't the weather,
it's the snags. Many's the boat lost her bottom on an un-
derwater snag, or got caught and had the devil's own time
gettin' loose."

"Thank you," Katlin said. "It's always nice to know what one will be facing."

"You're welcome, Miss. Always glad to oblige." The passenger ambled off. Colin looked down at Katlin who shook with suppressed laughter at the man's obvious misinterpretation of her comment. He grinned.

"I fear, Miss MacKenzie, that your wit was wasted on the gentleman."

Katlin laughed aloud. "I believe you're right. I also believe it's time we got ourselves on board."

As it turned out, they waited for an hour before the fog lifted enough to see the length of the bay. The wind rose, and the *James L Day* set out, slowly at first, gathering momentum as she left the shoreline behind her. Katlin watched Yerba Buena Island pass to the starboard side, then saw Alcatraz approaching to port. As the gentleman predicted, when the ship cleared the island, a stiff breeze struck her, and the rigging creaked with the sudden strain placed upon it. The ship heeled hard to starboard. Elena cried out in fright, and wrapped her arms around Henry. Katlin clung to the rail with both hands.

"Don't be frightened," she reassured Elena. "This ship has weathered the Horn. A little wind isn't going to capsize her. Just hold on so you don't fall."

Henry grinned. "You can hold on to me all you want, Miss Elena."

Elena blushed and released him. To cover her embarrassment, she pointed to the west. "Look," she said. "You can see out into the ocean."

As they watched, another sailing vessel entered through the Gate under full canvas. The sun, burning through the fog bank, shone on her rigging, and made little rainbows in the spray cast up by her bow. Katlin followed the boat with her eyes until the *James L Day* swept up the strait and a hill blocked her view.

"This strait's about six miles long, according to one of the seamen I was talking to," Henry reported. Katlin smothered a smile. Henry always managed to glean information from the crew.

"Connects with San Pablo Bay," he continued. "We'll pass some volcanic islands, two called The Brothers, then two more called The Sisters."

"How original," Katlin said, with a touch of sarcasm. The first two hove into sight and she gasped, "How lovely!" The sun striking the rock cast the islands in different shades of red as the shadows shifted with the angle of the sun. They next passed The Sisters, and entered San Pablo Bay.

"My, it really is getting warmer." Katlin loosened the scarf about her neck and unfastened the top button of her coat.

"Yes," Henry laughed, "and it will continue to do so, the farther upriver we get. They say it got up to ninety degrees in Sacramento City yesterday."

"Ninety! Oh, my. I said I wanted it warmer, but I would settle for a little less than ninety."

"I hear it cools off at night, though," Henry reassured her. He swept his arm around to encompass their surroundings. "According to my informant, this is a big bowl, about twelve miles wide. We must be making ten knots with that stiff breeze behind us, so it should take us about an hour to get across."

The captain joined them. "Good day, ladies. Not often I have the honor of transporting lovely young misses like yourselves. Allow me to point out the sights." He waved his arm. "The Napa, Petaluma, and San Rafael Rivers all empty into this bay."

Katlin followed the sweep of his arm with her eyes. Tall reeds hid the sloughs, so she could not tell exactly where the rivers entered. Thousands of ducks and geese mingled with the ubiquitous seagulls, crowded so close together they covered the water completely.

"And over here, Miss," the garrulous captain continued, swinging his arm to the side, "is Mare Island."

"Mare Island? Why did they call it that?" Katlin asked.

"Story goes, someone saw a wild mare headin' up a band of elk." He chuckled. "'Course, another story says a mare belonging to an army major got swept down river and he found her there. You know how stories get started, then get better with each teller."

She laughed. "Yes, I know. I like the one about the band of elk better."

"We'll be entering the Strait of Carquinez here soon. That's where the San Joaquin and the Sacramento Rivers join. Lotta water goes through the Strait. Gets all the water from all of the rivers that drain the whole Valley. Will you ladies join me for a bite of dinner first?" He gallantly offered Katlin his arm.

She took the proffered arm with a smile. "The ladies would delighted, Captain."

After a good dinner, for which they paid a dollar apiece, they returned to the deck in time to see the bluffs of the Strait passing on both sides. The early afternoon heat wafted over them, tempered a little by its passage over the water. Katlin could imagine how hot it must be farther up the river. The hills, brown and barren, stood as a gaunt monument to the lack of rain.

"Soon's the rains come, Miss MacKenzie," the captain assured her, "the hills turn green and pretty. Wildflowers cover the hills in sheets, especially the poppies and the wild mustard."

From the Strait, they entered Suisun Bay on the way to the Sacramento River. The captain pointed out the town of Benicia, nestled in a glen on the port side, and, a little farther on, Martinez, on the starboard side.

"There were them as figured Benicia would be a rival to San Francisco. Got a good anchorage, excellent site for a town, but too far from the markets. Army and Navy like it, though. Both of 'em got headquarters here." He waved his arm in the direction of the headland. "You can see General Smith's house from here."

Katlin made out a cluster of buildings on the far shore and nodded. "And that mountain to the west?" A lone peak rose majestically above the surrounding hills, purple in the distance, across the vast expanse of the bay.

"Oh, that's Mount Diablo. Lots of stories about how it got called that, but Salvio Pacheco's land grant in '27 were called Monte del Diablo, so I suspect that's the most likely reason for the name. Afore that, they called it after the Bolbones injuns, as was livin' there when the Spanish come." He removed his cap and wiped his forehead. "Startin' to get warmer as we get upriver. Old Diablo now, they tell me it's an extinct volcano. You can see it from all over the Sacramento area. Now, if you'll excuse me, Miss, duty calls."

An hour later, the rattle of the chain in the hawse pipe told Katlin they had reached the rendezvous point where they would meet the steamer *Sacramento* for the last leg of their voyage. She saw three houses on the shore, one of which stood three stories tall.

"And where are we now?" she asked Colin, who had joined her at the rail. A mosquito buzzed her ear and she swatted at it.

He grinned. "They tell me this place is called 'New York of the Pacific'. Pretty optimistic name if you ask me."

Another mosquito circled and Katlin exclaimed, "This may be a good anchorage, but how can anyone live here if the mosquitoes are this bad?"

Colin laughed. "Just be glad we only have to stay here until the *Sacramento* arrives."

Darkness had descended before the steamer, a small, light craft some sixty feet long, pulled along side of the *James L Day*. By the time all of the passengers and their gear had been transferred to the smaller vessel, midnight approached.

"At least the breeze has blown away the mosquitoes," Katlin sighed with relief to Elena.

The girl yawned in response. "There is a place we can sleep, yes?"

Katlin chuckled. The child could barely keep her eyes open. She turned to Henry. "That little den of a cabin by the engine compartment. Do you suppose they have bunks? Elena is exhausted." And I wouldn't mind a few hours of rest either, she thought.

"I'll check it out," Henry began when Colin rejoined them.

"I already did," he said, "knowing the ladies would like a place to rest. It's a filthy little spot, only about six by eight feet. The bunks are planks with a couple of rough blankets which I suspect are crawling with vermin, judging from the looks of the place. Besides," he grinned, "they want five dollars apiece."

"Five dollars!" Katlin gasped. "That's robbery."

Colin nodded. She could barely make out his features in the shadow of the lantern light. "I've secured a place for us and our gear in the bow where we should be reasonably comfortable. I suggest we go there now before someone else finds it."

Katlin woke at daybreak with a start, stiff from sleeping in the cramped space on the hard deck. She glanced at her companions. Colin had already risen, and stood looking across the bow. Elena slept, curled up against Henry, who had a protective arm wrapped around her. Her long, dark lashes curled against her cheeks and she looked even younger than her fifteen years.

A warm surge of love for the two young people washed over Katlin, amazed at the maternal affection she suddenly felt. We'll make it, children, she thought. We'll make it.

"We are approaching Steamboat Slough," Colin said. He offered Katlin his hand to help her rise. She grimaced as pains shot up her legs. They had gone to sleep from the cramped position she had been forced to maintain all night. Wiggling her toes, she tried to get some feeling back into them.

"They tell me this cuts some twenty miles off of our journey," Colin added, with a sympathetic grin at her obvious discomfort. "I know the accommodations were not the best, but you did manage to get some rest, I trust."

She managed a grim laugh. "Some. I fear, from what I understand, that sleeping arrangements are not too likely to improve much."

"Probably not," he nodded in agreement, "but I hope at least to be able to stretch out full length, even if it's only under a tree!"

A blast from the little vessel's horn startled them all. Elena awoke with a frightened cry and clung more closely to Henry.

"Relax," Katlin assured her. "We seem to be pulling over to the bank. We are not to Sacramento yet."

"We appear to be stopping for wood," Colin observed. "I see piles of it along the bluff, and we are backing up."

"These squatters cut the oak and sycamore and sell it to the steamers for twelve to fifteen dollars a cord," said a gentleman who stood nearby. "You can see the fellow's cabin over there in that clearing." He raised his arm and pointed. "Make a pretty good living, they do."

"I would think so, at those prices," Colin observed. "Who owns the land?"

"Guess it's part of Cap'n Sutter's land grant, but fellers have been squattin' all over it, so it'll be somethin' for the courts to settle. There are those that are sayin' Sutter's not got the right to claim it, since it were a Mexican land grant, and the United States owns California now. Sutter's let the Injuns live where they always have. You'll see a small village where the slough heads back into the main river. They make their huts with the tule reeds that grow all over here." The man chuckled. "Squatters say if Sutter let's the Injuns stay, why not them?"

The man moved on, and Katlin turned to Colin. "A young painter Elena and I met in San Francisco said something similar, that squatters were moving in all over Captain Sutter's claim."

A loud blast from the ship's horn drowned Colin's reply and the little vessel again swung into the middle of the river. The slough soon rejoined the main river. At the junction, they saw the Indian village the gentleman had referred to. Several naked children played joyfully in the water at the edge of the bank and stopped their play to point and stare at the passing intruders. A woman nearby smiled at them indulgently as she washed clothes.

Katlin watched them for a few moments as the steamer swept past, its wake making little eddies along the bank, thinking how the influx of thousands of gold seekers was bound to change their way of life, for better or for worse. As they entered the Sacramento again, she looked up and down the river, contemplating its beauty, with the rich foliage along the banks, and the groves of stately trees.

Three miles above the town of Sutter, a small cluster of thirty or forty houses, Katlin got her first view of Sacramento. Masts and spars lined the embarcadero, so many clustered together she could hardly tell where the ships left off and the land began.

Colin laughed as Katlin stared. "Looks like they've turned half of the ships into shops and houses!"

Katlin observed the tangled mass of spars, masts, and tree limbs lining the shore. Cables ran from the ships to the trunks and roots of the trees. Signs directed passers-by to shops and residences. She shook her head.

"Well," she mused, "I must admit it is different from any-place else I have ever seen." She wiped the perspiration from her forehead, for the climate had turned decidedly warmer. "I suppose living on a boat is better than under a tree, but it must be hotter than the pits of Hades below deck." She swung her arm to indicate the shoreline. "Look at those magnificent trees that have been burned out! Can you believe anyone would be fool enough to build a fire at the base and destroy such a welcome source of shade?"

"World is made up of fools who would do just that, Miss MacKenzie. I suggest we concern ourselves with finding a place to spend the night."

Katlin nodded, her mind suddenly on Caleb. Was she close to him now? He would surely have gone to the gold fields, but Sacramento was the main source of supply for the miners in the camps. What if he came to town? What would she do if she came face to face with him?

And Colin? Inevitably some day Colin would hear about Caleb. Would he disappear from her life as soon as he learned what had happened? She did not want to think so. Surely the Colin she had come to know would understand. Or would he?

She sighed and dismissed Caleb from her mind, prefer-ring to think, with eager anticipation, of the possibility of a warm bath and a night's sleep in a real bed.

# Chapter 25

KATLIN AND ELENA, with Henry beside them, sat on their trunks in the shade of one of the towering oaks, waiting for Colin to return. Mules, oxen, drays and buggies milled about them with all manner of goods and people. Mexicans, Chinese, Chileans, and Kanakas hauled everything from lumber, furniture, books, and barrels of flour and molasses to sacks of potatoes and cases of brandy and pickled oysters. Everything, goods, people and mules baked in the afternoon heat. By the time Colin returned with a cart and driver, sweat dripped down Katlin's face and trickled down her back. Henry obviously suffered from the heat, but Elena seemed unaffected.

"Look," she giggled to Katlin, pointing at a Chinese man passing by. "His hair, it go almost to his feet!"

"Shh," Katlin hushed her. "He'll hear you. I'm sure it is a great source of pride to him. Come on, Mr. MacDougal is waiting."

Colin assisted both girls into the seat while the teamster loaded their trunks into the back. "We can stay at the City Hotel, according to this gentleman. He says it's not finished yet, but does have rooms available." He laughed. "I doubt it will be very luxurious, but should be better than sleeping under a tree."

"After last night, anything would be an improvement," Katlin agreed.

As the cart bounced along the rutted road, the mules' hooves kicked up little clouds of dust with every step. Katlin felt it sticking to her sweaty face, and coughed frequently as the dust-laden air found its way into her lungs.

Colin grinned in sympathy. "He assures me it's not far."

"Is that it?" Katlin asked as the cart approached a magnificent brick edifice.

"Oh, no, ma'am," their driver advised her. "That there's the Anchor House. First brick buildin' in Sacramento City, it were. George Zins, him as has a brick factory over Sutterville way, makes right fine bricks, he do, he built it back in '47, for his bride. Married Doris Wolfinger, he did, her as bein' one o' the survivors of that Donner Party. Feller name of Winters just rented out part o' it. Unnerstand he plans to run a boardin' house there, but he ain't open for business yet."

"That's too bad," Katlin murmured as they pulled to a stop in front of an unprepossessing three story building which bore a lopsided sign announcing 'The City Hotel'. "I'm sure it would be better than this."

Colin chuckled. "Don't be too hasty. I understand this is considered the headquarters of Sacramento society. They held a grand ball here last Fourth of July where the men were even required to wear swallow-tail coats."

"Really?" Katlin murmured. "These men don't look like any of them would even own such a coat."

Colin shrugged. "I only repeat what I've been told. I guess there are some equivalents to landed gentry around the outskirts of the city." He chuckled. "Believe it or not."


By the next morning, Katlin's dire predictions had proven true. As exhausted as she had been, her sleep had been broken every few moments by the cries of unhappy children, or the shouts of mule-skinners, who seemed to depart at all hours of the night. In the few moments of quiet in between all the noises, mosquitoes had buzzed in her ears, or some small creature, whether fleas or bed-bugs she could not tell, had kept biting.

She looked across the table at Elena, and could tell by the circles under the girl's eyes that she had not fared much better. As Henry and Colin joined them, Elena yawned prodigiously.

Henry grinned. "Guess no one got much sleep. Just the smells in this place would keep one awake, to say nothing of the noise."

"And the creatures!" Elena exclaimed. "They keep biting me. All night!"

"This place is obviously designed for profit, not comfort," Colin laughed. "Notice the spaciousness of the dining room and the saloons. Even spaces for monte and faro dealers. And notice the quantities of liquid refreshment available. The money is not being made from lodgers, believe me."

"They sure didn't waste any space on the sleeping rooms," Katlin sighed. "I thought our room in San Francisco was small. This one, by the time I got myself and my trunk inside, the room was filled. A narrow bed, a slim washstand, one narrow chair, and me!"

"There is always the dormitory," Henry suggested helpfully. "Bunks four tiers deep all around with a common wash-stand in the middle of the room."

"Thank you," Katlin grimaced. "I'll take my cell. At least I can shut the door!"

"I guess today had better be spent finding a place to live," Colin chuckled. "I, for one, plan to look for some land to buy. Got to be a good farming area, from what I hear. The long dry season has to make this an ideal place to grow wheat. And they're importing wheat now. All these miners coming are a ready market for flour."

"Not going to the gold fields?" Henry asked.

"That's too hard a life for me," Colin grinned. "I've grown too soft to sleep on the ground and spend all day digging in the heat."

* * *

Shortly after finishing breakfast, the four of them stood in front of the hotel, ready to begin the search. Katlin glanced at the sun, already high on the horizon and shook her head.

"I'm afraid today's going to be another scorcher," she sighed, opening her parasol. "A little of the cold in San Francisco would be welcome."

Colin grinned in sympathy and offered her his arm. "They tell me it's the San Francisco cold we can thank for that welcome cool breeze every evening. Seems that ocean breeze blows the cool air right up the delta."

Katlin chuckled. "Well, I suppose we should be grateful for that much. Where shall we begin?"

"Front Street, I suppose, then we can cut back and forth and be sure we see the whole city, such as it is."

By late afternoon, after trudging streets ankle deep in dust all day in broiling heat, they sat gratefully in the shade of a huge oak tree.

"I'm afraid we may be forced to spend another night at the City Hotel," Colin remarked. "Our search has proven remarkably unproductive. None of the buildings I have seen so far look any better. They seem to consist mostly of a few sticks of wood and some canvas. Canvas roof I can understand, but canvas walls seem a little flimsy to me."

"And the cart drivers! They try to knock you down," Elena exclaimed.

Henry smiled in sympathy. "It's just because there are so many of them, and they're all in a hurry to get someplace."

"Everything is so expensive," Katlin exclaimed. "Someone said the City Hotel was built as a sawmill for Captain Sutter, and the present owner had to pay a hundred thousand dollars for it. A hundred thousand dollars for a sawmill!"

"I heard he only paid fifty thousand," Henry interposed helpfully.

"Fifty thousand, a hundred thousand, whatever. Why, in Maine, I could have built a ten room house for two thousand."

"Yep," Henry nodded, "and the City Hotel's only thirty-five by fifty-five feet. But at least it's built solid, and has three stories. A lot of these so-called buildings are just frames with canvas sides and roofs."

"With lumber selling at up to a dollar a square foot," Katlin sighed, "it's no wonder we see so much canvas." She shook her head. "What's going to happen when winter comes?"

Henry shrugged. "At least it never snows."

"Well, thank heavens for that." Katlin rose to her feet. "Let's get back to our so-called hotel. I, for one, am ready for a little supper. I even think I may sleep through the drunken revelries of the mule-skinners tonight."


A short nap, a bath, and a surprisingly tasty supper revived Katlin's spirits. When she and Elena joined the two men in the dining room, they found them engrossed in conversation with a jovial gentleman in a broadcloth suit, who rose with a smile as the two ladies joined the group.

Colin introduced them. "Miss MacKenzie, Senorita Velasquez, allow me to present the good Doctor Morse. He has been regaling us with some stories of early Sacramento."

"I'm sure he has some stories to tell, if what I have seen and heard in our short stay is to be believed," Katlin said with a smile as she extended her hand.

Dr. Morse bowed gallantly over the proffered hand. "Believe them, Miss MacKenzie. Believe them. Sacramento has become a perfect lazar-house of disease. All these men come from all over, many arriving in the last stages of scurvy, typhus, and dysentery. And fathers abandon sons, sons abandon fathers, even brothers, in the madness to chase the gold, will abandon each other to die alone." He shook his head.

Katlin recalled poor James McFee, and thought of the faithfulness of Will Martin, who stayed by his brother. Somehow, it comforted her to know that not all men were as Dr. Morse described.

"Better now," the good doctor continued. "The Odd Fellows formed an organization to care for the sick, and since General Winn was made president, a great amount of relief has been dispensed. He even sees that every man who dies is given a coffin for burial. Before that, men often died with no one in attendance, and were frequently buried without even the dignity of being sewn into a blanket."

"*Que barbara,*" murmured Elena with tears in her eyes. "It is so sad. To die alone, it is not right."

"Only hospital is one at the Fort, but the doctor who runs it charges so much only a few could afford to go there," Dr. Morse continued. "Council has to pay sixteen dollars a day for every patient. My partner, Dr. Stillman and I, plan to build another hospital on a piece of property at Third and K. There we will be able to charge a great deal less. And we hope to do it before the rains begin." He rose to his feet. "It has been a great pleasure to meet you lovely ladies. Now, if you will excuse me, I must depart."

"We wish you the best in your plans for your new hospital," Katlin smiled in response. "It certainly sounds like there is a real need."

They watched Dr. Morse leave, then Colin turned to Katlin. "He also informed me that, while most consider California good only for raising cattle and for her mineral wealth, some, including me, feel the future here will be in agriculture."

"So you plan to obtain land and go into farming?"

"Yes. Dr. Morse told me a Captain Weber bought a large section of a Mexican land grant, San Jon de los Mokelumnes, from the wife of the owner, and is selling parcels. It's located south of Sacramento, along the Cosumnes River. I obtained Captain Weber's direction from the good doctor, and plan to write to the gentleman tomorrow." He grinned. "I, too, have found the accommodations here a bit wearing."

"Well, if you can pronounce that name so well, Weber should be happy to sell it to you," Henry chuckled.

"And even if I am forced to pay sixteen dollars a day for a carpenter, *MacKenzie's Mercantile* is going to be constructed by the end of the week," Katlin declared.

"Hear, hear," Colin grinned, raising his wine glass. "I'll drink to that."

# Chapter 26

On SEPTEMBER 23, 1849, one month after Katlin's arrival in Sacramento, the first rain struck. As the clouds built and the wind mounted, Katlin could not believe it. With a roar like a freight train, the rain poured down upon the canvas roof of their flimsy shelter.

"I thought they said the rains never come until November," she gasped to Henry, who ducked through the door, soaking wet.

"Fellows down at the Round Club tell me the local injuns say it's gonna be a wet winter. They've been tellin' folks the river's gonna go over its banks. Say the signs are all there, and rain this early is one of 'em."

Katlin shook her head and looked around at the boxes and crates of merchandise she had received from Mr. Walker just the week before. She had carried out her plans, and hired a young carpenter from Vermont to construct the building on land she leased from Peter Burnett and his partner. Since her funds were limited, and she had been forced to pay the carpenter sixteen dollars a day, the building was similar to many of its neighbors.

The canvas roof flapped in a sudden gust of wind. She shivered and peered anxiously at the ceiling, watching for leaks. Seeing none, she sighed with relief. So far, so good.

"Come in, quickly, and get into dry clothes." She pulled the boy towards the blanket that served as a makeshift wall to separate his sleeping quarters from Katlin's and Elena's. "Go." She gave him a little shove. "Do you suppose we should move some of the goods out to Mr. MacDougal's, just in case?" Colin had succeeded in buying a hundred and twenty acres from Captain Weber, and had moved into the small, three room house located on the property. She glanced up. The rain no longer pounded on the roof.

Henry emerged, pulling a dry shirt over his head. "Seems to have stopped. Musta been a freak shower." He grinned. "Besides, if we moved all this stuff to Mr. MacDougal's, where would he put it?"

Katlin sighed. "You're right. He really has no space for it either. But his home is up on a knoll, higher than the rivers. Highly unlikely he will get flooded. Maybe you're right. Maybe it is just a freak shower. I certainly hope so. But the Nisenams have been living here for a long time. I would be inclined to take their warning seriously. What other information did you gather while you were there?"

Katlin often thought she would like to visit the Round Club, as it sounded like a very interesting place. Except for all of the paintings of naked women, of course, she thought with a blush. But she also knew quite well no ladies ever went there.

"Did hear the reason the City Charter got voted down was all the gamblers turned out to defeat it. According to my informant, none of them want to see law and order brought to the city. Guess they think the next thing will be church folks trying to shut down the gambling halls."

Katlin shook her head. "From what I hear, some of them should probably be shut down."

"That's where the money is, Miss MacKenzie," Henry chuckled. "All those crazy miners work and slave to get those little bags of gold, then lose it all in a weekend."

Katlin thought of Caleb. Is that what you are doing, you rat? You used my money to get yourself here, now are you going to gamble it all away? And then go find yourself another gullible widow?

She broke off the thought as she realized Henry had spoken to her again. "Sorry. My mind wandered. What did you say?"

Henry grinned. "You did seem to be miles away. I said, my informant at the Round Club is a monte dealer - and a former preacher."

"Preacher!" Katlin gasped. "How could a man of the church be dealing cards in a gambling house? Especially a den of iniquity like that Round Club."

The boy shrugged. "As you've said, there's easier ways to get gold than to dig for it."

Katlin just shook her head. Another cloudburst poured rain upon the roof. She lifted the flap of canvas that served as the door and looked out into the street. The thick dust had turned to mud. The city grew by leaps and bounds around her. She knew the population had increased to around ten thousand, from the four houses she had been told the city had contained the previous April, before the miners started arriving in droves. The sound of hammers and saws rang out all day.

Wagons of immigrants from the overland routes had begun reaching the city, and Katlin knew the coming months would see many more. She felt a strange pity for the poor oxen who had pulled those wagons over all those dreary miles. The poor creatures had a patient, accepting look that seemed almost human. She frequently saw cows mixed in with the oxen in many cases, forced to do equal duty.

The men complained loudly of the suffering they had endured on the crossing, but the women, Katlin had often chuckled to Elena, seemed, like the oxen, to accept the hardships of the journey as just a part of the experience.

As she gazed out at the rain pouring into the already muddy street, she thought of the coming winter. "Henry," she said to the boy beside her, "there have to be hundreds more of these poor souls on their way in the mountains.

Many of them won't arrive until at least October. What about them? If the storms come early, won't some of them be trapped like the people in poor Mr. Donner's group?"

"Captain Sutter has thought of that too. He's sent some men out with supplies and to help hurry 'em along." He grimaced. "I hear the reason the Donners got trapped is they spent five days recruiting on the Truckee before coming over, 'stead of just two, like they should've. If they'd started over the top three days earlier, they'd have made it ahead of the storm."

Katlin shook her head. "On such a tiny detail, the fate of so many rested. I suppose they thought they had plenty of time."

"Yep. First storms don't usually start until November. Mr. Sutter, he's been helpin' so many it's like to broke him, from what I hear." He chuckled. "And a lot of the ones he helped show their gratitude by squattin' on his land and stealing his cattle. No wonder he handed the whole affair over to his son and retired to Hock Farm, his place up on the Feather River."

"The poor man," Katlin sighed. "It must be discouraging to do so much for people and have them turn around and steal from you."

"Yep. Gonna be more trouble, too. Remember that house Robinson built on the levee at I Street? The one the city authorized Brannan and his bunch to tear down a couple of weeks ago?"

Katlin nodded. "I thought Brannan cleared out the whole area."

"He did, but now a lot of the squatters are claiming that was public land, not part of Sutter's grant at all. In spite of Sutter putting out a notice in the *Placer Times* last May giving the boundary lines of his property." They both paused and glanced up at the ceiling as another gust of wind shook the canvas roof.

"I just hope it doesn't get any worse," Katlin muttered.

"The squabble or the wind?" Henry grinned.

"Both," she laughed. "I suppose there is nothing we can do about the quarrels, but do you suppose we should do something about the rain? What if the river should overflow?" She glanced around at all the boxes again. "I wish we had a second floor."

"We can rent some space from someone who does have a second floor - if we had a thousand dollars or so to spare."

Katlin grimaced. "I'm afraid that is out of the question, at least until we start moving some of these goods. With only five or six buildings in town with a second floor, such space is going to be very expensive." She sighed. "We'll just have to face whatever comes. Maybe we can sell some of this merchandise right away." She rummaged in the crate that served as a make-shift desk and brought out her paper, ink, a quill pen, and started to write.

"As soon as the rain stops," she said, shaking the sand from the note she had penned, "go down to the steamer office and send this note to Mr. Walker. I've told him not to send any more goods until we see if the river really does flood."

Henry looked ruefully at his boots, caked with mud in spite of his efforts to clean them. "Rain on all that dust is turning all the streets to mud."

Katlin sighed. "Just what we need. Here we have goods to sell and no one can get through the mud to buy them."

"At least no one can say they don't see our sign."

That was a joke among them. Katlin had insisted the sign that read *'MacKenzie's Mercantile'* be a large one, easily read from up and down the street. "No one will buy our merchandise if they don't know we are here," she had declared. She had also placed a notice in the *Placer Times*.

They had moved some of the goods, mostly things the miners needed, such as pans, shovels, axes, and blankets.

She hoped to concentrate more on fine linens and fabrics, but knew the city needed more women before such things would be in much demand. She had sold some linens to a few of the ladies from arriving wagon trains, as much of theirs had been dumped on the trail to lighten the loads to get over the mountains.

Elena emerged from behind the curtain, holding a lovely china teapot. "Look," she cried, "how pretty! We can keep it, no? We do not have to sell, yes?"

"Yes and no," Katlin laughed. "We can keep anything we want, but we have to pay Mr. Walker for the whole shipment."

Elena burst into giggles. Katlin and Henry stared at her, puzzled, unable to she what she found so amusing.

"I give up," Henry finally said. "What's so funny?"

"You, me, us, all this," she managed to gasp between spasms of laughter. "I am now a merchant, yes?"

"Yes," Henry agreed, "but I can't see why it's something to laugh about."

"Oh, but you did not grow up en *Espana*, trained to be a fine lady *en la casa de un* aristocrat. My father, he was a Don. It is like you say in England a Lord. My father, he looked with scorn upon the trades-people. They were beneath him. Only the servants dealt with such people." She went into gales of laughter again. "*Si mi papa podria a verme ahorita!* If he lived, he would say no *hija* of his could be seen in the company of merchants." She looked from Henry to Katlin. "And now, not only am I in their company, I *am* one!"

Henry gathered her in his arms in a bear hug and rocked her back and forth, shaking with laughter. "That's my girl!" he beamed.

Katlin watched the two youngsters with a smile, marveling at their resilience. She remembered her thought as she watched them sleeping in the bow of the steamship.

We'll make it, children, she repeated in her mind. We'll make it.

She looked up as a man dressed as a miner lifted the flap and entered. "You open for business?" he asked.

"We certainly are," Katlin smiled. "What can we do for you?"

"Need one of those India Rubber ponchos. I hear they keep off the rain, which is, unfortunately, coming all too heavily at the moment. And a couple of new blankets. My present blankets are sadly worn and tattered." He smiled, showing gleaming white teeth in his darkly tanned face, a contrast to the tobacco stained teeth the miners usually displayed. "The weather at my claim up at Long's Bar will soon become very cold." Dark hair hung in waves almost to his shoulders, and his thick mustache quivered as he nodded. Turning to Henry, he asked, "You MacKenzie?"

Henry shook his head. "Not me," he said with a grin. "I just work here. Miss MacKenzie is the owner." He indicated Katlin with a wave of his hand.

"Excuse me, Mademoiselle." He swept off his hat and bowed. "Jean Baptiste Ruelle, at your service."

"You're French," Katlin exclaimed.

"French-Canadian, Mademoiselle," he responded. "I have been trapping in thees area for many years. I am the first to discover the gold on the South Fork of the American, back in '43. I show it to Capitan Sutter, but he brush me off. I tell him, he stake me to a mule and some gear, I go and find him more. He refuse, and I have no money, so I leave." He tugged at his mustache. "When Mr. Marshall, he find the gold in '48, I try to tell Capitan Sutter I am first to find, but he ignore me." He shook his head. "So James Marshall, he is famous, and I, Jean Baptiste Ruelle, am nobody, grubbing for a few ounces on my poor claim at Long's Bar."

Katlin could think of nothing to say. She watched as he

selected two blankets from one of the crates on the floor and accepted the India Rubber poncho Henry handed him. He watched solemnly as Henry carefully weighed out the proper amount of gold dust he offered in payment.

As he turned to leave, he bowed over Katlin's hand again. "I bid you welcome to California, Miss MacKenzie. We have great need for ladies here. Also, my Nisenam partner tells me the rivers will be overflowing this winter. I advise you to heed his advice and be prepared. Good day."

Katlin turned serious eyes to Henry, who carefully poured Ruelle's gold dust from the small scales into a cloth bag which he then tied securely to be sure none of the precious flakes escaped. "That's another warning. What shall we do?"

Henry shrugged. "Not much we can do except leave stuff in crates so's we can stack it if the water comes. Water shouldn't hurt much of it too bad, long's we can get it dried out quick. And it doesn't float down the river," he added.

She sighed. "I suppose you're right. I don't know what else we can do." She grinned suddenly. "Do you suppose Ruelle is telling the truth? That he really did find gold on the American River back in '43?"

"Probably. Been my experience the man who gets all the credit's not necessarily the one who deserves it." Then he grinned. "But it hasn't made Sutter or Marshall rich either. In fact, it's almost ruined Sutter. Ruelle may be the one who got off best after all."

Katlin laughed. "You're probably right. Let's concentrate on finding ourselves a good stove to take some of the chill off of this place. I have a feeling it's going to be a cold winter."

In November, a Post Office opened in Sacramento.

"At last," Katlin remarked to Elena when she heard the

news. "If Sacramento is going to be a major city, we certainly should have a Post Office."

"Especially if we're going to be a State," Henry said. "They tell me that assembly Governor Riley called down in Monterey signed a constitution. Gonna vote on it soon. I hear it's outlawed slavery."

"That's good," Katlin remarked, immediately thinking of Malcolm. "Slavery is a shameful practice."

"Might cause some trouble getting California admitted to the Union, though," Henry cautioned. "All the Slave State Senators will oppose it, because that will give the North more states than the South. And it is setting a precedent, going straight to statehood instead of being a territory first."

"Is President Taylor for or against?"

"We'll see. Guess it depends on how much support he can get."

"Who did they select as Senators?"

"William Gwin and John Fremont."

"Fremont? The one who started that disgraceful Bear Revolution and put General Vallejo in jail? And disobeyed his commanding officer?"

Henry grinned. "That's the one. I guess the fact that his wife is the daughter of Senator Benton from Missouri probably helped. I hear she pushed real hard to get him selected. And was real unhappy when they gave him the two year term and Gwin the six."

Katlin sighed. "Well, I guess we'll just have to wait and see. I don't suppose their new constitution says anything about allowing women to vote. That would sure settle the slavery question fast, if women had anything to say about it."

The boy shook his head. "Don't think that occurred to any of 'em," he grinned. "But they did put in that married women have the right to own property, instead of having to turn it all over to their husbands."

"That's good. What made them think of that?"

"Guess it's a Spanish tradition. They didn't want to go too much against customs that have been common practice around here for over two hundred years."

Katlin immediately thought of Caleb. If Maine had passed such a Constitution, she could have gone to the law when Caleb had stolen her money. She felt a sudden stab of apprehension. Would the weather drive the miners from the gold fields into the city? What if she found herself face to face with Caleb? What would she do? Or, more important, what would his reaction be?

She shook her head and noticed Henry watching her closely. She pulled herself out of her thoughts with an effort and smiled brightly. "And so now we have a Post Office! You can write to your parents and tell them how much your health has improved. I'm sure they've been very anxious."

# Chapter 27

The RAIN CONTINUED, and cold winds swept down on them day after day. The three of them spent most of their time huddled by the little Franklin Stove trying to keep warm as the wind whistled through the flimsy canvas walls.

By mid-November, the roads were swamped, so transportation came almost to a complete halt. And still the rain continued, turning warm and threatening to melt the snows piled high on the Sierra Nevada Mountains to the east.

Henry returned one cold, miserably wet day to report the State Constitution had been approved by a vast majority, and a delegation had left for Washington to present California's petition for Statehood. "Now we just have to wait and see how they argue it out," he said, warming his hands over the little stove. "Take a while, with all the opposition they'll get from the South."

They struggled to survive from day to day. Katlin worried about Henry's health in the cold and damp, but he seemed no worse. In fact, he seemed to cough less each day. Maybe everyone was right when they said the climate in California helped cure consumption. She and Elena both fussed over him, and made sure he got plenty of rest and wholesome food. Maybe, just maybe, Katlin wished fervently, we dare to hope for his recovery.

One day early in December, a young man entered the store with a packet for Katlin, and introduced himself as James Stolles.

"Opened myself a one man mail service from the new Post Office to the mining camps," he said. "Deliver mail all up and down the diggin's, as far up the east fork of the Feather River as Taylor's Bar."

"What a clever idea!" Katlin exclaimed. "How much does it cost?"

"Charge a dollar in dust to deliver a letter, half a dollar to take one back to the Post Office here in Sacramento. Cheap at twice the price. Miners are right glad to pay it. Saves 'em comin' all the way to the city just to see iffen they got mail."

Katlin looked at the packet, but could not imagine who would be writing to her from the diggings until she remembered Malcolm. Memories of his easy friendliness washed over her.

"Feller up at Bidwell's Bar asked me to be sure this got to Miss MacKenzie at *MacKenzie's Mercantile*," he said, handing her the packet with a bow. "If you have a response you wanta send, I'll deliver it fer a dollar's worth o' dust."

Katlin opened the packet, and a brief note read:

> "Miss MacKenzie, one of the other miners up here at Bidwell's Bar wrote this fer me, since I can't write, but I'm askin' you to please keep this gold dust until I can get me enough to pay for my freedom. I figger it'll be safer with you than here in the camp. Most of the miners are pretty honest, but I feel better with you keeping it, now there's a way to send letters back and forth. Your good friend, Malcolm"

Malcolm's broad smile and expressive dark eyes flooded her mind. So he had remembered her after all. He was doing well, if the size of the bag of dust she held in her hand was any indication.

"Yes, Mr. Stolles," she said, "I do wish to send a reply. Can we offer you some refreshment while I write? Henry, measure out a dollar's worth of dust for the gentleman. Elena, bring Mr. Stolles a piece of pie and a cup of tea. We want him to get out of the city before the mud won't let him go."

"Gettin' right bad, it is, Miss MacKenzie," Stolles said as he sat at the little table. His eyes gleamed at the sight of the wedge of apple pie Elena placed in front of him. "Saw a team of oxen stuck right up to their bellies. None of the freighting companies are coming into the city. Closest they come is out to Sutter's Fort. Ground's a little higher there. Even some talk of movin' the city off more towards Brighton.

"Not likely to happen though," the garrulous Mr. Stolles rambled on. "Brighton too far from the river. All that stuff comes up by steamer. What they gotta do is see about haulin' in some rock, or buildin' some plank streets so's at least the main roads kin carry a wagon."

"Is anyone thinking of doing so?" Katlin queried, glancing up from her letter.

"Not so far as I've heard. Hardin Bigelow, now, he's a-talkin' about building levees. Says if the river's gonna go high enough to go over the banks, the thing to do is make the banks higher."

"That makes sense," Katlin nodded, folding her letter into a packet. "But I suppose no one is paying any attention to him either."

"Not yet," Stolles grinned. "But I betcha they will after the river goes over."

"You think it will?" Henry asked, with an anxious glance out the doorway at the leaden sky.

"Oh, sure, all the Maidu, every tribe all up and down the rivers, say the same thing. Say early rain is the first sign. And they been livin' here a lot longer than these so-called city fathers who only been here since last summer." He joined Henry at the doorway and glanced up at the sky.

Katlin joined them and handed Stolles her letter for Malcolm, addressed only 'Malcolm, Bidwell's Bar'. "It looks like it's going to rain again any moment. You'd better get going."

She and Henry stood together and watched the horse struggle through the knee-deep mud. Katlin thought of her snug cabin back in Maine, surrounded by the lovely pine trees, and sighed. *Caleb, you rat, that's one more thing you owe me for.*

Two weeks later, the sun broke briefly through the cloud cover and Katlin looked up from washing dishes to see Colin striding though the door. Her heart leaped at the sight of him, as handsome as ever.

Elena rushed to him with both hands outstretched. "Señor MacDougal, it is so good to see you. You have been, how you say, the stranger for so long!" Colin laughed and seized her in a bear hug, then set her back on her feet as Henry reached him.

"She's right, you know," the boy grinned as he grasped Colin's hand firmly. "It has been too long since we've seen you."

Colin turned from Henry to Katlin and bowed elegantly over the hand she had quickly dried on her apron. His aquamarine eyes met hers and she felt her heart turn over as she returned his smile.

"Yes, it has been a long time," she said. "Come in, come in. Elena found a lovely china tea set in the goods Mr. Walker sent, and we have yet to use it. She has been saving it for just such a special occasion."

Elena had already pulled the teakettle forward over the heat and bustled about setting the makeshift table they had made from boards placed across wooden crates. As she walked past the crate Colin had seated himself on, she wrinkled her nose. "That smell! What it is?"

Colin laughed. "I'm sure it's my boots. I've hired a light cart to haul some of your merchandise out to my place until we see what the river does." He removed the offending boots and set them outside the door, and returned to his seat in his stocking feet. "I had to walk through several inches of the most noxious mud I've ever encountered. Between the cattle and the horses and the men who've never learned to use an outhouse, it's a wonder the miasma hasn't made everyone sick." He smiled as Elena poured steaming hot tea into the cup in front of him.

Katlin's mind was on his earlier words. "Will you have space? I thought your house was kind of small."

"Compared to what I had in New Orleans," he grinned, "it certainly is. But I don't have much myself. We'll manage."

"Thank you. It will be a relief to have at least some of the goods safe if the river goes over. Are you sure you can get a cart through the mud? The streets are in terrible shape."

"That's why I rented the lightest cart I could find. If we don't pile it too heavy, and if we are careful to pick our way around the worst spots, I think I can get at least some of the more fragile items, like linens and blankets. Pots and pans and picks won't suffer from the water too much."

Katlin sighed. "There is one crate of the damask table linens, which probably won't be selling soon anyway, not until the town gets more civilized. The damask would be ruined if it flooded. And the whole case of the new Colt pistols. Water would not be much of a problem, but all that mud . . . ." She shuddered.

"We will do our best," Colin replied. "I brought my hired hand along to drive the cart. I swear I pay him more money than I make myself. Fifty dollars a month and room and board! He's a jolly Irishman with a brogue so heavy I can hardly understand him, but he is a good worker. I told him by the end of five years, he will have made all the money and will own the farm. So I asked him, and then what shall I do? He just laughed and said, 'I'll hire you to work for me, and you will soon have your farm back.' "

They all laughed and Henry said, "That reminds me of what one of the fellows at the Round Club was saying. He runs a boarding house, and says all of his guests never miss a meal or pay a dime. He told them he couldn't afford to keep feeding them unless they paid, so what should he do? Their advice to him was to sell out to someone who could!"

Colin chuckled. "Well, when Peter Burnett gave his inaugural address down in San Jose, he said he believes, as I do, that California's future will be in agriculture, not minerals and cattle. We'll see who's right. I just wish these fools would stop killing every coyote and snake they see. The squirrels are overrunning the whole place. They're not like the tree squirrels we have back East. They dig holes, and the cattle and horses step in the holes, to say nothing of how they dig up the fields. I can see them becoming a major problem."

Elena set a wedge of golden apple pie in front of Colin and his eyes lighted up.

Katlin laughed at his expression. "Elena has finally mastered the Dutch oven. I really should see about getting a girl to help us. There is too much work for the three of us. But I want to wait until after I see what the river does."

"I can be back tomorrow for another load if the weather holds."

"And you must plan to join us for Christmas dinner."

He laughed. "I'll do better than that. I'll bring the goose. I've got a pond on my place with hundreds of ducks and geese."

Nature smiled upon them briefly, and the sun came out. Christmas Day sparkled in the golden light. As Colin carved the goose, Katlin, her hopes rising, raised her glass. "Here's to no more rain for at least a month."

Henry chuckled and raised his glass as well. "Hear, hear. Let's give everything a chance to dry out."

When Colin departed after the festivities, he took Katlin's hand in his and said solemnly, "If the three of you would like to stay with me for a few weeks, the offer still stands."

Katlin's heart turned over, but she said, "Thank you, but I don't dare leave my inventory."

He shrugged. "As you wish. Good luck." Their eyes locked for a long moment, then Colin released her hand. He turned on his heel and departed.

Katlin, Henry, and Elena celebrated the New Year with a toast from one of the bottles of champagne out of the case Mr. Walker had included with the shipment. "For good luck," his note had read.

"So far, so good," Henry said, as he and Katlin clinked glasses. "Maybe the river won't go over after all."

"Oh, I hope not," Elena cried. "I do not like the rain. I wish for the sunshine to come back."

Katlin took them both in her arms and hugged them fiercely. "I love you both so much. Maybe our luck will hold."

By the following Tuesday, a violent southeast storm rocked the city, pouring rain down upon the canvas roof with a vengeance. Katlin woke to howling winds that threatened to take the roof off its eaves. Elena opened her eyes wide, then snuggled deeper into her blankets.

"Stay in bed and stay warm," Katlin ordered the girl. "Henry," she called as she struggled into her boots. "We have to check for leaks."

"Coming," he responded. He emerged from behind the blanket wall just as Katlin reached the center of the room. Together they peered anxiously at the flapping roof. The rain dripped through the saturated canvas in a number of places. Katlin eyed the situation with dismay.

"We can't possibly catch the water from all of these leaks," she said, shaking her head. "Every time we move some-thing, a new leak will start up. We'll just have to let it go."

"Good thing we got most of the stuff water can damage out to Mr. MacDougal's," Henry remarked.

Yes, Colin, my love, Katlin thought. One more thing to be grateful to you for. As so often before, she thought of how much she had come to love him and rely upon him, and how hopeless her love was. He would never under-stand what had happened with Caleb. And he kept himself aloof. Sometimes she felt he wanted to say something to her, but always held back. She often found herself won-dering if something had happened in his life that made him afraid to admit he loved her.

She shook herself out of her musings. He probably was being so helpful just because he was a gentleman. No point in building up dreams that would never be fulfilled. "Henry, we need to know how bad this is getting. Bundle up so you don't take a chill. Put on one of those India rubber ponchos to keep dry and go out and see what's happening."

Elena handed Katlin a cup of tea, and the two of them waited in silence for Henry's return, listening to the drip, drip, drip of the rain plopping onto the crates of merchan-dise. Every few minutes, a drop would land on the hot stove and sizzle itself into steam.

Henry returned an hour later. "River's overflowing at I Street, between First and Third," he reported. "Pouring in at a ferocious rate. Maybe," he added wryly, "we should have taken Mr. MacDougal up on his offer." He shrugged. "Too late now. Doubt we could get there even if we tried."

The day dragged by. Evening saw a lessening of the storm, to Katlin's relief, but by then, water ran down most of the streets. In late afternoon, Henry again went out to reconnoiter.

When he returned, he said. "It's getting worse. That new zinc building of Montgomery and Warbass has water running under it. Going to cut away the whole foundation. Torrents are rushing down Second and Third." He shrugged off the dripping poncho and laid it over one of the packing cases. While he warmed his hands over the little stove, he added, "And it's gonna get worse, too, because it's raining in the mountains and melting the snow. I think we should think about getting to higher ground. We can't get out of the city. We're surrounded by water."

"Mr. Johnson's building in the next block has two stories. Could we make it to there?"

Henry grimaced. "We may have to." Then he chuckled. "Boys at the Round Club are taking odds. Most of the money says the river won't get any higher. We'll see who's right pretty quick, I suspect."

Wednesday's weather repeated Tuesday's, with rain continuing to pour down upon them, and the water in the streets reached the doorway of many of the buildings. Katlin watched anxiously, the thought that Henry was right, that they should have accepted Colin's offer to stay with him for a few weeks until they saw what the river would do nagged at her. But Katlin had not wanted to abandon her merchandise, and, in spite of the weather, shoppers continued to drift in. She never for a moment forgot the money she owed to Mr. Walker, and, while he had said nothing, she wished to pay him as soon as possible. Of course, if all of the merchandise floated down the river . . . . She forced her thoughts from that possibility and turned to the boy beside her.

"Henry, if the water goes any higher, we will make for Mr. Johnson's building."

Henry shrugged expressively. "Guess we'll have to. Water seems to be rising slow-like. Current doesn't seem too bad." He paused, then added, "Yet."

Katlin laughed ruefully. "You're encouraging. I think you're right. We should be prepared to evacuate. Tie things as securely as possible. Elena, pack our haversacks with some food and extra clothing. I'll leave the lamp lighted. And sleep in your clothes tonight. We don't want to have any delays should we have to run for safety."

Elena and Henry scurried to obey. Katlin gathered the lists Mr. Walker had sent with the merchandise, the records of everything she had sold, and all the gold dust. She tucked the items in her haversack and stowed it at the end of her bed where she could reach it quickly.

When they could do no more, she persuaded Henry and Elena to go to bed. She checked the lamp to be sure it had plenty of tallow, then, worn out, she stretched out on her bed and snuggled into the blankets. We can't do any more, she thought. Whatever happens, we'll face it as it comes. Her last thought before sleep claimed her was the memory of the tingles that ran up her arm as Colin held her hand.


Early Thursday, sometime before dawn, a wild clanging of the alarm bell roused Katlin from a sound sleep. She rose from the bed to find herself standing ankle deep in icy water.

# *Chapter 28*

"ELENA! HENRY! Get up. We've got to get to higher ground." Katlin pulled on a pair of dry socks and stuck her feet into her boots. She waded to the table where the lamp stood, thankful for its comforting light. In the dim glow, the flickering light danced in Elena's frightened eyes.

"Come on," Katlin urged when the girl sat unmoving, staring back at her. Katlin felt a moment of panic flash through her. Had they waited too long? Had she risked the lives of Elena and Henry for the sake of the crates of merchandise stacked about her? She shook off the feelings of doom. Too late for self-recriminations now. They had to get moving. "That's why we didn't get undressed last night when we went to bed, remember? We suspected this might happen. We have to get over to Mr. Johnson's."

"And hopefully his building is not one of those the water has undermined," Henry commented as he joined them, blankets and India rubber ponchos in his arms. "I'd hate to be on top of a building when it toppled over."

Elena's face paled. "That can happen?"

"Hush, Henry," Katlin admonished. "Don't frighten the poor girl any more than she already is." She wrapped a blanket and a poncho around herself and picked up the heavy haversack containing her records and her gold. Henry wrapped Elena snugly and helped her get her boots on. When all was ready, they waded toward the entrance, Henry in the lead. He placed Elena's right hand securely on his belt. "Hold on," he told the shivering girl. "No matter what happens, don't let go!" He hoisted her haversack to his other arm with a grunt of surprise. "What did you pack in this? It weighs a ton."

Katlin followed Henry and Elena as they stepped out into the street. The wind tore at them, threatening to rip the blankets from their bodies. Katlin hugged hers more securely and struggled to keep up with Henry, who half led, half dragged Elena along behind him. They could barely see in the dim, pre-dawn light.

"Hurry," Henry urged. "The water is getting deeper. That warm rain must have melted the snow. Water probably pouring in at a terrific rate."

They had not gone half a block when the water reached their knees. They struggled to cross the open street. Katlin found it harder and harder to keep her footing. She stifled a scream as her foot rolled on a rock beneath her and she almost fell. The mud threatened to suck her boots off with each step. The current increased with each passing moment. She gasped with relief when they reached the other side of the street and were next to a building once again.

"Keep a hand on the wall," Henry ordered.

"Are we almost there?" she gasped. The water reached the middle of her thighs and tore at her skirts, reminding her of crossing the swollen river in Panama. She tried to drive the image from her mind. "Thank heavens we have a little light from the moon." As if to answer her, a darker cloud moved across and the moonlight faded.

Henry chuckled grimly. "It was good while it lasted. I counted yesterday. I think it's three more buildings until we reach Johnson's. I know he has a second floor."

"I'm glad you checked it out. I'd hate to be floundering around out here with no idea where we were headed." Katlin felt her heart pounding in her chest, so loudly she swore she could hear it, even over her labored breathing. A block and a half had never seemed so long! Just as she felt she could not take another step, the water reaching her hips, Henry turned into a door way.

"Come in," he urged. "The steps should be along this wall. Ouch! I just found them Or, I should say, my shin found them."

Katlin slowly moved across the wooden floor, not wishing to bark her shin, too, until she found the first stair and thankfully started to climb. At the head of the steps, a man appeared with a lighted lamp held high.

"Come on, get the ladies up here," he urged Henry. "They'll be safe. We got a bunch already, but the more the merrier."

With the last ounce of her strength, Katlin pulled herself and her haversack up the remaining rickety steps and collapsed in a heap.

Henry shook her shoulder as she lay trying to get her breath back. "Miss MacKenzie, I know you're worn out, but if you and Elena don't get out of those wet skirts, you're liable to take a chill."

Katlin sighed and forced herself to move. "He's right. Come on, Elena. Get that sopping wet skirt off and wrap yourself in a dry blanket. Get the boots off, too. We've got to get them tended to or we'll never get them back on again."

The sun broke through the cloud cover the next morning. Henry and Katlin climbed up to the roof of the building where they had taken refuge and saw the city stood under at least four feet of water. Bodies of cattle and mules floated on the current, along with tents and houses and boxes and barrels of goods. The water reached as far as they could see.

"I hope none of those crates are from *MacKenzie's Mercantile*," she commented to Henry, her eyes fastened on the floating merchandise. "But I suppose that's wishful thinking. I'm sure if others have lost their goods, we will too."

"Good thing we got as much as we did out to Mr. Mac-Dougal's," Henry said. "Seemed like a lot of extra work at the time, but looks like it's paid off."

"Are you sure he'll be all right?" Katlin felt a sudden fear that possibly the flood had affected Colin as well.

"Should be. He says his place is on high ground." He laughed. "But I'll bet he's stuck there. He'll be high and dry, but on a island in the middle of all of this."

They returned to the corner of the room where Elena sat with their belongings. She had managed to turn the little square into a cozy room, with blankets on three sides. She had found a small crate, and on it sat their breakfast of crackers and beef jerky. With no way to heat anything, Katlin feared cold fare would be their lot for a least a while.

She heard Henry laugh and looked again at the little table. Elena had set out the teapot and the four china cups on their saucers. She had rescued the little tea set she had grown so fond of. The creamer sat empty, but the sugar bowl held four lumps of sugar.

As Henry and Katlin squatted on the floor by the make-shift table, Elena scurried away and returned in a few moments with a kettle of boiling water which she poured into the little teapot. A cheerful steam arose, and the welcome aroma of brewing tea greeted Katlin's nostrils.

Henry hugged Elena as she beamed proudly over her little triumph. "Now I know why that blasted haversack was so heavy!"

The following morning, Henry, grinning from ear to ear, came for Katlin. "You've gotta see this." He led her to the roof and pointed to the corner of Second and J. She saw that Wesley Merrit's fine new brick building had been so undermined by the rushing waters that it had tumbled over onto Masset and Brewer's auction store.

"Quite a sight, isn't it?" Henry commented. "Glad we weren't in either one of those buildings. Sure hope this one is secure."

Katlin's eyes covered the scene before her. People on boats, baker's troughs, India rubber beds, and makeshift rafts of all descriptions floated about, dodging the debris. Women and children huddled in the flimsy craft, which made their way to the few two story buildings.

"The poor souls," she murmured, her heart filled with pity for the wretched creatures. "I'll bet they've lost everything they owned."

Henry nodded. "Probably. Lots of folks have. Be interesting to see how the city fathers plan to prevent a repeat performance when the snow melt comes in the spring." He chuckled. "To see some of these fellows carrying on, you'd think this was one big frolic. Half of 'em are drunk. And I've even seen some of 'em roll into the water just for the fun of it, yet not a one has made any effort to save some of the barrels and crates floating down into the river. Kind of sad, and funny at the same time."

"I suppose it's just a reaction to all they have been through."

Henry only shrugged. "Maybe. I heard the patients at the city hospital were abandoned to drown. A feller name of Sherwood happened by in a boat and took the poor wretches over to Dr. Morse's new hospital at Third and K." He shook his head sadly. "I guess some of 'em are in pretty bad shape, and likely to die from the chill they took."

"That's a shame. I'm sure Dr. Morse will do all he can to save them. That lovely new hospital! I hope it's a sturdy building."

Henry grinned. "I hear they pay $1500 a month in rent. The building cost Priest & Lee $15,000 to build. You could build a better barn back home for about $2,000, but costs out here are outrageous. I'll bet the fancy bleached muslin they lined the walls with is ruined. They'll never get all of this smelly muck out of them."

"At least they have a second story. I'm sure Dr. Morse is thanking himself for his foresight."

That very gentleman made his appearance later on that afternoon. "Miss MacKenzie," Dr. Morse said, bowing over her hand. "I have come to ask you a favor. I had so hoped you survived the deluge in good health. In addition to my regular patients, and every ill person who presents himself at my door (or window, in this case), I have taken in a number of wretches from the city hospital. Many of them were left in an unspeakable condition. They need nursing care. There are so few women in the city, and they are in no condition to help, most of them having children to care for."

He sighed. "So many have appeared at our window, begging us to take them in, or at least to store their valuables for them We take in only the sick, however, but none of those are turned away. Thank heavens Dr. Stillman has joined me. He tried his hand at mining, but, like many others, has found it is better for a man to do that for which he has the training and talents." He smiled ruefully. "But I digress. Could I persuade you to come with me, for a day or so at least? Most of the poor creatures will probably die, but I would like to see them at least comfortable during their last hours."

Katlin hesitated. "But I have no nursing experience."

"All they need is bathing and someone to ladle some soup down their throats. Dr. White is out of town, or he would never have allowed them to get into such a state. I especially need you for one poor lady. She is the only female patient we have, and we have partitioned her off in one corner to give her some privacy, poor soul, but she needs a woman's care. Please come."

"Has she no family?" Katlin felt her resistance weakening.

"Widow lady," he replied, shaking his head sadly. "Lost her husband on the trip out across the plains. Has been supporting herself baking pies, but got flooded out, and then took sick."

"Go ahead, Miss MacKenzie," Henry urged her. "Sounds like they really need you. I'll stay here with Elena and our belongings. They'll be safe, I promise."

Katlin shrugged. What could she do except go with the doctor? "Okay, I'll try," she said, after a moment more of hesitation, during which Dr. Morse looked more anxious than ever.

The doctor sighed with relief when she finally nodded her consent. "Oh, thank you, Miss MacKenzie. I have a boat waiting to take us back."

Nothing in Katlin's life had prepared her for the sight that greeted her as Dr. Morse assisted her out of the boat into the upper story of his hospital. The garret was one big room, with two half windows on the sides and a full window at each end. It was the front of these two windows through which they disembarked. A sheet partitioned off one corner. Up to forty men lay shivering on the floor. Only a few were covered with dry blankets. One old man raved, wailing out words unintelligible to Katlin.

She crossed the rough boards to his side and knelt to smooth the tangled hair back from his forehead. His eyes focused and he looked into her face.

"Gabriel, I'm comin'," he muttered. "Here's an angel I see."

"Shh," she soothed. "I'm not an angel. I'm Miss Mac-Kenzie, and I've come to help Dr. Morse get you well."

Her glance took in the enormity of his condition. The filthy clothes were little more than rags. He was so thin his hip bones protruded from his trousers, every rib plainly visible where his shirt lay open. He shivered with cold, and the smell from his clothing told her he also suffered from dysentery. He reeked of urine. He had evidently lain helpless for some time.

Katlin rose and approached Dr. Morse. "We need dry sheets and blankets, and I need a basin for water so I can clean this poor old man up."

"I have hired a boatman to take my partner, Dr. Higgins, around the city to bring me all the dry blankets and clean linen he can find. Do the best you can until he returns. I hope he is speedy, for not only do we need the supplies, the owner of the wretched boat is charging me thirty dollars an hour."

Katlin remembered the two cases of blankets she had been forced to leave behind at *MacKenzie's Mercantile*. Forget it, she told herself grimly. They are probably halfway to San Francisco by now. She thought of the boxes and barrels she had seen floating by their place of refuge. No one seemed to pay any attention. With all the splashing and playing around in the water she had observed, she felt someone could have made some effort to retrieve at least some of the merchandise.

A fair-haired young man of about thirty approached with a smile. Dr. Morse introduced them.

"My partner, Dr. Jacob Stillman, Miss MacKenzie."

Dr. Stillman bowed over Katlin's hand. "So kind of you to offer to assist us, Miss MacKenzie." He grinned wryly. "We have many offer to work with us, but they all wish to be paid. Since most of these poor wretches will probably never pay a bill, we would be hard pressed to hire any more help. Bad enough we pay $300 a month for the apothecary and $250 for the cook."

"I had no idea there was so much sickness," Katlin frowned, appalled to think how isolated from the community she had allowed herself to become. "I have been so busy running my store . . . " her voice trailed off.

"Oh, yes, do not feel badly. You are not alone," Dr. Stillman advised her. "Many people have no concept of the suffering that surrounds their city. I spent two months in a vain search for my fortune in the yellow metal, and learned a great deal about conditions. Hundreds are encamped with nothing more than a flimsy tent for shelter, with only scanty supplies, not nearly enough to keep them properly fed. Many of those begging for employment were driven from the mines by hunger. Overwork and bad food contribute to the problem as well, not to mention disappointment and homesickness. So many came with such high hopes."

Katlin thought of Caleb. Would he be among those driven from the mines by the weather and starvation? She looked over the wretched mass of humanity, half fearing she might find him among their numbers. What would she do if she did? With relief, she realized none of the poor souls huddled on the floor shivering looked familiar to her.

She shrugged off her thoughts and returned to the old man's side. He had lapsed into unconsciousness, and she could get no response from him. His breathing became shallow and rapid, and his lips took on a bluish hue.

Tears streaming down her cheeks as memories of her father's death threatened to overcome her, Katlin held the old man's hand and stroked his forehead until the breathing stopped.

Dr. Morse patted her shoulder. "I'm sure he died happier, knowing you were with him, Miss MacKenzie. It is a terrible thing to die alone."

"What are you going to do with his body? There's no way we can bury him."

"We sew the remains of those who die up in blankets and submerge them in the water on the first floor."

"What?" Katlin's face registered her horror.

Dr. Morse shrugged. "What choice do we have?"

Katlin shook her head and walked to the corner where the lone woman lay. She knelt by the woman's bed and took her hand.

The eyes opened slowly, and a faint smile hovered on the woman's lips. "Thank you for coming," she whispered. "Dr. Morse said he knew of a lady who might come to help. I'll die easier, knowing there's a woman who will tend to my . . . my . . . ." the voice faded into silence.

Katlin smiled. "Hush. No more talk of dying. You have to get well to help me with all of these men."

A soft chuckle was her reward.

Two days later, two of the men from Dr. White's hospital had recovered sufficiently to be moved out of the hospital to higher ground, and the rest had died. Katlin, numbed by so much tragic death, for some of the men had been very young, accompanied Dr. Stillman on one of the burying expeditions. The doctor hired a whale boat for $40.00, and they took three of the bodies.

"Are you sure you wish to go with the men, Miss MacKenzie?" Dr. Morse looked concerned. "It will not be a pleasant task."

"I don't expect it to be." But, she thought, if I don't get out of this charnel house and get a breath of fresh air, I'm going to start screaming. Not wishing to tell him her real reason, she just smiled and said. "I feel I owe it to the men to be present as they are laid to rest." It was not really a lie, since she also felt obligated to go since none of those who died seemed to have anyone else. It would be a terrible thing to be buried with no one present who really cared.

The boatmen found a patch of ground above water close to Mr. Sutter's abandoned fort. There they dug a large grave under a majestic oak tree, using an axe to free a gigantic root. The cross-shaped root formed a ready made marker. After the three bodies were laid in the pit, Katlin murmured a little prayer as the grave was filled in. The root was driven into the ground to mark the spot.

"And we have no idea who they were, or any way to notify their families," Katlin sighed as Dr. Stillman helped her back into the boat for the return trip.

"Unfortunately, no," he agreed. "But we have done the best we could for them."

Katlin shrugged in resignation. "I suppose you're right." She looked back at the grave, covered with the soft green sod. Such a beautiful day! Meadowlarks and blackbirds surrounded them, filling the air with song. A flock of geese fed on a nearby knoll. Somehow, the beauty of the day and the beauty of the spot chosen for their final resting place seemed to lessen the sadness.

That evening, she watched Dr. Morse pour a little brandy in his ink as he sat at his desk writing. Puzzled, she asked him why he did so.

He laughed. "To give spirit to my letter, Miss MacKenzie."

"What?"

He laughed again. "Dr. Stillman puts laudanum in his ink, to still any apprehensions his letter may awaken in those who read it."

Katlin shook her head and went to bed. She lay on her blanket on the hard floor for a long time, listening to the howling of a dog who had been abandoned by his master. Somehow, the mournful sound seemed an appropriate way to end the day.

By the following morning, the water had receded enough to expose the first floor. There they found four barrels of pork, one of beef, and a case of wine. Dr. Higgins laughed as he broke open the case of wine and held aloft one of the bottles. "Providence has repaid us for the support we gave to so many destitute people with this small contribution to our depleted larder."

Katlin laughed. "I don't see any merchandise from *Mac-Kenzie's Mercantile*, so I am going to assume my work has been sufficient reward for my room and board for the past days."

"More than sufficient, Miss MacKenzie. Your assistance has proved invaluable."

"Thank you, Dr. Higgins. I'll remember that should I require your assistance in the future."

He grinned and popped the cork from the bottle. "Here's to your continued good health." He took a swig from the bottle. "Good journey to you."

That afternoon, Dr. Morse returned Katlin to Johnson's Building.

"I cannot thank you enough, Miss MacKenzie," he enthused. "Your very presence made the last moments of those men so much easier." He bowed over her hand after she alighted from the boat. "If you ever wish to seek employment as a nurse, I would be most pleased to have you."

"Thank you," Katlin smiled, thinking if she never had to go through that experience again she would be forever thankful. "I think I will stick to *MacKenzie's Mercantile*."

Henry and Elena greeted her with enthusiasm. Elena looked at Katlin closely, taking in the lines of fatigue on her face and the bedraggled clothing she wore. The girl frowned with concern.

"You look the tired. You have work very hard, no?"

"Yes," Katlin replied grimly. "We only managed to save two of the poor wretches that were abandoned at Dr. White's hospital. How anyone could let their patients get into such a miserable condition I will never understand. Fortunately, many of the others were not nearly so bad off. The one lady recovered sufficiently to take my place, thank heavens."

She shook her head and changed the subject. "The sun has been out for two days now. The first floor of Dr. Morse's hospital is already below the water level, but I think he's on a little higher ground than we are. Is the water beginning to recede? Can we check to see if we still have a store?"

"By tomorrow we should be able to tell."

Katlin pulled off her boots and stretched out on her blanket. "Wake me up when it's tomorrow."

# Chapter 29

Elena PULLED a blanket over Katlin's shoulders and tucked it around her carefully. "You sleep, or you, too, will be sick. My Henry and I, we will keep the guard, yes?"

"Yes," Katlin murmured, half asleep the moment she lay her head on the folded blanket. She had been working so hard for so long she had not realized how exhausted she had become until she stopped. "Sleep. I feel like I could sleep for a week."

The next morning, Katlin and Henry left Elena with their belongings and descended the stairs to the street. They emerged from the building into sunshine so brilliant it hurt Katlin's eyes.

"Thank goodness the water is finally going down," Katlin sighed. She tried to ignore the body of a mule just emerging from the receding water in the middle of the street, envisioning the smells and disease that would result from all the animal carcasses that surely would appear as the water receded.

"Water's not all the way down yet, but we should be able to see if there's anything left. Be careful." Henry took her arm and guided her to the shallowest spots along their route. In a few minutes, they had their answer. The walls had collapsed, but the canvas roof lay over what must have been the interior. Streams of water ran between what appeared to be either crates or parts of the walls.

Katlin surveyed the tangled mass in mute dismay.

Beside her, Henry broke the silence. "Looks like most of it's still there. Gonna be a lot of work, diggin it out."

Katlin sighed. "What a mess!" She shook her head. "The water has to go lower before we can start. Let's go back and get some food. I suspect we're going to need all the strength we can get."

Three days elapsed before the water receded from the wrecked remains of *MacKenzie's Mercantile* sufficiently to allow them to begin the onerous chore of clearing the debris. They began by trying to scrape the mud from the top of the canvas.

"We'll never get the smell out of this," Henry advised Katlin. "Better figure on new canvas."

"No," she said firmly. "We're going to rebuild with brick, and we're going to have a second story. As much as I hate the idea, we will do it even if I have to borrow the money."

The following morning they returned to the site to continue their labors. The sun again shone with a brilliant radiance, sending diamond sparkles across the remaining puddles of water. The beauty of the day almost belied the destruction that it so clearly portrayed. All around them lay the ruins of the city. Lines of green slime at eye level on the side of the building told her how high the water had risen.

Katlin sighed. "If it only didn't smell so bad." She could not describe the odor. More than outhouse or dead animal, instead, a sickly sweet smell of decay.

About noon, as Katlin and Henry toiled among the ruins of the store, Colin rode up, accompanied by Michael.

Katlin looked up at Colin, and their eyes met. Colin said nothing for a long moment, just sat on his horse shaking his head.

Michael, in his thick Irish brogue, murmured, "Oh, my, oh, my, oh my, and what a mess. Who'd 'a believed a little water could do so much!"

Colin grimaced. "More than a little water, I fear, if the amount running down the Cosumnes was any indication." He smiled at Katlin and she felt her knees weaken. "We came to see if we could be of any assistance."

Katlin laughed shakily, struggling to keep the tears at bay. "As you can probably see, we can use all the help we can get."

Colin and Michael pitched in, and the job of cleaning went quickly. Colin sent Michael to round up some able-bodied assistants, and soon a dozen men grasped the edges of the sodden canvas and peeled it off, revealing the destruction beneath.

The little stove lay on its side. Henry hastened to set it upright on its sturdy little legs again.

"Stove's fine, Miss MacKenzie," he assured Katlin. "Little elbow grease to polish off the rust and it'll be as good as new."

The beds and the little table had collapsed, and lay in a tangled mass of mud and debris. With a sigh, Katlin lifted one corner of a sodden blanket out of a case. The smell again threatened to overwhelm her, and she dropped the blanket back into the case. "We may as well discard them. We'll never get the stench out." Tears filled her eyes as she viewed the destruction.

Colin patted her arm in sympathy and said in a gentle voice, "It's a mess, I know, but remember, I took a lot of your merchandise with me, and it's safely stored. In fact," he grinned, "it takes up about half the space in my house." Putting his hands on her shoulders, he met her eyes. "I think a general store would be a good investment. Could I lend you the money to re-build?"

Katlin shook her head. "Remember Mr. Shakespeare's advice, 'neither a borrower nor a lender be?' What if I can't re-pay you?"

"Very well, then. Let's do it this way. If I got a crew over here to erect a two-story brick building to house your establishment, would you consider a fifty-fifty partnership? I know you have the skill to make the store a success, and I think you could give me a good return on my investment. Is that better?"

Katlin almost choked. Partnership? Return on investment? Can't you say you want to help me because you love me? Apparently not, She smiled brightly, hope flaring anew within her. At least they would have a sturdy building and be back in business. She held out her hand to Colin.

"Put her there, Partner. You've just made a deal."

"Hear, hear," Henry proclaimed. "Here's to the re-birth of *MacKenzie's Mercantile* and to the success of the new partnership." He held up an undamaged bottle of Mr. Walker's champagne, wiped it off on his shirt, and popped the cork. The effervescent wine bubbled over the lip of the bottle. "Sorry there aren't any glasses." He offered the bottle to Katlin.

Laughing, she took a sip and passed the bottle to Colin. From Colin, it went to Henry, then to Michael, and the bargain was sealed.

Three weeks later, Katlin and Colin stood side by side and watched the workers hoist the new sign into place. The sign on the two story brick building that had risen almost like magic from the ruins of the first store proclaimed to the world that *MacKenzie's Mercantile* was again open for business. Michael watched from the seat of the cart he had driven, the back laden with crates of merchandise for the newly reopened store.

"Are you sure you don't want the sign to read MacKenzie and MacDougal?" She had offered to share the name, but he shook his head.

"I prefer, Miss MacKenzie, to remain a silent partner." He

grinned suddenly. "Besides, by providing the building, I can finally move your boxes out of my parlor!"

Elena and Henry, delighted with the new building, and the idea of private living quarters on the second floor, had eagerly awaited its completion. The three of them had taken up residence as soon as the floor had been laid, putting up a tent for Katlin and Elena while Henry slept under the stars until the carpenters finished the roof. They had not wished to impose on Mr. Johnson's hospitality any longer than necessary, and were eager to be away from the crowds of people.

"I just hope this building doesn't topple in the next flood like several others did in the last one," Katlin observed with a touch of irony. "I trust someone is trying to do something to keep the city from flooding again."

Henry laughed. "If Hardin Bigelow has his way, we'll be protected by a series of levees. He's been out working on them himself, and persuading as many to help him as he can. He's been in the saddle night and day to keep the work going. I understand he's even resorted to threats to get men to work for him."

"Well, I certainly hope he's successful," Katlin responded with a heavy sigh. "I'd hate to go through another week like that again, especially so soon after the last one."

Colin grinned. "You're going to get your money back quick, with this box right here." He patted the case of Colt revolvers on the back of the cart. "I hear these are going for seventy-five dollars apiece."

"Seventy-five dollars! Apiece?" Katlin gasped. "Why, that's five times what I paid for them. Are you sure?"

"I'm sure. One of your competitors has one in his front window for sale for just that sum. And he'll get it, too. Just appreciate your good fortune," Colin advised. "The gun has gotten quite popular, and most of the merchants lost their merchandise. The ones that managed to save some, like *MacKenzie's Mercantile*, can charge pretty much whatever they want. I can't say how long it will last, but enjoy the boom while you can."

Katlin laughed merrily. "We'll re-open tomorrow," she avowed, "and with a special on Colt revolvers for only seventy dollars!"

"I knew I invested wisely," Colin chuckled. "Your business sense far exceeds mine." He twisted his mouth wryly. "I'm afraid this has not been a good year for farming. Half of my fields are under water, and the other half are so sodden that I can't get on them to plant. And they are predicting more flooding as soon as the snow melts on the Sierras."

"Oh, I hope not," Elena cried. "I do not like the water."

"I just hope Mr. Bigelow gets his levees built in time," Katlin said fervently.


Colin helped Michael unload the cases of merchandise into the storage room in the back of the new building, and took his leave of the little group. As he looked back to wave once more before turning the corner, he had to admit he missed the camaraderie the four of them had shared on the trip from New Orleans. And Miss MacKenzie? He could not help feeling she wanted them to be more than friends, but he kept remembering his first impressions, that some passion had driven her to California.

He sighed. Until she resolved that passion, whatever it was, there would be no place for him in her life. And if she did? What do you really want, Colin MacDougal? Do you want to love again and risk repeating the loss you suffered at Michelle's death? He wondered, guilt washing over him. Could he ever get a woman with child again, knowing perhaps it would be his child who killed her, as his son had killed Michelle?

He did not notice his horse moved slower and slower until Michael pulled the cart up beside him and waved cheerfully. "And it's a fine building ye've built for the lass, Mr. MacDougal. And she's a good head on her shoulders. She'll do well by ye."

He eyed Colin shrewdly. "Aye, and a good looking lass she is, too. Lady through and through, she is, I'll wager, or I'll never touch another drop of good Irish whiskey."

Colin had to laugh at Michael's shrewdness. "You're right. It's a fine lady she is." He exhaled a long, heart-felt sigh and shook his head. "We'll just have to give her some time."

# *Chapter 30*

The CITY SPRANG UP around them again with re-markable rapidity. A few weeks after the raging waters had disappeared, tents and canvas houses quickly gave way to large and commodious buildings and stores.

"I guess we're not the only ones determined to have a second story the next time the river goes over its banks," Katlin remarked as they watched the activity about them.

By mid-February, stage lines had opened throughout all of the valleys to service the mining camps. The town erupted in a frenzy of parties, bull-fights, horse races, and theatrical shows.

One evening, towards the end of February, Katlin and Henry sat upstairs in their snug dining area after supper. Elena had taken the dishes downstairs to wash. Having the pantry and dish cabinets upstairs created extra work, but Katlin wanted to be able to live comfortably upstairs should the river flood again.

"It seems they are almost trying to deny that such a thing as the flood ever existed." Katlin shook her head. "Don't they realize another couple of weeks will bring the snow melt down and we could be flooded again?"

"Hardin Bigelow is still trying to convince many of these fools that a levee is the only way. Most of them are from the North, or the Atlantic seaboard, and know nothing about that type of a construction. They just make fun of him, but give him credit – he is persisting." He shook his head grimly.

"But those squatters are going to cause trouble yet. Charles Robinson built another house on the bank, down at Front and I Street. Sam Brannan just tore it down again. They had a big meeting over land titles back in December, just before the flood, but the flood only slowed the issue down. Going to be trouble, there is, mark my words."

"Oh, I'm sure they'll settle it somehow. After all, Captain Sutter has abandoned his fort and moved up on the Feather River. Maybe it'll just all die down."

Henry shrugged. "Maybe," he said, his voice expressing the doubt in his mind. "We'll hope so."

The rain began again in March. Katlin thanked heaven, and Colin, that they had a sturdy roof over their heads.

Henry came through the front door shaking the water off of his poncho. "Coming down in buckets," he declared. "Sloughs are already starting to rise." He looked around the room. "Mr. Bigelow is like a madman, driving his crews, but I think we might do well to get our merchandise up on the second floor."

"You're probably right," Katlin nodded. "We are certainly better prepared to face a flood now than we were in January. Let's start with the things in the storeroom."

A cold wind whistled, driving the chill through the building. Katlin, shivering, wrapped her shawl tighter and urged Henry to put on another sweater.

"Elena is upstairs huddled by the little Topsy stove. She is fretting that you might take a chill. You've been doing so well lately, I think she is afraid you might lose what you have gained."

"I really do feel great, Miss MacKenzie," Henry said, his face lighting up. "Maybe what they say about California climate is right."

"I suspect, since this has been such a wet winter, that good food and rest have probably done you more good than the climate. But whatever it is, we want you to keep on improving."

"Do you really think I might get well?" the boy asked, so wistfully that the hope in his voice wrung Katlin's heart. "Do folks ever get well from the consumption? I mean, *really* well?"

Katlin laughed to hide the pain she felt. "We'll have to pose that question to Dr. Morse the next time we see him. I do believe he thinks it possible. So I don't want you exhausting yourself lugging cases up the stairs. Go out and find a couple of those loafers that hang out by the Round Club and tell them we'll give them a dollar apiece and supper to do it for us."

As Henry headed for the door, she added, "And go by Mr. McGuire's Iron Works. See if you can get him to sell us a metal door and some shutters for a decent price. If that river does go over, I think a good, sturdy door would be a good thing to have, and if we cover the windows, it should help keep the water out."

The boy grinned. "You're probably right. I'll see what kind of prices I can get him to give us."

By the time the river really threatened to flood the city again, in the middle of March, Katlin was ready. The heavy iron door and shutters were in place, and all of her extra stores were stowed on the second floor. She kept just a few of each item of merchandise on display so everything could be quickly moved upstairs should the need arise.

The next morning, the cloud cover vanished and the sun came out. Katlin's spirits rose with the sun. Maybe they would be spared another flooding. The bright sunshine encouraged her, even though, as she looked across at the sun sparkling on the distant Sierras, she realized the sun on the mountains would melt the snow just as fast as rain.

James Stolles appeared with yet another packet from Malcolm with more gold dust. He greeted Katlin and Elena

cheerfully. "River's gonna go over again, she is," he announced. "The side rivers are risin' all up and down both
the Sacramento and the American. And both are already at
flood stage with all the melt water comin' down."

"We've got our fingers crossed, hoping Mr. Bigelow's levees will hold the water out of the city," Katlin said. "But,"
she added with a little chuckle, "we have moved all of our
extra stores upstairs just in case. It's not that we have no
faith in the levees, but we're not going to be caught like we
were in January."

Elena set a piece of apple pie in front of Mr. Stolles and
he sighed with pleasure. "Sure do miss your pie, Miss Elena,
when the weather keeps me in the camps an' won't let me
get into the City."

Every time Mr. Stolles appeared on his deliveries, it had
been on the tip of Katlin's tongue to ask if he met Caleb in
his travels. He would be in a good position to know, since
he covered most of the camps and had ample opportunity
to meet most of the men.

Each time she resisted the impulse for two logical rea-
sons. One, she had no idea what last name Caleb used,
since he seemed to change it frequently. Two, she had no
desire for anyone to know she sought him, not wanting to
have to make any explanations. If Mr. Stolles started asking for anyone fitting Caleb's description, it would arouse
curiosity, if nothing else. And if Caleb heard someone was
looking for him?

She kept telling herself she would have to make the effort
to find him some day, or she would never be able to close
that episode. After all, her whole purpose in coming to California was to find him. He had stolen her entire inheritance.
Could she just let him get away with it? And what about the
poor widow he duped? And the others who would no doubt
one day become his victims, since the procedure seemed to
work so well for him. Could she abandon her search after

coming this far?

The practical side of her rose up and told her the best course might be to forget the whole affair and just get on with her life. What could she do if she did find him? There was no law to speak of in California, and it would be her word against his.

But what if she did forget about searching for Caleb? If Colin asked her to marry him, could she agree without knowing whether or not Caleb would reappear? And what if he should show up on her doorstep one day? He did not know she knew of his duplicity. He could claim her as his wife. She would have no way of proving anything. She could be accused of bigamy.

She saw Mr. Stolles watching her closely. Not wanting him to guess at the turmoil that raged within her, she asked about Malcolm's health and fortune.

"That one's a worker, let me tell you. Seems to be good for him, too. Must be a tough one, the hours he puts in. Claim keeps on producing, though, and he keeps on paying me to bring his stash down to you." Stolles shrugged. "My business has been fallin' off since the stages now go to most of the camps, but Malcolm, he says he trusts me. So do some of the other fellers, so I guess I can keep goin' for a while." He rose to his feet with a grin. "I'll keep doin' it long as it pays. Sure beats grubbin' for gold."

Katlin nodded, thinking of the preacher turned monte dealer. "Many have found easier ways to get it than to dig for it. At least, your way is honest."

He finished his pie and wiped his sleeve across his mustache to dislodge the bits of apple and crust clinging there. "Got to get outta town before the river goes over. Your letter ready?"

"Give Malcolm my regards," she said, handing the man the packet. "I've told him if digging for gold ever palls, he is welcome here. We could certainly use a good worker!"

*   *   *

After Stolles departed, a young woman barely out of her teens entered. She glanced around the room, and exclaimed, "Maggie was right! This god-forsaken hell-hole really *does* have a decent store with a lady to talk to."

Katlin, a little startled at the girl's language, smothered her impulse to laugh, and greeted her cordially. Her youthful exuberance was like a breath of fresh air. "I am glad your informant was correct. How may I help you?"

"I need some fine linen, preferably a lawn, to make myself some new chemises and drawers. How can I explain that to a man?"

"How, indeed," Katlin laughed. "I have some very fine lawn which fortunately did not get washed down the river in the January floods, and some of the latest patterns. I even have needles and thread and such if you are in need of notions."

"I certainly am. We came across in a wagon last fall, from Missouri, and Pa wouldn't let us bring hardly anything. I smuggled my little etui in with my stockings, but I am almost out of thread. And I haven't a single hook and eye." She extended a hand. "Jenny MacFarland."

"A fellow Scot," Katlin grinned and they shook hands. I might have known, Katlin thought. Blue eyes and blonde hair like ours come only from Scotland. "Katlin MacKenzie," she returned. "Welcome to Sacramento. Where are you living?"

"Pa's got himself a spread out close to Jared Sheldon's place, on the Rancho Omochumnes land grant Mr. Sheldon got back in '44, before the Americans overran the place. Nobody's said he's got no claim to it, like the problems other folks have had. He's been selling some of it, I guess figuring to get a little money out while he can." She chuckled. "At least we were above the water when the floods came.

Mr. Sheldon, he's talking about building a dam on the Cosumnes River, to keep it from flooding and to give some
water for irrigation in the summer. Problem is, that would
flood some of the miners off their claims, so they object."

She laughed merrily. "I'll let the men argue that one out.
My main complaint with the place is that there's nothing out
there, to speak of. The little store doesn't have any decent
yard goods at all. Mr. Daylor has a little store, runs it with
goods he buys from Mr. Brannan here in Sacramento, but
when all the miners came, they found they could make more
money running cattle up into the camps to sell, so he's talking about closing the store.. So as soon as the rain stopped,
I borrowed Pa's horse and rode in."

"Alone?"

"Oh, no, Pa insisted on sending one of my brothers in
with me, but I made him wait outside. He grumbled a bit,
because he wanted to go see some of the sights, but I told
him I'd tell Pa if he wasn't there when I got done shoppin'.
I'd have been here sooner, but my friend Maggie just told
me about you havin' this place here last week."

Katlin smiled. "I had hoped word would spread. I guess
it has. As more and more ladies come to California, I plan
to make *MacKenzie's Mercantile* the store they choose to
patronize."

"Well, I'll be back, you can bet on it. And I'll tell all
the other ladies. Any I see, that is. Not a lot of ladies
around where we are. Of course, there is Mr. Sheldon's
wife, Catharine, and her sister Sarah as married Mr. Sheldon's friend Mr. Daylor." She fondled the ecru lawn and
lifted the bolt to her cheek to savor its softness. "I'll take the
whole bolt." She looked about. "I trust you have more?"

"Oh, yes. The bulk of my stores are upstairs, in case Mr.
Bigelow's levees don't keep the river in check."

Jenny laughed merrily. "Very good," she approved. "Did
you lose a lot in the floods in January?"

"Not as much as I could have." She really is a delightful girl, Katlin thought. I hope we see her often. "A friend stored a number of cases of my merchandise at his home until the flood passed." Her heart missed a beat as she thought of Colin. She tried to keep her face from betraying her reaction.

The girl looked at her shrewdly, but only said, "He must be a *good* friend. The floods, now, they were terrible. Mr. Daylor, he runs a ferry so folks can cross the river to get to his little store, and his brother-in-law, Sebastian - - Sebastian, oh, I forget his last name, anyway. He was real young, and got washed off the ferry and drowned. Real sad." She returned to her inspection of Katlin's merchandise. "I'll take this bolt of damask as well. It's been so long since we had a decent cloth on the table my brothers are forgetting their table manners."

When Jenny waved goodbye and turned her horse towards the east, her brother trailing along behind her obediently with the laden saddlepacks, Katlin stood at the doorway and waved back. She felt refreshed. Jenny was one of those people who brought sunshine wherever she went.

A week later, Henry came for her. "You have to see this, Miss MacKenzie. Come on. Elena, watch the store for a little while."

Katlin followed Henry to the wharf area. Boats tied at the docks strained to escape their dock lines as the river tore at them. The current raced past, the furiously churning waters carrying debris from the size of twigs to whole logs. Foaming waves doubled back on themselves as the raging turmoil tore at the banks on both sides. As Katlin watched, a huge chunk of soil tore loose from the opposite side and fell into the river, carrying a large sycamore tree with it. In seconds, the whole tossing mass disappeared.

"Scary, isn't it," Henry grinned as Katlin watched the raging torrent in a mixture of horror and fascination. "Anyone fall into that, they'd be a goner. But this is what I wanted you to see." He led her to a built-up embankment. "This is one of Mr. Bigelow's levees. He's got half a dozen blocking the spots where the river went over the banks in January. And, so far, they've held back the water."

"I certainly hope they continue to do so," Katlin murmured with a shudder. Turning away, she tried to shut out the sound of the turbulent water.

"So do a lot of folks," Henry said. "There's even talk of electing him mayor if he does succeed in saving the city."

Henry told Katlin the results of the voting a week later when he brought her a copy of the April 1 edition of the *Sacramento Transcript*. He quoted from the paper in his hand. "'Today a grateful citizenry thanked Mr. Harden Bigelow for his services to the community by electing him the first mayor of Sacramento City.'" He chuckled. "Since his levees were a success and the city didn't flood again, the 'grateful citizenry' forgot all about the scorn they heaped on him while he was trying to get 'em built."

He gave her the paper with a grin. "Here you are, Miss MacKenzie. First edition of a brand new newspaper. Mr. Fitch, Mr. Upham, and a couple of others started it up as a rival to the *Placer Times*. Say they're going to publish three times a week instead of just once like the *Times* does. Say Sacramento needs news oftener than once a week."

Katlin perused the paper. "It does seem to be well written and well edited, I will give it that. Can Sacramento support two papers?"

"I understand you can buy a fifth interest in it for $5000.00, if you're interested in supporting it."

Katlin laughed. "No, thank you. I'll stick to what I know." She continued to scan down the pages, then gasped.

"Henry! Listen to this." She read the announcement aloud, "Valuable Negro girl, age 18, bound by indentures for two years, amiable disposition, good washer, ironer, and cook. For particulars, apply Vanderbilt Hotel. J.R. Harper." She looked up. "That poor girl. She must be frightened out of her wits, being offered for sale in this lawless land with all of these men. And we have been saying we need someone to help with the household chores, especially the heavier work like washing and ironing." Katlin did not say so, but she detested ironing.

The boy looked puzzled. "I thought you didn't hold with slavery."

"I don't, of course, but see, if we get her, we can set her free. And then we can hire her to help with the work around here."

"What if she wants to go home after you tell her she's free?"

"Back to the South, where she'd be a slave? I doubt that."

Henry shrugged in resignation. "Whatever you say, Miss MacKenzie."

"Go to the Vanderbilt and talk to Mr. Harper."

# Chapter 31

"THIS IS CELIE, Miss MacKenzie."

Katlin turned at Henry's voice and came face to face with one of the most beautiful girls she had ever seen in her life. Large brown eyes met hers, the smile showed white, even teeth in a heart-shaped face with smooth skin the color of coffee with lots of cream. A quadroon, Katlin thought.

She returned the girl's smile and took both of the work-roughened hands in hers. "Welcome, Celie. We'd be happy if you would come to work for us. There's far more than we can do by ourselves, and decent help is so hard to find."

"Henry here paid off my indentures to Mr. Harper, ma'am. I'd be grateful iffen you'd take me in. I got nowhere to go. Mr. Harper, he . . . he . . . " she hesitated. "He wanted me for a while, then he said I wuz a nuisance, and he wanted to be shed of me. I wuz skeered when Henry come, but he told me you was a fine lady, and would treat me right." She offered Katlin a shy smile.

"All she's got is what she's wearin', Miss MacKenzie," Henry growled. "Harper said he didn't hold with pampering, so he never gave her anything more."

"You poor child," Katlin exclaimed. "Well, we have a whole store full of yard goods and patterns. I think your first job will be to get yourself something decent to wear." She laughed. "Would not speak well for *MacKenzie's Mercantile* if the help is not decently clad!"

Three days later, on April 4, 1850, Katlin awoke to the loud clanging of the alarm bell. She jumped from bed and dressed as fast as possible, calling for Henry. They met in the hall. Elena, still in her nightdress with her robe pulled about her, followed at his heels, crying *"Que es, que es?"*

"We don't know yet. There is no threat of flood. It must be a fire. Come on." She hurried down the stairs and headed for the front door, Elena and Henry following closely behind. Smoke rose high into the sky from the direction of the river, and the scent of smoke filled the air.

"Seems to be several blocks from here," Henry commented. "Must be down on Front Street. With a brick building like we've got, not much danger from fire, but I'd better go check. You ladies stay here." Henry ran toward the billowing smoke.

Elena wept as his figure rounded a building and disappeared from sight. *"Vaya con Dios, mi amor,"* she murmured, crossing herself.

They waited, watching the column of smoke anxiously. Flames shot above the surrounding rooftops. Elena clung to Katlin, weeping in fright.

"My Henry, he will be burned," she sobbed.

"Hush, of course he won't be burned. I'm sure he has sense enough to stay away from the flames." I hope, Katlin thought. And all of this smoke has to be bad for his lungs. He has been feeling so well lately I think he is forgetting to be careful.

Soot drifted down on them as the air thickened, covering their hair and their clothing, making breathing harder. After what seemed an interminable length of time, and just as Katlin began to think she and Elena should retreat to the safety of *MacKenzie's Mercantile*, Henry returned. Elena threw herself into his arms and wept with relief.

"Don't cry, my sweet. I never got within half a block of the fire. I just smell like this because of all of the smoke. The men that formed that new Mutual Hook and Ladder Company proved their mettle. That fire engine of theirs kept the fire to eight buildings and saved the rest." He pulled his huge handkerchief from his pocket and wiped Elena's eyes. "Let's go home. After all that excitement, I'm ready for breakfast." He wiped his face with the handkerchief and looked ruefully at the ash and soot. "And a bath."

Celie settled in quickly. It took Elena a while to accept her, but after a week, Katlin heard their voices raised in song together as they washed clothes in the bright morning sunshine in back of the building.

Henry, busy unpacking a crate of china that had arrived from Mr. Walker just the day before, met Katlin's eyes. The sounds of a Negro spiritual echoed through the room. Elena picked up the words and the tune as she caught the rhythm. Her soprano harmonized with Celie's contralto.

Katlin smiled. "I'm glad they are getting along. I never dreamed how much help Celie could be. Would you believe she has finally caught up with the ironing?" With any luck, Katlin thought, I'll never have to iron again.

"Speaking of Celie reminds me. Did you hear about the case of that Southerner who brought his slave out here and put him to work in the diggings?" Henry chuckled and started stowing the packing materials back into the empty case. "Seems the Negro discovered he had rights here in California and left his master. He went off and staked his own claim to provide for himself."

"Oh, yes, I believe I heard that. The master claimed he was just passing through California on business, that he did not intend to stay, and that since he was not a resident, the Constitution guaranteed him the right to keep his slave. Did the court reach a decision?"

"Yep," Henry grinned. "Said that since the man put the Negro to work in the gold fields as soon as they arrived, he had obviously brought him here for that purpose and declared him free."

"Wonderful," Katlin chuckled. "So the Negro won. There is some justice in this demented country after all."

"And that was not the end of it. They then tried to charge the poor fellow with resisting an officer of the law because he protested when he was arrested. The Justice ruled that since the officer had no authority to arrest the man, the charge was dismissed."

"Good. And speaking of freedom, that last batch of gold Mr. Stolles brought down should be almost enough to pay off Malcolm's owner. We'll have to check to make sure, then ask Malcolm to give us the man's direction. Adams and Company can transfer it back to the States for him."

"Don't they charge ten percent?"

"Yes, but at least we know nothing will happen to it, like the steamer sinking or something."

"Or no clerk along the way deciding he needs the money more than Malcolm's owner!"


The next day, while Henry unpacked yet another crate, one filled with bolts of lace and spools of velvet ribbon, the door opened and Jenny walked in. Katlin noticed her effect on Henry. He stopped with a bolt of lace half way to the shelf and gaped. Jenny was a vision of loveliness, with her porcelain fair skin, her pert nose with its light sprinkling of freckles, the blonde curls escaping from the confines of her bonnet, her cheeks pink from the ride.

Jenny did not even notice the effect she had on Henry, but Elena, who been helping Henry unpack the crate, certainly did. Katlin stifled her impulse to laugh at the look of pure venom Elena cast in Jenny's direction. She hastened to perform the introductions.

Henry managed to find his voice enough to stammer a mumbled, "pleased to meet you." Elena remained silent.

"Oh, what lovely lace!" Jenny took the bolt from Henry's

numb fingers. "Just what I am looking for." She cast a merry glance at Katlin. "And the velvet ribbon, too." She laughed. "Would you believe this benighted country has finally produced an acceptable swain? The last batch of settlers to arrive included a young man who can not only read, he can speak like an educated man. Says he's a school teacher, and wants to open a school for the young ones."

"How wonderful for you," Katlin managed to stammer.

Jenny rattled on. "And he's taking me to the church supper this Sunday, and I wanted some lace and ribbon to make myself a new pelisse so I'll have something proper to wear. So I told my brother I had to come back here, because *MacKenzie's Mercantile* is the only place this side of San Francisco where I can get a decent bolt of lace." She held the bolt in triumph. "And here it is. I knew you would not fail me."

At this recital, Elena recovered some of her poise, and asked politely if Jenny would like a cup of tea.

"Oh, no, thank you. I have to get back, for I want to get started on my outfit. Would never do if I didn't have it ready for Sunday. And I have to bake a pie for the supper, too."

She counted out the coins, gathered her purchases, and breezed out the door. "Bye for now! I'll be back to tell you how the courtship with Mr. Cootes is progressing." She flung a merry smile back at them. "Maybe even to invite you to the wedding." The door slammed behind her and she was gone.

Henry smiled at the stunned Elena. "I think maybe I would like that cup of tea."

Katlin could no longer contain her laughter.

But even as she laughed, a sense of loneliness crept over her as thoughts of Colin washed over her mind. Jenny's happiness in a prospective suitor only made Katlin more aware of the hopelessness of her own love. Colin had not been by the store in some time. Maybe, Katlin thought, he has found someone else. But she rejected that. No, she tried to tell herself, he is probably busy planting, or clearing his fields, or building onto his house, or any of a thousand things.

But deep inside, she knew it was more than that.

# Chapter 32

BY JULY, the sun burned down upon them every day with a vengeance. The grass turned brown and crisp, and the hot air took the moisture out of everything.

"Thank heavens for the breeze from the river," Katlin panted, fanning herself with one of the fancy Oriental fans she had taken from the case Mr. Walker had sent, with the comment that folks in Sacramento had more use for fans. Remembering the chilly summer weather in San Francisco, Katlin had to agree there was probably not too great a demand.

All of the windows and doors stood open to catch even the slightest bit of cool air. The streets were quiet. The day before, the town had been filled with the sound of Fourth of July celebrations. Drunken miners had paraded up an down the streets until Henry, at Katlin's request, put out the 'Closed' sign and bolted the door.

"Probably not going to get too much business today, Miss MacKenzie," Henry chuckled. "Miners all sleeping off yesterday, and the ladies won't want to come out in all of this heat."

Suddenly, a figure filled the doorway, and they both looked up. For a moment, Katlin hesitated, then recognized the man and cried, "Malcolm!" She rushed forward with outstretched hands. "I almost didn't know you! You've filled out, and put on weight."

"Hard work will do that," he chuckled. "And not everyone starved in the mines, Miss MacKenzie. In fact, the spot where I staked my last claim has grown into quite a community of folks. Even got us a store. Buncha miners as came after I'd settled in named the place 'Timbuctoo', which they tell me is some place in Africa. I dunno, as I never had no schoolin'. But I kinda liked the idea of them namin' the town for me."

"I think it more than appropriate. Have you just come to visit, or do you plan to stay?"

"Actually," he grinned, showing his even white teeth, "I was kind of hopin' your offer of a job might still hold. Got enough gold to buy my freedom, and diggin' is mighty hard work. Claims are starting to wear out now, gold for easy pickin's about gone. Too many men, too few really good claims."

"Of course. I was just telling Henry that now we are so well established we really should have a delivery driver and handy man. I've already spoken for a small delivery cart."

"Glad you didn't get washed out in the floods. I heard it got pretty bad here in the city."

"We lost a lot, but fortunately had stored most of our goods out of town with Mr. MacDougal, so we were able to recover quickly. And, as you can see, we now have a building with a second floor, so if the river goes over again, we will be ready."

Henry chimed in with the story of the slave who had won his freedom in the courts. "So maybe you could just declare yourself free, like he did," he concluded, "and save yourself all that money."

Malcolm shook his head. "Bargain's a bargain. I told my old master I'd send him a thousand dollars in gold in return for my papers sayin' I be a free man, and that's what I'll do."

"I knew you were a man of your word," Katlin said with a smile. "We'll be proud to have you with us. We can send the money to your old master through Adams and Company. They pay $14 to $16 an ounce for dust and, for ten percent, will send the funds anywhere in the States we tell them. And you've more than enough stored here to take care of it. Maybe even have some left over." She laughed. "It seemed like every week or so Mr. Stolles was here with more bags of dust to add to your collection. In fact, so much came in that Henry began to think he should join you."

"I just sent all I had with him each time he came through. The ones as made the money were them as run the tradin' posts. The Injuns didn't have no notion what the gold wuz worth. Feller as ran the post at Parks Bar, David Parks, he'd swap the Injuns a cup of gold fer a cup of sugar. He headed back for New Orleans with over $85,000 in gold coins. Sure wish I coulda made that kinda money. But I got me enough." He set his pack on the floor and fumbled in his pocket, drawing out a worn piece of paper. "I'd sure appreciate it if you could take care o' sendin' Mr. Andrews the money, Miss MacKenzie. I've got his direction wrote here on this piece o' paper he give me when I ...."

At that moment, Celie joined them, carrying a tray laden with sparkling china. "I've finished washing these as you asked, Miss MacKenzie. Where do you want ...." Her voice trailed off as she noticed Malcolm standing in the room, staring at her as if he had seen a ghost.

Katlin smothered a smile as she introduced them. I'm a born romantic, she thought. These two are perfect for each other. And Celie could never find a better man than Malcolm. "Malcolm is going to work with us, Celie. We are going to add delivery to our services, and he can also help you with some of the heavier work."

"Yes, ma'am, I'm a right good wood chopper," Malcolm grinned as he took Celie's hand. "Year in the gold fields, a man learns to do a lot he never dreamed he'd wind up doin'. Learned how to sew on buttons and patch holes in my pants. Even bake a pretty good pan o' bread, if I do say so myself."

Katlin laughed. "You can start by cleaning out one of the storerooms upstairs so you'll have a room to sleep in. It's not luxury, but it is under a sturdy roof."

Malcolm hoisted his pack to his shoulder. "After tent livin', it'll be luxury to me. Be good to get away from the ague, too. Lotta the miners spent as much time in their blankets shiverin' with the ague as they did diggin'. That or the scurvy or the flux. But the ague seemed the worst."

"I'm afraid you won't escape it completely in Sacramento City." Katlin shook her head ruefully. "We, personally, have been fortunate, and none of us have been afflicted, but many people here in the city suffer acute attacks of the ague. In fact, I've heard some say the ague here is the worst they have ever known."

"Doc name o' Justin Gates, he's got himself a pharmacy on wheels. Moves his wagon from camp to camp, treatin' them as needs healin'. Swore by a formula o' his, he did, said it wuz the best fer the ague. Mixture o' blue pill, quinine, and oil of pepper, take it reg'lar fer three days. Did seem to help some o' them as took it."

"We'll have to remember that."

On August 14, the trouble with the squatters Henry had predicted for months erupted. Three days before, James Maloney and Charles Robinson re-instated Murphy on a lot the sheriff had removed him from previously. Sam Brannan immediately razed that building as well. They put the County Counsel and two others in jail on board the prison ship *LaGrange*, tied up at the dock, charging them with treason.

In response, forty mounted squatters led by Maloney and Robinson marched on the *LaGrange*, with the intent of freeing the prisoners.

Rumors flew. Henry came running in and told Katlin Sheriff Maloney and Mayor Bigelow planned to confront the mob.

"They'll be killed," Katlin gasped. "That big a mob, someone is bound to shoot. Is anybody doing anything to stop it?"

"I guess MacDougal has gone to San Francisco to get help."

"Our brave Lieutenant Governor ran for help instead of sending someone?"

Katlin's sarcasm was not wasted on Henry. He chuckled. "Yep. Boarded the steamer *Senator* and headed down the river. And I hear they've declared martial law in the city. Want me to go find out what's going on?"

"Absolutely not. I want you and Malcolm to stay right here. If any bullets start flying, I want to know both of you are safe."

Henry hesitated, but Malcolm grinned obediently and said, "As you wish, Miss MacKenzie. I always felt it a good idea to stay out of the way o' bullets."

A volley of shots rang out, followed by shouts and screams, then silence. Kalin rushed to the doorway, Henry and Malcolm at her heels. Elena hovered behind them. Nothing moved in the street, as far as they could see. They waited.

Finally, Dr. Stillman came by. Katlin sent Elena for lemonade for the doctor and his two companions and asked him for a report.

"A couple of the squatters were killed, including the leader, Maloney, and a number wounded. The carnage was a dreadful sight, Miss MacKenzie, men lying bleeding all over the street. Mr. Woodland was killed instantly, and Mayor Bigelow received three wounds, which we fear will be mortal."

"No!" Katlin gasped. "How could that have happened?"

"He didn't think the squatters would shoot. He wanted to talk to them, reason with them. I warned him. I know

some of those men. I knew they would shoot. I understand
Dr. Robinson was also wounded, and is hidden in a house
over on Fourth Street. Washington is acting Marshall, and
he asked me to get some help and take him, dead or alive.
We are on our way there now." He indicated the two armed
men beside him. "Robinson has done more to instigate the
problems than any other man."

"Be careful," Katlin urged. "We don't want any more
killing. And you are too valuable a man to lose in such a
silly quarrel."

He smiled and bowed over her hand. "Thank you, Miss
MacKenzie. I hope to avoid getting killed myself. And we
thank you for the delicious lemonade. In this heat, it was
most refreshing. Now, we must go, although if Dr. Robinson is wounded, I doubt he will be going anywhere." He
turned and strode off down the street, followed by his two
bodyguards.

They watched the men stride up the street, rifles swinging
at their sides. Henry shook his head grimly. "It's not over
yet."

Katlin and Henry attended the funeral of Mr. Woodland,
close to the oak tree where she and Dr. Stillman had buried
the three unfortunate souls who had died at the time of the
flood. Although she had known Mr. Woodland only slightly,
she felt since he had died in defense of the city, he had
earned their respect.

Dr. Stillman saw her standing a little apart from the
mourners and joined her.

"Why are these men so well armed for a funeral?" she
asked, concerned at seeing so much weaponry surrounding
her. She hoped nothing would occur to induce them to start
shooting.

"Because rumor said the squatters were going to bury
their dead here at the same time, so Captain Sherwood

thought it best we have an armed force. Needlessly, it would seem, for all is quiet."

"Good. I hope it stays that way."

He chuckled. "I hope so too, Miss MacKenzie. I have discovered I am a doctor, not a soldier. My knees knock together at the thought of facing an armed force. I fear I am not nearly so bold as our brave mayor."

"And how is he?"

"It appears he may recover, but he has lost his thumb, and we fear his injuries are so severe he will have to resign his position as Mayor."

"What a shame," Katlin exclaimed. "And after he saved the city from the floods, and was so conscientious about doing a good job. That's what put him in harm's way."

"And Dr. Robinson, who was heard shouting to the men to shoot the mayor, will recover from his wounds."

"I hope they hang him for murder," Katlin muttered through clenched teeth.

"I wouldn't count on it. He's got a lot of political friends. Some of the judges are on the side of the squatters. We'll have to wait and see." He shrugged his shoulders expressively. "As soon as the services for poor Mr. Woodland are over, Sheriff McKinney is taking an armed party to arrest some of the squatters said to be holed up about seven miles up the American River."

"They had better be careful."

About nine that night, shortly after Katlin had lighted the lamps and was preparing for bed, pounding echoed on the metal door at the front of the building. She heard Malcolm clamber down the stairs and cross to open it. When he did so, she recognized Dr. Stillman's voice, and hurried downstairs, pulling her robe around her as she went.

"Miss MacKenzie," the doctor greeted her. "Please, do not be alarmed. Several of us are patrolling the area to ensure no one decides to torch the city during the unrest. We only wanted to reassure you that you will be safe, that we are going to protect you."

"What unrest?" She heard a little gasp from Elena behind her.

"Colonel Kewen rushed into the Common Council meeting tonight to report that Sheriff McKinney and ten men were killed, and that reinforcements were needed, for the squatters are marching into town in force." He shook his head sadly. "I fear there will be more bloodshed."

"Sheriff McKinney killed?" Katlin sighed. "Oh, I hope not. His poor wife, such a dear little thing. She was here in the store less than a week ago." Buying material to make a new shirt for her husband for his birthday, she thought, sadly remembering the girl's bright smile as she described how she planned a surprise party. Katlin shook her head. Instead, it appears she will use the new shirt to bury him in.

"It's just rumor, so far. I have found that it is better to wait until further confirmation before anything is said to his wife." He turned to continue his rounds. "Please do not be alarmed. We have armed patrols watching every man who comes by. We will protect you."

"Thank you." Katlin turned to Elena. "Go back upstairs. Where's Celie?"

"Prob'bly hiding under the blankets," Malcolm chuckled.

Katlin laughed. "The only smart one among us. Back to bed, everyone. We'll sort this out in the morning."


The next day, a contingent of fifty troops arrived from Benicia, placing the city under martial law, and the conflict was over.

A sober Henry returned from his morning news gathering. "The rumor was partly true," he reported. "Sheriff McKinney got killed, but no one else. A man named Allen, one of the worst of the squatters, shot him, then got clean away, in spite of all the men the Sheriff had with him. Supposed to be hiding along the river somewhere, but no one can find him, wounded though they say he was." Henry gritted his teeth. "I hope he dies, the scoundrel, for killing our Sheriff."

Tears filled Katlin's eyes. "Poor man. So brave and so young. How sad for his dear little wife! We will have to attend his services. When are they to be?"

"I'll find out," he said gently. "Just be glad we got through this with as few deaths as we have."

"Yes," she agreed, "but I doubt that will be of much comfort to the Sheriff's bereaved widow."


McKinney's funeral was the largest Katlin had seen in all the time she had been in Sacramento. His widow, scarcely more than a girl, walked bravely behind the men carrying the coffin. Katlin stood where she could see her face, with her jaw set, dry-eyed, as though determined to show the world it could not defeat her.

Poor little Mrs. McKinney almost lost the battle when the first clods struck the top of the coffin as the men began filling in the grave. Katlin thought that hollow thump the most dismal sound in the world.

When one of the men raised his voice to sing 'The Old Rugged Cross', Katlin lost the battle herself. Tears ran down her cheeks at such a tragic loss of such a fine young life. The widow placed a single red rose on the top of the new mound, then rose to her feet in a daze, and walked blindly away. As she reached Katlin, their eyes met, and the girl's tears overflowed. Katlin gathered her into her arms, and the two of them wept together.

# Chapter 33

FATE LOOKED UPON them kindly for a while after everything settled down and General Winn felt safe returning his soldiers to Benicia.

"Although," Henry laughed when he reported their departure, "many of them said they would just as soon stay here. Not much life around Benicia except for the mosquitoes."

"I remember the mosquitoes very well," Katlin grimaced. "And I'm sure those young men will find Benicia quite dull after the night life here in Sacramento. I just hope the town stays quiet. We don't need any repeat of the unrest."

"Guess Robinson's still in prison, from what I hear. And Mayor Bigelow has resigned and moved to San Francisco. Says he wants to be there when the steamer comes in with the news that California has been admitted to the Union."

"Optimistic, isn't he? I'm sure all of the Southern Senators are going to be opposed. It will give Free Staters more votes than Slave Staters."

Henry shrugged. "Guess we'll have to wait and see."

The three of them looked up in surprise as Colin burst through the door. "Miss MacKenzie, Henry, Elena, are you all right? You were not injured in all the fracas?" He seized Katlin's hands. His eyes bored into hers. "I've been so busy I've paid no attention to news until Michael came from Mr. Hicks' Post Office to say that the squatters were killing everyone and burning everything." He looked around.

"Obviously that was an exaggeration, but we were understandably concerned." He dropped her hands as though just realizing he had been clinging to them.

Startled at his sudden appearance, Katlin did not quite know what to feel. She smiled to herself, her mind a jumble. *He does care for me. He just needs time to sort things out for himself. Maybe by then I'll have some news of Caleb. Maybe,* she thought, the feeling no less intense because it was mute, *I'll find out he was one of the many miners who have died of scurvy or dysentery or the ague. It would serve him right.*

"Please," she invited, getting herself back under control and remembering her manners, "come and have a cup of tea. Business is picking up, and we have hired two more helpers since you were here. Remember Malcolm?"

"Quite well," he laughed. "I remember you defending him against that Mississippi ne'er-do-well with your trusty Colt."

She shrugged, "Well, yes, I suppose you would remember that, since you came to my rescue."

"From what I noticed, my dear, you were not really in need of rescue."

"I recall being very glad to see you, however," she laughed. "Anyway, Malcolm has earned enough to pay off his old master, so we have sent the money to Mr. Andrews back in Alabama. We hope and pray the steamer that brings the news of statehood will also bring Malcolm's papers declaring him a free man."

"He's already a free man, Miss MacKenzie. The State Constitution says so."

"We tried to tell him that, but he insisted he promised his old master the thousand dollars. After all, the man did not have to give him the chance. And so we have hired him as general handyman and delivery driver."

"I suppose it speaks well for Malcolm's integrity, that he felt obligated to fulfill his promise." Colin's eyes widened as Celie entered the room. "Hello," he smiled. "And who might you be?"

Katlin smothered a chuckle, as Celie's beauty had obviously smitten Colin. "This is Celie. Celie, Mr. MacDougal, a long time friend who came with us across the Isthmus." She turned to Colin. "We paid off her indentures, and she has agreed to work for us." She removed a pile of blankets from a chair and said, "Please, sit down. Is Michael with you? You will stay for supper, won't you."

He nodded. "Yes, I will be pleased to stay for supper. I told Michael to reserve rooms for us at the Eagle, and he is off tasting the pleasures of the more decadent parts of the city. I told him I planned to spend the evening with my good friends at *MacKenzie's Mercantile*." He grinned. "After all, I had to check up on my investment, didn't I?"

They passed a pleasant evening. Elena and Celie sang while Katlin played the little harpsichord Mr. Walker had sent in one of his shipments and Elena had insisted they keep. After Colin returned to the Eagle and everyone crawled into bed, Katlin lay awake for a long time, thinking. Colin obviously cared for her. His face when he entered the store that afternoon had told her that. He had been genuinely concerned for her safety, far more than for his return on his investment.

But what would she do if he did want to expand their relationship from friendship to marriage? With the matter of Caleb still unresolved, how could she ever accept a proposal from Colin?

She turned over for what seemed to be the twentieth time, still unable to sleep. The room seemed stifling. She rose and stood by the window, letting the breeze from the delta waft over her, cooling her overheated forehead. I do hope I'm not taking a fever, she thought. The ache in her heart deepened.

Remembering the schooner she had seen wrecked on the shoals of Cape Hatteras, she thought of her reaction at the time.

"I wish you had been on that ship, Caleb Parker or Martin, or whoever you really are. I wish you were dead," she muttered to the silent room. But I have to *know*, she thought. I have to *know*.

Time passed, but it brought her no closer to a solution. Colin became a regular visitor, and the musical evenings spent together became more special. The romance she had hoped for between Celie and Malcolm blossomed, and Celie frequently asked permission to accompany the young man as he made his deliveries throughout the city.

Business increased as more and more settlers flocked into Sacramento and more disappointed miners returned from the gold fields. As Katlin had hoped, more arrived with families or sent for their families, and the women flocked to her store.

September drifted into October, and the leaves began to turn. Evenings became chillier, and autumn would soon be upon them.

Katlin slept soundly the morning of October the fifteenth. The sound of gunfire and shouts roused her from her bed with a start. She lighted a candle and looked at the clock. One-thirty in the morning. Pulling on her dressing gown, she rushed into the hall to meet Henry and Malcolm as both emerged from their rooms.

"What in the world is going on?" Katlin gasped. "I thought the squatter problem had settled down. It's too early for floods. Do you suppose there is a fire?"

"Want me to go and find out, Miss MacKenzie?" Henry offered.

"Not until I know more. Can you make out what they are saying?"

The shouting came closer, as revelers passed down the street in front of the store. Henry grinned as he caught the words.

"News just came in on the *Abby Baker*," he reported. "California has been admitted to the Union."

Katlin shook her head. "I'm glad. Now I'm going back to bed."

The next morning, Dr. Morse came by to deliver the news to Katlin in person.

"My partner, Dr. Stillman, is returning East to visit his family, and he was in San Francisco when the *Oregon* arrived with the news that California was admitted on September 9th. The information took over a month to get here." He smiled. "Jacob also sent me a note which I received in this morning's mail. I understand there was quite a celebration in San Francisco when the *Oregon* docked with banners flying and the band playing."

"It took them long enough." They paused in their conversation as Elena entered with a plate of doughnuts and a pot of tea. "Thank you, Elena." Katlin poured a cup of tea for Dr. Morse. "Because the Southern States objected, I suppose."

"Yes, but apparently reason won out. After all, California is a very rich state, and Mexico has not yet given up all hope of reclaiming her. None of the Senators, not even the Southern ones, wanted to see California's gold fields reverting to Mexico. In fact," he chuckled, "to keep Mexico from learning the news, the papers concerning statehood were smuggled across the Isthmus in an umbrella by Elisha Crosby's daughter Mary Helen. John Bidwell entrusted the documents to Mr. Crosby, and that gentleman felt the least likely person to be questioned by Mexican officials would be a young girl."

"Clever. I'm sure admitting California to the Union would send a warning to Mexico to keep her hands off. I can also see why Mexico might not want the news to get through to anyone in California."

"Jacob also said," Dr. Morse added with a frown, "that when the *Oregon* arrived, she had twenty-two cases of cholera on board, and fourteen of them had proved fatal."

"Oh, no!"

"He wished to warn me that someone with cholera could easily have boarded the *Abby Baker* for the trip to Sacramento before becoming ill, and could bring the dreaded disease to our fair city."

She sighed. "I suppose all we can do is pray."

Their prayers were not answered. Five days later, Malcolm returned from his deliveries to report the first victim, an immigrant from the *Abby Baker*, had been found dead on the bank of the levee.

"It's in the city for sure, Miss MacKenzie," he reported. "We'll have to be mighty careful none of us takes it. They buried the man where he lay, and burnt up ever'thing he had touched, cuz they wuz all so skeered o' the cholera."

Elena began to weep, burying her face in Henry's shoulder. "We will all die," she wailed. "All of us will die, like my *dueña* in New York, and the poor man on the trip across to Panama."

"Hush," Katlin soothed. "You didn't die in New York when your *dueña* did, and you didn't die on the Isthmus." The sight of poor James McFee dying at her feet, his face blue, rose to haunt her. At the memory of the smell as he died she barely suppressed a shudder. "We will just have to wait and see what happens."

"Can you imagine, we were a State for over a month

before we knew about it?" Henry shook his head. "If we're going to be a member of the Union, we'll need a better means of communication than waiting for these boats to get all the way around."

"What we need," Katlin responded, "is a train across."

"Actually," Henry said, "a good stage road would help. Several local businessmen have been talking about one, Ben Halladay for one."

"They's been talk of a railroad, Miss MacKenzie," Malcolm offered, "but ev'ryone says the Sierras are too high, can't no one ever build a train track over any mountains that steep."

Katlin chuckled. "I'll bet someone will figure out how to get over them, if there's enough money in it."

Four days later, seven cases of cholera were reported. Five of them died. People fled the city in panic as more reports of deaths and illness came in.

Katlin listened to the news with trepidation. Should they flee? Or would they be better off staying where they were? The streets were almost deserted. Customers stopped coming to the store.

Henry reported three of the big gambling saloons had shut down. "Must be real scared, Miss MacKenzie," the boy grinned. "The amount of money those places make, I never thought anything short of a flood or a fire would persuade them to close their doors."

"I believe this is worse than a flood or a fire. We can never tell where it will strike." Katlin drew a deep breath and shook her head. "What can possibly happen next in this benighted country?"

Dr. Morse came by the following morning. He lacked his usual debonair appearance. His coat was rumpled and a stubble of reddish beard covered his face. "The victims of this dreadful disease are not confined to those of intemperate and irregular habits. A number of doctors have succumbed to the illness, Miss MacKenzie, but we are all staying by our posts." He paced about the room, and finally turned to face her. "Miss MacKenzie, I hate to ask this of you, but we have been forced to burn so many of our blankets we are running out."

Kaltin drew a sigh of relief. She had feared he planned to ask her to help take care of the sick again, a task she had no desire to perform. She also knew full well she would never have the courage to refuse the good man anything he asked.

"Of course," she replied. "I have several cases of very good blankets that I just received from Mr. Walker last week. How many do you need?"

He cleared his throat. "Well, a case or two would be a big help, but I, er, um, we, er, uh . . . ." His voice trailed off.

"What you are saying is you don't have any money to pay for them."

"So many of our patients are unable to pay, especially those as pass on, and most have no kin to pay either." He stopped and took a deep breath. "I know we've no right to ask you for charity, Miss MacKenzie, but if you could find it in your heart to give us credit, we would be eternally grateful."

Katlin laughed. "Dr. Morse, as much as you give to the community, the least I can do is contribute a few blankets. I'll have Malcolm deliver two cases to your hospital this afternoon." She smiled at the relief on the man's face. "I just ask one thing. Don't make poor Malcolm carry the cases inside. He's terrified of the cholera, and is firmly convinced that if he goes inside the hospital he'll die for sure."

"Just tell him to leave them on the stoop. And thank you for your help. If I can ever return the favor, you have but to ask."

"Thank you. I just hope I never have need of your services. Is there anything else you need? Linen? A few lengths of the India rubber sheeting?"

"Anything you can spare, Miss MacKenzie, will be very much appreciated. And now, I must return. My services are much in demand. I must ask you to defer your offer of some of your delicious tea until a more opportune moment." After a quick bow over her hand, he scurried out the door.

On the 30th of October, the *Alta California* announced there had been nineteen deaths from cholera in the city. Henry repeated this news to Katlin. "But they say the papers have been reporting a lot of deaths as fever and dysentry, when the folks really died of cholera. They're trying to keep folks from giving in to panic." He grinned. "They might as well not bother. About eighty percent of the folks have already run."

Katlin sighed. "We've been lucky so far. We'll just have to hope."

But their luck ran out. That night, as Katlin entered her room to prepare for bed, she heard Elena call her name, a panicked cry that made Katlin's heart miss a beat. She rushed into the girl's room to find she had vomited all over the counterpane. The smell told her she also suffered from diarrhea.

"I have the cholera," she wept. "I know I have the cholera. I am going to die, no?"

Panic swept through Katlin's body, and she wrapped her arms around the girl in a fierce hug. *Did I kill her by bringing her here? Should I have gone back directly back to Maine?* She had never even heard of the cholera in Maine. She shook her head to drive away the paralysis. *Think,* she told herself. *Think.*

"Not everyone who takes it dies, Elena," she assured the girl with a confidence she did not feel. "Just remember we love you, and you are very special to us. You must get well. For all of us. Especially for Henry. He loves you. Remember that." She picked up the cloth from the commode by the bed. "Now, let me wash your face and get you cleaned up. You'll feel much better."

Celie's frightened face appeared in the doorway. "Is she gonna die, Miss MacKenzie?" the girl whispered, her eyes wide, her face showing her fear.

"No, Celie. She's not going to die because we won't let her," Katlin replied firmly. "Please, go into the kitchen and make some tea. Actually, make an infusion of blackberry leaves. The Nisenam swear by that for dysentery, and I haven't seen anything the American doctors have tried that works any better. We're going to try the Indian method."

By morning, Elena was only semi-conscious. Henry stood in the doorway with tears running down his cheeks as he watched. Katlin kept urging the girl to drink the spoonfuls of the blackberry leaf infusion, and kept Celie busy making more.

Dr. Morse came by that afternoon. Katlin still sat by Elena's bed, pressing the tea upon her. She seemed no better, but, Katlin thought, taking some comfort from the knowledge, she seemed no worse. She could still rally enough to swallow, and, while the diarrhea continued, at least the vomiting had stopped. And the dreaded blue pallor had not yet appeared.

"I heard the young lady had taken this terrible disease, Miss MacKenzie, and felt I had to at least come by to see how she fared. How long has she been ill?"

"Since last night, about nine," Katlin replied, her voice hoarse in her fatigue.

"And you have been with her all that time?"

Katlin nodded.

"I must encourage you to let Celie spell you, or you will become so fatigued you will become ill yourself."

"Celie is terrified to come into the room, and I don't wish to force her. I have been lying on a blanket on the floor in between the times when Elena needs care."

He shrugged. "As you wish. I know the difficulty in getting help to nurse the victims. I am very well aware, as you have probably read, that the papers are reporting only small numbers of deaths, but I can assure you the actual numbers are much higher. Has no one else in your household shown signs of the ailment?"

"Not yet, thank God," Katlin responded.

"We will pray it remains so. When she rouses a little more, give her sips of barley water. That has been the only thing I have discovered which has proven efficacious. What are you giving her now?"

Katlin laughed grimly. "An infusion of blackberry leaves. One of my customers has a Nisenam partner who says all the Maidu swear by it. I felt it worth a try."

"I will have to try it myself. Nothing else seems to do any better. But do try the barley water. It seems to increase the patient's strength once he begins to show signs of relief from the cramping."

"Will anything relieve the cramping pain? She suffers so whenever the spasms strike."

"Peppermint tea, and a decoction of ginger root. Those are the only two I have found to be of any benefit. An infusion of raspberry leaves is also recommended, but I am sure there is little difference between blackberry and raspberry."

"Thank you." Katlin turned to the hovering Henry. He needed something to do. "Henry, get Celie started on some barley water, and get to the apothcary for some ginger root and peppermint leaves." She held the boy in a fierce hug for a moment. He returned her embrace with a sob.

"Elena is gonna get well, isn't she, Miss MacKenzie? Please tell me you think she's gonna get well." His voice caught. "I thought I was gonna be the one to die, but now that I'm so much better . . . ." His voice caught and he could not continue.

"Please, don't give up yet. She is still alive, and we are going to do our best to keep her that way." She released him with a little shove. "Now, go get started on those things I need."

The boy scurried away and Katlin returned to Elena's side. Bleak despair swept over her. The three of them had been through so much together. The idea of losing Elena was more than she could bear. Surely God could not be so cruel. She recalled her feelings as she had watched them on the voyage up the river.

No! She would not let it happen. Determination swept over her. Elena would get well. Stroking the girl's hair back from the sweaty forehead, Katlin smiled into the dark eyes that looked at her with mingled fear and trust.

"We'll make it, children," she murmured. "We'll make it."

# Chapter 34

THREE DAYS PASSED before Elena began to respond to the treatment. Katlin, although exhausted to the point of collapse, never left the girl's side, sleeping on a blanket on the floor beside her bed. The faithful Henry hovered about.

John Bigler came by briefly to see how she fared. He carried a sachet of camphor which he held to his nose periodically.

"Does the camphor help keep you from taking the disease?" Katlin could not help wondering if anything, other than blind luck, detemined who took the disease and who did not.

He smiled. "Some say yes, others no. The way I reckon it is, no harm done, and if it helps, so much the better. I have been visiting the sick since this dreadful epidemic began, and, so far, have been fortunate." He shrugged his shoulders. "Some say it is God, some say the camphor. If those who say it is the miasma that causes the disease are right, the camphor should help." With a chuckle, he added, "And I confine my visits to speaking. I don't touch anything, in case those who say it is spread by contact are right."

Katlin recalled what she had observed in Havana Harbor. Were the Spanish doctors right? Then why hadn't she, Katlin, taken ill? She certainly had close enough contact with Elena during these past few days. She shrugged her shoulders. What will be, will be.

After the good gentleman took his leave, Henry chuckled to Katlin. "Bigler wants to be Governor of the State, now that we are a state. That's why he's making such a show of how concerned he is for the citizens, visiting all the sick folks and all."

Katlin returned to spooning more of the barley water into Elena. "At least he is brave enough to stay in town. Maybe he would make a good Governor."

Their next visitor was Colin. Katlin had emerged from Elena's room for the first time and gone downstairs to get some clean linen for the bed. The store was empty, for the population remained depleted and customers rare.

"Miss MacKenzie."

Startled, she turned to face him, immediately aware of how disheveled she must look. Her hair had not been combed for days, and she still wore the same dress, rumbled and spotted, that she had been preparing to take off when Elena became ill. She automatically put up her hand to smooth the tangled mass of hair back from her forehead.

Colin frowned, his concern showing in his eyes. "Have you been ill? Did you take the cholera? I heard it was a terrible time. I should have been here sooner ..."

She interrupted him. "No, I am perfectly healthy. I realize how I must look, for I have been caring for Elena. She has been ill for four days. Fortunately, she has been the only one." So far, she added in her mind.

Their eyes met. The sympathy she read there broke Katlin's reserve, and the tears overflowed. Colin gathered her into his arms and held her while she wept.

"Poor, poor brave Katlin," he murmured against her hair. "Always taking care of everyone, never a thought to taking care of yourself."

It felt so good just to cry, to not have to keep up the bold front she had to maintain with Henry and Elena that she let him hold her, taking comfort in his embrace, treasuring the love that swept over her. Even though she knew nothing could come from it, as long as the matter with Caleb remained unresolved, she savored the moment.

She came to her senses and pulled herself from his embrace. Fumbling in her sleeve for her handkerchief, she wiped her eyes and blew her nose. "Thank you," she smiled. "I guess I needed a good cry. I have been so worried for so long. But I do believe Elena has turned the corner now. Please, come up and see her. She will be pleased to know you have come."

Colin followed Katlin up the stairs, his thoughts jumbled. While she was in his arms, the love he felt for her surged though him with such power he almost lost his head and asked her to marry him. It was well she pulled back, or he would have done so. And then what? Michelle had been gone for a long time. She would have wanted him to marry again. She felt so strongly he should have a son.

But something told him Katlin was not ready. He had felt it before, when they had been so close to declaring their love for each other. He did not doubt she loved him. He could see it in her eyes. He also knew he loved her.

He shook his head to clear it. Whatever it was, she was not yet willing to confide in him or, as far as he could tell, anyone else. She kept it bottled up inside. Of course, he had to confess, he had never confided in her either. She still did not know he had been married before, did not know of his loss of Michelle and little Colin MacDougal III.

Should I tell her? He wrestled with the decision until they reached the top of the stairs. No, he decided. Not yet.

Once Elena began to convalesce, she recovered with the resiliency of youth. Henry's devotion never wavered. He waited on her hand and foot, encouraging her to eat the restorative soups Celie prepared, reading to her when she was bored, or just sitting beside her holding her hand.

On November 9, the wild clanging of the alarm bell sent Henry and Katlin running to see what had happened.

Smoke and flames billowed high into the sky, whipped by a fierce north wind that roared down the valley with hurricane force.

"Not another fire," Katlin muttered. "We should build everything out of brick, and stop this nonsense."

"Everything's dry as tinder, Miss MacKenzie, what with all the heat all summer, and the rains haven't started yet."

"And last year they started in September!"

"Yes, and we got the floods, just like the Injuns told us we would," Henry grinned. "But with this wind, any fire as gets a good start is bound to spread. Probably take a whole block."

"At least the wind is blowing the smoke away from us. Let's walk down a bit and watch our brave fire fighters in action."

They strode to where they could see the New York Hotel engulfed by a mass of flames. The fire crackled and hissed, the smell of smoke filling the air. Soot drifted down on them as they watched the Eagle and the St. Francis start to burn. The Mutual Hook and Ladder Company #1 frantically pumped water onto the Galena, in a futile attempt to save it. They were joined by the Confidence Engine #1, Sacramento's second team of fire fighters.

"Something to watch, isn't it, Miss MacKenzie?"

"Look at all those poor people that have been dislodged," she said, noting displaced lodgers clinging to the meager armloads of belongings they had rescued from the inferno, watching with sad faces as the flames devoured the four hotels. "I hope everyone got out. It would be horrible if someone burned to death."

"Oh, I think they got everyone out. Not many people were there to begin with, 'cause most folks haven't come back yet. There is still some cholera in town." Henry shrugged expressively. "Guess this was about the best time for 'em to burn, if you look at it that way."

The efforts of the fire fighters kept the damage to those four hotels. As it became apparent the fire would spread no furthur, Henry and Katlin returned to the store to reassure Elena, Malcolm, and Celie the fire would not reach them.

On November 17, the papers annnouced the epidemic had run its course. On the 28th, the news also reached them that Hardin Bigelow had died of cholera in San Francisco on the previous day.

"The poor man," Katlin exclaimed when she heard the sad news. "To be shot four times and survive, to have a hand amputated for gangrene, then to die of cholera. Losing his hand must have weakened him, and made him more vulnerable." Although, she thought, the disease had taken some who were in the bloom of health.

Henry nodded. "Funny how things work out sometimes. And there's talk of running Robinson for Assembly."

"What? How in heaven's name can they be thinking of such a thing? The man should be hung for murder."

The boy just shrugged. "I told you he had political friends. And some of them favored the squatters all along. Sutter never was very popular. Too arrogant." He chuckled. "You remember the Jared Sheldon your friend Jenny told you about?"

"Quite well."

"Seems his friend William Daylor got into a row with Sutter because they were both after the same Injun girl. Sutter had Daylor arrested and hauled off to Monterey and locked up. Sheldon intervened, and Governor Michetorena just laughed and released Daylor from jail."

Katlin laughed.

"But the best part is, Daylor got even. He took $15,000 out of his claim at Dry Diggings and loaned $6000 of it to Sutter to bring Sutter's family over from Switzerland." Henry chuckled. "Guess from what the fellows say, his wife is a real termagent. He kept telling her he didn't have money for her passage. When Daylor loaned him the money, he couldn't use that as an excuse any longer. I guess that's one reason why they moved up to Hock Farm. His wife wanted to keep him away from all of his Injun girlfriends."

Katlin only shook her head.

Once the fear of cholera disappeared, Sacramento returned to life with remarkable rapidity. Customers began returning to the store, and business was brisk.

One morning toward the end of November, the door opened and Jenny breezed into the room, with her usual rush of energy, followed by a timid looking young man.

"Oh, Miss MacKenzie, I'm so glad to see you are still here! We heard the most dreadful rumors, about how everyone in Sacramento was dyin' of that wretched cholera. Mr. Shelton's good friend, Mr. Daylor, he took and died, poor man. He'd found a man dying of it, total stranger he was, and tried to help him. The man died anyway, then Mr. Daylor took it and died too. Dreadful. Poor Mr. Shelton, he was all broken up, 'cause I guess him and Mr. Daylor had been friends for ever so long. And Mr. Shelton has got his own problems, what with him wanting to dam the Cosumnes, and the miners in such a row over his plans."

Katlin began to run out of breath just listening to this narrative, when Jenny broke off with a little laugh.

"But here I am running on, and not introducing you!" She pulled the young man forward. "This is Jeremy Cootes, Miss MacKenzie, and we're engaged. He asked me to marry him just last Sunday after church services, and of course I said 'Yes' immediately."

"Of course," Katlin murmured.

The young man took Katlin's outstretched hand with a shy smile. "Very pleased to meet you, Miss MacKenzie. Jenny places great faith in your store, and has assured me

I can purchase supplies from you for the little school I plan to open."

"I have some paper and pens and inkwells. Books I would have to order, but I have a supplier in San Francisco who can get me almost anything I want. Give me a list, and I will send it on to Mr. Walker. It usually takes about a week to get most items. Of course, if he has to get it from the East, it will take longer."

"We will do the best we can with what we can find, Miss MacKenzie. I have a few books."

"Oh, and wonderful books they are," Jenny chimed in. "He's been reading to me from some books by Mr. Dickens. I cried when that Mr. Carton took the place of the young man of the girl he loved, and died in his place, because she loved that young man more than she loved him. Wasn't that noble of him? And so romantic!"

" 'Tis a far, far better thing I do than I have ever done before,'" Katlin quoted, glad she knew the story, for figuring it out from Jenny's narrative would have been difficult.

"Oh, you've read it, too?" She rattled on. "And poor little Oliver! I felt so sorry for him. It must be dreadful to be hungry. I remember coming across the plains, they said we might run out of food, and I thought that would be awful. But luckily, we always had enough. Although," she shuddered. "it wasn't always that tasty. I got so tired of beans!"

She flitted from bolt to bolt, checking out all of the cloth Katlin had displayed. "I've just got to find a really nice length of material to make myself a wedding dress, and some lace for a proper veil. My friend Maggie, now, she married a young man, miner he is, and they live in this dreadful little cabin with only one room, and she has to cook outside, she didn't have any decent cloth to make a gown, so she got married in her best calico print. She said it didn't matter, she was in love, all that mattered was she would be with the man she loved."

Katlin liked Maggie better every time she heard about her. She sounded like a sensible and practical young woman.

Jenny rambled on. "But I think your wedding day is so special you should have a *very* special dress, don't you think, Miss MacKenzie?"

Katlin and the young man exchanged smiles. "You're right, of course. We must find you a very special material. I think I have a length of lovely satin I have been saving for just such an occasion." She had been saving it in hopes Elena would need it, but decided she would just have to order more. She would probably need more anyway, with all of the new people coming into the City. All of these men had been without women for so long there would surely be some weddings coming up.

She enlisted Malcolm's aid to help Jenny and Mr. Cootes pile all of their purchases into Mr. Cootes' buggy.

"I'll invite you to the wedding," Jenny cried over her shoulder as they drove off, waving back. "I hope you can come." They disappeared around the corner in a cloud of dust.

Katlin reentered the store and collapsed onto a chair, rocking with laughter. "I declare, Malcolm, every time she leaves I feel like I've done a whole day's work! Please, ask Celie to bring me a cup of tea."

# *Chapter 35*

A FEW DAYS LATER, as Katlin totaled her sales for the month of November, Malcolm approached Katlin shyly, leading Celie by the hand.

"Miss MacKenzie," he began with a broad grin, "Celie here has consented to be my wife."

"That's wonderful, Malcolm." She hugged Celie. "I'm so happy for both of you."

Celie burst into tears and returned Katlin's embrace. "Oh, ma'am, iffen you hadn't bought off my indentures, who knows what woulda become o' me?"

Katlin laughed. "Oh, I'm sure Malcolm would have found you. Love has a way. I do hope you'll continue working for me. I don't know what I would do without you."

"Oh, yes'm. We'd never think o' leavin' you, Miss Mac-Kenzie. And since Mr. Andrews sent me my papers, I'm free to marry." He hesitated. "Only got one problem."

"And that is?"

"Got me no last name. Preachers as marry folks always wants a last name. Do you s'pose there'd be a problem if I jest picked one?"

Katlin thought of Caleb and the number of last names he had no doubt gone through in his career and smiled. "I'm sure, Malcolm, in this town you can select any last name you choose."

"My old master, he was good to me. Do you s'pose he'd mind iffen I used his?"

"I'm sure he would be proud if you did. And Mr. and Mrs. Malcolm Andrews has a fine sound to it."

But as she watched them stroll off hand in hand, their happiness only made Katlin more desolate at the thought of her own helpless love for Colin, and fury with Caleb for leaving her in this dilemma surged through her again. I'll get even with you, Caleb, you rat, she muttered under her breath. That is, if I ever find you. She pressed her clenched fists to her forehead in frustration. How was she ever going to know if he was one of the many miners who died, many buried in unknown and unmarked graves? There was no way to trace him. She had no idea what name he used out here, and no way of finding out.

She sighed and returned to adding the column of figures.

In mid-December the rains began at last, and the danger of fire lessened,

"Locals are now sayin' we're gonna have a drought year," Henry told Katlin as they stood together in the doorway watching the light rain sprinkle down, making tiny drops in the thick dust of the street. "Say it usually happens that way, heavy rain one winter, then two or three years before it comes again."

"Well," Katlin sighed, "I certainly don't want to go through another winter like the last one. But it would be nice to get at least one good, soaking rain so we don't have to worry about fires all the time." She glanced up at the cloud cover already beginning to dissipate. "But this hasn't been enough rain to even settle the dust in the street."

"Gonna be a lot o' disappointed miners. They've spent all summer slaving away in the heat, digging up mounds of dirt to run through their sluice boxes as soon as the rivers rise. If the rains don't come, lot of 'em are going to lose their shirts."

"I never thought of that. I'm so glad Malcolm got all he needed before this happened."

"So is he," Henry grinned. "I've never seen a happier man. He's so besotted with Celie he can hardly keep count of the boxes he's delivering."

Katlin smiled. "Yes, that does seem to be a match made in heaven. Celie is so happy she got such a good man she goes around singing all day. Did you see that length of red satin she's making her wedding dress with? I told her brides usually wore pastels or ecru, but she wanted the red."

"She'll make a striking bride, no doubt about it. Did they say when they want to get married?"

"I guess as soon as she finishes her gown," Katlin told him. "Maybe when Colin and Michael come for Christmas."

"Got to go tell Elena. She keeps asking." The boy turned and ran up the stairs.

Katlin watched him leave, her heart bleak. She knew she should be happy for them, for Henry and Elena, whose love seemed to grow stronger every day, for Malcolm and Celie in their new-found joy. Somehow, their love only made her feel more despair at her own futile love for Colin. What made it harder was the realization that Colin felt the same for her. She could see it in his eyes. She sensed it when he held her during Elena's illness.

Something kept him from speaking. In a way, Katlin knew she should be glad. If he proposed, she would be forced to tell him about Caleb or refuse his offer, neither of which she wanted to do. Whatever ghost in his past kept him silent, it was a blessing. But Katlin wished she knew what it was. Something, or someone, had hurt him. She felt his reserve, as though he feared being hurt again.

With a sigh, she returned to the task of straightening out the wooden reels of ribbon. The last two ladies who left the store had insisted upon looking at every spool she had before making their selection.

"At least," she chuckled to the empty room, "they finally bought something." Not like Mrs. Maloney, she thought, who looked at every spool of ribbon, every packet of lace, and every bolt of cloth before announcing she preferred the merchandise at Mr. Smith's store. Katlin had barely resisted the impulse to tell the good lady she was welcome to take her business to Mr. Smith at any time.

Malcolm returned from his deliveries and grinned as he handed her the coins and receipts from his rounds. "You know that Maloney woman who's always fussin' about your stuff not bein' as good as what Smith has over to his store?"

"Yes, as a matter of fact I was just thinking about her. Rewinding all these ribbons reminded me of all the times I've taken every reel off of the shelf so that fussy old woman could feel each one of them to 'check fer quality', as she put it. I doubt she'd recognize quality if she saw it."

"Thought you'd like to know Smith says the same thing about her. Says she always grumbles at his displays and tells him yours are much better. He says he told her to come and see you, then, iffen she'd rather."

Katlin's spirits rose. "Thank you, Malcolm," she chuckled. "I needed a good laugh."


Colin and Michael came for Christmas, laden with a goose for the holiday dinner and gifts for everyone. Again Katlin felt the camaraderie they shared. After the feast, Katlin played the harpsichord and they all sang some of the old, familiar carols, reminding Katlin of the happy evenings with her parents before her mother died. Strains of Silent Night and The First Noel rang throughout the building. Colin had a pleasing baritone, and Michael sang in his thick Irish brogue with great enthusiasm, if slightly off-key.

*  *  *

As the evening's festivities drew to a close, Colin took Katlin's hand and said, "There's a beautiful moon tonight, and it's not very cold out. Would you come for a walk with me, Miss MacKenzie?"

Something about the look in his eye made Katlin's heart leap. Was he about to propose? What could she say if he did?

But the first words he spoke when they were alone startled her. He stopped and faced her, holding her hands so tightly he hurt her. He did not seem conscious of the strength in his grip. Katlin, not wanting to break the spell, said nothing.

"I have to tell you why I left New Orleans."

She waited in silence.

He released her hands and turned away, but not before she caught the glint of tears in his eyes. She remained silent.

"I grew up in New York," he said, "but after my mother died, I had no other family there, so I decided to try something different. I took the rest of the money my father had left us and bought a plantation just outside of New Orleans. There I met a French girl, daughter of one of the other plantation owners." He paused and took a deep breath. "You have to live there to understand them. They had this little group of landowners, and everyone else was outside of the circle. Even the slaves of the landowners looked down on the rest of the population.

"Anyway, since I was a landowner, they immediately accepted me. Michelle and I fell in love." He smiled faintly. "You remind me of her in some ways, although she had sparkling dark eyes and shiny black hair. She . . . she was so in love with life. I can still see her, scandalizing the neighbors by riding astride, with her hair flowing free. Then when our son was born . . . ." He stopped, unable to continue.

He did not need to say it. Katlin knew. She put her arms around him and said softly, "And you lost them both."

He nodded, unable to speak. They remained silent, holding each other, until Colin regained his composure. "I felt you had a right to know," he finally whispered.

"Thank you," she said softly.

They remained locked in the embrace for several moments then, in silence, returned to the store. At the door, Colin wished her a good evening, and took his leave. Suddenly, he turned back and, with a sob, clasped her to him. He held her for just a moment, then just as suddenly released her and strode away.

Katlin watched his figure disappear into the darkness then, with a long sigh, started up the stairs to her room. She looked about. What had always been such a cozy haven to her seemed stark and cold in spite of the heat from the little Topsy stove in the corner. A shiver ran up her spine. She had never before felt so alone and so desolate, not even after her father died.

"Someday," she murmured to the silent room, "Someday, Colin my love, we will be able to bury our ghosts."

# Chapter 36

B Y SPRING OF 1851, *MacKenzie's Mercantile* had established itself as a successful enterprise. More and more men had brought their wives and families from the East. With the arrival of more ladies, the demand for Katlin's quality of merchandise rose. She had repaid Mr. Walker, and, with her success, found herself able to buy her own goods from the manufacturers in the East and have them shipped directly to her.

Colin remained a frequent visitor, but never again referred to the wife and child he had lost. Katlin wondered how long they could go on keeping their love at bay, he through his fear of again losing someone he loved, she through her fear of Caleb reappearing on her doorstep.

"You're running away from your past just like I am, Colin my love," she murmured to the empty room. "Will either one of us ever be able to put the past behind us?"

The bell over the door jangled, and two ladies entered. Katlin brushed her thoughts from her mind and greeted them. "Good morning, Mrs. Lowe, Mrs. Adams. And how are you this fine morning? I have some very fine Chantilly lace, just arrived from France. Can I interest you in taking a look at it?"

Day followed day in a never ending pattern. The romance between Henry and Elena continued to blossom. The arrival of summer reminded her it would soon be two years since she reached Sacramento. The city grew rapidly around her. Every morning she awoke to the sound of hammers and saws. She found herself thinking more and more of Caleb. Would she ever find him? Did she want to? Perhaps she should just close that episode of her life. But she knew she could never marry Colin until she somehow resolved the problem.

With a sigh, she got out her 'spider stick', as she called the pole with a cloth wrapped on the end. She used it daily, in her never-ending battle, and cleared out yet another web in the corner of the ceiling. She had swept down more spider webs in a month than she did in a year back in Maine.

She chuckled grimly. In a way, the persistent spiders reminded her of the problem with Caleb. No matter how many times she tried to sweep him away, he kept returning to haunt her.

Henry and Elena returned from a stroll along the waterfront. Elena never tired of watching the activity in the busy port, and Henry never lost his love for ships. They frequently walked along Front Street.

On this particular occasion, Elena's face shone, and she immediately scurried up the stairs. Henry lingered and paced about the store until the two ladies buying material for curtains finished their negotiations and departed.

Katlin, amused, suspected what had happened, from Henry's nervousness and the heightened color on Elena's face. She waited until Henry finally stopped pacing and faced her.

"Elena turned seventeen last January," he began, then stopped.

"Yes?" Katlin prompted. This was obviously not the news he wanted to impart, for they had feted Elena with a party. Even Colin and Michael had come.

"And we, er, we've been talking, and, and . . . ."

"And you want to get married," Katlin finished for him.

"She's got no folks except you, Miss MacKenzie, so I told

her I'd ask you. She insisted I get your permission, for no proper Spanish girl, especially a member of the nobility, which I guess Elena was, would ever marry without the consent of her family." He grinned at Katlin. "That's you."

Katlin smiled and hugged the boy she had grown so fond of during the two years they had been together. "You not only have my permission, you have my blessing."

"I'd never 'a brought it up if I didn't think I was going to get better. They were right when they said the climate of California is good for those with the consumption. I hardly ever cough anymore, and I don't get the fever in the afternoons like I used to." He returned Katlin's hug with enthusiasm. "And you've been so good to us." His face beaming, he turned and started up the stairs. "Got to go tell Elena."

Katlin watched him go with tears in her eyes. She knew she should be happy for them, but somehow their love only made her feel more despair at her own hopeless love for Colin.

One June morning, she decided to take a stroll down the shops on 'J' Street. She had not taken a look at the competition for some time. She liked to see what other businesses were starting up around her. As she walked past the pawn shop, she glanced in the window and gasped aloud. There, featured prominently in the window display, lay her grandfather's onyx ring.

Katlin recognized the ring immediately. She stood, transfixed, staring at the proof Caleb got at least this far. Her heart beat so loudly in her chest she feared passers-by would hear it. Her feet refused to move. For a moment, she felt she might faint. The thought that he could be close by both frightened and excited her. Could she finally put Caleb behind her and be free to marry Colin if he should ask her? Or would his reappearance in her life only create more problems for her. She could not, as a married woman, own sole property. If she acknowledged her marriage to him as valid, he could claim the store. And no doubt would, she thought grimly. He had already taken one from her.

Yet, if she denied the marriage, and word got around that they had lived together in Maine . . . . She pushed the thought from her mind, took a deep breath, and forced herself to move. Tearing her eyes from the ring, she entered the little shop.

"Morning, Miss MacKenzie. And how are you this fine summer day? Business still good?"

"Yes, thank you, Mr. Greenwood. And a good morning to you as well." She took a deep breath to slow her pounding heart and clenched her hands so he would not see how they shook. "That onyx ring in the window, with the large diamond in the center. How long have you had it?"

"Jest about a week now. Fine piece, ain't it? Man as pawned it seemed right loathe to let go o' it. Assured me he'd be back. Made me promise not to sell it, but I jest had ta put it on display. Thought maybe it'd bring in business, show folks I got me some quality stuff here."

Trying to keep her voice steady, she said softly. "It's mine. It belonged to my grandfather."

Mr. Greenwood looked startled. "Are ye sure, Miss Mac-Kenzie? Lotsa rings look a lot alike."

"I'm positive, and to prove it, look inside. You will find the initials A.M. for Angus MacKenzie engraved there. Also, there is a slight chip on the lower inside corner of the onyx."

The pawnbroker picked the ring up and examined it. "You're right." He stared at her. "But . . . but what if the owner comes back?"

"He's not the owner. He stole it from me. He also stole a lot of money, which I am sure he has spent by now. But I want my grandfather's ring back. It's a family heirloom. Actually, the "A.M." is for the original Angus MacKenzie, my great-grandfather. My father brought it with him when he came to New York in '26."

"Do you – er – uh, have any proof of what you say? I mean, you could'a sold it to him, and are now a-tryin' to get it back." He looked embarrassed. "Not, that is to say that I'd ever suspect you o' nuthin' underhanded, Miss MacKenzie, but . . . ." His face flushed a bright red.

"But you will have to explain to the man who pawned it your reason for giving it to me?"

"You do see what kinda position you put me inta, don't you, Miss MacKenzie?" Mr. Greenwood looked at her anxiously over the top of his spectacles.

"Would you like me to call the sheriff? He could take it for me, and relieve you of the responsibility."

"No, no, it'll be fine. You take the ring. Ye've convinced me it's yourn." He wiped the beads of sweat from his forehead with his rumpled red handkerchief. "Said he only needed the money fer a piece, that he'd be a-gittin' it right back. Gave his name as Caleb Smith, but I reckon that were an alias."

"He told me his name was Caleb Martin and some one else Caleb Parker, but I suspect those were aliases as well. I doubt anyone knows his real name." She found herself wondering if he needed the money to woo another unsuspecting widow with a little property.

"Said he'd be back fer it right soon. What'll I tell 'im?"

"Tell him the rightful owner claimed it." Just don't tell him where to find me, she thought. Clutching the ring tightly in her hand, she left Mr. Greenwood staring after her and returned to the street.

As she walked back to *MacKenzie's Mercantile*, she found herself looking at all the men she passed, half expecting Caleb to appear before her. If he pawned the ring, he must have been short of funds. She felt a momentary panic. What if he came after her? She had no way of proving their marriage was invalid. She had never told anyone, so she would have no witnesses.

She reached the shop and locked the door. He wouldn't dare come after her, would he? She usually had Malcolm or Henry or both with her most of the time, and Colin made a habit of dropping in for a cup of tea with fair regularity. She could only pray Caleb would never find her alone.

But if Caleb was in town, he obviously still lived. Her wish that she would find he had died had proven futile. What would she do if he reappeared in her life? Would she be able to finally cut her ties with him and be free to marry Colin? Or would he just create more difficulties for her?

Shaking off her misgivings, Katlin cut a length of ribbon from the reel on the counter and strung it through the ring. She hung the ribbon around her neck and tucked the ring inside her bodice.

One week later, the bell on the front door clanked and Katlin looked up to find herself face to face with Caleb.

He caught her alone. Malcolm had gone on his daily deliveries, taking Celie with him as usual, and she had sent Henry and Elena on a picnic by the river, feeling a day of rest in the sunshine would do them both good.

A smile lighted Caleb's handsome face. Turning on the old charm, she thought. Well, I won't fall for it again, believe me.

"What a surprise, my dear wife. Who would ever think you would follow me clear out here? Then, of course, you always were a strong-willed woman."

"Follow you?" He knows I have the ring, she thought. How else would he have known where to find me? Determined to put on a bold front, she added, "Why would I follow you? Perhaps to get my half of the money from my father's store?"

"Put that money to good use, I did, little wife o' mine. Planned to send for you as soon as I got myself set up good, you oughta know that. I just tried to spare you a hard trip."

He smiled at her. "Got me and my partner to the gold fields and staked us until we got our own claim workin'. We just never reckoned how much it would cost us to live out here."

"Are you telling me you don't have any of the money left?" She looked him straight in the eye. "How about the money from the poor widow you married just before you found me?"

His eyes widened, then narrowed to slits. The handsome face turned ugly. "And how'd you learn about that?"

"Her brother followed you. He showed up at my place three days after you left." She smiled, a movement of her lips that did not reach her eyes. "What's the matter? Having trouble finding another gullible widow to marry? Can't make it if you try to earn your living honestly?"

The charm vanished and he snarled. "And what do you think you can do about it?"

"Probably nothing, if the money is gone. I'd hoped to be able to send something back to that poor widow. She's probably destitute." Maybe, she thought, fighting down the panic swelling up inside of her, perhaps she could convince him she did not have the onyx ring, so she said, "And what have you done with my grandfather's ring?"

Her hopes vanished as he scowled. "You know right well where that ring is. I got me a few bags of dust and went back to reclaim it. Man as owns the pawn shop says you accused me of stealin' it."

"And what would you call it?"

"Told him I had every right to it, bein' your lawful wedded husband." He grinned, an evil, triumphant look crossing his face. Katlin found herself wondering how she could have ever thought him handsome.

She felt the blood drain from her face as she realized the damage he could do to her. He could claim the store, or spread rumors around and ruin her reputation, the reputation she had fought so hard to maintain. The ladies of the town would stop coming to her store to buy calico and lace. The men would lose their respect for her, and she would have trouble collecting the money due her. And Colin? She tried not to think of Colin.

She remembered the Colt on the shelf under the cash drawer. Kill him, a little voice in her head told her. Kill him before he destroys what you have built up for yourself here.

No! Every fiber of her being cried out against it. I can't kill another human being, she thought. Especially not in cold blood. It would be wrong, no matter how much of a threat he presented.

While Katlin wrestled with her conscience, Caleb came around the end of the counter and began walking towards her.

"Where is the ring?" he asked, his voice menacing. "And after I got that ring appraised, I figgered the jewelry I left in that box had to a' been valuable too. I was a fool to leave it. Should'a knowed it would be valuable. What'd you do with it all?"

"I had to sell it to get money for my passage. If you will recall, you ran off with all of the money from the store."

He laughed harshly. "Those earrings you're wearin' right now was in that case. Guess you didn't sell everything. If you don't want to give me the ring, fine. I'll take the earrings."

"No! They were my mother's special favorites. They're . . . they're not valuable. They just mean a lot to me."

"Not valuable, huh? Well, we'll see," he sneered. "I'll just take 'em and see what Greenwood has to say about what they're worth."

She backed away from him to the end of the counter where her Colt lay. As she reached the shelf, with one quick motion, she brought the gun up and leveled it at him.

"Stay away from me," she ordered. She cocked the pistol, the snap loud in the silent room.

"And would you really kill me, wifey dear? After all, I'm not armed. It would be murder. Think what folks would say if you kill your husband." He laughed, an unplesant, jeering sound. "Maybe even get you hung for murder, even if you are a pretty woman."

She backed farther away, around the end of the counter, back towards the door, praying someone would come in. Maybe if she could get outside, someone would help her.

He lunged for her and grabbed her wrist, wrenching her arm upward. The pistol fired, the bullet whizzing harmlessly into the ceiling, the sound echoing around the room. His grip on her wrist tightened. She clung desperately to the gun. He seized her around the waist with his right arm and pulled her to him. His face close to hers, he leered, "And now what, my little Scottish spitfire?" He squeezed her so hard she gasped in pain. "You *are* my wife, you know. I could have you right here and be within my rights."

She gritted her teeth and clung to the Colt in spite of the pain in her wrist. She knew only too well it would be her word against his. Colin, help me, she pleaded in grim silence.

As if in answer to her prayer, she heard running footsteps on the board walkway and Colin's voice came from the doorway.

"Katlin, I heard a shot! What's going on?"

Caleb whirled to face Colin, shoving Katlin away. She staggered and almost fell, the Colt still gripped in her hand. She caught herself, then watched in horror as a little gun appeared almost by magic in Caleb's hand. He fired and Colin fell backwards to the floor.

Katlin screamed. She saw Caleb, with an evil leer, grinning down at Colin's prostrate form. With no conscious effort on her part, the pistol fired twice in her hand.

# Chapter 37

CALEB CRUMPLED to the floor, but Katlin paid no attention to him. She raced to Colin's side and lifted his head. The bullet had struck just above his left eyebrow. She could not tell if it had penetrated his skull or not.

"Oh, Colin, Colin, Colin my love. Don't die. Please don't die," she sobbed. "I love you." Tears poured down her cheeks and spilled onto his as she stroked his face and pleaded with him not to leave her.

Henry appeared from nowhere. Katlin heard Elena screaming, "He cannot be dead, oh, please Beloved Virgin, he cannot be dead."

Henry squeezed Katlin's shoulder. "I'll fetch Doc Morse," he promised. "It doesn't look like the bullet went into his head. It was just a little pop gun. Good thing he didn't get shot with the Colt. I think he's just knocked out." He glanced over at Caleb's body. "Who's the dead man?"

"Dead man?" Katlin looked at Henry in a daze. My God, she thought. Caleb. I killed him. Now it will all come out, the whole sordid story. She stared at Colin's still, white face and shook her head. It doesn't matter. Colin will believe me, and the rest of the world can think what it will. She closed her eyes. And if Colin dies, nothing else matters anyway.

She opened her eyes and looked at Colin to find the aquamarine eyes open and fixed on hers. With a slight smile, he whispered. "I'm harder to kill than you think, Miss MacKenzie. And were your declarations of eternal love real, or were they only because you thought I was dead?"

Katlin, almost hysterical with relief, laughed and cried at the same time.

He took her hand and raised it to his lips. "Michelle has been gone for four years. As she would say, could she be here, life is to be lived. She would not want me to be alone for the rest of my life. And," he grinned wickedly, a sparkle in the aquamarine eyes, "she wanted me to have sons."

Katlin blushed.

# EPILOGUE

## *June, 1852*

ONE YEAR LATER, Katlin rose early and walked out onto the porch to watch the sun rise across the fields of growing wheat. She never ceased to marvel at the beauty of spring. The runoff from the river still flowed over many of the lowlands, but wildflowers covered any land not under water or planted. Purple and white wild radish, yellow mustard, an occasional shooting star, orange poppies. In the afternoon, the purple four-o'clocks would come out.

As she stood watching the sun rise behind the snow-covered mountains of the Sierras, she recalled the events of the past year. Colin had recovered quickly from his injury and claimed that he, not Katlin, had pulled the trigger that killed Caleb. He said he had found Caleb threatening Miss MacKenzie, and Caleb had pulled a gun. Since Colin was a solid citizen, and Caleb virtually unknown, the inquest was mercifully brief. With the man dead, Katlin could refute his claim to Mr. Greenwood, when he came to retreive the onyx ring, that she was his wife. Katlin had no trouble getting Mr. Greenwood to believe that Caleb had said she was his wife only to try and regain the property he had stolen from her.

She shuddered to think of the problems he could have created for her, had she not killed him. She tried to feel some guilt, but her only emotion since that fateful day had been relief that it was over at last and she was free to marry Colin.

Caleb's body lay in Sandhill Cemetery along with the victims of the flood of January and cholera epidemic of October of 1850. Katlin erected a small stone marker. She felt she owed him that much. Since she had no information on where or when he had been born, and did not even know his real name, the stone read simply, "Caleb Smith, died June 11, 1851".

Her whole life really began that day. Colin admitted he had loved her since their trip across the Isthmus, but, sensing her reservation and not knowing the source of it, had feared his feelings were not returned. He had felt she loved him, but not until he heard her sobbing out her love for him as he lay felled by Caleb's bullet had he been sure. He also admitted he had, at first, been reluctant to fall in love again after losing Michelle, but could not help himself.

Before she would marry him, she told him the whole story of Caleb and his many wives. He had insisted she put it behind her. He even sent money to the widow Caleb had bilked in Maine.

Henry and Elena married shortly after Caleb's death. The two of them, with Katlin's advice, had taken over the management of *MacKenzie's Mercantile*, leaving Katlin free of the day to day operations as soon as she and Colin married. Malcolm and Celie lived above the store and worked for them. She and Colin made at least one trip a week to Sacramento to oversee the store.

Katlin smiled as she thought of how quickly Henry had learned. She thought of their handshake on the *Panama* sealing their partnership. A good choice. She had never for a moment regretted that decision. And Elena had matured into a charming young woman. The love between the two glowed about them like a halo.

As she stood there watching the sun rise, Colin came up behind her and put his arms around her, his cheek against her hair. He put one hand on her abdomen, and the baby moved within her.

"Penny for your thoughts, my darling," he smiled.

She placed her hand over his on the baby. With the other, she reached back and stroked his cheek.

"I was just thinking how fortunate I am to be so happy, my love. I hope it lasts forever, but if not, let's plan to live for today. Let tomorrow take care of itself."

"It's a good philosophy," he murmured against her hair.

They stood together in silence as the sun's rays moved across the porch and bathed them in its golden light.

*Katlin's Fury*

# BIBLIOGRAPHY

*Gold Rush Letters of J.D.B. Stillman*;
(Lewis Osborne, Palo Alto, 1967)

*Letters of James M. Gibson to His Parents, 1850 to 1852*; Compiled and copyrighted by Eloise Gibson Spencer.

Gudde, Erwin G.; *California Place Names*,
(University of California Press, 1949)

Holden, William M.; *Sacramento: Excursions into its History and Natural World*,
(Two Rivers Publishing, 1988)

Holliday, J.S.; *The World Rushed In*,
(Simon and Schuster. New York, 1981)

Kelly, Esq., William; *A Stroll Through the Diggings of California*, (Biobooks, Oakland, California, 1950.)

Kemble, John Haskell; *The Panama Route 1848-1869*,
(University of South Carolina Press, 1990)

Kloss, Jethro; *Back to Eden*,
(Back to Eden Books Publishing Company, 1939)

Stevens, Errol Wayne; *Incidents of a Voyage to California 1849* (The Western History Association, 1987)

Taylor, Bayard; *El Dorado, or Adventure in the Path of Empire*, (The Rio Grande Press, 1967.)
Originally published in 1850

[over]

Taylor, Bayard; *New Pictures from California*,
(Biobooks, Oakland, California, 1951)

Thompson & West; *History of Sacramento County*,
(Thompson & West, 1880)

*Katlin's Fury*

# About the Author

The author, a graduate of Stanford University School of Nursing, lives in Southern California where she is in business with her oldest son. She has been published in professional journals, and several of her short stories have been published or won awards. *Katlin's Fury* is her third novel. Her first, *Matilda's Story*, a biographical novel based on thirty years in the life of her great-grandmother, Matilda Randolph, has won critical acclaim. Her second, *Susan's Quest*, a historical romance like *Katlin's Fury*, has also been well received.

The author is also active in community affairs. She is President of Liga International, Flying Doctors of Mercy, and flies once a month to Mexico to provide care to the rural poor. As a nurse, she is also a member of CA1 Disaster Medical Assistance team, and has responded to disasters in Hawaii and North Dakota. She has also been on mercy missions to Russia, Mali, and the Philippines.

As a member of the Board of Directors of the Natural History Association, she is actively involved with the Orange County Natural History Museum, and is also on the Board of Directors of the Laguna Chamber Music Society.

Work has begun on her fourth book, a sequel to *Matilda's Story*, entitled *Matilda's Story: The California Years*, which will cover Matilda's life from 1867 to 1906.